COURT OF TALONS

FANG & FIRE BOOK ONE

JENNIFER CHANCE

OLIVERHEBERBOOKS

All rights reserved.

No part of this publication may be sold, copied, distributed, reproduced or transmitted in any form or by any means, mechanical or digital, including photocopying and recording or by any information storage and retrieval system without the prior written permission of both the publisher, Oliver Heber Books and the author, Jennifer Chance, except in the case of brief quotations embodied in critical articles and reviews.

PUBLISHER'S NOTE: This is a work of fiction. Names, characters, places, and incidents either are the product of the author's imagination or are used fictitiously. Any resemblance to actual persons, living or dead, business establishments, events, or locales is entirely coincidental.

Court of Talons Copyright 2024 © Jennifer Chance

Cover design by Dar Albert at Wicked Smart Designs

Published by Oliver-Heber Books

0 9 8 7 6 5 4 3 2 1

For Ayn,
Forever

CHAPTER 1

The way of the warrior is death.

And if my chicken-brained brother keeps slowing us down, I may have to kill him myself.

"There!" He points, destroying any hope I have of ignoring his latest outburst. "What's that over there?"

Merritt pulls his warhorse to the side of the crumbling trail for what has to be the fifty-seventh time this morning. I watch him with barely controlled irritation, keeping my head ruthlessly still beneath my hooded cloak. If I make any sudden move, the jewel-encrusted coils of my thickly braided hair will tip me right out of my saddle.

My brother has no such constraint. He bounces in his stirrups, then strains to see over the tumble of vegetation, his eyes bright and his smile wide. He's every inch a seventeen-year-old off on his "first true adventure."

"Patience, Talia," my handmaiden mutters beside me. "He has the attention span of a gnat. Three bronze say we're back on our way within the half-hour."

"Done." I'd never take Adriana's coins, of course, but she's wrong. I know Merritt better than he knows himself.

We'll be here a while.

Merritt's stallion huffs and stamps, driving a hoof into the broken stone. All around us are jagged piles of rusted metal, burned-out husks of what may have once been vehicles. Hollow buildings leer at us from either side of the collapsed road, redolent with long-ago death. Merritt seems not to see anything but the hulking wrecks, while I study a thin, fetid stream of goo that moves sluggishly along the bottom of a choked gutter, bubbling from a dark hole I don't want to think about too much.

It's a cursed place, salted with the fear of the forsaken who vanished from these same streets hundreds of years ago. So *many* died in the onslaught of the Western Realms before the Protectorate rose up to hold the line between order and chaos.

We shouldn't be here...

But it's also a shortcut to pass through the Shattered City, and we needed to make up the time.

"We have to keep going," I call to Merritt, forcing a grin when all I want to do is shake him into deep unconsciousness. "We're already arriving after dark, and that's if we push hard."

"Well, what's the rush?" Merritt wheels his warhorse part way toward me, his mood immediately souring. "You'll be married off tomorrow anyways, whether we get to the Twelfth House at sunset or midnight. Who cares when we arrive? Go water the horses or whatever, and let me see what's what."

With that, he's off again, angling Darkwing around a fallen metal beast. The priest Nazar moves after him, always the grimmest shadow. Merritt is the old man's charge, but Nazar also glances my way with steady eyes. I know what he's asking of me. *Scout the perimeter. Make sure no one is watching.*

It's the one task the perpetually grouchy priest has let me take on during this journey, and I won't disappoint him.

"Adriana." With that one-word order, my handmaiden falls in line behind me. Both of us have been relegated to fat-bellied ponies by order of my father, but they're sturdy enough, and try their hardest to keep up. Meanwhile, Father is back at the Tenth

House, drinking to his new wealth, while I—for the first time in all my twenty-one years—am *free*.

At least until we reach the Twelfth House.

My own "first true adventure" will only last the day.

"Are you supposed to protect him while wearing your bridal finery too?" Adriana asks me drily as we plunge into the forest that butts up against a huddle of gutted buildings. There's a sort of outraged wildness here that seems to mock the stump of a rusted marker still visible beside the almost-trail. Whatever lettering or symbols the sign once boasted are long faded away. As are all the ghosts who made them or once read them. The forest, however, lived on. Violently, eagerly, chewing up what little of the doomed civilization remained behind.

I grin. "Only if I'm lucky." I'd take any chance to put my secret combat practice into action, but there will be no need for it on this scouting expedition. "Not that we're likely to find anyone here. Still, the tournament is barely a few days' ride from this city. If anyone from another house heard about my marriage and thought Merritt might be traveling with me to the Twelfth House first, they could maybe want to see if he was worth worrying about."

Adriana scoffs. "He's not. He's as useless as—"

Her words die away as I lift my hand. Since Merritt could crawl, I've permitted only myself the occasional pettiness to say anything negative about my brother. He may be overindulged and a little exasperating, but Merritt's boisterous affection for me and my mother's stalwart commitment to us both are the main reasons I'm still alive. That and my docile willingness to go along meekly with whatever indignity my father demanded of me, including this absurd marriage to a house even more backward than our own.

Adriana breathes out a quick apology, and I accept it with an even quicker smile. Her easy candor is my fault. I've been too careless with her, but she's the closest thing I've ever had to a friend.

I follow my smile with a chuckle. "But *they* don't know that, yeah? To them, Merritt may be the newest entrant in the Tournament of Gold, not just passing through to secure fighting men for our house."

"Well, *I'd* like to travel to the Tournament of Gold," she points out, reasonably enough. "Not be stuck at the Twelfth House watching you try to play dutiful wife."

"Not try," I remind her as she draws up next to me.

She sighs. "Not try, no. You'll be the perfect bride and helpmate, Lady Talia. A blessing to all you meet."

"Yes." And I will. I have to be, to ensure the heresy of my birth is finally buried for good. After twenty-one years of shame, I'll at last have a chance to bring honor to my house—even if it's only as the bride-in-waiting to a boy of barely fourteen years, whose house is the weakest of the Protectorate.

I'll take that chance. I'll make the Twelfth House strong. Eventually, I'll make both our houses strong.

For now, however, I must remain careful, quiet, and small beneath my stupendous pile of hair. When news of this marriage finally trickles out to the rest of the Protectorate, it'll be the merest footnote: Merritt's supposedly sixteen-year-old sister Talia, second of the Tenth House line, married in accordance with the Lighted Path. Forgettable, forgotten. Still a lie, in many ways. But a lie that keeps me breathing.

Far better to be the second-born daughter hidden away in obscurity, than the firstborn girl who should never have lived.

"Straighten up there." Adriana's order breaks through my thoughts. "Your hair is listing."

That makes me giggle, and we spend the next quarter hour in relaxed companionship, picking our way through the tangled forest. Eventually, we come upon a babbling stream, and I think about Merritt's direction. It isn't a bad idea.

"Water the ponies," I tell Adriana. "I need to take off some of these clothes."

She doesn't remind me to be careful. She doesn't need to. If for any reason I don't successfully reach the Twelfth House and complete the marriage ceremony awaiting me there, my father will end my life without another moment's thought.

After helping me out of my long cloak and its restrictive hood, Adriana turns away to hang the garments while I head deeper into the trees. I can't strip off the rich green gown that falls from my chin to my ankles, cleverly split to allow me to ride, but I wish I could. Instead, I grumble dark curses against its maker, punching down the voluminous cloud of material as it catches at every branch and twig. I'll be dragging half the forest with me by the time we reach the Twelfth House. But that's not my fault now, is it?

"Orlof won't care about my clothes," I mutter to myself, maybe a little bitterly. "He won't notice anything but the hair."

"He might notice that you talk to yourself when you think you're alone."

I turn in one movement at the sound of the unfamiliar voice. Twin daggers snick out of my wrist sheaths and slip into my palms like the unfurling of a heron's wings. I see the man's movement as I whirl, judge, and aim true upon my exhale, releasing the first blade with a practiced jerk of my right wrist. It cleaves through the air then buries itself into a sturdy trunk a scant three inches away from the arrested face of a man I've never seen before, a man dressed in cloth of gold and glittering ebony.

I swallow hard, staring at him. This man is undoubtedly a threat, a villain.

He's also as jarringly beautiful as an angel fallen straight from the Lighted Path.

My forbidden training reasserts itself in half a heartbeat, and I quickly take in more relevant details. This is no common marauder. He's young—maybe just shy of twenty-five years—rich and well-fed. He's also taller than most any man I've ever seen, broad-shouldered and long-limbed. Slender, yes, but sturdily built. His hair is jet black, his skin as shimmering bronze as the coins Adriana wagered so foolishly back on the trail. His eyes glint gold above a generous rose-granite mouth and iron-forged cheekbones. He grins at me, and his teeth flash white and even.

Additional assessments flow in. He's not only rich and healthy, his gold and black garments mark him as a member of the First House. His breeches are heavy but well made—a rider then, for all that he's now on foot. Whether he's truly First House or no, he comes from one of the larger houses, I think, some holding in the middle of the fertile plains that doesn't know privation.

He's a lord, too, not some soldier. I'd bet my hair on it. There's something about the smugness of his grin that speaks of long years of fulfilled expectations.

The shock of my blade impaling itself so close to his perfect jaw doesn't seem to faze him.

"You missed," he informs me.

"Did I?" I slide a second blade into my palm to replace the first, and I turn it to catch the thin stream of light flowing through the trees. "Should we try again?"

"Not yet." He pulls the blade free from its trunk, examines it, then leans against the tree. Leans! As if we're in a courtyard and not a wild wood. Distantly, I wonder if Adriana is watching. "There aren't any markings on this blade. One would think you wouldn't want to lose it, yet you don't claim it as your own. And it's not often that I find a lady who's also a marksman."

I know better than to answer all his unspoken questions. The blade is unmarked because I'm not allowed to have a weapon on my person sharper than a paring knife. My safety lies in my lineage. No man would dare risk my father's wrath to touch me.

Then again, we're no longer in my father's house.

"Perhaps you don't know many ladies from the borderlands." I gesture to the knife. "Return it, if you would. I have more need of it than you do."

He doesn't. Instead, his gaze drifts across my face to rest on my uncovered hair. I watch him count the rows of silver and jade beads that thread through it, taking their weight and measure. Yes, definitely someone from a larger house. I'm sure of it.

"So fierce," he murmurs, studying me. "You're heading to the

Tournament of Gold?" His gaze drops to my gown of emerald green.

"Right now, we're traveling through a forest we expected to be empty. What brings you this far from the plains when the tournament is so close? Surely, the First House must be missing you."

His brows shoot up in surprise, and I know that once again, my aim is true. But the question still remains. *Why is he here?*

Deliberately tucking my blade into his belt, his expression remains easy, unconcerned. He carries no obvious weapons, but I don't see his horse—or his men. Someone dressed so well would have both.

He gestures to my gown. "There are no warriors at the tournament wearing Tenth House green. Is this about to change?"

"No," I say flatly. "Nor will it for years to come."

Something in my confident tone finally seems to rankle him, because his lips twist with disdain, those gorgeous golden eyes going hard. "As if you'd know anything about it. It's Lady Talia, yes? Of the Tenth. Daughter of Lord Lemille, sister of Warrior Merritt. You must be off to be married, dressed like that. And based on your path, I'd wager you're heading to the Twelfth. That's a waste."

Indignation and all-too-familiar rage at my unfair plight boils within me. I bank it just as quickly, and execute the barest shred of a curtsey, my back as stiff as a board. "And you must have overheard your betters, to know all that," I shoot back just as coolly. "Lord Rihad of the First has no children that he claims—or first-blooded warriors, for that matter."

Surprise blanks the man's face, then heat rushes into his cheeks, sharp and intense. I clench my knives as he steps forward—

"Huzzah!" The far-off shout of pure and utter joy draws the man's too-keen eyes up—up!

Fear rabbits through me. He's looking to the sky, and if he's doing that, he *knows*—knows I'm not traveling alone here, knows my brother journeys with me.

This man's no villain, maybe. But he's still someone I should manage and contain, not taunt with rudeness. *Fool*!

"Fair enough, you guessed true!" I blurt out breathlessly, startling his attention back to me. I still don't trust myself to bow, not with my colossal coils, but I sink down into a far more respectful curtsey. "I *am* off to be wed to Lord Orlof's son, and I'm ever so nervous. Please accept my apologies for being awkward. My own lord calls. I have to go."

That makes him blink. "Your lord—"

"Not my lord for long, by the Light. But always my big brother," I burble on, doing my best imitation of a girlish smile. "You'll bless me, yes? With the might of the First House, however you come by it? Despite my teasing, you *are* a warrior, I see that plain enough, though I don't...I mean I don't understand how you know so much if you're not Lord Rihad's son. But as you say, I wouldn't." I simper, blush, and all but bury the man in words, but I want him to *see* how foolish and unsophisticated I am. I want him to discount both me and the boy whose laughter rings out even now in the distance, as excited and full-throated as if he had no care in the world. *See me. See us. We are unworldly nobles from the mountains. We cannot hurt anyone.*

The fallen angel of the Lighted Path looks at me, then smiles.

"You are so blessed," he declares. His tone is solemn and true: the tone of someone who's given this grace many times before.

A chill snakes through me. Who *is* this man who wears the colors of the First House so easily? I know of no noble warriors that represent that house other than Lord Rihad himself—a man my father's age. So, who is he, and why is he traveling in the mountains instead of taking his ease at the Court of Talons?

Oblivious to my racing thoughts, he bows to me and continues, "May you and your new husband walk ever in the Light."

His final words are lost in Merritt's bellowing whoop. "It's a practice field, has to be!" my brother calls out.

My hope of a clean escape turns to ash. "I must—" But I no longer care anything for the First House man, I care only for my brother, my idiot brother, who wants to play at being a warrior without any understanding of what it means.

I whirl away from the man and rush back to where Adriana has the ponies ready. In another few moments, I'm cloaked, covered, and back in the saddle. Then we're off, galloping through the woods, aiming toward the sound of my brother's voice.

We rush up a gentle slope of fragrant sweet briar and beyond a rocky promontory and cheerful stream—and I see exactly what has excited Merritt so much.

The once-forested slope beyond the Shattered City is bleak. Devastated. A huge stand of trees completely flattened—and not from some long-ago war. Only a rough circle of fallen timber remains, trees uprooted and barreled over as if a sudden, raging storm had erupted in the middle of the mountains...erupted and then vanished without a trace.

This kind of destruction could be the result of only one thing.

A banded warrior and his massive Divh.

"Talia! You're back. Whose was it, d'you think?" Merritt's voice rings with eagerness as he dances Darkwing in a tight circle, his face alight. He scans the surrounding mountains, as if they'll tell him who passed before us, both man and monster, heading to the magnificent coliseum of the First House, where the Tournament of Gold is held every year. "The Seventh—or the Fifth? The Fifth, I bet. I've heard their first-blood's Divh can clear a whole army with the swipe of one paw."

"We should go, Merritt." My voice, always low, now sounds like gravel. I don't want to think about Divhs as big as this, so much larger than our own. The lesser houses, like ours, have only one Divh—bonded to the first-blooded and firstborn son. The greater houses, such as the Seventh and the Fifth, have more, Divhs that belong to warrior knights and even banded soldiers.

But in every case, the house's firstblood Divh is the largest Divh of the holding...and from everything I've heard, some of these Divhs are truly massive. I don't want to imagine my starry-eyed brother one day facing such a creature in combat, even within the carefully restricted pageantry of a tournament.

At Merritt's frown, I press my point. "Truly, it's past time. The sooner we get to the Twelfth House, the sooner you'll be done with me."

He stiffens at that, then gapes at me. "But I don't want to be done with you!" he declares, his voice suddenly betraying his youth in a heartbreaking quaver. "Are you so ready to be done with me?"

I blink, my breath stolen away from me. I take in my baby brother's bright, earnest eyes, his flushed cheeks. "N-no, Merritt." I say, too truthfully. "I'm not."

"See?" His face clears, and he gestures again to the devastation before us. "And besides, a *Divh* was here—and not just any Divh, but one of the biggest, I'm sure—*practicing* for the Tournament of Gold." He pulls up his horn and issues a sharp, cutting blast, calling back our other scouts. I can't help thinking of the man in the forest, the First- or Second-House lord. "We'll stop for a bit! I've a mind to practice too."

"Practice for *what*?" Forgetting my place despite our priest and retainers drawing near, I once more become Merritt's older sister. A role I can never truly disclose or impose, of course. But one of us has to be sensible, and that's never been my brother's strength. "Your purpose at the tournament is to buy soldiers, Merritt, nothing more. And we're to travel discreetly, remember? Father said we mustn't be noticed."

"Yes, well, Father's not *here*," he reminds me with a grin. "Besides, there's nobody around for a hundred miles. The mountains will cover me, and the Tenth House hasn't competed in the Tournament of Gold in a generation. It's *more* than past time."

"Lord Merritt." The priest Nazar has ridden up to us, his calm voice cutting across our standoff. Though he travels with us solely to ensure that my wedding ceremony is blessed by the Light, I'm glad to have him intervene now. The priest's body is rigid and straight in the saddle despite his age, his long white hair as hidden as mine beneath his own hood. "Is practicing now the wisest choice? We've several hours' hard riding ahead to reach the Twelfth House."

"Oh no, no, no. Not you too," Merritt groans, waving at the stream that froths around the nearest rocky promontory. "Do what you want. I'm *practicing*." He dismounts with a light hop then unbuckles his sword and lets it fall to the ground.

I wince; beside me, Nazar also whispers a soft rebuke.

I should say something about the man in the forest, dressed richly in gold and black. Even if he's no threat whatsoever, I should speak. But I only stare as Merritt bounds toward the small hill, scrambling up it to gain a better view of the devastation beyond. Meanwhile, one of our retainers picks up my brother's sword and clutches it close, every inch the dutiful squire.

We have a pitifully small retinue of soldiers with us—only five, and not the strongest five of our house. But our father, above all else, wishes to draw no attention to our company until they are well and truly free of me. Until we reach the Twelfth House, we're supposed to be ghosts.

Nazar and I dismount as well, but the priest makes no move toward the cheerfully babbling stream. Instead, he watches Merritt.

Since he first came to our house ten years ago, Nazar's role has been to lead us in the rites and ceremonies of the Lighted Path, including the sacred transfer of our family's Divh from Father to Merritt when Merritt turned twelve. The priest offered to oversee Merritt's training as well, but Father told him he was far too old. He allowed Nazar only to speak aloud from the sacred book of war, while Father wielded both sword and stave.

Meanwhile, I watched them both. Whatever I heard, I memorized. Whatever I saw, I practiced silently and secretly in the shadows. My father isn't that great of a warrior, but he could teach well enough, and I suspect he simply didn't want to give up his influence over Merritt—his only son.

Four children died in my mother's womb before I was born;

after Merritt's birth, she could bear no more. Two years ago, she passed into the Light, which means that now, only my marriage contract keeps me breathing. Yet another reason we should keep moving on the road to the Twelfth House.

Alas.

The priest squints as Merritt reaches the top of the hill. "This is self-indulgent folly," he mutters. "He has no intention of genuine practice."

Like so many other things, it's forbidden for any woman to speak of Divhs and training and battles. Despite my better sense, though, I can't hold my tongue.

"Even if he did, what's the point?" I grouse. "Merritt's not allowed to enter the tournament, and he shouldn't. I know Divhs aren't supposed to get truly injured anymore when they fight in the tournament games. But this—" I wave at the destruction around us. "Whatever destroyed this valley must be five times the height of our manor house. Merritt's nowhere near ready to face a creature so powerful, and our Divh is far too small to be of any use in that kind of battle."

I shiver. Was the man I saw in the forest a banded warrior after all? Was it his Divh who caused the destruction here?

I should tell Nazar about him—but the priest turns sharply to me, his scowl dripping ice.

"Are you saying a first-blooded warrior knight shouldn't enter the Tournament of Gold?"

"Well, I...no," I stammer. Is Nazar testing me? I'm not sure. Nevertheless, I must tread lightly. There's no need to irritate him further.

And what's the harm, really, of what I found? The man I met was no villain, he was a nobleman of the First House—that much was abundantly clear. There are rules among the houses to keep all nobility safe, but I'll be robbed of all my freedom for the rest of this trek if I reveal I was talking to some stranger like an idiot child.

I clear my throat. "I'm saying Father's already made the decision. Merritt isn't going to the tournament to compete, not this year. He's going to purchase soldiers. That's all. Light knows we need them."

That shuts up Nazar for a breath, and for good reason. With every season, more marauders seem to be weaving through the forests at night, more criminals and refugees streaming across the borders from the east. This marriage alliance we're forging with the Twelfth House will help strengthen our two border holdings, but not as much as a garrison full of able-bodied men will.

And to get those men, we need to go to the Tournament of Gold.

"Talia," Nazar murmurs, and I realize he's not looking at me anymore.

I quickly return my attention to the embankment and can't help the surge of excitement that overrides my dismay. Every time Merritt summons the Tenth House Divh, it's as if the very air carries a song of pure possibility. My breath catches, my pulse jumps. *We're in the mountains. No one will see—well, except a fellow nobleman to whom we are no threat.*

In fact, maybe it's a good thing if that man sees Merritt and his Divh. Maybe he'll decide we are of no interest to Lord Rihad and his Court of Talons. Merritt's too young to fight, our Divh too small. He'll see that and ride away, and we will be safe in the mountains. Safe.

Besides all that, Merritt is *summoning his Divh!* And this time, I'll be allowed to see it, up close and in the light!

"Secure the horses," I bark as my brother thrusts his left fist into the sky.

The men comply, more out of fear than any loyalty to me. It takes a trained battle mount to accept a Divh, and even Merritt's warhorse swings his head as I race by him, his wild eyes also staring at the summit, his nostrils flaring.

Atop the ridge, Merritt claps his right hand to the thick leathery band that wraps tightly around his left bicep beneath his tunic.

"Gent!" he yells with delirious joy.

It's his Divh's name, a name I've never dared speak, not even in whispered imaginings as I've played at being a warrior knight. Certain indiscretions can be overlooked—but not that one. Though women can speak of Divhs in general terms, the name of a Divh is death to any female who utters it, no matter her blood or standing.

Merritt shouts it again.

"Move your ass, you lazy beast!"

The very air around us ripples with the force of the creature's arrival from its spectral plane. My head rings with its scream.

Not yet, not yet! I want to see! I clamber up the rocky hill, barely clearing the promontory when the monster roars again. The ground suddenly shakes, sending me reeling. Dust swirls all around me, and I stagger upright—then gawk at the goliath before me.

I've *never* been this close to it.

Merritt's Divh is twice as tall as our manor house and nearly as broad. It looks most like an enormous, sage-haired bear, except a single horn sprouts up from its nose, thick and pointed. Also, the monster's body is hopelessly out of proportion to be a bear's. Its neck is too thick, and even though it is standing tall, its forelimbs are far longer than its hind legs—so long they hang forward, the heavy paws knuckling the churned-up soil.

Scarcely able to breathe, I peel my eyes wide, determined to imprint this memory forever on my mind. As the Divh wheels around, my heart surges—not in panic, not in fear, but in a wild, exultant joy unlike anything I've felt before. In the brief second its gaze passes over me, I drink in its strength as if it were my own, filling me up, making me whole. Whispering in my mind that *I* am the monster, *I'm* the mighty power. That *I* can do anything and everything simply by opening my heart and hands and willing it to be so.

"Gent!" Merritt cries a third time, shattering the moment.

With an exultant laugh, my brother drops his arm, setting the beast into motion.

The Divh scrambles around on its powerful hind legs as if to get its bearings, then springs forward, employing its oversized arms and legs to launch across the shattered forest. It lands in a crouch next to a scraggly copse of trees.

I jerk my glance back toward my brother. This jumping maneuver is Merritt's favorite move with his Divh. More than once, he's done it too near the Tenth House manor, sending dishes bouncing off their shelves and fine pottery crashing to the ground —until my mother ordered cabinet doors built to protect anything that might be broken, and rushes doubled up on every floor.

Now Merritt swings his arm in a swooping arc, directing the creature to dive headfirst into the last remaining section of standing forest on the slope. My fists clench tightly—Merritt should be more careful! The two of them are linked mind to mind, body to body. If his Divh is injured, Merritt will be injured too. But my brother's face is rapt with excitement, jubilant in the surge of power that marks his sacred bond with the giant protector.

And I realize as I watch, I *want* this happiness for him. This unfettered, unabashed joy. I want him to grow and find love, success, and real, lasting honor. He is my brother. I love him no matter what trick the Light played on us all those years ago, bringing me into the world first in violation of our sacred traditions. I love him no matter how foolish his notions are, believing that he could pit our Divh against the mightiest in the land— and win.

I love him no matter how much he likes knocking things down.

Merritt yells again, and the Divh bellows in response, whether in pain or frustration, I've no idea. Still, it does what Merritt orders and hurls itself forward. Its roar echoes off the mountains and shakes rocks free from the upper heights. Then it turns its shoulders into the remaining trees, toppling them.

Again and again, Merritt forces his Divh into yet more ambitious acrobatics—jumping, rolling, diving. With each punishing strike to the ground, dust billows up around the beast, only to be caught by the wind and scattered. The mountains seem to wince and shrink away as more rocks tumble and the beast's bellows vibrate through the valley. The Divh responds each time in perfect service to my brother's commands, though I cannot see the value in them. Instead of directing Gent to slash and tear, my brother treats his Divh like an overgrown pet, rolling it around the valley, causing maximum damage to anything that can't fight back.

Nazar suddenly pushes by me on the ridge and takes several long strides toward Merritt. "Lord Merritt," he shouts, and I've never heard the priest's voice so loud, so curt. "If you're going to train, you should—"

"Watch this!"

My brother shoots his hand into the sky once more, making another fist, and the Divh leaps. As it descends this time, however, Merritt runs toward the edge of the promontory, knowing the Divh will break his fall when he leaps, knowing it will catch him in its enormous paws.

Unreasoning fear jolts through me as Merritt races so thoughtlessly toward the open air. He'll be fine, I know he'll be fine, he's done this stupid trick a hundred times. Running at his Divh, knowing it will do anything he asks, and yet...

My heart is pounding so loud as Merritt jumps, I barely notice the flash of brightness in the air beyond him, the stab of light racing through the sky. It looks almost like...but no, that's impossible, that cannot be.

Merritt!

I try to cry out the name, the warning, but my breath stalls in my throat, my hands lift up, my blood congeals. Time seems to rush too quickly, only to stop, halting completely as I lurch forward, too late—too late!

The stab of light is an *arrow*.

No sooner do I see it than it's already reached its target, already ripped into flesh and muscle, piercing through my brother's back and out his chest, Merritt's body convulsing midair as his Divh's roar shakes the whole world.

"No—" I start to run. Gent leaps. Its massive sage green paw swipes for my brother—swipes and *misses*, the Divh's immense body also jerking mid-reach, mirroring Merritt's agony—

No! My mind refuses to accept, my eyes refuse to see, every inch of me bursting with the wrongness, the impossibility of this scene. I race on, heedless of the terrain, tripping over my cloak, my hair, my own feet until I reach the promontory's cliff.

I scream with helpless outrage as the mighty Divh makes a final heaving grab for my brother. The goliath and the boy collide together beneath the bold and brilliant sun, both of them twisting, turning, tumbling as they...

Fall.

CHAPTER 2

"Merritt!"

I'm thrown backward with the impact of the Divh's crash back to earth. Another eruption of dust explodes skyward. I think I hear Nazar's voice, but I have no time for him.

My head canting dangerously to the side with the weight of my braids, I scramble over the promontory's edge, ignoring the rocks and the scrubby brush that rips at my clothes and hair. The mighty Gent didn't catch Merritt after all. Instead, my brother lies in the shallow lee of a rocky outcropping. The Divh sprawls on the far bank of the stream, knocked back into the ruined forest, trembling violently. I gape at the monster, then back at Merritt as I race down the slope.

My brother has rolled to his side, his body outstretched. The arrow is embedded in his back, its dull gray flanges sticking out wide like a horse's plume, terrible and dire.

"Merritt," I gasp, dropping to my knees. The cold, cruel point of the arrow juts from his chest, stained crimson with fast-flowing blood. Merritt's eyes are wide and glassy. I take his hands, wishing I could give him my strength, my stubbornness, that he might live and I might suffer in his place.

The Divh groans in the clearing by the stream, its breath heavy and harsh. My brother's body shudders as Gent's does, the two of them still echoing each other's agony, and I grip Merritt's hands more firmly.

"You will not die, my brother," I command as his wild gaze finds mine, this bright and foolish boy. There is no more superiority in his eyes, no more youthful disdain. Instead, there's fear. Fear and hope and endless yearning for my words to be true. "You will not die but rise in glory, defending the Tenth House as our champion. From the steps of the Exalted Imperium to the farthest borders of the Western Realms, you will ride forth. You will not die."

"Talia," he whispers. Panic chases through me. I've dressed animal wounds after vicious attacks—men's wounds too, when marauders ambushed our riders. I know death, and I know the burst of blood that spills from Merritt's mouth, painting the world in red. Still, I can do naught but hold this fragile warrior child in my grasp. He is my brother, and he cannot die. He is my brother, and—

"You will not die," I say again, more sharply. Merritt's pain-filled stare drifts back to mine. He seems ancient in this moment, not a boy at all anymore, but a man who's learned too late the wisdom of the world, too late and too soon at once. I sense him slipping away and I pull him awkwardly close, trying to avoid the tip of the brutal arrow that seems to have cleaved its way through even bone, so firmly has it punched through my brother's suddenly too-small body.

I shudder as Merritt collapses into me. I've been taught not to cry, but the unbending of my brother's body is my undoing as well. Tears spill forth, sobs wracking through me. I can almost imagine Merritt's spirit, desperately fighting to leave, but I am equally desperate. *You cannot die.*

Finally, my mind registers that something else is wrong. *Where are our retainers, come to help with Merritt? Where is Nazar?*

Then a new sound penetrates my ears.

Screaming.

I whip around, but I can't make anything out beyond the promontory's peak. Still, I mark the crash of battle on the other side of the rocky outcropping—the clatter of swords, the pounding of horses' hooves, the cries of men. *Marauders!*

The warrior! As soon as his image flashes into my mind, I cannot unsee it, I cannot undo it. No one else was in the forest, was there? I rushed back too fast, too fast! I didn't ask his name; I didn't ask his business. I let myself be turned around and now...and now...

I suck in a huge breath. I have no sword, no shield. But they'll be coming—for me, if not for Merritt. No one will believe my brother has survived that arrow through his back. If I can hide him in plain sight, hide us both...

Hauling Merritt against me, I drag him along the rocky slope. Several paces on, I see a shallow ditch flanked with boulders. I stumble into it, half pulling Merritt's body over mine, facedown so the arrow's foul gray plumage is easy to see for anyone looking. If they think he's dead, they'll not glance twice, I know. They won't look for either of us.

My brother convulses again, though the breath has all but left his body.

"Shhh, Merritt, shhh," I croon, clutching him close. "Lie still. They'll think you're dead. They'll leave and we'll find help, I swear it."

The cries of battle surge closer. Above me, pressing down as if to cover me more completely, my brother shivers again.

Or...not exactly shivers.

Squinting hard, I fix on the point just below his left shoulder, where beneath his tunic sleeve, Merritt's warrior band is deeply embedded in his bicep. He received that sentient cuff when he was twelve. I hadn't been a part of that ceremony, of course. I know next to nothing of the private, sacred ritual. But now the loose fabric of my brother's sleeve trembles violently, shifting as something moves beneath it. In my mind's eye I can see his warrior band, wriggling against Merritt's skin as if to shuck itself free from my brother's dying arm, an arm it no longer considers worthy of protecting or defending.

"Stay with me, Merritt." To keep him steady, I grip Merritt's shoulder with my right hand, then entwine my left hand with his as his fingers slacken. "We'll get you help, we will."

Where is Merritt's Divh? I can't see anything from my hiding place. Another shard of panic knifes through me. Divhs die when their warriors die, disappearing back to their own plane. So, if the monster is still here—if it lives, then there's hope.

I lift Merritt's body a bare inch to peer out, but the Divh no longer sprawls across the river, its enormous bulk gone. And when I look back at my brother, I know the truth.

By the Light, no. Merritt's eyes have turned distant and cold, staring into nothing. His body is yet more diminished, thinner than it was, a mere shroud of the boy who'd fairly burst with laughter and chatter and life. I try to speak, to cry, to do *something*, but I'm locked in place, covered in Merritt's blood. Everything around me is frozen still, except... I frown in confusion. Except Merritt's warrior band.

I reach out to lock my hand in his, drawing it close as I stare at his upper left arm. I transfer his hand to my left and slide a new knife out of my right wrist sheathe and into my palm, then cut his tunic sleeve away. What I see makes my mouth go dry.

While the rest of the world has stopped, my brother's band, that sacred symbol of the bond between warrior and Div...keeps *moving*.

Squirming, almost. Slipping and writhing like a living thing —then snapping free with impossible speed to race down his arm.

"What—"

I jerk back but can't dislodge my left hand in time.

My skin seems to melt into Merritt's, my finger bones on fire. The warrior band appears to be a simple circlet of leather as wide as my hand, but it might as well be a fire snake as quickly as it moves, and before I can pull back, it leaps with sudden viciousness onto my wrist.

"No!"

I can't escape it, though. The acid from the band slices through my skin with a savage heat, searing me bloody. It tears its way up my left arm, shredding my tunic sleeve, burying itself into my bicep like some flesh-eating monster.

For a moment, I register nothing but the shock of it, then that too is burned away with a roar of such agony I start to scream. Only I can't seem to catch my breath, can't clear my eyes as smoke and fire wrap around me. Nausea then horror flood over me by turns; time seems to stop, sputtering and cracking—or is that the sound of my bones breaking? No sooner does it pass then another scorching wave strikes me, over and over again.

When I finally manage to make any noise at all, it's little more than a ragged pant, my gasp barely squeezing by the rising gorge in my throat. I'm coated in sweat and blood and suddenly cold...so cold.

I crawl out of the ditch, out from underneath Merritt, but I've lost all sense of place. Where am I—and why is Merritt so still and small below me? Why am I surrounded with the smell of charred and blackened skin?

New shouts ring out in the distance, curdling death cries that cut through my delirium. Agony swamps me in ever-sickening waves as I wrench my gaze away from Merritt's empty eyes.

The truth of my position crashes back down on me.

I can't stay hidden another moment. I have to go—to fight!

I turn away from Merritt's shallow grave, struggling to ignore my throbbing arm as I stagger forth. My legs are too heavy, my head too light despite my blood-soaked hood and filthy cloak. I sway beside Merritt, a stranger in my own skin, the heat from the warrior band biting all the way to the bone. Another cry of raw pain rises in my throat, but only a tortured groan escapes.

A horse screams again beyond the hilltop, and I lurch forward almost blindly toward the sound. I follow the edge of the rocky promontory as it runs along the banks of the stream, until I'm splashing through shallow water at its end. With every step, my head clears, my senses sharpen. I finally emerge from behind the small hill and take in the field before me.

It's utter chaos. More than two dozen marauders are striking down our scant five soldiers, who are obviously no match for the attack. Adriana lays in what looks like a dead faint off to the edge of the field.

No...not a faint, I realize, as bile rushes up into my throat. Blood coats her hair, and her face is misshapen, her body collapsed and still. *No.*

"Adriana!" I scream, but no one can hear me. Men and horses crash together, swords clang, and everything's washed in dust and blood. I even see Nazar—*Nazar!* Rushing on foot into the melee, his hands clutching a sword I know the old man has no hope of wielding. Fury spikes through me. *He'll die. They all will die!*

With an instinct I can neither understand nor control, I clap my right hand to my left bicep, my need to stop this—stop *all* this—so great, so terrible—

"No!" I cry. My voice grows and grows, filling the canyon with a bellow loud enough that the very trees flatten before me, the mountains tremble, the air fractures and flows away.

Except...it *isn't* my voice that's roaring with such unfathomable force.

Or not my voice alone.

A wall suddenly crashes down beside me, thudding into the ground so hard, I go flying—only to rebound off another wall that's solid, smooth, and...*green.*

I yank myself back from its surface. It's warm to the touch, warm with the texture of hairless hide, like the skin of a lizard or a snake, but it's a wall...a *wall*. A wall that's closing in on me!

I whirl around, seeking a way out, but the wall ends not in thin air but in the smooth ebony of a new surface that ends with the cruel jutting curve of...claws? Yes, jet black *claws* stretch out from the ends of these hide walls, and I instinctively crouch down, lifting my arms to protect my face, even as the dust chokes off my vision and the booming noise continues to rage above me.

I can't stay here! The creature above me draws in another breath to bellow, and I scurry forward like a beetle, bursting out from between the walls of sleek black talons.

Before me on the field of battle, I can see the truth. I am too late—far too late. A dozen or so riders are racing away in fear, none of them wearing the distinctive green livery of the Tenth House. I thrust my feeble arms forward, unable to do more than scream.

The giant above me leans forward as well, his own arm sweeping down in a grasping arc a mere handspan behind the desperately fleeing horsemen—but they escape into the forest. If any of them had originally thought to return and give fight, those ideas are drowned in the full-throated howl of the monster above me, a thunderous tide that almost reminds me of—

"*Gent?*" I whisper, the word so soft, I'm not sure I'm even speaking at all.

The howling stops.

I stagger forward, unable to fully comprehend the sudden silence of the field in front of me—*how can so many men lay so still?* Then I turn and slowly crane my neck, peering up...up...dizzy with confusion as I stumble back several more steps, trying to see, to understand.

Above me, three times taller than Gent had been, stands...a colossus.

A giant. A god.

It's—it's *almost* like the Gent I knew before, but impossibly, insanely different. Still bear-shaped with improbably long front limbs, still horned. But where Gent's fur was a muddy sage, this Divh is cloaked with deep silver fur over dark green skin. Where Gent had a single horn protruding from its snout, this Divh sprouts horns from its temples as well—and its shoulders, elbows, and knees that I can see. This Divh *can't* be Gent. Everything about it seems mightier, especially its upper body, its arms now thicker than our entire manor house and, yes, long enough to sweep an army from its path. Unbidden, Merritt's excited declaration about the Divh who'd been in this valley before us comes back to me, icy horror on its heels.

"Gent," I say the forbidden name again, my voice still far too raspy to do more than die in the dusty air. Still, the giant Divh hears me. It cocks its enormous head forward and slowly, laboriously drags one foot away from me, then the other, its talons scoring deep fissures in the earth as I stagger fifteen more steps away from it. In that one small step, it's now well beyond the stream, back amid the shattered trees, its movements almost tentative as its huge black eyes focus on me behind a central ebony horn.

Then it drops to the ground so heavily, I'm thrown several paces, crashing to the ground in a heap. The earth shudders with the booming impact of Gent's knees as they flatten splintered tree trunks and dig into the ruined field. The goliath lowers its head, still watching me as it stretches its thick paws forward.

All at once, I finally understand what's happening, and a fierce, unbridled wonder sweeps over me for the barest moment, forcing back the wrongness of all I've seen this day.

The Divh...is *bowing*.

To *me*.

CHAPTER 3

I stare, transfixed, my throat clamped tight. The Gent I knew was big, yes. Strong, imposing. But this creature's heart thuds in his chest with the sound of war drums, its breath pushes me back with the strength of a stiff breeze as it huffs through its fangs, its chin on the ground. Its outstretched claws are only a few scant paces away from me, each razor-sharp talon as tall as I am.

Someone steps close. The priest. "Place your hand on the warrior band, Talia," Nazar orders, his words too loud, too harsh.

"I—" Grit chokes me; I can hardly breathe. Nazar grunts and grabs my loose right hand, slapping it to my left bicep. Another searing pain jabs me to awareness.

"Send it home," he orders. "Home, Talia. Say its name to release it back to its plane. Now."

"Go," I gasp, turning back to the ferocious god before us, and once more speak the forbidden name. "Go back, G-Gent. Go home."

The words are more question than command, but a moment later, all the air in the valley is sucked away. My hooded cloak whips violently around me as the Divh—the mighty, enormous, gloriously reborn Divh of the Tenth House—vanishes into nothingness.

Nazar catches me as I sway.

"Where is your brother?" he demands.

"I—what?"

I blink at Nazar, suddenly, damningly aware of what I've done, the crime against my family and the Light. More than one crime, too. More than one! I twist away from the priest, hiding my bloody, burned arm.

"Nazar, you have to understand," I begin, my teeth starting to chatter. "I didn't mean...I didn't—"

"Your *brother*," he says again.

I turn toward the jumble of rock, all that's left of the promontory after Gent's passage, and point.

"There," I finally manage. "He's... I left him. There."

Nazar nods, then glares at me. "The horses fled into the forest in the attack, Darkwing too. The well-trained ones will still be close. Find them and wait for me."

"But the rest—"

His face hardens. "The rest are dead. The men. Adriana. All of them." He lifts a hand toward the distant tree line. "Get the horses. I'll bring the boy."

He strides away.

I turn a half step toward the forest but don't move at first. Instead, I stare at the ruin of the clearing.

We'd ridden into this valley not an hour earlier filled with laughter and dreams. Now the valley is strewn with bodies—known and unknown, old and young, horse and rider alike. I pick out the dark green cloaks mounded over silent forms, and my stomach churns. Anyone who stumbles upon this clearing will know that something dire has happened to the Tenth House. Something terrible and final, an arrow through our very heart.

We'll be attacked. There's no doubt in my mind. We're one of the farthest houses on the eastern border of the Protectorate, cut off from the larger houses to the west by mountain and forest. The marauders and brigands have already been worse this spring than ever before. If they hear...if they somehow learn...

Bile rises in my throat, and I stagger away, not stopping until I'm back over the crest of the destroyed valley and once more in the shadow of the forest. I strain toward its embrace, seeing death in every tree, every blade of grass, and almost cry with relief when I make out Merritt's horse—and three others just beyond.

"Darkwing," I snap, harsher than I intend. The horse's head comes up, his eyes rolling as I grasp his bridle. Angrily wiping away my tears, I duck under Darkwing's head and move quickly through the forest, securing any other animals I can find—whether ours or the marauders. I try not to think about the riders of these steeds, lying somewhere in the field behind me. I pull the horses together to wait.

By the time the priest reaches me, my brother in his arms, the entire valley has fallen still. Not even the birds chatter in the trees.

Nazar lays Merritt's body on the soft earth. With a strange, almost surreal detachment, I realize the priest has already removed the gray feathered arrow from Merritt's body, already bound my brother's wounds with long strips of his cloak. Merritt's hair is matted to his skin, his brow caked with sweat and dirt, but no life remains in his pale face.

I tear my gaze away from him, stare at Nazar. "They're all dead?"

"All. Five Tenth House soldiers and Adriana, six attackers." His face is drawn, and he looks impossibly old to me. "When Merritt was struck, I was on the ridge with you. The others were down at the water, on foot, most with their swords still strapped to their saddles. By the time I reached them ..." He grimaces. "Our fallen are avenged, but they are still dead."

He speaks as if he holds himself to blame for the death of five fighting men and an untrained handmaiden—him, a priest of the Light. But I don't deny him his guilt, any more than I can deny myself my own. *Five Tenth House soldiers...Adriana...*

And by the Light... *Merritt.*

The world wavers, darkness surges, but before I can slip away completely, Nazar's voice brings me back into focus.

"There's water in the skins," he says curtly.

I nod. My brother shouldn't go to the Light dirty and broken. He should be sanctified, his face wiped clean, his hands clasped over his heart. Pulling my own tattered cloak from my shoulders, I use its cleanest sections and gently, so gently, prepare my brother not for a life of tournaments and champions, but for eternal Light.

Nazar returns sometime later, his tunic stained with fresh dirt, no doubt from the graves of our fallen retainers and Adriana. Numbly, I watch him lift Merritt's still form and carry him to where he's made a makeshift pyre of branches and the cloaks of our retainers.

"Pray over your brother, Talia of the Tenth, and we will give him a warrior's death," the priest says. "Then we must be gone before anyone else comes to this place."

"Adriana?" I whisper.

His voice is hard as flint. "Struck in the first pass. Her grave remains open; it's yours to close if you wish it. You can say your goodbye to her but remember—every moment with her takes you from Merritt, and he is your brother and lord."

"My...lord." I swallow hard, but glance to where he points, and stumble over to where there are five mounds in the dark, crumbling soil. Five mounds and one trench, with an oddly small, heavily wrapped form lying within it. How can death shrink a person so quickly?

I pick up the small shovel Nazar has left beside the trench. It's meant for covering over campfires, not graves, but it clearly has done the job. I push it into the rich earth, pull up a surprisingly light mound of loose dirt. The forest is willing to take our offering, it seems, even if we don't want to give it.

I drop the first mound of earth upon my only friend.

"Adriana," I whisper. I can't get past her name, tears falling thick and hot as I shovel dirt over her. Sorrow washes through me, chased by anger, then pain, then more anger, over and over again, rolling tides of loss and rage. With each scoop, I feel a part of us is being covered over and hidden away, obliterated forever. Our laughter. Our chatter over visiting bards and lords. Adriana's hissed warnings whenever someone came too close while I was battling shadow warriors in the dark. Our giggled assessments of men and boys. Our wishes and hopes. Our fears. Our plans for a shared future now buried in rich forest soil.

"Adriana," I manage again, the words of the Light a blur to me, mumbled and hissed and moaned over her. I finally drag myself away from the freshly formed mound and trudge back to Nazar.

For a second time, I stare down at a body prepared for death as Nazar begins the sacred rite of passage, his chant as haunting as the wind on a barren winter's night. Merritt seems impossibly wrong, lying there. Like Adriana, he's too small, too still, especially on his pyre of gathered branches, his body offered up to the open sky. When Nazar strikes flint to stone and sets the pyre ablaze, I can almost hear Merritt's laughter once more, can almost see him riding, proud and strong. Can almost see him leaping into the air to jump—knowing he would be caught. Knowing he would never die.

Tears well up again, and despite the dishonor and my own returning fury, I let them fall. Here is my brother, my only brother. Here's all the hope I've ever had.

Nazar doesn't speak for several long minutes as the fire burns down. Doesn't move, in fact, from my side. But when I finally step away from the darkening embers, the priest lifts a hand to stop me.

"You're banded," he says, his voice as punishing as a fist.

And just like that, I know.

There's still more dying to do this day.

CHAPTER 4

"I didn't want it," I protest, already hot with shame as Nazar glares at me beside my brother's smoking pyre. "I didn't."

"No?"

I wince, this single word a new and deadly cut. Because Nazar, of course, would know.

Though I'd always tried desperately never to be seen, I *had* mimicked Merritt's movements in the hidden corners of the keep when I thought no one was looking. Nazar has caught me more than once in my shadow dancing. He could have—should have—had me lashed for my transgression. To my surprise, he never did, merely watched me with the same dark-eyed gaze he so often turned on Merritt. A few times, he even corrected my form with the barest word, the slightest shake of his head.

I treasured those secret, stolen instructions more than he probably ever imagined, rose-gold threads embroidered into the endless gray tapestry of my life.

Now those threads ensnare me as damningly as the cuff upon my arm.

I extend my shaking left hand, my chin up, the grubby tangle of my once-beautiful hair nearly overweighting me. There's no denying the band sunk into my bicep. It's still wet with my blood, my skin scorched black around it.

"I *didn't* want it," I say again, more forcefully this time. "I still don't. Can...can you remove it?"

"Here?" Nazar's face is implacable. "No. Without the unbanding ritual or a warrior to take on the sacred charge, only death can part a warrior from his band."

"But this is a mistake." I reach up for the offending band, my fingers digging into my ruined, blistered skin despite the spike of agony. "I don't want it!"

"No!" Nazar's horrified shout barely reaches me.

I grasp the band to wrench it free as scorching fire explodes through me, punching the air from my lungs and turning my bones to milk. I wheel back, dizzy with pain, and fall to the ground. I try to get up, but my legs won't work, my limbs instead jerking at awkward angles, my hands, my feet, even my tongue quivering as I fight to breathe, to speak.

Nazar watches me shake uncontrollably from a short distance away, never moving.

At length, when my body ceases the worst of the spasms and merely quakes, he speaks. "I suggest you don't try that again. If you need more incentive, know this: a forced unbanding ceremony is one of the most agonizing experiences a warrior can ever endure, both physically and mentally. Once you are separated from your Divh through any other act than the normal transfer of father to child, your heart will never beat normally again, your feet will never be fully sure upon the ground. It's a weight like stones upon your lungs, a loss that keens forever in the depths of your soul."

I bleat out a pitiable moan. I know of course that Gent was once banded to my father, but I'd been forced to remain deep inside the manor house whenever my father had summoned him. I'd only managed to watch Merritt work with Gent in secret—and never once had thought about the transfer process of the band, forced or otherwise. "How do you know all this?"

He grimaces. "I saw it happen decades ago, by order of the emperor. Only once, thank the Light. But it was memorable."

"Right." I groan with a last, indulgent whimper of abject misery as I force myself to face the path that lies before me. We must return to the Tenth House as fast as we can. Which means my father will see me. See me and know the extent of my betrayal. That I didn't protect Merritt. That I allowed him to die and stole the band from his broken body, though I didn't want it—didn't know—could never have imagined—

"Very well." When I finally speak, I don't recognize my voice. It's dust and rocks and emptiness, which is all that's left for me. "We'll go back. The band will be transferred in this...unbanding ritual. And then I'll—perhaps I'll return to the Twelfth House and marry after all." If my father allows me to live after my betrayal. I don't hold out much hope for that.

To my surprise, however, Nazar shakes his head. "There's no time," he says flatly. "Your house needs soldiers, now more than ever. With the loss of these five, the Tenth only has five remaining fighting men—our strongest, but still nowhere near enough. The soldiers we need can only be found at the Tournament of Gold."

"But..." I turn back to the field of the dead, forcing myself not to shrink away. "These were only marauders. They'll scatter. No one will know of this attack."

"No." The old priest's face is resolute. "These were not marauders. That arrow was shot by a house soldier."

A new, impossibly colder wave of queasiness sluices through me as I think of the man I saw—the warrior in gold and black. "You're wrong," I declare. "That's against the Rule of the Protectorate. No warrior would kill Merritt."

My voice is resolute. Nazar isn't Protectorate born. He came to us from Hakkir, the capital city of the Exalted Imperium, in the summer of my eleventh year, long after the deceit of my assumed role as Merritt's younger sister had been woven into the fabric of our house. But even though he's not native to our land, the priest knows our laws, our traditions. Still, I say the words aloud to scrub out his accusation. "It's illegal for any Protectorate house to strike another house outside the Tournament, on penalty of death."

"That doesn't change the truth of this attack." Nazar's words are quieter now, though no less absolute. "These men didn't fight foolishly but with set purpose. First the initial shot to take the warrior knight by surprise, ideally to kill him and remove his Divh from the battle."

He motions to Merritt's pyre with a curt wave. "Then the rush to kill our horses with arrows. Soldiers on horseback followed with swords and clubs—a swift and focused attack. That's not the mark of marauders, Talia, hungry and desperate for food or weapons or silver. That's the mark of trained fighters."

"But...no." I shake my head, outrage sparking through me at his stubborn denial. "No house kills another house's warrior knight. It's against the law."

Nazar's eyes remain fixed on me, bleak and hard. "It's against the Light as well. But it's what happened here. None of the attackers wore any symbol to betray their house, but those that fell told their truth. Their nails were unbroken, their bellies full, their bodies strong. They were not marauders. They belonged to a holding, and a wealthy one. It's a question solely of which."

"No," I insist. Again, the priest isn't Protectorate born. He's wrong. I know he's wrong—and I'll prove it.

I wheel away from Nazar, stalking out of the forest to return to the battlefield.

The sight of the horsemen still laying on the ground shocks me more than I expect. I'd seen them fallen in the heat of the battle, but now, up close, it's so much worse. I force myself to stare hard at the attackers who lost their lives in their cowardly assault...

And I see what Nazar sees. These men don't look anything like the marauders who have plagued the distant holdings of the Tenth House. Those were rough-skinned outlaws, their hair matted and coarse, their teeth black. But these men...

For all that they wear no colors, these men look like house soldiers. They're young. Strong. And above all, well-fed.

Which means someone with money and power sent them out here to do this. Someone ordered this attack on the Tenth.

And I saw a warrior who wasn't wearing gray, I think. I saw a warrior in gold and black, a First House warrior in this very forest.

How can that be possible? How could I not have realized the danger racing toward us?

I hear Nazar step up beside me, but I don't turn. I can see nothing but the image of the Tenth House in my mind, shadows drawing closer to it with every breath.

"If what you're saying is true, we're already doomed," I say quietly. "The house—whatever house it is—*knows* that Merritt has fallen. They'll attack us outright."

"No," Nazar says. "If anyone was watching this battle, they'll know two things: that the attack on our house happened, and that Merritt did not die."

"Did not—" I swivel my head back toward Merritt's pyre. Nothing of it remains. Even the ashes of the Tenth House retainers' cloaks are destroyed. We have buried the bodies of our men and left our enemies for the carrion hunters to scavenge, but Merritt's body is well and truly gone. By the time we leave, there'll be only charred and overturned earth in that spot. "You burned him."

"No," Nazar says. "Merritt was struck down and rose again, cloaked in righteous fury. He reviled his attackers, who fled like the dogs they are. That's the tale that will come out of this battle, if any tale is whispered at all. That the firstborn of the Tenth House was shot and did not die. That he roared forth with an even mightier Divh, who made the mountains tremble."

I jerk as if struck, the image of that same enormous Divh branded on my mind. "Why *did* that happen?" I demand. "This— that wasn't the Tenth House Divh who appeared above me. It couldn't have been—it was far too big. And it would never bond itself to me. It's forbidden." Even as I speak, I recognize the stupidity of my words. The Divh *had* responded when I'd called its name—had bowed to me. But...how?

"When the warrior's need is great, the Divh responds," Nazar says evenly, but he refuses to be distracted from his point. "You stood in front of a sacred Divh, wearing the cloak of the Tenth House with your hood up. You turned the attackers back. To any who looked, you were Merritt."

He folds his arms. "To any we meet at the Tournament of Gold, you must be Merritt as well."

I snap my gaze to him, this new impossibility assaulting me like a never-ending storm.

"*No*," I say, and here I know I am on solid ground. "No. You must be the one to purchase soldiers for the Tenth. I'm a first-blooded *daughter*, Nazar. No one would take me as a boy. Not with this." I grab the trailing edge of my braided hair and shove it toward him, its thick, knotted length now gray with dirt and ash. "I am a *daughter*. I'm getting *married* tomorrow."

The priest lets the silence between us lead me to the next realization. Obvious and clear and such a violation, it takes my breath away.

"You want me to...to cut it off?" These sacred coils are a symbol of my first-blooded birth, instant proof of my value to another noble house. Without them, I'll never marry. Never leave the Tenth House, never truly live. Even if I somehow survive my father's wrath, he'll never let me see the sunlight ever again.

Nazar scoffs at my horrified expression. "You're worried about your *hair*? Do you know what will be left of your arm once the band is ripped from you? Rags, Talia. The muscles completely cut through, the bone broken, the entire length of your limb from shoulder to wrist scarred with twisted, mangled flesh. Many—*most* warriors die during a forced unbanding ceremony if they aren't transferring the band to their own child, which is why it's rarely performed. Many—most of those warriors die before the band reaches their wrist, where it sinks into the bone and *stays* there, if their Divh decrees it must, even if their bond is officially broken. Divhs don't give up their warriors easily, once such warriors have been chosen. And you *have* been chosen. As clearly as if you participated in the sacred rituals. You will likely not survive your unbanding. Even if you do, you'll be forever scarred."

If he means to scare me, he's succeeding. And he continues relentlessly. "If Merritt dies on this battlefield without sending reinforcements back to the Tenth, his house dies with him. The only way you can save your family, your people, is if you secure men for them. Death is the way of the warrior." He points to my arm. "If you are to die, then die with honor. Protect your house."

I swallow, looking away. *Honor,* I think bitterly. Honor for my house, in the only way now open to me. I have no other choice, if I want to honor Adriana's and Merritt's deaths. If I want to make the Tenth House strong.

And I *will* make the Tenth House strong.

"Cut it off," I growl at last.

Nazar doesn't hesitate. A few moments later, he's at my side with a hunting knife, putting his hand into the great mass at my nape. Rather than uncoiling it from its bands and knots, he slices deep, sawing his way through the thick mane. At first, I feel nothing but the tug of the sharp blade. Then he pulls away.

My head springs forward, and I lift my hands to either side of my head. "Oh!"

"Turn around," the priest mutters. "You look like you've been mauled."

I know the moment he sees the thin scar stretching across my throat, so narrow beneath my chin as to be almost invisible unless you're looking for it, but ending in a vicious, puckered whorl beneath my left ear. The scar that both my high-necked tunics and the thick, artfully arranged coils of my hair have long served to cover, a relic of the first—and last—time I strayed too close to my father when he was in one of his black moods. Nazar hesitates a long beat, studying the rough and crumpled skin.

"Your voice," he says at last.

I shrug, keeping my chin up, my eyes cold, my expression as empty as the winter's sky. My father's knife hadn't sliced my throat deeply enough to kill me, but my low, husky voice still bears the mark of his rage. So do my legs, for that matter, but those scars are more easily hidden. "I couldn't speak for months after the injury. When I finally did, I sounded...different."

Nazar doesn't respond but bends once more to his task. He works the knife to either side of my face, then back around my neck. I struggle to hold myself still. The breeze against my neck prickles my skin, and my head feels lighter than it ever has, almost wobbly on my shoulders. When Nazar finally steps back, I teeter with my hands out wide by my side, uncertain how to balance.

His critical glance takes in my altered appearance, and my mind races at what he must see. My sacred hair had always been my most valuable attribute, proclaiming me as a woman of worth. My face had always seemed attractive enough, at least with my scar hidden beneath all those glorious, coiled braids. *Beautiful*, my mother had proclaimed, more than once. I had no fear of being rejected by the child of the Twelfth House. But now...

Now my hair is so *short*. My face is thrown into sharp focus and the scar along the left side of my neck exposed, this last a silent testimony to the shame I must never speak aloud.

No one would find me beautiful now. No one.

My chin lifts another notch.

Nazar stares down at the mass of hair in his hands. "We'll keep this."

I scowl. "Like a pet?"

"No. It's got your dowry sewn up in it, and we may have need of that."

I curl my lip, but he's not wrong. If the hair was cleaned, the adornments reset, it could be sold—or broken apart for its stones. And we have soldiers to buy.

Nazar has already transferred his gaze to me, though. "You're built straight enough. Your back is broad and strong. In breeches and loose gear, you'll pass." He grimaces. "Your low voice will help as well. You are the warrior son, Merritt. Firstborn of the Tenth House."

Firstborn, I think hollowly. One falsehood undone; a new, far worse deception begun.

And I'm not alone in this new lie either.

"Why are you doing this?" I ask sourly, shifting my gaze to stare into the priest's inscrutable, pale eyes. "If the truth is discovered, I won't be the only one punished. You'll be killed as well."

"Why doesn't matter," Nazar says. He turns me back to the smoldering remains of Merritt's funeral pyre, then lifts his gaze once more to the mountains looming over us to the west. They are our last barrier to the Tournament of Gold, and to the fate the Light has dealt us.

"You are Merritt, warrior knight, first-blooded direct descendent of the founders of the Protectorate," Nazar says, my shorn pile of hair spilling over his hands. "Your feet are on the Lighted Path, the way of the warrior before you. From now until you take your dying breath, *that* is all that will matter."

CHAPTER 5

The journey over the mountain pass to the Tournament of Gold takes us three hard days' travel. I barely notice it. My dismay over my shorn hair fades with the plodding of Darkwing's hooves. It's replaced by the twin daggers of grief and fury at Adriana's senseless death, and at the loss of Merritt with his whole life in front of him. Those rake over me by turns, as sharp and jagged as the broken arrow in my saddle bag.

Someone—somewhere—loosed that arrow. And though finding that killer cannot be my focus, the anger that builds within me against the slinking coward who took my brother's life eventually crowds out everything else…leaving behind only deep, immovable rage.

My left arm throbs every time I jostle it, too, blood seeping out from under the bandages Nazar has carefully fashioned for me. He says it will heal quickly, but I don't see how. Especially since I shouldn't have been banded at all. At least I didn't share Merritt's crippling sickness when he first bonded with his Divh. He'd been ill for days, a shivering, quivering mess. I only feel pain.

Yet another sign I am unworthy. As if I need more reminders.

The priest ignores me, mostly, for most of the first day. After that, when he speaks at all, it's to tell me of this city or that, this house or the other, soft murmurs of a world I've never known except for the brief scraps of information I'd overheard through the years and ferreted away. No woman needs to learn about the politics and structures of the Protectorate. But first-blooded and first-born warriors must. And I *am* a warrior, at least for these next few days. I sop up his every word like it's my last meal.

At length, I tell Nazar of the man I saw in the forest, dressed in First House colors. He's shocked, then outraged, of course, and he rails at me, driving nails into the wounds of my own guilt. His sneering rebuke shreds through my weak protests and half-formed defenses as if they were made of cobwebs. He rants for a solid three hours, then abruptly stops, falls silent.

What's done is done, he says. The warrior can only move forward.

His lessons begin anew—and more of them now, histories and heroes, politics and power. I learn that Lord Rihad may have no sons, but he isn't without his banded warriors—some of them almost as noble as the Lord Protector himself. He speaks of a nephew yet unbanded, too—Fortiss. A fighter of great renown, from an honored family, who is still without a Divh, for reasons Nazar doesn't know but which plainly confuse him.

I think of the man I met, his golden eyes, his noble face. Is this Fortiss to blame for my brother's death? I think of the gray-feathered arrow in my pack, shot true and far into the sky until it buried itself in my brother's back. It's finely made by any account, and so was the bow that shot it, I suspect. Not a marauder's arrow, either. A nobleman's.

Fury knots within me, as thickly coiled as my cut-off hair, but nowhere near as beautiful.

Gradually, Nazar's quiet, lulling voice helps me box up the last of my pain, bury it deep. In this sacred soil, I plant iron-tipped resolve, fledgling shoots strengthened by the priest's stoic presence. I will go to the tournament. I will secure the soldiers we desperately need. Once that is done, I'll return to my father and face his punishment.

Even if I don't survive that punishment, I *will* bring honor to my house.

By the third day of our journey, the pain from my arm has diminished to a dull ache—or maybe I'm simply distracted by the changes all around me. The road we're following has grown crowded. Excitement rushes through the air, everyone's tongue bearing tales of the coming Tournament of Gold. It's to be the largest one ever, they all say, and the boons to the winning houses will be extraordinary. The Court of Talons will be full to bursting with warriors eligible for the winged crown—the award given to the winning warrior, if Lord Protector Rihad judges him worthy.

Nazar never stops to ask for any details beyond what we can overhear. Neither do I, of course. Every time a traveler stares too long at our small company—a boy, a priest and five additional horses, our dusty packs and empty saddles draped in Tenth House green—I brace myself. We are hardly a procession worthy of one of the great houses of the Protectorate. At every sidelong glance I expect to hear the cry that I am a thief, a liar, a criminal wearing the rightful band of my brother.

But no one stops us; no one speaks. Instead, we simply ride.

It's late afternoon before we crest the final ridge. With a subtle gesture, Nazar points me toward the roped and cordoned campsites clearly occupied by the visiting houses of the Protectorate, their warrior knights and their banded soldiers come to fight in the Tournament of Gold. The lesser houses, like ours, have only one Divh, bonded to the first-blooded and firstborn warrior son of the house lord. The greater houses have more—Divhs that are bonded to lesser noble warrior knights and even to non-noble banded soldiers. The Divhs of the first-blooded and firstborn warrior knights are always the mightiest, by far. But any Divh, even one commanded by a banded soldier, would be awesome to behold.

The campsite's layout mirrors that of the Protectorate itself: the First House flags flying in the center, surrounded by the Second, Eighth, and Fourth Houses to the west, the Third, Seventh, and Ninth Houses to the south, the Eleventh, Tenth, and Twelfth Houses to the east, and the Fifth and Sixth Houses to the north.

Even now, I can see the red and white banners and tents of the Second, the sky-blue flags of the Fourth, the rich purple of the Sixth House. I've only heard of these great houses from the bards. Seeing them now feels wrong somehow, like a story ripped from its pages and scattered on a field. I search to see how large a space was allotted for the Tenth House, and yet—what would we raise? We have no banners or tents, no flags to fly. We've barely kept more than our bedrolls and grave shovel.

Still, I can't dwell on that depressing truth for long. Because beyond these rich encampments, the thriving city of Trilion bursts forth like a swarm of bees startled from its hive...and for a moment, I can only stare. I've never seen such a place—never even *imagined* it.

Trilion isn't a city proper, Nazar has told me. Now, taking in the buildings and streets below me on the third afternoon since my brother's death, I understand better what the priest has been trying to explain during our journey.

Most every city, from the capital of the Exalted Imperium on down, is a tightly wound body built around two hearts: its market, and its buildings of official commerce and law. Inns and taverns, shops and artisans' stalls expand in ever-widening circles around this double-beating center, hemmed in by rivers or mountains or the sea.

But Trilion's hearts beat differently, and the city that has sprung up around them throbs with a rhythm all its own.

Soaring high above the city is the First House, home of Lord Rihad and the Court of Talons. The First Lord of the Protectorate governs not only the city at the base of his mountain stronghold, but the whole of our border nation; he answers only to the Emperor of the Exalted Imperium, who has not stepped foot in the Protectorate for the past hundred years. At the base of Lord Rihad's mountain, there's a wide swath of wasteland—open ground unplowed or built upon, I assume by Rihad's own decree. Then the city proper of

Trilion begins: inns, taverns, shops and smithies, crafts holds and kilns, all of it spreading out in a teeming tide toward the second great structure of the city: the tournament coliseum.

Fully three hundred galloping strides long on each side, the coliseum of the Tournament of Gold consists of two great stands carved out of a bedrock of limestone, reshaping what had once been two bulbous fists of rock jutting out of the earth into massive semicircular foundations for seating.

It's rumored that a great city once stood on these grounds, and a stadium for sport as well. But unlike the cities tucked into the mountains to the east, still somewhat intact despite the long centuries of rot and decay, the open plains were cruel to all relics of the past.

By the time the Exalted Imperium pushed back its enemies and secured the Protectorate as a buffer zone between the empire and the chaos of the Western Realms, there was very little left of the civilization had existed before. And so the first Lord Protector and the Twelve Houses of the Protectorate built upon those ashes and transformed the limestone monuments into stadiums to celebrate their fabled warriors.

According to Nazar, these stands can hold five thousand souls. Even from this distance, the coliseum seems impossibly huge. Mighty Divhs do battle there, and I clench my fists as I look at the enormous structure in the distance, my pulse pounding. Gent would have competed there, were Merritt still alive.

"Declare yourself!"

The voice is so loud, so close, I nearly fall off Darkwing. As it is, I flinch back roughly, then whip around to gape.

A tall, thin, severe-looking man stands in front of us on the path in richly embroidered robes. Beside him, a shorter, equally thin man in a tunic and heavy breeches holds a massive open book. They are dressed in the colors of the First House—gold and black.

Gold and black! My mind immediately flies to the warrior in the forest, and then to the gray-feathered arrow in my saddlebag.

This must be some seneschal of the First House, sent to record all the visiting houses. I could show him the arrow, explain the attack, demand justice for Merritt—

Except...that won't work. Because *I'm* Merritt.

"Declare yourself!" the man barks again, his eyes narrowing on me, not Nazar.

"Merritt," I blurt, my rough, low voice made harsher with panic. "Lord Merritt of the Tenth House, son of Lord Lemille, first-blooded and—firstborn."

The man bends over the book to scratch my name onto a page, his assistant holding the tome securely. "Come to enter the Tournament of Gold," the seneschal says, speaking in a haughty, privileged tone. It's not a question.

I trade a quick glance with Nazar. The priest's headshake is only barely perceptible. "No," I say. "We seek only to hire soldiers this year. No more."

The seneschal peers up at me, his beetling brows lifting high on his gaunt face, but the next words I hear aren't from him or his assistant. Instead, a called-out greeting rolls across us with the rich indolence of spilled wine, seeping into all the empty spaces of my life I hadn't realized were there.

"Merritt of the Tenth House. Well met."

I turn in my saddle, pulling Darkwing around—then jolt upright.

It's the warrior from the forest.

I want to scream, to flee, or to faint straight out of my saddle. I do none of these things, instead remaining stoic and still as the warrior stares at me with an insufferably cocky smile. Everything about him is the same: the confident carriage, the broad shoulders, the rich vestments of gold and black. His burnished skin practically glows in the harsh sunlight, his curling black hair lifts gently in the breeze, and his golden eyes seem to see right through me. All the saliva dries in my mouth.

There's no question, now that I see him in the light. This is a true warrior knight, first-blooded and firstborn, I know it in my bones.

The man is flanked by two attendants—clearly soldiers, with blocky faces and flat eyes—the three of them on snow-white horses that fairly glow in the bright sun. They all wear gold tunics trimmed in black.

Were these attendants also with him in the forest? My mind practically burns with the question. Was one of them the archer who murdered my brother?

"Who..." I begin lamely, but the warrior mercifully cuts me off.

"Fortiss of the First, nephew of the Lord Protector," he announces, confirming Nazar's suspicion in one breath. "And of all the warriors in the Tournament, I'm probably the only one glad to see you here."

Fortiss, I echo in my mind, twin streams of fire and ice stiffening my spine. The unbanded champion of Lord Rihad—his brother's child? Sister's? Nazar hadn't told me this. There's too much Nazar still doesn't know about the politics of the First House. I can feel the priest's keen attention on the man in front of me, for all that he makes no sound.

Fortiss holds his hand out to me, and once again I freeze. I've never shaken a man's hand as an equal. Then Darkwing stamps, clearly picking up on my nerves. I thrust my hand forward, awkwardly clasping Fortiss's. He clamps it hard, and his grin widens as I jerk my arm back once more.

"Rumor has it your caravan was waylaid by marauders," he says, false concern shading his words. "Judging from the state of your horses and packs, I believe it. Has your party split up to find lodging?"

I grit my teeth, hearing the lie in his voice. *Rumor has it, my ass.* He was there in that forest, as sure as he's standing in front of me right now. Why would he lie about it? "We were waylaid, as you say." My rough voice slices the air, cold and blunt in the sunshine. "We mourn the loss of many good men, and a woman too."

"Woman?" Fortiss's face registers genuine shock, and he

glances to Nazar, then to the horses, then finally back to me. "Not your sister, surely? Lord Rihad had wondered if she was traveling with you."

"No." There's really nothing else I can say about that, and no ready lie springs up to explain where in the Light I've hidden a full-grown woman and all her wedding hair. Instead, I glare at Fortiss until he shifts his glance again to Nazar.

"Lord Protector Rihad bade me keep watch for any riders in the trappings of the Tenth House green. He'll be glad to know you've arrived safely after your trials on the mountain pass. No tribute will be required of you when you make your presentation to him tomorrow. Rather, it's his profound hope that you will regain your losses and more in the Tournament of Gold."

"I'm not here to fight," I say quickly. "Only to hire."

"As you say." Glancing back to me with inscrutable eyes, he gestures to our pitiful clutch of horses. "Again, this isn't your entire encampment, is it? Your sister—was she hurt? Tell me she is well."

I am struck dumb, and Nazar speaks in my place.

"She remains at some distance, safe," he says gruffly. "This is no place for a woman."

Fortiss barks a sharp laugh. "That's certainly true." Does he sound relieved? Dismayed? Or simply astounded that the Tenth House line is still intact?

By now, I've finally regained my tongue. "And how has Lord Protector Rihad heard of this attack?" I scowl, glaring at him. "We saw no one but the *marauders* whose bodies remained after."

Fortiss only shrugs. "Maybe not, but you were seen. A passing caravan claims they witnessed the attack from high on the pass above you. They shared the breathless tale to any who would listen —including talk of the enormous Divh the Tenth House brought to bear."

"Too late to save the lives of my people." My words are bitter and sharp, and Fortiss's gaze meets mine.

"True enough. But if your Divh is anything like what the

rumors say, you can gain more men in the tournament—more, and better men—"

"*No.*" I'm more forceful this time. "I'm here to buy soldiers, not to fight. That can wait another year." It can wait a lifetime.

Fortiss frowns, then his face clears. "Ah! No wonder you're so insistent. You don't know, do you?"

He leans forward again as if to confide in me, and I force myself not to lean in as well, a witless moth to his flame. "The Tournament of Gold—it's different this year. There are boons to be had by those who win unlike any that have ever been granted. The deeper you get into the tournament, the better your chance for freshly minted banded soldiers—soldiers paid for by the First House, not your own coin."

I blink in surprise at the unexpected largesse of the First House —banded soldiers we don't have to pay for? Could that be possible? At the Tenth, my father holds our coin in a tight, two-fisted grip, loath to spend any of it for anything. He would leap at this chance to get able-bodied men for free, I have no doubt.

Fortiss laughs at my expression. I try to school myself back to disinterest, but he's not fooled. "I thought you'd care to hear that. Far better to keep your coin and get solid men for free, than to spend your money needlessly, eh?"

Unreasonably annoyed by his tone, I return his grin with a growl. "I'm not here to compete, Fortiss of the First." Once again, I think of the arrow in my saddlebag, proof positive of a grave betrayal among the very houses this tournament celebrates.

Fortiss is the nephew of the Lord Protector, who is the governor of our entire territory, *and he was there.* I should show him the arrow, demand an explanation—but something stays my hand. I am, after all, a woman dressed as a man...and I am bound with a warrior's band. If that band was discovered, nothing I could say would change the fact that I'd be arrested, imprisoned, and probably killed.

No. I need a better plan.

I turn to the seneschal, who's not yet put away his book. "I'm here to buy soldiers," I reiterate. "Nothing more."

"Stubborn to the end," Fortiss overrides the end of my declaration, his voice still maddeningly confident. "While you're here, though, at least take a look around. The Tournament of Gold begins with a few days of competition among the rank and file; men and boys seeking their fortunes in the garrisons of the great houses. But there will be a warrior and Divh battle or two as well—merely exhibitions—to whet the appetites of the crowds. Something to watch, if you are thinking of fighting in the two-day competition between high-level warriors at the end of the tournament." He raises both hands at my black look. "Or even if you're not."

Throughout this recitation, Nazar has edged forward, and I glance at him, not missing the keen interest in his eyes. "What else should we know about the tournament?" he asks.

Fortiss turns to him then straightens as he takes in Nazar's deep-blue cloak, flipped back now to reveal its gray lining.

"Priest of the Light, you honor us," he says. "Forgive me, I didn't realize—"

Nazar waves him off. "You say the tournament has changed this year. How, specifically?"

Fortiss remains respectful, but there's no denying his excitement. His horse stamps and shifts beneath him. "The Tournament of Gold has always showcased the best warriors from all twelve houses—those who participate, of course." He eyes me as he says this last, and I feel the blood creep up my cheeks. I grit my teeth but say nothing.

"This year will be the greatest spectacle yet. After the preliminary battles among the fighting men are done, the warrior knights and banded soldiers who qualify—if any do—will undertake two days of one-on-one competition. Two men and their Divhs will take the field, face off, and whoever triumphs advances. In that way, the field will be winnowed down from more than fifty to eight."

"More than fifty," I echo hollowly. I had no idea there were so many warrior knights and banded soldiers coming here to compete. Most houses have garrisons of men to protect them in the absence of their mighty Divhs, but still, it seems rash to leave so many houses without their warriors.

"The eight remaining combatants will fight in a configuration of Lord Rihad's choosing—though you can bet it will be tailored to please the crowd—until there remain only two. Those two will fight for the tournament's ultimate prize."

"The winged crown?" It's my voice, not Nazar's, that breaks in as Fortiss pauses. I grimace at the warrior's knowing grin.

"Often promised, rarely bestowed." He nods. "But this year, like I said, is different. The crown brings with it a dozen newly banded soldiers—the top non-noble finalists in the lower levels of the tournament. Something else to consider, no?"

A horn sounds, and Fortiss lifts his head, turning as if he can see who's making the distant call. His profile seems chiseled in stone, and wariness tightens my stomach. A new, unfamiliar, and definitely unwanted doubt fills me. This is a warrior knight I need to stay far away from. This whole place is a danger I can ill afford.

"New houses arrive," Fortiss announces, glancing back at me, "and so I must greet them. But welcome to Trilion, Lord Merritt of the Tenth." He studies me intently for a long moment, then nods. "To Trilion, and to the Tournament of Gold."

CHAPTER 6

We set up camp, erecting a central tent that is large enough to hold ten men. No one needs to know we don't fill it with anything but air and, with any luck, we'll soon have men to spare. Nazar spends some of our coin to pay for a messenger's swift ride to the Twelfth House, with a letter to Lord Orlof advising him of our detour to the tournament and assuring him of my eventual arrival. Neither of us speak of how I plan to hide a warrior's band from my future *husband*, of course, but that's a challenge for another day.

There's also the niggling issue of my sister lodging in some Trilion inn, but Nazar waves off my concern over this. Women have no place at the tournament. No one will come looking for Talia here, he insists, only Merritt.

By the Light, he better be right.

The next morning, I set off with new resolve to play my role and secure my house. To my surprise, Nazar's prediction has been borne out: the deep cuts on my arm caused by Merritt's warrior band have closed, thick dark scabs replacing the red welts. Eventually, he says, the black scorching will fade, and this time I believe him.

With the sun bright and full, the morning breeze playing through my cropped hair, I find myself willing to believe anything. It's nearly a half hour's journey from our camp to the coliseum, but I don't mind the walk. Besides, I need the practice.

Riding like a man is easy enough—far easier than as a woman, truth be told. But walking? More difficult than I ever imagined, especially in leggings and boots. If I'm to make a presentation to Lord Protector Rihad later today, as Nazar informs me I must, I have work to do.

But all may not be lost, if I can keep my focus. With a skill I didn't know the priest possessed, Nazar has fashioned for me thickly padded breeches and a tunic made of heavy material that gives me bulk while straightening the curves of my chest and hips. I carry my sword slung low on my waist, which forces me to walk in a wide, sweeping swagger, and my dark green cloak flows around me in rich, Tenth-House green. I feel ridiculous, but if I go slow, I can manage it.

The tournament grounds are teeming with people this morning, shouts and laughter mingling with the stentorian tones of an official crier reciting the history of the tournament—how it honors the ancient battle between the warriors of the Exalted Imperium and the vile armies of the Western Realms. I barely listen. Even as far away as the Tenth House, I've heard this story often enough.

The man's voice grows more strident as I approach. "Our imperial warriors were allied with the Light, and through a battle of unimaginable ferocity, they conquered the Darkness. In return, we were granted the service of the Light's mythical beasts, the Divh!"

At these last words, my warrior band flares with sudden and unmistakable heat, and I stop short. A few people around me seem to take notice and edge away respectfully. Respectfully! I struggle not to apologize to them, to tell them they need take no extra measures for me. That I'm only a second-born, a daughter, a woman.

Except, I'm not, by the Light. Not in this place. Here, I'm a firstborn son. A warrior knight. Though Nazar has actually taken something away from me—my hair—he's also apparently added impressive bulk to my size in all directions. It's a strange and unsettling truth, both thrilling and, in its way...deeply irritating.

The crier continues his tale, refocusing me. "But the war had taken its toll. The forces of the Exalted Imperium withdrew to its capital city to regroup, leaving behind a Protectorate of twelve great houses whose firstborn sons commanded mighty Divhs, as well as noble families throughout the land who were also granted Divhs by divine decree. No one dared challenge the might of our great beasts, so there was no more fighting. But the twelve houses and their noble families dared not rest! To keep our alliance with the Divh strong, we brought the Way of the Light to our great Protectorate. Under the careful watch of the Lord Protector, Divhs were transferred from one generation of sons to the next. Invoking the imperial right granted only to him, the Lord Protector then used his own band to create new bands, summoning Divhs for worthy fighting men—making them banded soldiers. And then, finally, the First House established an extraordinary proving ground for both the warrior knights and their mighty beasts: the Tournament of Gold!"

Cheers go up all around me, the spell of the man's tale finally breaking. Though he continues on about the glory of the First House, I force myself to start moving again. *How much Merritt would have reveled in the pageantry of this place,* I think, unexpected sorrow lancing through me. *How much he would have loved every moment of this.*

My heart a rough stone in my chest, I make my way toward the coliseum—not to make a purchase right away, but at least to scout out the area. As I walk, my gaze remains fixed on the enormous structure. The crowd is already whispering about the day's tournament trials, and despite myself, I burn with curiosity to see them.

The banded soldiers and their Divhs won't be summoned for fights such as these, they say. Instead, it will be men and their horses, tilting for a chance to gain a position in a house's garrison. A house like the Tenth, I resolve. If I can gather the men we need quickly, in the midst of the pretournament confusion, my deception may not be uncovered.

I'm jostled to the side as my mind is swept away by thoughts of battles and beasts, and stumble into a small group of people. Someone in the crowd shoves back.

"Watch your step, boy," comes the surly snap.

I straighten, willing myself not to react. Here's yet another person taken in by my disguise! A tremor of hope chases through me. Here in Trilion, I'm not a crime, not an abomination...I'm an ordinary boy, someone meant to be here. No one knows my truth in this city. No one knows my shame.

No one will know anything but what I show them.

As long as I never again cross paths with other true warriors like Fortiss of the First, I will survive this place.

Squaring my shoulders, I aim once more for the tournament stands when a flurry of activity to the right catches my attention. There are shouts and cries of excitement, and small, lumpy sacks held high in grimy hands. Money bags, I realize instantly. A fight must be underway, or some game of sport to keep the interest of the mob at bay until they can wager on the tournament proper. Nazar has warned me to stay away from everyone other than the soldiers whose services I must buy, but I'm a man now. A firstblooded, firstborn warrior, in fact. I can go anywhere as long as I don't stay too long, don't fix my attention on anyone, or let them fix their attention on me.

I shoulder my way through the crowd until it shifts before me, giving me some view to the open space beyond.

It *is* a fight—my very first of the tournament!

A tall, strong boy brandishes a long, well-turned sword. His face is set in a snarl of outrage, thick lips pressed back against his teeth. He wears no helmet. A shiny chain mail shirt hangs from his shoulders, and his breeches are sturdy and well made. This is a warrior knight, I realize instantly, cut from the same cloth as

Merritt and probably the same age of seventeen years, no more. I don't think he's first-blooded, more likely a warrior knight from lesser noble family, but his sword is well made, and heavy enough to make the boy's arms wobble, for all his apparent strength.

"You dare to speak to me, *cripple*, about anything?" he demands in a shrill voice, staring hard at someone I can't see. "You dare?"

I stand up on my tiptoes to see his opponent—and gape.

Facing the warrior knight is an even younger boy of maybe only fourteen years, but not one dressed in chain mail or heavy clothes. He's wrapped in rags that look stitched together from several different shirts and pants, and in place of a sword, he holds a long stave in his right hand. But though I've fought many mock battles with rods, the boy doesn't fling out his left hand in the same manner I have done.

Because he has no left hand. He has no left arm.

His face is a mass of old bruises and cuts, and there's blood on his ragged shirt as well. He doesn't back down in the face of the young warrior attacking him, however. Instead, he eggs him on.

"Come at me, then," he cries, his face creasing in a wild grin that seems more desperate than joyful. "Come at me. You've got your sword, Hantor. All I've got is this stave. Hardly a threat, yeah? Come at me!"

Chuckles ripple through the crowd at this, and the young warrior knight stiffens. His colors are red and white, the standard of the Second House. *Is* he first-blooded? He's arrogant enough to be, anyway. Does he already have a Divh? I strain to peer above the shoulders of the men in front of me and miss the next taunt of the one-armed boy—the one-armed boy who surely knows better.

Then his laughter sounds again. "Come at me, you *girl*. Let me show you—"

The one-armed boy can't finish his jibe because the taller youth screams in outrage and races toward him. A loud cry goes up from the watchers. Bags change hands, and a rush of chatter fills the space as new bets are made, the boys in the circle now engaging in a furious clanging of sword and stave.

I watch, wide eyed, as I watched every training battle of men or boys I could at the Tenth House, always from the shadows. I could never train formally, of course, but I would sneak out when all was dark and quiet and lift the heavy rods in the middle of the night, thrusting and striking at wooden posts driven into the ground, while Adriana stood watch. I'd always take care to miss the posts, so as not to make any noise, until one day I found a stave had been wrapped with a thick blanket of sheep's wool. Striking it made no sound at all.

My lips twist as I recall my delight of that night's discovery, and all the subsequent training I'd done with that blunt weapon. I'd assumed it was a training tool one of our men had devised and forgotten about, but now I think of Nazar...and wonder.

Another shout goes up, recalling me, and I shove into a pocket of space between two arguing spectators. As I do, the one-armed boy steps out of the way barely in time to avoid a long slashing lunge then cracks his wooden stave against the back of the taller boy. The young warrior knight stumbles and goes down on one knee. The crowd yells louder. The knight scrambles back up to his feet, his face a mask of rage and dirt. I stare at him in surprise. I've never seen anyone that furious before, and over—what? A sparring match?

But the warrior knight's anger is his undoing. He surges forward, and the one-armed boy flicks his stick in exactly the way I'd do it. The knight apparently has not been spending his time with staves, and his sword tips up, slipping out of his grasp and tumbling to the ground.

A great cheer rises, and the boy grins, his face transformed in that moment to one of sheer joy as he flourishes the stave, then drops it to signify the fight is over. Money changes hands at a swift pace, laughter and taunting cries gilding the air around us.

A movement behind the boy propels me forward.

"No!" I shout instinctively, stepping closer to the open space of the fighting pit. The taller youth has picked up his sword and now lunges toward the younger boy, who, without his stave or a second arm to protect himself, can only twist in shock as the warrior knight comes at him.

Instantly, I see Merritt before my eyes. Merritt, tall and straight, laughing and brash and joyful and now, impossibly, *gone* because I didn't act—didn't move quickly enough to protect him. I *won't* be too slow again.

Pushing the one-armed boy out of the way, I scoop up his abandoned stave and bring it forward in an underhand swing as the young warrior knight's sword comes down. The stave is sturdy, a thicker, heavier wood than I've ever used in my play-acting behind our manor house. The sword clangs against it and bounces back, wobbling in the knight's inexperienced grip. The young man attacks me in a fury then, slashing and thrashing. I hold up the stave to block him, but still he comes on, each clang of his sword jolting me to my bones. Then I pivot to the side long enough to bring the stave around in a jarring crack to the knight's skull, and he loses his sword completely.

His sword, but not his fury.

He rushes me.

I've never grappled with anyone before, and the boy advances with his fists up and hammering, suddenly far too close for me to use my stave. Instinctively, I drop the stave and lift my forearms to protect my face, but not before the warrior knight cracks me directly beneath the eye, a blow hard enough to make my vision scatter into a million fragmented pieces. The pain surprises me almost as much as the violence of the blow, and I taste blood in my mouth. Blood! With my arms positioned so high, he tries to pummel my stomach, but Nazar's padding saves me there—saves me and gives me the space of a breath to regain my senses. I lunge forward, shoving hard against the boy's body until he crashes to the ground.

Once again, that seems to be the wrong thing to do. We roll, and distantly I hear the cheering of men. Then suddenly, I am on the bottom and the boy is on top of me, his fists battering down on my forearms. He sits heavily on my stomach, too heavily, and a new kind of agony grips me, this one tinged with hysteria. I can't breathe, can't think! I fling my right hand out to scrabble away and my fingers connect with something round and slender—the stave.

As I flail for it, however, I leave my face open, and the boy's blows rain down harder, each one thudding mercilessly, his fists seeming to follow me even as I try to twist and jerk my head away. My hand grips the stave now, but it's too long for me to do anything normal—its arc would soar too high and too slow. Instead, I heft it in my grasp until a good four inches extends to the near side of my fist.

I grin, and the sight of my teeth flashing between my bloody, split lips seems to take my opponent off guard. His eyes widen—and I strike. I lift the stave off the ground and yank my arm in tight, cracking the boy in the temple with the rod's thick base.

With a furious cry, the young warrior knight topples off me. Even as I scramble away, fear blanking my pain for a blessed moment, a strong arm snakes around my waist and a voice as fast as a galloping horse chatters into my ear.

"We go, we go now! Hantor's stunned, but he'll get the others, he'll get the others and they'll be furious. He'll kill us, they'll all kill us; you're an idiot, so we go!"

Still babbling at an almost manic speed, the one-armed boy half drags me into the crowd. Delighted onlookers part easily for us, cheerfully letting us escape into the throng. The boy doesn't stop, however, until we're in the shadows of the enormous coliseum walls.

"You're an *idiot*," he says again after he dumps me unceremoniously on the dirt. The sting of my injuries crashes down with me, an avalanche of rocks that seems to have landed mostly on my face. "You know that, right? An idiot."

"I'm an idiot," I moan. I roll over onto my back, and the boy whistles long and low.

"Your sword—Holy Divh, you *did* have something in that scabbard. "Why didn't you use it? You're an—"

I let him carry on as I try to assess the damage. My face is a mushy pulp, but my teeth appear to be intact. My body is not at all damaged. The knight hadn't gone for my wrists or hands, which were the most unprotected part of me after my face. He's also spared my neck, which *feels* unprotected but mostly because I no longer have a thick pile of hair wrapped around it. I'm bleeding from a long scrape along my scalp, but I've been injured enough to know that such blood doesn't mean much. My vision dances and my head feels stuffed with straw, but I'll live.

I haul myself up to a sitting position, and the boy opposite me shuts up. I squint with the eye that hasn't yet swelled shut. "Who are you?" I ask.

He grins despite his own split lip, which bleeds anew as he holds out his one good hand to me. "Caleb. I'm a squire for the Second—well, I used to be with the Second House." He shrugs his left shoulder, causing the flap of cloth to flutter. I expect to get queasy at the sight, but I don't. Mainly because Caleb keeps talking.

"My arm's a bit of a challenge for people to work around. So these days, I'm more of a squire for hire by any house that needs me, scurrying about, doing whatever needs doing. Gathering supplies, chasing away thieves, all of it." He grins again. "But I can fight better than anyone gives me credit for, and that helps. I'da made more on that scrap if you hadn't come along. 'Course, I might've gotten clocked too. No one wants to bet on a cripple once he gets beat up, I tell you plain."

"Your house lets you—where are your clothes?"

"My—oh." He sighs, and a little of his stuffing seeps out of him. I instantly miss it and curse myself for my thoughtless comment. "I can't wear a proper squire's garb anymore. Not a squire, you see, not really. And I don't have a family, not like a regular one. So—I make do. I think the Second'll take me back but till then, I..."

"Until then, you need clothes," I say, my voice far too sharp. "I've got extra."

Caleb bristles. "I don't want your charity. I don't even know you."

"I'm...Merritt of the Tenth," I say, forming the words awkwardly. "At least take me back to my camp then, hey? Before I go blind." I hold my hands out to the side as I try to rise—no easy task with a sword strapped to my side, and harder still with my ringing head. "Help me up? I'm not going to be able to see anything in the next few minutes."

Caleb moves quickly to my side and stands steady as I grasp his arm and pull myself to my feet. Beneath his rags, he's thin and wiry—definitely no older than fourteen, maybe only thirteen years. But someone I desperately need at the moment, all the same. "I can't tell direction," I mutter.

"Where are you camped?" He's already moving me back into the crowd, standing far enough away that I'm not hanging on him, but close enough for me to keep him in view despite my dimming sight. "This side of the coliseum?"

"Yes, on the road toward the village. No, off the road. Off..." I shake my head slowly, trying to stay focused. "There are trees."

He snorts. "Trees are a good start. Is there a stream as well? Or rocks?"

We move like that back through the crowd, Caleb stopping once to crack his right palm on the back of an apparent friend. Money bags are emptied and their contents divvied up, and I resolve to find my own way. I point myself in what I hope is the direction of Nazar's camp, unsurprised when Caleb catches up with me and turns me slightly to the left.

"Sorry, needed the coin," he says. "I find if I don't settle up right fast, it tends to slip away."

"You fight for money?" My words aren't forming correctly anymore, and my mouth has difficulty closing, my lips puffy and dry.

"Well, I don't fight for fun, if that's what you're thinking. And

I'm not in the tournament proper, can't be without an arm. Though that would be a thing, wouldn't it? Fighting for the right to join a noble house as a soldier, to have a chance at earning a Divh. This year, *thirty* men will get chosen as banded soldiers, to be parceled out to the winning house of the tournament, their first year's wages paid for by the First House! Twelve will go to the winner alone!"

I swing my head toward him, aware that it's taking me longer than it should. "Really?" I'd never heard of so many men being granted the honor of a Divh so quickly.

Was this what Fortiss had meant, saying the winners of the tournament could earn soldiers for their house of real worth? "Thirty banded soldiers, all at once?"

"*Thirty.*" Caleb nods. "It's unprecedented. The thirty best non-banded combatants at the tournament will undergo a ritual with Lord Protector Rihad and his priests to become banded soldiers. Then they'll be free to serve a house. Rumor has it that all the houses are coming who need more men, which is most of them now." He eyes me meaningfully, then frowns and fumbles at his side. "Here, take a sip of this."

He holds something up to me, and I try to sniff it, but my nose is clogged with blood and gore. "Just water," Caleb says. "You get spirits in you, you'll fall down. And I won't be able to carry you, I'm thinking."

The water tastes like the finest liquid I've ever drunk, and I take two long pulls on it before I push it back. "Yours," I say. "You need it too, with this heat. But thank you."

"You really are an idiot," Caleb says again, but there's something in his voice that catches at me, something important. Then I stumble into him. How am I this hurt? I wasn't hit that hard, I'm sure of it.

"Sorry," I grunt, and Caleb picks up the pace, threading through the crowd with nimble ease, chattering all the way as my heart begins to hammer and my eyes water. I don't realize I've hunched over until I squint hard and the tips of Nazar's boots finally swim into view. I nearly sag to my knees, but Caleb's strong arm holds me, and his high, clear voice bursts out.

"Your knight, sir." Caleb shuffles back, taking me with him. His voice quakes as he speaks more quickly, all in a rush. "Sir, I did him no harm. He saved my life—my life! In the crowd today. I could do naught but bring him back to your camp. He saved my life, and I brought him back—hey!"

I slump to the ground.

CHAPTER 7

My face swells to half again its size by the following morning. Caleb's gone when I awake, but Nazar doesn't leave the campsite. Instead, he layers foul-smelling poultices over my face, covering my eyes, and slaps my hands away when I try to pull off the soaked cloths.

"At least now no one will mistake you as a warrior knight," he says grimly. "Merely an unhoused grit trying for a noble station."

I manage short sentences, my mouth slowly regaining the ability to form distinct words. "I fought well and hard. Caleb has one arm."

"It was not your fight."

"He beat the red knight fairly. The boy came after him. But the fight was already over. It wasn't fair."

Nazar hesitates for a long time, and I almost drift off into sleep again. Then his words pull my mind back. "You didn't draw your sword."

I snort, half coughing as the air lodges in my swollen nose. "I don't know how to use it."

"That's the first sensible thing you've said in days," he snaps, and a moment later, the true source of his anger becomes clear. "You were to meet with Rihad yesterday."

He catches me before I can lurch upright. "Lie still. I told the men who came 'round that the ride and the attack in the mountains has caught up with you, and that you would honor Rihad more by healing before he sees you. It's true enough, and the Lord Protector seems inclined to give you both grace and space." His tone implies I deserve neither, and I wince. He's right.

"Lance my bruises." I wave my hand at the poultices. "I'll heal faster."

"No," he retorts, with the sharpness of a teacher driven to the edge of his patience. "You'll heal faster but imperfectly, with scars beneath your eyes."

Defensively, I point to my neck, though the blood rushing to my face makes my head throb. "I'm already scarred. What's one more?"

The priest doesn't speak after that. I fall into a fitful sleep. At one time, I can almost hear voices. Nazar's calm and measured tones, Caleb's—I think it must be Caleb's—high and earnest patter. But mostly I draw in the fragrant smell of mint and cloves and the strong tang of garlic, so strong I'll taste it for days, I'm sure.

When I wake again, I don't move, but Nazar is there anyway. He peels away the top cloth to uncover one eye, and I blink up at him, almost able to see him through the slit that's opened up. The swelling has diminished. My head is clearer, my senses sharper. I have to be improving.

"Lie still." Nazar's words are clipped, and regret scores through me as he resettles the rags. I went out yesterday to buy soldiers, not to get my head bashed in. The priest pulls the cloths off my mouth and wipes at my lower face, then I feel the press of a cup against my lips. The water is clean and pure and tastes like air.

"I'm sorry, Nazar," I say when he pulls it away. "I only wanted to help Caleb. I was foolish."

"You fought with your fists and the stave."

I don't know how to respond to that, so I consider the soft breeze upon my face instead, the smells of ginger and cloves and cooked meat. I've no idea how long I've slept, but my mouth feels different now. My teeth are secure in their sockets, my tongue no longer too thick. I blink my eyes wide open beneath the cloths and can see more of the brightness of the full sun. The swelling is nearly gone.

At length, Nazar speaks again. "Why did you fight with your fists? You're not as strong as a man—or even most boys. You'll never be as strong."

I frown. I stretch my fingers out and curl them back again. They're sore, but nothing seems broken. "I used the stave as well. I'm good with the stave."

"You'll never be as good as a trained man with the stave either. At least one wielded by your hands. You're not meant to *attack* with such tools. Only defend."

I wonder if something has gone wrong with my mind. Nazar's speaking and I can follow his words, but I don't understand what they mean. I listen to the quiet gurgling of my stomach. I'm hungry, I realize. That has to be good. That has to mean I'm healing. That has...

When I drift back awake again, I'm sitting up. I blink my eyes open and can absolutely see Nazar through my left one. It's not that difficult. He stands directly in front of me, his lined face not three inches in front of my own. When I flinch back, his eyes crinkle. He straightens and hands me a bowl. "Eat."

It's a porridge of rice and honey and gingerroot, and it smells wonderful. "Slowly," he directs as I take the bowl with shaking hands. "You can eat it all, but not all at once." The waterskin beside me is full, and at Nazar's nod, I pick it up too. I don't deserve his care. My throat closes up, and I focus on the meal so Nazar can't see my face.

"You know nothing of how a warrior knight fights in a tournament."

Nazar says the words without censure. They bite just the same. I'm glad my face points away from the priest but wince as embarrassment brings the blood to my cheeks in a flare of pain.

He's right, of course. I've never seen a tournament. I've rarely been allowed to hear the tales of the bards firsthand. And I was too proud to ask the servants to recount the tales, contenting myself with overheard snatches of poorly remembered details.

That same pride now stings me to speech. "Tournaments are simple enough. There are knights on warhorses with a lance and a sword. They race toward each other."

"Yes, for show," Nazar says mildly. "How do they fight when the parade is done?"

"The parade?" My shoulders drop. I've eaten all the rice, but I stare at the bowl, lost. The tournament play I've seen in our own yards had been nothing but boys riding toward each other with fake lances and swords. That's all I've seen, in truth. All I've been allowed to see.

"True warriors don't fight with their fists. They fight with their minds."

I lift my head at that, scowling at the priest. "Caleb wasn't getting his *mind* beaten in, Nazar. He was getting pummeled on his actual body."

"Neither he nor the other boy were true warriors."

"Well, the other boy had a fine sword and the clothing of the Second House, red and white. He looked like a warrior knight."

"A warrior knight." The priest's disdain is palpable. "Fighting for money against a clearly impaired squire."

He has a point. "Caleb could have drawn him into a fight for pride or rage."

"He could have." Nazar nods. "But if so, the boy is still clearly not a true warrior knight, no matter what his house calls him. Because he would have known better, or at least would have been afraid of what could happen. As you should have known better and been afraid of what could happen."

"But—" I shake my head, confused.

"His Divh," the priest says quietly. "If in his panic or pain he summoned a Divh into the center of that crowd…"

My eyes snap wide as Nazar sighs. He seems to make a decision. "You will go to the coliseum today, with coin this time. You can secure the men we need."

"How will I know what to do?" I ask, finally putting voice to my biggest fear. I can bluff my way through a crowd, fair enough. But I've never spoken to true fighting men before—certainly not those who didn't already serve our house. *What will I say? How should I act?*

Nazar doesn't have a chance to respond.

"Merritt!" A bright voice sails out of the trees, and a moment later, Caleb bounds into the center of our camp. He's still dressed in his hodgepodge of colors, but his cloths are clean and his smile delighted. "You're awake. It's about time."

He looks to Nazar. "I've found a group of good prospects. Together, but not together, if you know what I mean."

The priest nods, and I stare at Caleb in bewilderment. "I don't know what you mean, no."

"The soldiers you're seeking for your house," he says, puffing up with importance. "You want them coming from different areas of the Protectorate so their allegiance will be to your house and not each other. If we could get a banded soldier, that'd be a coup, but I'm thinking any who'd be allowed to come here are the best and brightest of their houses. Any interest they express in being wooed away from their current patrons would be all for show now—they'd cost far too much, especially if they want to compete in some of the lower tournament games. Toward the end of the tournament, though..." He shrugs, fully the wise sage. "Then there may be a chance."

"Oh," I say, as if I understand what he's talking about. "Of course."

I straighten my shoulders, ruthlessly stamping down my confusion and weakness. I'll do this because I have to do this, and Caleb's words do make a certain amount of sense once I take a breath to consider them. A banded soldier would be a greater boon than I'd thought possible. Not just a fighting man, but one who commanded a Divh, even a small one? That would keep the

Tenth House safe. That would keep the border secure too. That would...

"Come on!" Caleb grins at me. "I told 'em you'd be coming and with coin to spend. No one doubts it, what with the marauder attack."

I blink my itchy eyes, and Nazar talks over Caleb's chatter, filling in what I've missed as I take stock of my arms and legs. Everything seems...better. Even my banded arm no longer hurts.

Then Nazar's words catch my attention. "The First House isn't the only party who knows of the attack. It's reached the people of Trilion as well."

"*Reached* them," Caleb scoffs. "It's already legendary—*you're* legendary. No one has seen a Tenth House warrior since your father fought here decades ago, and from all accounts, the Divh you're banded to is far more enormous than anyone remembers! You'll have no problem finding soldiers—men are lining up just for the chance to serve with such a powerful house and to rout the marauders who dared attack you."

"Marauders." I don't recognize the sudden cold anger in my voice. Caleb flinches, stepping side to side as if ready to bolt.

"Sorry. I know you lost good men," he says quickly. "But you've got more who're ready and waiting for you. I can tell you exactly what they're worth too. I know them all." He shifts his weight again, clearly eager to be off. "We've had marauders worrying the edges of the tournament grounds here, too, worse this year than ever," he says. "It'll be good to have more men allied with you when you set off for home. For protection."

I frown at Nazar, but he's already stepping up to me, handing me a purse heavy with silver. I weigh it in my hands. I've no idea how much is in it, no idea what the worth of a good man is. My mother taught me only what was necessary to run a household, what to pay for a chicken or a cow. Surely a soldier commanded more than that.

The priest speaks again. "Remember, this is the full portion we will spend," he says, as if we've already discussed this many times.

"Give more weight to older soldiers than young ones. Men of discipline and proven mettle."

"A few young ones would be—" Caleb shuts his mouth as Nazar sends a stern look his way, then tries again. "Sorry. Old is good. More than good."

I nod and pocket the purse. Caleb seems honestly eager to help us, but I can't help but wonder—why? Is it simply that I aided him in the fight? Or should I be warier of his good humor and cheerful prattle? He's slipped so quickly into our camp...

There's too much in this place I cannot trust, I feel it in my bones.

We're ready to go less than a quarter hour later, Nazar distracting Caleb long enough that I'm able to relieve myself behind the horses and ensure my costume is fully in place. Acting the part of Merritt grows more complex with each hour I undertake it, but the task of negotiation, at least, has become clearer. With Caleb along unable to keep his mouth shut, I suspect I'll learn all I need to know about purchasing soldiers without asking a single question. Maybe that's why the priest seems willing enough to let the squire help us, even if I'm not as sure.

Nazar goes one further and hands a long green tunic to Caleb before we leave. The look of wonder on the boy's face knifes through me, chasing away some of my doubt, but I keep my own expression neutral.

"These men know me," he says to the priest. "They know I didn't come here with you."

"Then they can know you've become our hired agent," Nazar replies dismissively. "Merritt is a warrior knight, not a tradesman. You will represent him."

Caleb nods, swallowing. He pulls the tunic over his shirt, smoothing it down with one dirty hand, for once struck silent as we leave our camp.

He proves his worth nearly immediately.

Setting off across the streets of Trilion toward the immense bulk of the coliseum, Caleb recovers his tongue and strikes up an unceasing commentary. "Nazar didn't give the rumors justice, I'm telling you straight," he says. "You're already famous. That Divh of yours has taken everyone by surprise. The old warrior knights swear that the Tenth House guardian was lighter in color and half the size of what's being reported, but—"

"How does anyone know differently?" I interrupt, my words unintentionally brusque as my mind shies away from the images his chatter conjures up. "No one came to our aid."

He echoes what Fortiss told me not two days ago. "There was a caravan, or so the story goes. High up on the pass, too far away to help. But they heard the roaring of the Divh, saw it from all that distance away. No one knows who first carried the tale to Trilion—Nazar already asked me. But once it reached the city's borders, it spread like fire."

I grunt. There *was* no caravan on the mountain pass. Nazar and I would've seen it. Which means members of the attack party itself must have come slinking back to Trilion to report—or Fortiss reported for him. They or their minders planted the story of the marauders, no doubt worried I—well, Merritt, anyway—would come seeking retribution. No one would believe a house broke the most basic of laws of the Protectorate by taking up arms against another house, but someone is making doubly sure the suspicion doesn't get raised.

Who would care if it did, though?

I lift my eyes toward the high castle stronghold, and Caleb follows my gaze. "Lord Rihad—he's heard of it too, it's said. Nazar said he deferred your audience with him with your face all…" He flaps his hand at my head, which needs no further explanation. It still feels like a crushed gourd. "He's probably waiting until you enter the tournament."

"I'm not entering the tournament."

Caleb's exasperated sigh tells me this isn't news. Undoubtedly, Nazar has already walked this path with him. "Seriously? Did you not hear me when I told you that the winner of the tournament will get their *pick* of the top-ranked banded soldiers? You wouldn't even have to spend your own coin—just enter and win out. The pit fights will be done in a couple of days, then some contests between the banded soldiers who aren't good enough to compete in the tournament proper—and then the real tournament will begin. All the houses who've committed will do battle until only one remains."

I scowl at him. "I thought no house struck down another house."

"Well, of course they don't," he says. "I mean that one will remain in a figurative sense. Warrior knights can die, sure, but—it's rare. Very rare. And it's never on purpose."

Never. My lips twist. Yet while these honored men don't strike to kill on the tournament field, some skilled archer from a noble house *had* pierced my brother's heart with a featureless gray arrow. Was the archer a warrior knight as well? A banded soldier?

Or merely a guard, a hired mercenary...

No. I discard this last idea as soon as it forms. Merritt's murder was a delicate act, for all that it was ruthless and of seeming cowardice. Guards fail. Mercenaries can be bought—or they can talk out of spite. To assassinate a warrior knight—and by extension his Divh—would be an act of highest secrecy. It would not have been trusted to someone not in the inner circle.

Is Fortiss my brother's murderer? Or someone Fortiss knows? He *has* to know him, which is crime enough—it's far too much to believe he's completely ignorant of what happened to my house.

But I can't ask. I know I can't ask—and it shouldn't matter to me. I don't have the luxury of seeking revenge. Not when I have a house to protect.

And yet...*could* I seek that revenge? Could I find the low coward who loosed that arrow from the heart of the forest? Could I trick Fortiss into revealing him...somehow?

Or into betraying that *he* was my brother's murderer?

"We'll be gone before the tournament starts," I say sternly, to banish those thoughts before they can take root. "These...

marauders were too bold. There's no reason they won't strike again."

Caleb snorts. "No reason other than their guts turned to milk on seeing your Divh, maybe. That's why they're marauders. They can only bite and snap in the shadows; they don't stand and fight when the odds are stacked against them."

As we wind through Trilion, the Tenth House's newest squire keeps up his relentless patter, in between useful observations about the best food carts and drinking houses, what corners to avoid and what warrior knights to recognize on sight. We pass another knot of men haggling in market stalls, and I ask the question uppermost in my mind. "Where are the women?"

He shoots me a startled look, and I know I've mis-stepped. I deliberately hold his gaze, daring him to challenge me. Was Caleb hired by some other house to unravel my story? Does someone out there know I'm not Merritt at all, but his untrained sister, desperately trying to protect her house?

Caleb's expression clears almost immediately, but not fast enough to keep my stomach from rolling queasily. "I keep forgetting, you haven't crept out of your mountain stronghold in so long, you might as well be from the Imperium itself. Girls,"—he flaps a dismissive hand—"women, whatever, they don't take part in the trade leading up to the tournament. It's not their place. You'll see 'em in the stands, of course, with their husbands and fathers—or at least their guardians—but not out and about. They belong in their tents if they're near the coliseum at all, I tell you plain."

I burn with a flash of resentment at this but keep my voice neutral. "Has it always been that way?" I think of my father, the fights I overheard between him and my mother as she pleaded for him to spare my life whenever he found fault in me, which was often. She'd begged him for years to sell me into marriage with another noble house versus kill me outright until he finally, blessedly agreed. I'd never thought about the inherent injustice of her needing to beg so frantically for my life...I'd merely accepted it. But now that I'm being treated as a boy, a man, with respect simply being offered up to me as a matter of course, I'm staggered by the difference.

Caleb merely shrugs. "Long enough. Women are for houses and holdings and the merchant caravans. Trilion is a civilized city. I mean, Lord Rihad does have a woman among his advisors, I hear, though most of the men are priests of the Light. I've never seen her, but that's what I'm told."

"How exotic of him," I say drily. It seems that—save for this lone councilor—a woman's place is as entrenched in Trilion as it is in our household. I don't know why I'm surprised.

Our conversation ends as we near the walls of the coliseum. Caleb slows, his body going straighter.

"These aren't all the soldiers available, but they're the best. They're trying to get to you first." He waggles his brows. "You want me to negotiate for you, in truth? I'm good at it."

I look at him, struggling to keep the relief from my face. "You know these men?" I ask quietly as they notice us. They, too, are standing straighter...because of me, I realize. Or the person they think I am. Merritt, firstborn warrior knight of the Tenth House, banded to a now-notorious Divh.

A sudden, sickening thought riddles through me. What if someone asks me to produce Gent?

Fear stiffens my spine. We need to get these men under contract then get out of this city. As terrible as my father's retribution might be, being caught in this city as a woman banded to a Divh would be far and away worse. The Tenth House would never get its soldiers then.

I square my shoulders. "I want ten men. Five to replace our fallen soldiers, plus the five we intended to purchase originally. And I want at least half of them young enough to still be trainable."

"But Nazar—"

"Half." Older soldiers can become set in their ways, and I can't risk Father rejecting these soldiers, no matter what happens to me —or to Gent, when the Divh is no longer banded to me. My father is proud and will want to feel like his power is absolute...especially once he learns of Merritt's death. I owe him that much.

Together, Caleb and I step forward, and the boy almost immediately starts talking. When it's over, ten fighting men are dedicated to ensuring the safety of my house. Half of them still green, the other half hard-bitten and sturdy. It's a good mix.

As the last of the earnest money is traded, the men set off with orders to prepare themselves for travel. I watch the last of them disappear as an earsplitting wail of trumpets sounds. I jerk back, startled, and Caleb laughs.

"It's beginning," he shouts, tugging me forward. "The exhibition. Come on—we'll go see!"

And without another backward glance, we join the crowd thronging toward the first celebrated event of the Tournament of Gold.

CHAPTER 8

Nazar waits just outside the gates of the coliseum. He meets my shocked gaze with a raised brow, as if of course he knew we'd find our way here. He carries a heavy satchel over his arm but otherwise looks like any of the other commoners on their way to be awed and amazed by the exhibition.

Though Caleb's fairly bursting with the news of our negotiation, he turns to me and bows. I look directly at Nazar, aware that anyone might be watching.

"It's done," I say, surprised at the real relief I feel, that our house is protected once more. "Ten men to the Tenth House, and enough extra horses to carry them. They'll be ready by tomorrow, and they're more than we'll need, judging by their looks."

Even as I speak, the horns sound again, marking the beginning of...something.

"Sorry, I must be going," Caleb says, pulling off his green tunic and handing it to Nazar. "I'll—I'll—" He stumbles, but Nazar merely nods to him.

"Go," the priest says, taking his tunic, as if he knows where Caleb is off to.

I don't, of course, but Nazar says nothing more after the squire dashes off with his usual frantic energy. Instead, the priest gestures me to follow him toward a rear entrance to the coliseum. Once we climb the dozen or so stone steps to slip inside, I stare up at the huge, groaning wooden infrastructure drilled into the bedrock, shaking beneath the pounding of many feet. It's dark back here and hung with shadows.

"What...?" I manage, but Nazar silences me with a look until he's convinced that we're well and truly alone.

"You can study your opponents like Merritt of the Tenth, but you can only gawk as Talia," he says quietly, shifting his satchel closer to me and opening it. Inside, despite the gloom, I see the coils of my old hair. "This way, you can do both."

I jerk my gaze up to him. "You want me to dress as *Talia?*" I squeak, barely able to believe it. "Why?"

He surveys me with steady eyes. "Because warrior knights don't sit in the stands. They stand on the battleground, ready to fight."

"But I'm from the mountains," I protest. "And the Tenth House isn't competing this year. No one would be surprised that I'm interested in how Lord Rihad runs his tournaments."

"It shows weakness."

"Well, we *are* weak right now." I shove the satchel away, but even through my irritation, I see his point. Merritt of the Tenth House has his own Divh, his own house to defend. He doesn't need to be entertained with the masses like some child. But Talia...

I ball my hands into fists. "There's no respect for women here. I expect that at home, but I thought..." I blow out a breath. "I thought it would be different in the city."

"And now you know better. Accept what is until you change it," Nazar says without inflection, pushing the satchel back toward me.

With a muttered curse, I give in. The gown is easy enough to swap into—a cut-down version of my travel clothes, thank the Light. But my hair...

I frown at the glistening wig, trying not to be unnerved by it. "Where's the rest of it?"

"You're not on your way to get married. I kept the bulk of it for later use."

"Mmm." Pushing away the thought of random coils of my hair sitting around our tent like serpents ready to strike, I lift the wig to my head. I pull it on tentatively, surprised at its snug fit. Then I squeak as Nazar steps up to me and yanks it roughly into place. He drags me out from beneath the stands into a sliver of sunlight, turning me this way and that. Then he nods.

"You'll pass, and your face has healed well enough that no one will look twice. If anyone asks after you later, we can say that your experience of the great exhibition has quite overwhelmed you, and that we have decided to send you back to the Tenth House ahead of our eventual return."

"Ohhhh..." I round my eyes and grin at him. "That's good. Do I need paint, do you think?" I wave vaguely at my face.

"Only enough to satisfy the briefest of glances." After rooting around in the satchel, he produces a pot and brush and hands them to me, and I do what I can in the shadows while he bundles Merritt's clothes away. Eventually, I present myself to him, and he nods again.

"It's enough."

Curling my arm into his, he leads me out of the shadows and down a long corridor until we step into the sunlight once more. Then he turns, and we mount the steep stairs that take us to the spectator seating. The massive rows of stands are sturdily built, for all the groaning I heard far below. How many battles have been fought here in the past three hundred years? I've no idea. There is still so much—*too much*—I don't know.

We jostle our way to where the crowd finally thins. Nazar sits at the edge of bench where we settle, his eyes keen on the field below. I squint to see over the mass of heads, fixing on the horses and riders far below who have already engaged in combat by the time we're seated. "They're too small to see."

He snorts. "This field wasn't meant for men."

I frown but the battle below has become a hopeless snarl, and I can make nothing out. I lean forward, straining, and at length, Nazar sighs and fishes in his robes. He withdraws a small enameled cylinder and hands it to me. "Put it up to your eye."

As I take it, I realize I'm not alone in my prize. Most of the wealthier spectators around us—male and female alike—have a similar tool, and I lift mine, turning it in my hand until I realize it's a lens of glass set into a long tube. I lift the narrower end to my eye, and the scene below me leaps into crystal clarity.

"Oh," I breathe. I can see every horse and rider, every stroke of the blade. My fingers tingle and my arm burns, which makes me sit up straighter. I've forgotten about the band wrapped around my bicep and am doubly glad for the heavy covering of my cloak to keep it from prying eyes.

The fight beneath us roils as more spectators flood into the stands, both on our side of the field and in the far distance where another bank of stone seats looms, now thronged with hundreds of watchers. I lift my glass toward those stands and see a constellation of glinting glasses in return. Even with all the seating, the tournament field is immense, and I sweep my glass along the crowd until another platform catches my eye.

It's carved into the stone embankment at the midpoint of the coliseum stands, nearly two-thirds of the way to the top of the wall. Before it on the battlefield are two towers made of wood, each with a broad rooftop space accessible by a door that clearly opens onto a steep stairway inside the narrow structure. The towers stretch up to just over half the height of the observation platform, but their rooftops are empty, both of them lonely sentinels standing between the melee and the coliseum stands.

The stone overlook directly above those wooden stands isn't empty, though. Several richly dressed noblemen crowd the space, each more pompous looking than the last. The glass makes them look as close to me as Nazar, and I gape as I take in their fine robes and heavy, jeweled belts.

One of them arrests my attention, and I stare openly. Fortiss. Standing among his retinue of men, his face stern, his gaze sweeping the crowd, he somehow manages to appear even nobler than he had on his white horse. He definitely looks more like a warrior knight than the idiot Hantor, who fought Caleb. He looks more like a warrior knight than I do too.

Beside me, Nazar notices my attention. He seems to not need a glass. "That's the company of Lord Protector Rihad, Master of the First House, governor of the Protectorate."

"Did you really think what Fortiss said was true?" I swing my glass to the crowd below. "That they're going to award *thirty* Divhs and banded soldiers to the top house of the tournament—twelve to the winner of the winged crown alone? Caleb also says it will happen."

"Caleb would know," Nazar says mildly. "There are already more than a dozen such men in the First House's barracks now, warrior knights and banded soldiers alike. To add more would make them powerful indeed."

Caleb said as much to me already, but now I pause, considering the ramifications. Someone—another house—dispatched its soldiers to attack the Tenth House, to kill Merritt. Were we the only house struck? If our attacker is growing secretly stronger while weakening other houses, what could that mean?

Thinking of the squire brings another concern to mind. I study the seeing glass in my hand for a long moment, then I push forward. "Can we, ah, trust Caleb?"

Nazar glances at me, his expression mildly surprised. "Why? Did he handle the money improperly? Steal it?" He frowns then, growing more concerned. "Did he guide you to hire weak soldiers? He seemed well pleased with your choices."

"No! No, nothing like that," I say hurriedly, instantly regretting my words. Caleb has done nothing but help me. "It's just—we don't know him."

"We don't know him," Nazar agrees, but he says nothing more.

Clearly, he's not worried, but that does nothing to assuage my own concerns.

Instead, I turn my gaze to the men on the platform. Once again, an unexpected thread of anger coils through me. My purpose here isn't vengeance but protection...and yet, I am close—*so* close to whoever took Merritt's life. Could I find that warrior? Force him to face justice?

I swallow. "Do you think it's the First House that sent the soldiers who...?" I don't finish the words. To even say them out loud seems sacrilege.

Nazar doesn't respond at first, pauses so long that I don't think he will.

When he does speak, it's to ask me a question, not provide the answers I crave.

"Why would they do that?" The priest's murmur is for my ear alone, and I instantly know it's a test.

I grimace. "I don't *know*, Nazar. That's why I'm—"

His mouth tightens, and I swallow my own hasty words. Even though I'm wearing a dress, I'm now a warrior knight, the protector of my house. There must be some reason why the priest is asking me to puzzle through the question. I sigh, then repeat what I've heard about these people, this place—not Nazar's scant few days of teaching, but the snatches and songs I've heard from the bards over the years. It's the only way I can think of to find the answer he seems to believe I already know.

"Lord Rihad rules the Protectorate," I recite. "The First House is the strongest of the twelve ruling houses. Those twelve houses are in charge of the Protectorate's security and by extension the security of the Exalted Imperium, shielding it from the threat of the Western Realms." I shiver as I say the words. No one knows what the Imperium discovered beyond the western borders of the Protectorate that halted their most recent attempt at expansion a hundred years ago. But whatever it was, it sent the imperial army all the way back to its capital city, ostensibly to rearm. They never returned. As it has for the last three hundred years, the Protectorate remained in place after the army's departure, our mighty Divhs arrayed against...something. But the attack from the Western Realms never came.

"How does the Protectorate remain strong?" Nazar prompts.

"Through its houses and Divhs, and, to a lesser extent, its unbanded soldiers." I gesture to the battle below us. According to legend, however, now gilded with three hundred years' gloss, ordinary soldiers hadn't saved us against whatever we encountered in the Western Realms. Only the Divhs and a dozen banded warriors had done that. "The tournaments give them an opportunity to practice for warfare, should it ever come again." By the Light, I pray it doesn't.

"And why would a house take on another house?"

"It wouldn't," I say instantly.

He's silent. I try to push on, but it's impossible to imagine, though I've seen it with my own eyes. "It...can't. It's not of the Light."

"We were attacked," he reminds me, and my heart hardens anew. Merritt's sightless stare, the dead gray arrow, so much crimson blood.

"To weaken the Protectorate overall by turning us against each other?" I finally guess. "That's the only reason. But how can that make sense?"

A roar goes up from the crowd around us, the fighting taking on a new level of frenzy far below. I see warriors fall, their horses twisting and stampeding. Men are getting injured down there, I realize. Maybe dying. Good, strong fighters—and for what? For entertainment?

I scowl at the carnage. "The tournament is supposed to be a training ground, I thought. Not a killing field."

Nazar doesn't reply, and I swing my glass again to the nobles and warriors assembled on the stone platform at the center of the stands opposite me. I see a tall man dressed all in cloth of gold, looking like the Light himself. Lord Rihad, I decide. Has to be. He's slender but conveys an implacable strength, and his left shoulder is bare, the heavy golden cloak thrown back. Not one but *two* sentient bands span his broad bicep, and I stare. Who can rule *two* Divhs? I've never heard of such a thing.

Fortiss stands beside the Lord Protector, and I study him again, my heart picking up speed. Something about the warrior knight draws my attention more than any other man on the platform—and they're all men, I realize with sudden awareness, feeling the weight of my mound of hair, my heavy gown. My lips flatten in a hard line. Even if they didn't do the deed, had Rihad and Fortiss ordered the killing of Merritt?

Even as I think it, I long to reject the idea. It would be the height of foolishness, on the eve of a tournament the First House itself was hosting, to take out a small house who poses no threat. Far more likely that it's another house, working in the shadows. If it's a house at all.

And yet, Fortiss was there. In the forest, wearing gold and black. Not hiding his affiliation to the First House at all.

Why was he there?

A horn blast sounds over the melee, not once but several times, and I snap my gaze back to the tournament grounds far below us.

Slowly, the men battling on the field pull apart from each other. Squires swarm forth, capturing horses whose riders have been knocked to the ground, helping men up and off the field. The area clears quickly. The other spectators lean forward in excitement, and I do as well.

Two tiny forms appear on either end of the mile-long field atop warhorses. The crowd erupts in cheers as the men race toward each other. As I strain to see more, however, I realize they're not holding lances, spears, or blades. They merely gallop in proud splendor, their plumage flying in the wind, cloaks stretching out long and theatrically behind them. Clearly these are warrior knights. Eventually, they slow their horses to a trot, then a walk. They meet in the center of the field and turn on point to face the central platform, each of them raising a hand to the Lord Protector.

The riders dismount. One of the knights is dressed in the rich purple of the Sixth House, a major holding whose livery even I instantly recognize, whose stronghold lies in the far northwestern reaches of the Protectorate. One wears sky blue—the Fourth House, I'm almost certain. To my eye, both warriors are strong and well made, their faces aristocratic.

There's movement at the base of the three-story-tall wooden towers that stand in front of Lord Rihad's imposing stone perch. Doors at the base of the structures pop open, and two figures emerge, dressed in gold-and-black livery. Squires of the First House. The squires hustle out toward the knights and take the warhorses' reins, then the warriors stride toward the towers amidst more cheers from the crowd. There is a near frenzy of anticipation building around me, and even I am up on my toes, desperate to see more.

The men pass through the doors at the base of the wooden platforms, and moments later they exit onto the rooftop platforms, facing each other. I frown. What are they doing? Beside me, Nazar remains unhelpfully silent as always, but I sense his gaze upon me, not on the men on the stands.

My attention, however, remains fixed on the warrior knights. They move to the center of the platforms. Each of them raises his right hand high in the air—then claps it to his left bicep.

An unearthly roar shakes the stands as the air snaps taut around us, and suddenly, cheers turn to startled shouts and everyone scrambles to better see the miracle before us.

I'm jostled as the crowd presses in tightly, but no one is stretching forward more eagerly than me. When I finally *can* see, I nearly drop Nazar's seeing glass.

By the Light, I certainly don't need it anymore.

On either side of the mile-long expanse before me, gargantuan creatures huff and blow, staring each other down.

Divhs.

CHAPTER 9

"Oh...*Light*," I whisper, snapping my mouth shut only when Nazar elbows me hard.

I don't need to ask him why he's chastising me. I know I should be more nonchalant, even as Talia and not Merritt. But these monstrous, impossibly *immense* Divhs are easily twice the size of Gent...well, the original Gent. Perhaps larger than whatever he's become too. I suddenly can't remember. Their shadows cover half the coliseum seats, and when they lift themselves to their full height, bristling and roaring with rage, they blot out the sun.

The creature on the right, the Fourth House Divh, looks like an enormous leather-skinned lion, but with hide the color of pale sky. Its skin is thick and covered with scars.

That Divh screams and flings its head high, then stamps its feet. Its head is a large shield-like platter and its mouth sprouts tusks at either corner. It has a half-dozen eyes spread over its brow, some directly in front, some to the side.

An answering scream comes from the other end of the field, and I jerk my gaze toward the noise, my breath stalling in my throat. The Sixth House Divh isn't at all like its opponent. A long, sinuous lizard, it's shaded deep purple in a violent series of arcing, rippling coils, and its wings expand almost to either side of the spectator stands. When it screams, it cranes its head far forward and its mouth opens, revealing a long red tongue—and a burst of fire.

The crowd bursts into another round of cheers, but a sudden knowingness sweeps over me, a call for my attention not to remain in slack-jawed wonder on the Divhs, but on an entirely different pair.

The warrior knights.

Nazar murmurs something beside me that's lost in the screaming, but I don't need his encouragement. I pull the seeing glass back up to my eye and stare.

The men have taken up position across from each other, their hands lifted as if they're about to leap at each other's throats across the broad gap between them. But they don't move otherwise. At either end of the long field, the Divhs scream and roar. The warrior knights' hands shift forward, and suddenly, chaos erupts, the sound of the lion's pounding paws against the earth momentarily drowning out the noise from the crowd.

My eyelids peel back so far, I'm surprised my eyeballs remain in my head. Peripherally, I'm aware of the monsters racing toward each other, but the men have barely moved on the stands—barely moved, and yet are clearly locked in sudden, deeply intense conflict.

Somehow, Nazar's voice reaches me, the priest leaning close to my ear. "Monsters capture the imagination of the masses," he says. "The crowds. Warriors fight with their minds, and their minds are what direct their Divhs."

"But..." The words die in my throat. They're *that* connected that the barest twitch, the slightest gesture sends these mountainous creatures hurtling forward? Merritt always overacted, throwing his body forth and screaming his orders for Gent to follow. These men...

The warriors on the platform remain completely still, each with a left hand outstretched palm up, a right hand gripped in a fist at his side. They could be statues, standing there, but through the glass, I can see their faces. They're set in fixed ferocity, glaring across the open space as if they are avowed enemies. My glance jumps to the center of the field where the Divhs collide in a rush of hide and bone, the winged fire lizard shifting to the right at the last minute, scoring its talons down the side of the pale lion. My gaze pings back to the men again. The sky-blue knight staggers back, a thin trace of blood blooming on his shoulder.

The crowd roars. First blood!

"They are *that* connected." Nazar's words batter my ear. "Life to life, death to death. You start the fight with fists and rods and sword, you end it with the mind. That is the way of the warrior."

The attack in front of me is suddenly replaced by the image of Merritt and Gent dropping from the sky, falling to the earth, sprawling out in the wrecked clearing of the practice field. Gent had disappeared—died, I'd thought—as Merritt breathed his last. Then Merritt's band had moved—moved with such speed and ferocity, and now I'm banded. I'm a warrior—a warrior with no clue of what these men are doing, no idea how—

"You do know, Talia. Look."

Whether Nazar is still talking, or the words are echoes of my own panic, I fix on the fighting creatures, my own warrior band tightening on my arm with a painful squeeze. I stare at them, and somehow—something opens up inside me; a door through which a thousand songs pour forth, each rising and falling in a hopeless jumble of noise, each building to a different crescendo.

One of the loudest of those songs belongs to the purple lizard on the field, I realize with a startled blink—another to the Fourth House's sky-blue lion.

The fight is raging with furious intensity now. The deep-purple lizard spins around, but its tail takes a few moments longer to clear its opponent. The light-blue beast lunges forward with a powerful paw, wrapping its claws around the tail and flipping it upward.

I swing my gaze back toward the wooden platforms, and in my mind's eye, the Divhs are superimposed over the warriors, their feverish battle overlaying the minimal, impossibly elegant movements of the knights. How can they...how do they?

But those answers aren't important now. What's important is the sudden, swamping connection I feel between these men and their Divhs, the weight of it nearly staggering me. The Fourth House warrior flicks his hand only an inch, but the Sixth House knight wheels back, staggering a few steps as his Divh goes crashing head over tail, making three full rotations before it regains its position and soars upward again.

The men reset, and I can both sense and see their incredible exertion, though it's their Divhs who slash and tear. Both warriors are sweating through their tunics, however, their effort plain on their faces and their trembling arms.

"Great warriors don't fight with their fists, nor with a stave or blade, for all that they may be wielding these when they go to war." Nazar's words are clearer now, closer. Somehow, his voice carries over the screech and howl of the crowd around me. "Great warriors fight with their minds. With their spirit and their hearts, yes, but mostly with their minds."

"But how—" I stare at the dance of death in front of me. The lizard has shot in close to the lion again, has buried its long snout in the larger animal's neck. It's not a big snout, but the spot is a sensitive one. Both Divh and its linked warrior on the wooden platform wheel back, arms and giant forelegs in tortured concert as the beasts grapple in the open field.

The Fourth House warrior knight breaks first, bursting backward and wheeling away. Blood now flows freely down his neck, and his face is a ghastly mask of pain as his creature bucks and roars, trying to dislodge the lizard. A chance crack of the giant lion's paw rakes across the lizard's gossamer wing. Twin screams surge over the crowd, and it's the Sixth House's warrior's turn to falter as the lizard finally opens its long jaws and blows back as if a puff of wind has caught it full sail.

This is a boon for the Fourth House Divh, but one that comes too late. On the field, the enormous sky-blue lion sinks to the ground, its forelegs trembling as it shakes its head, once, twice, clearly trying to get its bearings. The pain that reverberates from it is so strong, I can feel my own bones begin to quiver, and the band on my arm flares with another burst of heat.

On the platform, the men are affected as well. The blue-garbed knight of the Fourth falls forward to one knee. His right hand covers his left arm below the shoulder, only this time, his left hand comes up as well to form crossed arms over his chest. The purple knight of the Sixth, in contrast, remains standing, though he's clearly wobbly. He raises both arms high, and a figure in long black-and-gold robes steps forward on the First House's stone overlook. The figure lifts a horn to his mouth. A single clear note blows over the spellbound crowd, and everything stills.

Both warriors turn, their right hands finding their left shoulders. I hear their words in my own head, sending their Divhs back to their own plane.

The monsters disappear from the field.

The songs within me go silent.

Then the crowd catches me off guard with a new, startling roar. This time, they shout out a hero's welcome as attendants exit the doors at the top of the wooden towers and rush toward the warriors, apparently to give them aid. Both knights are surrounded. I try to see what's happening to them, but the crowd is surging around me now, the day's spectacle apparently done.

"Wasn't that great? Wasn't it?"

Caleb's at Nazar's side suddenly, bursting with excitement as I cringe back, trying to disappear. "The most amazing opening exhibition ever, mark me plain. Only fools thought the Sixth House would fall because the flying lizard was smaller than the lion of the Fourth. They were wrong. I knew it from the start. Small is often better. Small is fast, small is smart."

He bounces up and down. Rather than being irritated, Nazar turns to him, blocking me from view for another few seconds. "And why do you think that, Caleb?" he asks mildly. "Why is small smarter?"

"Because it has to be," Caleb shoots back. "Big will make you pay if you're not fast and savvy. Like Merritt with his trick with the cane, flipping it round so he could crack ol' Hantor in the head. Boy's brains are still probably rattling around in his skull. Where is Merritt, anyway—" he peers past Nazar and his eyes peel wide. "Oh, Light! Lady Talia, right? But...where's Merritt?"

I sense Nazar's gaze on me, but I have eyes only for Caleb. He's now wearing another borrowed tunic, this one deep yellow, the sleeve cut in such a way to allow for the stump that's all that's left of his left arm, without calling too much attention to it. The tunic falls in folds around Caleb's body, so that if he remains standing just so, you wouldn't even know he was missing an arm. Is this the tunic of one of the Southern Houses, come to fight in the tournament? Should I worry about who else is paying Caleb...and for what?

"Caleb, yes?" I offer, my voice as quiet and melodic as I can make it. "Your service to my brother has been very kind."

"He's a fighter—a warrior even!" Caleb says staunchly. "You should get him to compete. No one gets hurt, not really, and not for long. It really is more for show."

I nod at him with wide-eyed wonder, which seems to be the right thing. His obvious excitement pokes holes in my worries about him, at least for now. "There'll be no more exhibitions today?"

"Nope—not sanctioned, anyway. They needed that one to test the battleground, make sure everyone could see and hear, get in and out fast. There're more people here than ever before. They've widened the First House's balcony too." He gestures to the thick center ledge, still teeming with people, across the coliseum field. "So, um...will you and Merritt go up to the First House tonight? The culling begins tomorrow, you know."

"Culling?" That word sounds ominous to me. I try to shake it off, but it slithers along my spine in a whispering mockery.

Caleb doesn't seem to notice. "Make no mistake—today's exhibition was one of the grander you'll see. Not every warrior knight's Divh is like those. Some are big like that lion, some are far smaller than the fire lizard. The warrior knights too are different. For some, this is their first tournament, and don't even get me started on the banded soldiers. A few have never seen monsters as big as the ones down there today—but there're even bigger ones than that."

"Really," I say faintly.

"The stuff of legends, I tell you plain!" Caleb says. He looks at me with sudden curiosity. "I hear Merritt's Divh is larger than them all, though."

I tense at the pointed statement, but he merely laughs again. "No matter. I now have money enough to spread some rumors of my own about the strength of the Tenth House."

He pulls out a coin bag, and I leap onto the new subject, eager to turn the conversation away from myself.

"You bet on the outcome of the fight?"

Caleb preens a little. "Where there is a battle, there's a bet. Never bet against a fire lizard if you're thinking of making some coin yourself, though. Your money will have a way of eating themselves." His eyes widen, and he swings toward Nazar. "You know, Merritt should come with me tonight, now that his face has healed up. The fires will blaze high, with the tournament celebration beginning in earnest. I hear they've summoned the southern houses. It'll take a while for everyone to arrive, but the parties will start right away. The pickings are best earlier in the going—more money is spread out with fools ready to lose it. Where is he, anyway?"

I glance toward Nazar, sorely tempted by the idea of walking among all these warriors as one of them—not as a female. But Nazar, fortunately, is fielding Caleb's enthusiasm better than I am. "We've purchased our men, Caleb. We leave tomorrow."

Caleb snorts. "Those men won't be ready to leave until midday, earliest. They'll want to enjoy as much of the tournament as they can before you move out."

Nazar shrugs. "Then perhaps Merritt can spare some time

away. But Talia here..." He frowns, surveying me critically. "You seem fatigued, my lady."

"Oh, I am," I agree weakly, lifting a hand to bat at my hair. "I think—perhaps this is all too much to me. It's all so much."

"You're staying at an inn in Trilion?" Caleb asks quickly. "It's safer there, for sure. It's a lot for a woman to endure big crowds like this, I bet."

"It is." I keep my tone gracious, even appreciative, to hide the fact I want to punch him.

"So, where's your camp, Caleb?" I ask instead. The crowd has finally thinned enough to allow us to exit the stands ourselves and head back toward the distant ground. We stand and begin making our way down. "Where do you sleep after all the money has been made for the day?"

Caleb's awkwardness is suddenly obvious as he wobbles on the stair. Once again, it's Nazar who eases the boy's way. "We have need of a squire ongoing, if you aren't permanently committed elsewhere," he says, gesturing to Caleb's tunic. "Though it will be work, there's money and lodging in it for you, here and at the Tenth House manor, should you wish."

Caleb tries to appear nonchalant, but the look he turns on Nazar makes my heart feel suddenly large and ungainly, my throat too tight. "I could do that," he says, sending me a quick glance. "My commitments elsewhere aren't so good an offer as that. I'll just need an hour or so to make arrangements. And then I could go out with Merritt, if he's of a mind to explore."

"An hour, then," Nazar says gravely, and Caleb ducks away.

I swing my gaze to Nazar, whose face betrays nothing. "He *had* nowhere else to stay, despite his new clothes. You knew that."

The priest shrugs. "Then so much the better that we had need of him. And if your concern about him is warranted, then so much the better that we can watch him."

I nod, but I don't like the way my distrust makes me feel, tainting the genuine excitement of Caleb's eager words and earnest hope. Is this what it means to be a warrior of the Protectorate? To be constantly filled with doubt and suspicion, with the sense that every enemy's eye was upon you?

For me, it seems it is.

We make our way back to our own camp through the crowds as the music starts up around us, flutes and drums and long horns drawing down the distant night.

It would be relaxing—almost fun, I think—except for the clear assessment and dismissal I receive, time and time again. The same men and boys who hours earlier would have assessed and taken my measure as a warrior now drop me into categories far less worthy of anyone's time or attention. Irritation sparks and fans, and by the time we near our camp, I itch to pull the wig off my head, to swap out my gown for breeches and a tunic.

Fingers twitching, I reach for the belt of my gown when we're a dozen paces away, then hesitate as Nazar hisses out a breath.

"*Fortiss*," he mutters, and I jerk my gaze forward again. My blood freezes in my veins.

It's Fortiss, all right, still dressed in his pageant finery. He's seated himself outside our tent, propped against the grave shovel he's driven into the ground, looking for all the world that he might happily remain there all night.

He's here to see me, I'm sure.

But which me?

CHAPTER 10

Nazar snatches my hand again and curves it into the crook of his left elbow then lifts his right hand in greeting. "Lord Fortiss," he calls out while I try to keep from gawking. "Well met. I hope you weren't waiting long."

Fortiss looks up with a broad smile, sees me, and springs to his feet.

"Not in the slightest," he says as we draw near. "I came looking for Merritt, but it seems my luck has improved even over that option. Lady Talia, I'd heard you were staying in Trilion. I didn't know you had ventured this far into tournament grounds."

It's no difficulty to flutter and gape over him, and I do both in equal measure for another half-second until I regain control over myself. Up close, he's even more impressive in his rich and glittering silks than when I'd seen him on the tournament ground. And without my sword and boots, I feel woefully insignificant in his eyes, even though he regards me with more than a little interest. What's his game?

"Lord Fortiss," I say, and drop into a curtsey. "Merritt will be so disappointed to have missed you."

"As long as he's off enjoying the splendors of the tournament, I have no complaints." Fortiss grins, and I find myself unreasonably glad that my face has healed so well—then annoyed that I'm even thinking something so stupid. "Perhaps you'll allow me to show you some of it as well?"

He glances to Nazar. "I assure you, I'll keep her safe."

It's all I can do not to roll my eyes, but Nazar nods back to Fortiss, every inch my solemn guardian. "Your escort is much appreciated. She returns tomorrow to the Tenth House, to await her brother's return."

"The Tenth?" Fortiss asks with ease, turning his smirking gaze on me. "And yet a sneaky little bird told me you were intended for the Twelfth House when you were waylaid. If that's still your goal, we can arrange for an escort all the way there. Lord Orlof hasn't deigned to send any representatives to the Tournament of Gold in far too long. We'd like to make sure he still fares as well as we hope he does."

If this little speech is meant to get my back up, it succeeds, but once again Nazar saves me from saying something I'd surely regret. Instead, he continues to embroider the lie he's so deftly weaving around us. "It's a gracious offer, but no. It'll be good for the family to gather close again once we have a full complement of soldiers loyal to the Tenth house. The union of the Tenth and the Twelfth houses can wait a bit longer."

"Then I'll take full advantage of my opportunity," Fortiss says smoothly and holds out a hand. I'd sooner push him into the dirt than walk with him, but I accept his grasp and allow him to draw me away from our camp. He curls my hand into the crook of his elbow much as Nazar had done, only his grip is like iron, as if he's fully aware that I would flee from him at my first chance.

The moment we're out of Nazar's view, I test his hold. I attempt to tug my hand away, and he grips me closer still. "I've already had the pleasure of you running away from me once, Lady Talia," he assures me cheerfully, though steel now laces his words. "I have no wish to repeat the experience."

"Why?" I asked him, just as lightly. "Are you worried I might interrupt some new villain attempting to shoot my brother? What was the term you used? Oh, right. *Marauder*. Do you suppose these unknown *marauders'* tastes still run to small houses who pose no threat?'

He turns a much colder gaze on me. "Have a care, Lady Talia. The words you speak are treason at the Tournament of Gold. Lord Rihad takes his security very seriously."

"So do I. And so does Merritt, especially given how close he came to returning to the Light on his way to your vaunted tournament. Tell me, why were *you* in the forest by the Shattered City that day, Lord Fortiss? Of all the hills and valleys to hunt in, it seems a curious choice."

"I'd answer the question, should your brother put it to me. Alas, these aren't topics for a woman's ears, even one as fierce as you. But rest assured that no one was more pleased than me to see the villains thwarted that day. Your brother's health ensures the health of his house. And the health of all houses contributes to the safety of the Protectorate."

"Mmm." I don't trust myself to say anything more for a moment. Instead, I recall the words Fortiss used the first day I arrived at the tournament. How had he put it exactly? That unlike many, he was genuinely happy to see me—to see Merritt, anyway?

Merritt. We step into a wide square just as music starts up, and I'm struck again with the unfairness of it all. Merritt would have *loved* this. The torches, the color, the music and food—the people milling around, old and young, men and women. He would have reveled in the pageantry, and his place among his peers, celebrated and fêted, honored and cheered. I may not care for celebration, but he would never have wanted to leave.

Irritation crests anew. "Well, if our safety was such a concern to you, you could have stopped the slaughter of our men and my handmaiden. We could have used your sword in that melee."

"And if I had been at liberty to use it, I would have gladly done so. But once again we speak of things that are better shared with your brother, not you. Plus, if I'm not mistaken, you have changed your hair."

He steps away slightly to regard me, not quite letting go, and I tilt my chin up to meet his gaze. He doesn't know the half of the changes I've undergone since he saw me in that forest. "And you have changed your clothes, but not your colors," I counter. "Tell me, what house dares to try to assassinate a nobleman with gray arrows, Lord Fortiss? Have other houses been attacked? Is there a traitor in your midst?"

"Enough." Fortiss's grip tightens on me, and as his hand closes around my forearm, I count myself lucky that he has my right arm in his grasp and not my left. But how easy it would be for our positions to change, and my secret found out with a brush of his fingers across my warrior band?

Too easy. I should *not* provoke the man.

I draw in a fortifying breath and pray to the Light for patience. It doesn't fully work. "My apologies. I just have heard there's no end to your power and influence, and we lost good people that day. Seems like you could have helped."

He scowls. "I did help."

"Well, thank the Light you didn't help more, or my whole family would be dead."

"*Look*." In one swift movement, Fortiss sweeps me behind a tent where they are hawking spiced corn. He reaches out to grab me by my shoulders—presumably to lift me up and shake me like a witless doll. But my sense of self-preservation kicks in just in time and I jerk back. He pursues me until my shoulders brush up against the fabric walls of the food vendor's tent, and he leans forward, giving me no chance of escaping further. "I get the feeling there's a lot you think you know, Lady Talia. About everything—"

"It's a gift."

"But you *don't*," he continues resolutely, his eyes flashing as his jaw works. "You don't know the powers at work here, you don't know what it is to be a warrior, and you *don't* know how much your father has done your brother and your house a disservice by refusing to honor the Lord Protector. Everything Lord Rihad does is to support the houses, to keep us strong, and you stay up in your mountain hideout like you can't be bothered to interact with the rest of us. It's a problem."

I stare at him, my mind spinning. Has Father ignored the direct summons of the Lord Protector? It wouldn't surprise me. Father hasn't left the mountains since Merritt was born—not once.

Not once.

Unfortunately, Fortiss is still spewing on, unable to recognize my willingness to soften my stance on our discussion. "You should be grateful you're still alive out there in your fringe fiefdom, not making demands and expressing outrage that the forest is a dangerous place."

Well, so much for softening.

"The *forest* didn't attack us," I shoot right back, driving my finger into his chest, expecting to meet bone. It's not bone—it's muscle. A *lot* of muscle under his shiny gold shirt. But I won't be distracted by that. "A man and his dirty gray arrow did. And I—we —were lucky to survive that arrow and the assault that happened next. My handmaiden *died* in that attack, Lord Fortiss. Five of our soldiers did too. While you just ran. A. Way."

He grits his teeth so loud I can practically hear his jaw pop. "Well, you *did* survive. You and your brother made your way to the Tournament of Gold. Here, Lord Merritt can make your house leagues stronger. Especially if he steps on the tournament field to claim his birthright as a first-blooded and firstborn warrior. You should focus on that, Talia of the Tenth. Focus on building him up, keeping him strong. He's young, but his Divh—"

"You saw his Divh?" I can't help myself. I stop poking and flatten my hand on his chest, vaguely registering how hard his heart is pounding. "A-afterwards? After the arrow was shot? You saw him?"

Fortiss's gaze locks with mine. His face is so close, I can smell his breath—spices and mulled wine, the drink of those with money to spare and time to enjoy life's bounty. "Talk of Divhs is forbidden for any woman, Lady Talia," he murmurs, "or is that something else you've forgotten about, up in your mountain home?"

"Tell me!" I urge him, and now, somehow, both my hands are on his chest. It's a wide chest with plenty of room, but I'm still not quite sure how my hands took up residence there. The heat that pulses from it warms my cheeks, my neck, and sends spinning whorls of fire through my belly. "I've never seen it, not from a distance, not really at all. Was it—was it powerful? Was it fierce?"

"It was beautiful," Fortiss says, surprising me with the word—surprising himself too, I think. He dips his head lower, until his lips hover just above mine. "Powerful too." He leans a fraction closer and softly, gently, his lips brush my mouth, taste my fitful breath. Then he rocks back on his heels and grins down at me. "But, eh... not so fierce, I think."

"You lie!" But I'm laughing suddenly, and he is too, and he pulls me away from the food vendor's stall, spinning me into the crush of people thronging through the makeshift square. I'm out of my depth again, my heart pumping too fast, my mind churning with too many thoughts. I glance up—and blink.

A woman stands at the far end of the courtyard, watching me with cold and curious eyes. Her skin is deeply tanned, her mouth thin, and she wears no paint that I can see. She's tall and sturdily built, and though she's fully cloaked, her hair hidden beneath her hood, I sense she could shed that cloak in an instant and have daggers in her palms. I reach out almost blindly for Fortiss and meet his gaze urgently as he turns back to me.

"Who is..." I begin, turning back to where the woman stands—then break off lamely as I stare at the empty space. She's disappeared like a puff of wind, so fast I wonder if I imagined her. "Never mind." I shake my head, and Fortiss grins down at me.

"A truce, fierce Talia of the Tenth, for the short time we have together?" he asks. In that moment, laughing at me with his golden eyes, his easy smile, I think I'll never meet another man as beautiful as he is—and certainly will never want to. Just the sight of him turns my brains to mush.

"A truce," I agree. "And maybe—"

"Lord Fortiss."

We spring away from each other as if we were caught tumbling in a haymow, and I smooth my hands down my dress, shifting my left shoulder back as Fortiss's two retainers stalk up. The bigger one bows with deference, then straightens. "Lord Rihad requests your presence at once."

The soldier's gaze shifts to me, and his dark eyes categorize me as quickly as so many other men have tonight. A tendril of fear snakes through me. "I can escort your lady back to her camp." Beside him, his fellow solder takes my measure too, and the creeping sensation worsens.

"Ah—honestly, I'm good," I stammer, stepping away, but Fortiss merely nods.

"Yes, do that, Ginn." He looks to the second soldier, clearly forgetting me. "What's this about?"

"What ho, Lady Talia!" Caleb's bright, brash voice breaks over us as Ginn moves toward me. I whirl around to see my sturdy squire bounding up, sandy-haired and wide eyed. He's once more in Tenth House green, and he practically dances with excitement as he greets me, grinning ear to ear. I could kiss him.

"What *luck*," I say, far too brightly, but I don't care. I turn back to where Fortiss blinks at us and don't look at Ginn at all. "I'll just be on my way. Thank you, Lord Fortiss—and for your offer, sir—but don't trouble yourself, we're off—"

I practically drag Caleb away.

CHAPTER 11

Caleb deposits me back at the tent with Nazar, who tells him that Merritt will be returning soon before sending him off for spiced nuts and honeyed mead. By the time my squire returns a second time, I have re-established myself as Merritt, my face scrubbed free of paint, my legs back in Light-blessed breeches and boots. True to his word, Caleb takes me 'round the whole of the tournament grounds, where I watch and listen almost as much as I laugh. I don't see Fortiss again, nor the strange woman from the crowd.

I'm also no longer leered or sneered at. Not even once.

It's an instructive night for sure.

Later, much later, I dream of laughter and spitting campfires and song; a lifetime's worth of memories cobbled together in one night's revelry.

By the time I awake the next morning, one of our horses, a heavily muscled gelding, has been tied closer to our camp. Caleb, when Nazar informs him it's his, can't stop staring at the horse—at least until Nazar gives him a brush to groom it. Then his grin splits wide, and he starts up a nonstop flow of chatter as he works, almost without drawing breath.

"Lord Rihad's holding is the biggest castle you'll ever see, they say, this side of the Exalted Imperium's borders, and I believe it. Windows made of colored glass that turn sunlight into elaborate patterns, and the walls and floors cut of pure marble. And they don't dress like this"—he gestures at our simple tunics and breeches—"for all that this material is the finest I've ever felt, sir, begging your pardon."

His hasty words bring another smile to Nazar's face. I've never seen the priest so tolerant, and my own doubts are chastened further. But I can't help continuing to feel a vague disquiet about the squire, something that just seems...off.

"They wear state clothes all the time?" Nazar asks.

"To every meal and speech. And there are a *lot* of speeches in the Court of Talons. The Lord Protector assembles his house's soldiers at least three times a week to remind them of their importance to the Exalted Imperium and within the Protectorate themselves. Bards are instructed to tell only the high form of the battles of the Western Realms, and they have banquets once a week, whether there's anything to celebrate or no."

I frown, looking up at the enormous castle on the far rise. "It costs a lot of money to host so many banquets."

"They've got it, and to spare." Caleb waves again, taking in the bustling fairgrounds. "The Tournament of Gold has already been going on for days and days. There's money flowing freely, and you can be sure the First House gets its due. They've got their hands in everything, and what they don't drive themselves, they know about, for sure."

They've got their hands in everything, I think. Including who killed Merritt? Were they even now preparing an assault on the Tenth, seeking somehow to take over the farthest border house, the ancient gateway between the Protectorate and the Exalted Imperium?

But no, I follow hard upon my own words. No one considers the Tenth House a threat, regardless of the ancient role it served when the Protectorate was first created, to provide first news to the capital city of Hakkir of any threat within the Protectorate's borders. Now the Tenth is merely a small, lonely house, out in the middle of nowhere.

The First House could roll over the Tenth if it wanted to, it's simply too big. That's not who was behind Merritt's death. More likely one of the lesser, but more aggressive houses, one who felt it had something to prove.

My purpose here isn't to root out Merritt's killer, however. It's to protect the Tenth.

"We need to make sure the soldiers are ready—and not too drunk to ride," I say, renewed urgency tightening my words. "If we don't leave today, then we leave midday tomorrow, no later."

"Lady Talia, too?" Caleb asks, and Nazar fields that one as I blink.

"I've sent her to a proper inn with a small brace of men to prepare for her return to the Tenth," he says, his voice stony enough that Caleb turns to him with wide eyes. "You did well to bring her back last night, and I thank you again for it. Something in the manner of Fortiss's soldiers deeply distressed her."

"Well, Rihad's men are ass-mongers when it comes to women, everyone knows it." Caleb shrugs his left shoulder, causing his stump to bobble. There's barely three inches of his arm remaining, and he keeps the end carefully wrapped at all times. To lose a limb is virtually a death sentence, especially without expensive doctors at your beck and call. I can't imagine the pain Caleb must have endured when it happened.

"All of Rihad's soldiers live within the First House's gates, yes?" I ask, to pull my mind away from the horror of those images. "Or do you know?"

"Oh, yes, I know that for sure. Fifty fighting men and a dozen banded soldiers, plus another six or so warrior knights," Caleb confirms with a grin. "You don't see 'em out here, mixing with the people, right? That's on purpose. They have a certain status to uphold."

"A status."

"Not a good one. The whole lot of them are mean as snakes,

not a noble-blooded warrior among them except maybe the Lord Protector's nephew, and he's as grim-faced as the rest of them."

"You mean Fortiss," I say, his face emblazoned in my memory. "Is he noble in truth? First-blooded?"

"He's totally first-blooded, his family entwined with Rihad's, though I'm not exactly sure how. His father died young, if I have the story right, when Fortiss was still a boy. Fortiss himself was raised by the Lord Protector, even calls him uncle, but there's bad blood there."

"So they're not truly related," I echo, while Nazar prompts, "Bad blood?"

"Absolutely. No one talks of it, which means everyone talks *around* it, but all these years later, there's only whispers and dark secrets, none of it proven."

A horn sounds in the distance, and I turn. Caleb hops up from where he's been brushing down his new horse. The animal snorts, nudging Caleb's good arm.

"They're starting the pit battles," Caleb announces eagerly, patting the gelding. He turns to me, then Nazar. "If you don't have a need for us, Merritt should at least *see* that before we leave."

I make a face, remembering this term, at least, from the bards' tales. "Pit battles? That barbarism ended long ago, I thought."

"They truly taught you *nothing* at the Tenth House, did they?" Caleb laughs. "They still call them pit battles, but you're right, no one actually fights in pits anymore. They're up on platforms so everyone can see—and so that the ground isn't churned up for the real battles to come. But the fights live on—have to, to keep the flow of soldiers fresh. Accidents happen, people die. Even when there's no war, you still want a whole company of foot soldiers on hand, if you're smart, especially the houses like the First, where whole cities sprawl out around them. The pit battles make that easy. Everyone wants into a garrison, and this is the only way in. Once you're in, if you don't make banded-soldier status, it's the only way to *stay* in, unless you rise to officer ranks. Gotta keep your skills sharp, after all."

I shake my head. We have no garrison; we have no soldiers beyond our retainers, now numbering fifteen men. We should, by rights, have more defenses than the Eleventh and Twelfth House, at the least, but Father is tight with his money and tighter with his disdain of anything other than a first-blooded Divh.

I glance to Nazar, who's cutting up a garment of deep, dark green into cloth strips. My old hooded undercloak, I realize with a start, the one specially made to cover my enormous coils of hair. Now that mass is a tidy wig of ebony braids, and my undercloak is nothing but ribbons.

I couldn't be happier about that.

Before I can speak, the priest looks up. "Do you know how you would win in the pits, Merritt?"

"Win?" I blink at him. "I'd win by not entering them."

My response is met with a guffaw from Caleb. "Not enter them, are you mad? If you're a soldier and you have the chance to fight, you take it. Even as a warrior knight with nothing any longer to prove, you should be ready. You wouldn't get beaten up again like the first time. I can show you."

He tosses his horse brush to the folded blankets and squares off against me in the small space of our camp. Instead of rebuking him, Nazar stops his work and straightens. He watches as I jerk back, narrowly evading Caleb's opening punch.

Irritation sparks through me. "I'm not trained to fight this way, Caleb." In truth I'm not trained at all. Making war against posts driven into the ground only counts for so much.

"Of course you are," he jibes. "You fight with stave and sword. What are stave and sword but extensions of your arms and fists? What are your arms and fists but extensions of your head and heart?"

His words sound so like Nazar that I glance over to the priest, who's now regarding us both with greater interest. That glance is my undoing, as I see Caleb's jab from the corner of my eye but can't turn quickly enough to evade it. At the last minute, he pulls back, just tapping me lightly instead of walloping me, but I spin around anyway as he dances back.

"See? I do that with only one fist. You know how?"

"Because you're fast." I'm turning as well, my gaze not on his head, not on his nattering mouth, but on his stomach. That's how you keep animals in check. Their torsos move before their legs do. If you can focus on their centers, you can capture them more quickly than if you follow their heads or their hooves.

"Not fast—well, I am fast, that's true. But that's not the whole of it. The whole of it is that I keep my center tight until I decide how to move."

I smile with satisfaction. His trick isn't so much a trick after all. He twitches to the left, and though his legs seem to angle right, I follow his body and attack his right shoulder, shoving him hard.

He breaks back quickly, too quickly, and I stumble forward, turning the fall into a somersault as he also regains his feet.

"Second mistake. You went for my strength, not my clear weakness." He shrugs his left shoulder, his stump moving in its shortened sleeve. "I've gotten used to this, but no one else has. It's a misdirection."

He shrugs again, and my heart twists, but in that moment, he barrels forward, his head down, his body leading with his injured arm. Unsure how to move, I falter, and a moment later, I'm on my back, the wind knocked out of me.

"Ha!" Caleb leaps off me and holds out his right hand. "Be glad I don't have two stumps, or you'd already be dead."

I let him pull me to my feet, but I can't help the grin. "Have you been this obnoxious your whole life? Or merely since your injury?" It's the first time I've broached the subject of his arm, and the blood rushes to my cheeks even as I lean down to dust myself off.

Fortunately, Caleb seems unfazed. "I'll let you guess the answer to that." He bows to Nazar as I straighten. But Nazar's gaze is on me, not Caleb.

"Remember the truth of what you said to me," he says. "Don't enter the pits. It's not your place."

My place? I squint at him, then turn to meet Caleb's wide eyes. "What are you staring at?"

"Nothing—nothing." Caleb grins, his gaze shooting from me to Nazar. "The fights will be starting soon. We should go!"

Despite his excitement, Caleb picks his way almost casually through the crowds of the tournament fair, giving me the opportunity to look around more thoroughly. There are more women, I notice at once. Both old and very young, though not many my age. They're setting up makeshift camps and stalls, selling everything from food to tools to decorative trappings for horses and armor. Weaving among the stalls are the tariff takers as well, easily identified by their gold-and-black sashes.

Gold and black. The colors of the First House. The Lord Protector does have his hand in everything, it seems.

"What happens if the tariff takers find someone who's operating without paying their charge?" I ask as we turn into a thicker knot of people. The closer we get to the towering spectator stands, the more excitement hangs in the air.

"Doesn't happen much," Caleb says. "First time they run across a cheat, they shave his head and brand his scalp, then parade him around the field. Doesn't happen at all after that, not in any organized way. There's always someone looking to cut, cut, and cut the system, but the system only has to cut back once and you're done."

I nod. "And the tournaments always bring in all these people?"

"Like this big?" He rubs his face, considering. "The stands alone hold five thousand or so, but there're thousands more that throng to the Tournament of Gold, here more for the spectacle of people and goods and food than the fighting. And that's besides the people who actually live here year-round."

Thousands more? "Where do they all come from?" I ask, aghast.

"The closer houses, mostly. The Second for sure, the Fourth and Seventh. The Fifth, too. Not so much the Eighth. The holdings of all those houses span the plains of the Protectorate, and everyone who can spare the time comes to the Tournament of Gold at least once in their lifetime. Some come every year." He scratched his chin, looking around. "Still, I don't know that I've ever seen it this big. The last tournament to be close was three years ago. That one was big but nothing like this." His smile turns rueful, and I catch the undercurrent of his words.

"You were here?"

"I was here."

He ducks his head and reaches for my hand, pulling me into a thicker knot of people. "We'll never get there if we keep following this crowd. This way is shorter."

I grimace as he threads his way behind a series of tents. A small canal trails below, and the water stinks of rotten vegetables. I squint down the length of it, and Caleb tugs me on. "Canal system starts farther up the mountain, with snow runoff. They say the cisterns beneath the First House are epic—that there used to be a whole network of aquifers through here, back when this plain flooded on a regular basis. As it is, we still get enough. Water dumps through here and eventually makes its way to Murky Creek, which feeds into the Grand Garrapy River. The few weeks of wear the canal gets from the tournament it can handle, but it helps if we get rain."

The skies stretch out above us, cloudless. "So, this is going to get worse before it gets better," I say.

"A lot worse. But it's still quicker to cut through this way."

He's right about that. We climb out of the trench a few minutes later, and I realize we're right behind the coliseum. There's no one entering through this archway, which leads to a steep set of steps. "Where is everyone?"

"Not here. The pits are all ground level—well, not really pits, like I say. But cordoned-off fight zones. These stands were carved to watch the Divhs, not the fighters. Much easier to be on the ground for the pit fights. Lots more to see."

As if to reinforce his words, a cheer sounds dead ahead, and Caleb darts off toward another door. I find myself staring high at the immense coliseum walls. "They use this only once a year?"

"Yes, but it's maintained the whole year through," Caleb says, his gaze also going up, though for just a moment. "Otherwise, they run the risk of animals and squatters, which creates its own problems. Can't have a bunch of squatters here. Men with no good work to sustain them, and the women! Can you imagine a hundred or so of those, all of 'em with squalling babies, cooking and making a mess of everything? It'd stink to the sky inside of two weeks."

The comment is so off-handed, so casually disdainful, it nearly takes my breath away. "I hardly think—" I begin, but in truth I don't know what to say. How would Merritt respond to such a comment? Is this how my brother spoke with the other boys?

Caleb's now several steps ahead of me, and he shouts back excitedly. "Come on then! Here we are."

Before I can stop him, he races down a short corridor, where we have the briefest respite of darkness. Then suddenly we're out into the wide-open tournament field, filled with fighting men.

And it's madness.

CHAPTER 12

The entire length of the great tournament field is teeming with cheering, shouting people. The place smells of sweat and hysteria. Tight around my left bicep, my warrior band begins to chafe against my skin, and I shake the feeling off. This is not my place.

Easily a hundred platforms have been erected across the space, each surrounded by rings of people. There are no women here, I notice instantly, but men and boys of every age, all seeming to shout at once.

"Look, look!" Caleb tugs my arm and points to the nearest platform. Two boys, barely older than fifteen, grapple with each other in an almost brutal frenzy. "You have to be twelve to enter the pit fighting rounds for the first time, and no older than twenty-five."

"Twenty-five?" I look at him in horror. "They can't put those children against grown men."

"They don't. There's an overall winner, but also age winners. Everyone gets a chance, if they're good enough." His smile goes a little sideways. "Well, almost everyone."

A scream to my left draws my attention. One of the boys struggles upright, wheeling away from the first and holding his nose. Blood gushes between his fingers, and his eyes are wide and glazed with pain. My stomach churns as the first boy also staggers to his feet. He clenches his hands into unsteady fists, but a bell clangs to the side as he surges forward. Both boys stiffen, and a man wearing gold and black swings up onto the platform. He says something I can't make out over the cheering crowd and points at the boy whose nose wasn't broken.

While that one lifts his hands shakily above his head, the other boy seems to come back to himself. With a snarl of pure rage, blood still streaming down his face, he launches himself at the first boy again, and the two of them go down, kicking and punching. Caleb pulls me away as I see the first boy's head crack against the surface of the platform once, twice.

"No good can come from that," he says. "Let's move on."

"But the fight—it had stopped," I protest. "How can they keep fighting if the fight had stopped?"

He shoots me another odd glance, and once again I realize I've said the wrong thing. Panic pools deep in my stomach as Caleb eyes me, clearly expecting me to say more. When I don't, he fills in the suddenly fraught silence between us as if there'd never been a pause.

"You're looking at it the wrong way. Pit fights are supposed to mimic war, not some stupid game. While men still stand, they can fight. The official was slow and stupid, or he had a dog in the hunt, to handle the end of the round that way."

"A dog."

Caleb shrugs. "If he bet on the boy with the busted nose, he would've wanted to see him win. But once a fighter is dazed like that, the fight should be called. It's not interesting to watch anyone pummel a sack of meat."

Despite my best efforts, I make a face, but Caleb isn't looking at me anymore, thank the Light. He's on his toes to see the next platform. "If he wanted the boys to keep fighting, he got his wish, is all I'm saying. We should come over this way. There's something strange up there."

Conversation proves impossible as we plunge back into the

crowd. Since we've entered in the center of the stadium grounds, we're relatively close to the two large wooden towers and stone overlook where the Lord Protector had loomed above the banded soldiers in the first Divh battle. I stare up at the towers, stunned by their size. They'd seemed big from my vantage point in the stands, but with me on the ground, they dwarf me. Everything at the tournament is built to an impossibly large scale.

Caleb beats me on the shoulder. "Not up—over there. That's a sight, isn't it? Something big has to be happening for Fortiss to be—"

"Who?" The name jolts me to my toes, and I turn to where Caleb's pointing. My eyes round as I take in the gold-and-black bedecked figure standing in the center of a stage that apparently had been erected overnight, along with all the pit fighting rings. The platform is nearly four times the size of the small stage the boys were grappling on.

I frown. "I thought Fortiss was a warrior knight. What's he doing in a fighting ring?"

"That's not a fighting ring. It's for announcing the winners." Caleb stiffens. "Hold your ears. I hate it when they do this."

Horns suddenly blare around us, so intense, my bones vibrate. Agreeing with Caleb's suggestion, I clap my hands to my ears and screw my eyes tight against the pain.

As quickly as the blast begins, though, it's over. In its wake, utter silence reigns.

I peek once more at the stage. A man now stands beside Fortiss. He's as big as a bull, dwarfing the younger warrior, but Fortiss remains the more menacing of the two. Fortiss stares out at the crowd as if it's offended him. He nods to the giant, and the man puts his fists on his hips, then cries out in the loudest voice I've ever heard a man utter.

"Men of the Tournament of Gold, the First House commends you," he shouts, and a quick cheer rises up, cutting off sharply as the man-bull lifts his hands. "The Lord Protector seeks a new army of the best and strongest soldiers. Men who will be sanctified to band with the Divh. You are here because you think that there will be twelve such warriors accorded to your winning house, and eighteen more to the other top houses. But I say to you there will be *fifty*, apportioned to the highest-ranking combatants of the Tournament of Gold—and twenty to the house of the warrior who wears the winged crown!"

A wave of excitement sweeps through the camp. So not thirty, but fifty? With *fifty* banded soldiers in play, and if the warriors weren't distributed equally, one house could easily take over the others, if it wanted to—especially whoever won the winged crown. I've never even considered the possibility of house striking house before these past several days, but now it weighs on me heavily. By Protectorate law, the First House would never allow such a transgression—for no sooner would one house fall than others would band together in side alliances, to either defeat the original attacker or join forces with it, intending to establish a new ruling order. The First House wouldn't—couldn't—want that.

Then again, it's the First House who's proposing this new infusion of warriors, which will almost undoubtedly alter the balance of power among the houses. So…why?

If other houses have my same worry, then there's no way they agreed to this new influx of warriors—even those houses who are already represented in the Tournament of Gold. And for houses like my own, tucked into the mountains, far away from tournaments and monsters four times the size of our original Div… How could they even know what was happening until some new, unexpected army landed on their doorstep?

I'm not alone in my concern, it seems. Throughout the field, warriors dressed in formal livery stare at the First House crier, their faces stony. This is clearly news to them as well.

The giant isn't finished, though. "And who will rule this new army of soldiers? Who will claim these banded soldiers and their Divhs for their own house?"

He raises his hands again, but it's Fortiss who stands forward, his voice loud and clear, echoing across the tournament ground.

"Warrior knights of the Protectorate, I salute you," he cries out. He claps his right hand to his left bicep, and I'm jolted by the reaction in my own, an answering tremor that shoots down my arm, even though Fortiss is not truly banded. "You are the greatest collection of warrior knights of our generation. Whoever of your number is the winner of the Tournament of Gold, to his house will go fully twenty of these newly created banded soldiers. Twenty! Then seven to those who follow in the second and third positions, then five and then four, three, two, and one each to the final two place holders. Each house will see gain if they win at least one round in the tournament. And for your trouble, you will be awarded the best banded soldiers assembled in all the Protectorate!"

A cheer rolls forth, and I find my own voice raised as well in salute to the Lord Protector for his ample generosity. In truth, though, my head's still spinning. Fifty new warriors equipped with Divhs?

The horns sound once more, and I turn, then turn again. The battles have recommenced all around me. Men fighting each other if not to the death, then it might as well be, all of them under the careful or not-so-careful eye of the First House officials. Even given the possibility of graft, as Caleb suggests, there can be no disputing clear winners. Eventually, the cream of the crop will rise and be awarded a Divh. Even those who aren't made into banded soldiers will be invaluable as foot soldiers and guards.

Fifty banded soldiers. Fully twenty to the winning house. What would the Tenth House do with twenty banded soldiers—or even seven? Seven warriors with the protection of Divhs remotely close in size to Gent? We wouldn't need to worry and wait, hoping that marauders didn't come up from the south, or refugees from the east looking to escape the laws of the Exalted Imperium. We wouldn't need to cower in fear because my parents are too old to bear another son.

No. With twenty, seven, or even *three* banded soldiers in addition to the soldiers I've just purchased, my father could rule for years yet. Perhaps in time, a cousin would step forward, prove his worth, and my father would agree on a successor. With banded soldiers, he has options. With banded soldiers, our house will truly be safe, even without my brother.

Without my brother.

My mouth flattens, my fists clench, and I have to force myself to focus on what Caleb is saying now, hissing in my ear.

"—take it lying down, I tell you plain."

"What?" I blink at him. He's staring at me now, shaking my arm. "Take what lying down?"

"Fifty new warriors? That's not in accordance with Protectorate Law—and I know that law, I learned it back when I thought..." He waves off his own words. "Never mind. But I know it. Which means that the Exalted Imperium needs to sanction such a decision. Do you see anyone from the Imperium here? Because I don't."

I squint up to where Fortiss and the big bull of a man still stand. The battles roil around us, but Fortiss isn't watching them, exactly. He has the sense of presiding over the entire field, but he's not identifying the most viable men battling each other on their platforms. I pivot to track his gaze, noting as it shifts around the field, from man to man.

I'm right. He's not watching the fighters. He's eyeing the warrior knights. It's easy to pick them out, of course. They sit atop their warhorses, a wide berth given to them and their steeds. There are easily two dozen of them. None of them wear gold and black except for Fortiss...the sole representative of the First House, keeper of the law, upholder of the Protectorate's most sacred traditions.

Traditions. Anger spikes anew. There must be justice for Merritt's death in the First House, somehow. Rihad surely can't already know that one house has struck another. Once he does, how could he not help me? "How do you get inside the First House?"

"By showing up with a Divh on its doorstep."

I glance down at Caleb. "What do you mean?"

"I mean if you're a first-blooded warrior knight, you'll be welcomed with opened arms. You and your entourage given top-drawer treatment. The Lord Protector isn't an idiot. He wants to keep warriors of worth coming back, so he's going to treat them well. And once this new rumor spreads, I bet we'll see the last of the missing houses come out of the woodwork. The prize of more soldiers, especially banded soldiers, isn't one lightly made, for all that it's illegal. Unless there are agents of the Imperium up there in the First House, anyway." Caleb purses his lips, clearly considering the possibility.

Agents of the Imperium. I hadn't even imagined that. Would they...could I go to someone like that, tell *them* what happened to Merritt, show them the broken arrow? Would they hear my case, help me find justice? Perhaps even offer protection to the Tenth House?

Or, more likely, would they kill me on the spot for daring to wear the warrior band as a woman? The same as Rihad would, if he ever discovered my secret. Fortiss too.

Without warning, another blast of the trumpets nearly levels us.

"I hate that!" Caleb spits as we both slap our hands to our ears. We turn as one with the rest of the field, even the men on the fighting platforms breaking apart to stand at attention.

Fortiss calls again, his voice carrying over the silent crowd. "All warrior knights are honor bound to take part in the Tournament of Gold, for the glory of the Protectorate and the service of our people. Assemble now, that you may be officially entered!"

I freeze, even as Caleb bounces on his feet, his chatter starting up again. "Oh, that's good, that's smart. That'll reel in the ones on the fence, encourage more warriors to come running. Not all of them are here, of course, but a lot of them are. Even the Fourth House and Sixth House are here, you see?" He points. "Sky blue and purple."

"But the Sixth House already beat the Fourth."

Caleb shakes his head. "Solely a demonstration. If pressed, either side could say that they were acting for the entertainment of the crowd."

"Acting." I scowl. "The warrior for the Fourth House was *bleeding* by the end of that demonstration. That was no act."

Caleb shrugs. "I told you, he wasn't hurt that badly. And the exhibitions aren't official. Until the Tournament of Gold begins in earnest, everyone is on a level playing field. Even if they lose during the demonstration rounds."

I miss what Caleb says next as a large figure in red and white shoves me to the side, bowling me into the spectators surrounding us.

"Move aside, runt." He smirks with what seems like unreasonable malice, his teeth blackened and foul smelling. I'm not sure what he's been chewing, but he reeks of heavy spices and sweat.

"And you." He rounds on Caleb, who stands his ground, though his face has gone pale and bloodless. "I heard what you pulled with Hantor. Unless you want your other arm cut off, you'll be smart to stay out of the pits." He sneers. "Not that you'd have a chance anymore. Divhs thrive on strength, not pity. And pity is all you're good for now, isn't it?"

"On the stage, Jank," another man in red shouts down from the main stage, laughter in his voice. "You can taunt the horde another time."

The burly warrior grins and holds up an arm. His fellow Second House warrior pulls him up with a hearty tug. The second warrior's gaze falls on Caleb, and his face shutters. He looks away quickly, like a dog who's been whipped. Then, as if he's forced, he looks back, nodding at Caleb's green tunic. "You've found a new House. That's good."

"It is good." Caleb's voice is cold as flint, but there's still no color in his face as I glance sideways. What's going on here? Are these men responsible for his injury?

"Warriors of the Second, Fourth, and Sixth Houses, honor the Exalted Imperium!"

A roar goes up from the crowd, and I stare at the men upon the stage as they raise their left hands high into the sky, their right fists against their hearts. These aren't boys, in the main, though in their midst I spy the young Hantor, whom Caleb fought. Most of these warrior knights are grown men of twenty, even thirty years. Men who have trained to fight these battles, and who've trained the boys in their ranks.

My own arm band tightens painfully as my thoughts shift from the lines of men on the stage to the looming castle of the distant First House, high in its mountain embrace.

"Warriors of the Seventh, Ninth, and Eleventh Houses, honor the Exalted Imperium!"

I swallow hard as a second round of men on the stage raise their left hands, with more coming in from the crowd to clamber up. I've no idea which houses are still on their way to the tournament, or which won't send representatives at all. And, of course, the Tenth and Twelfth Houses have no representatives. The child warrior of the Twelfth House is probably still waiting for his bride in the northeast corner of the Protectorate. While the warrior of the Tenth House...

Anger boils up within me, thick and hot. *"Don't enter the pits,"* Nazar had said. That wasn't my place. But these men aren't standing on the fighting platforms. They're standing above them, on a separate stage. Honored by all who see them.

Honored.

I remember Merritt's words, so full of life and excitement. *"But I'm going to enter the Tournament of Gold and bring honor to our house..."*

A surge of emotion assaults me, leaving me dizzy with both a hollow grief and a razor-pointed rage. One of the houses on this stage took my brother from me. Took his dreams, his hopes and boyish fantasies, and speared them on the tip of a dead gray arrow. One of these houses committed the ultimate crime and would *never* pay for that crime unless I...unless I...

I wheel to Caleb, who's staring at me intently, the ghost of a smile curving his lips.

"Go ahead," he says, his certainty sending icy shivers along my warrior band. "This platform *is* your place, really and truly. Even Nazar knows it. He wouldn't have sent you here if he didn't, and he's smart, I'm telling you. I think he's *really* smart."

Fortiss's voice rings out again. "To all who would—"

"Wait!" shouts Caleb, before I can stop him. My heart thunders, but he's no longer standing beside me. Instead, he kneels and offers me his hand and shoulder and—almost without thinking—I step into his grasp and leap to the central stage as he stands again.

I land lightly on my feet. The men all turn, surprise evident in their features, and Hantor's reedy whine comes first.

"You! Get off the stage, you have no right—"

Fortiss's raised hand freezes everyone. This close, the head warrior of the First House looks impossibly perfect, chiseled from stone. His steady golden eyes take me in.

"Warrior Merritt of the Tenth House," he says, clear curiosity in his voice.

I nod hurriedly, and he smiles. An entirely different and unwelcome emotion punches through me. No one has ever smiled at me with such focus. I don't know what to do, how to act. It's all I can manage to keep my expression fixed and stolid.

"Warrior Merritt of the Tenth House, we're honored to have you fight in the Tournament of Gold," Fortiss says, bowing slightly to me. "You and your company shall join us tomorrow night in the great hall of the First House, to present yourself to Lord Rihad and partake of the warrior's banquet. Prepare your men."

Desperate not to betray myself, I stare gravely back, then bow my head as well. I can feel the outrage spilling off Hantor and Jank like spoiled wine, but they're the least of my problems.

Somewhere on this stage might be the man who killed Merritt. Who even now seeks to kill me, believing I'm my brother. And that murderer has me at a grave disadvantage, given how little I know about fighting and Divhs and...well, everything about this world of warrior knights. *What am I doing up here? What was I thinking?*

Then Fortiss turns to the crowd, and all my fears, my worries and denials are suddenly too late.

"To all you soldiers who would join these men," he cries, "I present you the warrior knights of the Protectorate. In the coming days, they will fight with their mighty Divhs to win your respect!"

A resounding bellow sweeps through the throng, practically lifting us off the stage. It's a cry of battle lust and excitement, and the band around my left arm spasms, a living thing.

As one, the warriors on stage lift their left arms high above their heads, their right hands crossed to their chests, fists to heart. We turn toward the mountain stronghold of the First House of the Protectorate and join our voices to the roar.

I have entered the Tournament of Gold.

CHAPTER 13

"This is going to be a tournament for the ages. You're going to show everyone, it'll be epic!"

Caleb hasn't stopped talking since I jumped down from the stage, the two of us disappearing into the crowd before Hantor can hunt me down. Despite my brave show, I don't want to fight the Second House knight again, or his friend Jank, the lunkheaded banded soldier.

They're not the only men I fear back on that stage, though. I try to remember who stared at me the longest and the hardest, in those few brief moments I stood among them. In truth, it was Jank who'd glared at me the most, once I'd declared myself. Hantor had, too—but Hantor was barely more than a boy. He'd never have been sent on a killing mission. But had Jank or one of the other warriors of the Second been given that charge? Had any of them been the one to shoot the arrow that cleaved through my brother's heart?

What was I thinking, to imagine I could enter the tournament without any real training? I'm as much of an idiot as Merritt.

"Caleb—" I try to interrupt.

He waves me off, pausing only long enough to give directions. "Turn here, back under the stands. We can breathe again."

I follow his lead, and soon we are in the cool half-darkness of a wide stone corridor, a distant light beckoning us onward, and more sunshine filtering down through long open slats in the ceiling. We move deeper into the stillness another twenty paces before Caleb stops and pivots to me. The smile on his face reaches all the way to his eyes, and he bounces up on his toes.

"Look, I know you don't think you're ready for this," he begins.

"I'm *not* ready for it."

"—And I know you're probably worried about the Seventh House's death worm—"

Death worm?

Caleb keeps going. "But we have time. There's another full week before the tournament proper begins, and maybe longer if they think they can get more warriors to show up."

I frown at him, my guts twisting. "What do you mean, more?"

"After today's announcement, you can bet that bards will be sent to all the houses not reporting in so far. That'll take a while. But at least now they won't have to go to the Tenth House and back—you're accounted for. That'll cut a good four days off the wait."

"Oh. Right."

He blows out a long breath then fixes me with a hard look. "Still, we'll have a lot to do in a short time no matter how you look at it. What with you being a girl and all."

My stomach drops so fast and so far, I'm surprised it doesn't fall out my feet. I can't do anything but stare back at Caleb in utter shock at his bold declaration, all my carefully constructed denials dying in my throat for one harrowing moment before I can recover.

But only a moment.

Chin up, eyes cold, expression as empty as the winter's sky.

"Take that back," I growl. I reach for my sword and Caleb's eyes light up with interest, the squire easily circling to my left as I haul out the long, slender blade.

"That was my first tip, you know," he says, keeping a good

distance between us, his gaze never leaving mine, his face now intent, more serious than I ever thought he could be. "I wasn't about to make a thing of it, since you'd just saved my ass and all. But you didn't draw your sword to fight Hantor, and any boy would've. Plus, you fought like you'd never been in a fight before. All defense, no offense. Only, no warrior son gets beaten up in the training yards. They're always the ones punching, while the other kids defend, because no one wants to get whipped for harming the favored boy. You're that favored boy, and you have been your whole life supposedly, but haven't *once* acted like it since I met you—not once."

Panic rattles through me, sour and sick, but I can't give into it. "You're lucky I don't kill you now."

"You're lucky I don't run off and tell the entire tournament that its newest celebrated combatant is a *girl*," Caleb shoots back, his tone sharp, almost angry, the threat in his words real and immediate to my ears. "Think about how much money would be in that little secret revealed, eh? Think about that."

Another surge of fear swamps me. *This is it*. After losing Merritt, after bonding with an impossibly mighty Divh, after standing on a stage and committing to fight against the greatest warriors in the country, I'll be undone by a boy. A boy I trusted and never should have. A boy I allowed to get too close.

But Caleb isn't finished. "And even with all that, I probably wouldn't have thought too hard about the sword and your abysmal fighting skills, but then your reactions at the pits—" he shakes his head. "Every single thing you cared about was wrong. So was everything you saw, things a warrior son wouldn't even *notice*. Certainly wouldn't comment on, no way."

"That boy," I mutter, and opposite me, Caleb nods, his face flushing. When he speaks again, however, his voice sounds very different. Quieter. Almost rueful.

"That boy. The injustices. Me. Maybe you considered me a cripple when you stopped to check out my fight with Hantor. But you didn't see me as a freak, something to laugh at and turn away from when things got ugly. You jumped in. You helped. And then..." He grimaces. "Then you let me help you. Asked for my help, even. Accepted it. You didn't dismiss me as a broken tool, useful but only so much. You leaned on me without even thinking much about it. I'd maybe get that from a seasoned warrior, someone older, more comfortable in his own skin. But not a boy of seventeen, desperate to show off at the Tournament of Gold. That doesn't happen. That shouldn't happen. But with you, it did."

I can't help myself, I stop, this last revelation cutting so deep and true I can't dispute it. In that moment I imagine Merritt, my beloved little brother, seeing Caleb for the first time. He wouldn't have been cruel, I don't think. He knew that terrible things sometimes happened to people. But he would've instinctively shied away from the squire, would've felt awkward every time the one-armed boy had approached. Whereas I...I know what it's like to be the one in the shadows, hoping desperately no one noticed me—but wanting to be noticed all the same. And I can't even imagine turning away someone's assistance, no matter who offered it.

Caleb has bested me. My shoulders slump as we face off against each other, the reality of his discovery a crushing weight. The way of the warrior is death, Nazar has told me. And death can come as easily inside the coliseum as beneath it.

"So why are you still here?" I finally ask, my voice leaden. "Why aren't you out there making all that money with this fantastic story, this secret so many people would pay real money to know?"

Caleb stares at me a long time after that, and his words, when they come, are quiet. Almost eerily quiet, floating to me like dust motes in the half-lit space. "Because you did stand on the edge of that pit where I was fighting with Hantor. And out of everyone there, all those men, all those boys, all those fighters who knew how to throw a punch and swing a sword...you were the one who jumped in to help me. You, who'd clearly never been in a fight in your life. You didn't jerk away from me in horror or even surprise as I ran with you through the crowd to get you back to Nazar, you just held on to me and let me guide you."

I smile ruefully. "I *was* nearly blind, if you'll recall."

"It doesn't matter. You accepted my help then, and every moment after. Even and including making sure that ass-monger Ginn didn't get his hands on you, letting me take you away. And what's more, yeah. You do react to things you shouldn't—and you especially make comments you shouldn't—but the thing is...your eyes are still open. You saw injustices in those tournament pits that I'd long ago stopped seeing. Even after I lost my arm, I'm still blinded by my desperate need to *belong*. I should never have stopped seeing those things. Things a true warrior worth his salt would care about."

He pauses. "Merritt died in those mountains, didn't he."

His words are blunt, but they don't hurt as much as I expect them to, more like a blow coming at me from a long way away. Once again, I see my brother leap, his laughter bright and full. Once more, I see the arrow pierce through him, shattering the sky.

"He did. I—his Divh bonded to me. I don't know why or how. After that..."

Caleb nods, his expression solemn. He knows, I think. He understands. "After that, yeah. You're a dead woman. Might as well fight for your house while you can."

I wince, the squire's words an eerie echo of Nazar's. "I will bring honor to my house," I say hollowly, glancing away. Even the shadows shrink back from me now, offering me no place to hide.

Silence fills the space between us, but Caleb doesn't—or maybe can't—remain still for long. And his voice is different when he speaks again. The bright and chattering voice of the Caleb who'd raced with me through the crowd, holding onto me as my eye had swollen shut.

"Hey," he says, and when I meet his gaze, his grin is back as well. Awkward and lopsided, but no less firm than it'd been before we'd rushed into this darkened space. "Is your name really Talia?"

I hesitate, this admission the final failure. But I force the words out. "Yes. It's Talia," I say, the word almost foreign in my mouth.

"Talia." He tests the word on the air, seeming to savor it, then shrugs. "Eh. I think for right now, I prefer Merritt. And Merritt, we've got a *lot* of work to do, if you're going to hold your own in the Tournament of Gold."

I blink, taking a step back, and now Caleb's smile splits his face wide. "That's right. I've never missed a bet yet, and I've decided I'm keeping my money on you." He points at my sword. "Put that away, though, and save us both the trouble. We don't have that kind of time. You're damned good with the stave, and your instincts aren't completely hopeless, but the sword... Well, you better pray you never have to pull that thing for anything but show. We can work with the rest, though. You've got heart, and you're idiot enough to rush in where no one else would. Sometimes that's all you need to win, eh?"

"You—" Despite Caleb's rush of enthusiasm, and the words that ring with such authenticity, I have to ask the question, have to know. "You're not going to tell? There's money in it, you said. A lot of money."

"There's *so* much money," Caleb agrees, flinging his good arm wide. Then he winks at me, and I know he's teasing—that he'd never seriously thought of betraying me, despite all my fears.

That said...he's still one of the savviest opportunists I've ever met.

Caleb grins, as if he's reading my thoughts. "But you know, if I place my bets right, there's a lot *more* in backing the scrawny warrior knight from the border, attended only by his old-as-dirt priest and squired by a one-armed boy. That's a bet I can make some scratch on, I tell you plain."

He laughs and turns away as I stare at him, beckoning me toward the sunshine.

"Come on. Like I said, we've got a lot to do. I'll even teach you how to fight one-handed, which is all you'll need to manage Hantor."

I fall into step beside him, suddenly feeling far older than my seventeen years...older but curiously lighter too. Caleb is—a friend, I decide. My second friend, ever. "I'm not worried about Hantor," I mutter. "I'm worried about his Divh."

Caleb snorts. "Don't be. It's about as frightening as Hantor is."

And after another dozen steps, we emerge into the bright and brilliant day.

CHAPTER 14

The crowd is much thinner here, outside the coliseum. The fighting has resumed in the pits, and I recall the two young boys I saw. One of them will move on, but as to the other, how will he fare? Will he have a home to return to, parents who care for him, though he hasn't excelled in the pits?

I think about Merritt being forced to fight that way. How would he have performed, coming to this place as anything but a feted warrior son? He had no idea of the world that existed outside the walls of the Tenth House. Clearly, I didn't either.

I need to do better, and in a hurry.

"When do you want to train with your Divh? I can be there for that too. I can help, you know. Even, you know, with this." Caleb's words cut through me, refocusing my attention. Not so much for what he's saying, but for the unexpected emotion that lifts from him like a wall of tears, for all that his tone is light. I blink as I take in his earnest expression.

"Of course you can help, at least I think you can," I say. "I'd be honored for you to assist me."

Assist me with what? I have no idea. I've barely seen my Divh myself. How am I going to use Caleb in any meaningful way? Merritt didn't have a squire assist him with his actual warrior training. He didn't need to. Merritt and his Divh were symbols of the Exalted Imperium, a warrior pairing intended for display, not use. The Tournament of Gold was a symbol too, I'd assumed...but clearly, I was wrong. There's no denying the undercurrent of danger and unrest I felt on that stage. These men will fight to win.

Caleb seems like he's waiting for more, and I shake my head, trying not to sound as helpless as I feel. "You have to understand. At the Tenth House, we held no tournaments. We fought in no battles. I don't know the first thing of how to fight like the warrior knights of the Fourth and Sixth Houses that we saw here yesterday. I don't know the proper movements or the protocols."

"You'll pick it up quick enough—and you won't be the only one feeling a step behind. Tournament rules change from place to place, so there's always something to learn. Keep your eyes sharp, watch everyone around you, and sneer a lot. I'm telling you, the sneering is half the battle."

Before I can protest, the crowd closes in around us, stifling our conversation. It's another hour before we reach our camp. The priest is there, and our horses, but no one else, thank the Light. I don't realize how much I've missed this oasis of calm until I've returned to it.

Caleb bounds up to Nazar then bows deeply to him. I wonder at that, but Caleb is excited, and he does owe Nazar his position. Plus, Nazar is a priest. Though his role in the Tenth House is limited to the ancient rites, perhaps here in Trilion, the position holds more sway.

"*Merritt* has entered the Tournament of Gold, just like you said he would," Caleb says, placing a slight emphasis on my brother's name, enough to make me wince.

Then his words catch up to me.

"What?" I stiffen as Nazar turns to me. "You knew I'd enter? How?"

The priest shrugs, his gaze inscrutable. "It's the surest path to honor, and your truest path. You merely needed to find it."

"It's definitely the surest," crows Caleb. "And speaking of, we've got to head up to the First House tonight. They'll be making room for us in the barracks, and the *feast*." His eyes dance as he clutches his hands to his stomach. "You've never eaten so much."

"Not tonight," Nazar says, watching me as I try to hide my panic. This is happening. Really happening. I've entered the Tournament of Gold. "We're not required so soon, surely."

Caleb pauses, shifting his glance between us. "Well...no. Technically, we're not required to appear until tomorrow, where Merritt will be presented at the grand banquet. There'll be other warriors coming in as well, I think, so there will be more honor banquets throughout the week. But Merritt's will be tomorrow."

"We shouldn't still be here at all," I groan, unable to help myself. "I shouldn't have entered. We should be getting back to protect the Tenth House."

"The Tenth is already protected," Nazar says, startling me. "The whispers have grown into a reinforced wall."

I scowl at him then cut my glance to Caleb, who's doing his best to look innocent, and failing utterly. "What whispers?"

Nazar gestures expansively. "It appears that the warrior knight of the Tenth has sworn retribution on the marauders who attacked his party—and on any others who dare harass his house. Any with ears to hear will wait now and see the outcome of the Tournament of Gold to see how much pain they are inviting onto themselves by troubling the mountain keep of the Tenth House. One knight and his Div...or a veritable army."

"As if I have any shot at winning." But I stare at Caleb, and he stares back, his grin unabashed. He knew the truth about me when he spread those rumors. He at least suspected it. Was he simply trying to drive the bettors into a frenzy?

"Yours is the way of the warrior." Nazar's words recall me, his tone completely neutral. "And so tomorrow, we go to the First House. Tonight, we prepare."

By prepare, Nazar clearly means "clean." Every dish, bowl, blade, and piece of tack is dragged into the center of our encampment, and Caleb and I spend the rest of the day inspecting, repairing, and running all manner of errands to fetch new leather lacings or metal hooks, ensuring all is in perfect condition. I bend myself as earnestly to these tasks as Caleb does, though I sense his intrigued gaze upon me, and I see what he sees. Here I am, a warrior knight, doing the lowest work asked of me without complaint. If he hadn't already guessed my secret, this wouldn't have helped.

My lips twist, but in this, at least, I understand Nazar. In a few days' time, I'll be asked to use these weapons and trappings of war. The more I'm comfortable with them, the better off I'll be.

Then again, I won't be entering a cleaning competition, but a...

I fumble my bridle, my hands dropping to my lap. Nazar looks up, then shakes his head slightly, clearly suggesting I need to stiffen my spine. He's right, of course. I've put myself upon this path now. All that's left to do is walk it, step by step.

The way of the warrior is death. I must face it fiercely.

Nazar's gaze moves to Caleb, for all that the squire is paying us no mind. Instead, Caleb's happily brushing down Nazar's mare, telling it of all the grand adventures that await us at the First House. The horse's ears flick back and forth, indicating that she's listening too, as Caleb warns her of the majestic warhorses in the First House's stables, along with the finest oats and fresh apples and softest brushes.

We work long into the evening. As we prepare for nightfall, Caleb helps unstitch me from my tunic sleeves, and I force myself to let him, even though he winces to see the dark and damaged skin around my warrior band. It looks far worse than it feels, now, only twinging when I jostle or press against it. I wonder if it will always hurt to the touch.

When we at last break for a meal, Nazar uncovers a cooking pot that's gone unnoticed in the embers of the fire. The rich, savory scent of meat swirls around us as he takes off the lid. He portions out the meal and I stare at it. I've never eaten anything so fine, or so much of it. This is a meal fit for warriors, I realize. As Talia, I wouldn't have eaten this.

Nazar watches as both Caleb and I dig in, though the priest's food goes untouched. Instead, he takes out his long pipe and lights the fine-smelling leaves within it. He gives us both cups of a sharp-tasting drink, which makes my nose crinkle. I set mine away instinctively after the barest sips, and a moment later, Nazar replaces my mug with a second, this one filled with hot water. Caleb receives no such new mug, and his laughter grows broader and less restrained as night falls heavily on the camp. Within an hour, he's too muzzy to stand, and I push him toward his pallet.

"No," he protests, trying to rally. "I'm...your squire. I hassss to help you."

"Then do a squire's work." I laugh and nudge him again, and he stumbles to the right. "Tonight, that means you rest. Nazar wouldn't have given you that wine if he hadn't intended it to put you to sleep."

That makes Caleb's eyes go wide. "Perhaps I'll dream of Divhs!" he says, and once again, the longing in his young voice hurts my heart.

"May your dreams bring you great happiness, then. Now go, get on with it. "

I watch him stumble to his pallet. I don't know that I can trust him—he's just a boy, and for all that he's clearly endured, he could say the wrong thing at the wrong time, betray me in a moment of panic or heat. I have to be aware of that.

But none of that matters so much right now, as I hear him telling his horse of how, one day, a mighty Divh will choose him as his warrior knight, and all will stare in wonder.

I'm still smiling as I finish the last of the camp chores, everything falling silent as the rich smell of Nazar's pipe plays on the night breeze. I'm grateful for the tasks, for something to focus my hands on even as my mind dips and whirls along impossible paths. But I can't say I'm truly surprised when Nazar finally stands. I look at him then glance back to where Caleb is lightly snoring. "He won't do much to watch the camp."

"I've hired other watchers. Come."

"No—wait," I say hurriedly, not wanting this secret to be shared beyond the reach of our own fire. "He knows, Nazar. About me. That I'm…" I swallow. "Me."

The priest squints at me, his pale eyes flat and unimpressed with my revelation. "Of course he does. Yet here he remains, pledged to Merritt of the Tenth. Would that you bring honor to his choice, as well as to your house."

With that, Nazar picks up his walking staff and turns toward the darkness. I scramble to my feet and follow him. The night is bright, the pale gray of his long tunic easy to keep in front of me. We make our way through the twisting maze of other camps that dot the tournament grounds. There's laughter and revelry in some, banked embers in others, each according to their needs for the following day.

At length, we arrive at the now-empty coliseum. The fighting platforms remain, littering the center of the field like leaves on a fall day, but no guards stand watch. The place has its own oppressive feel to it. I doubt anyone would seek to desecrate or loot it.

Nazar, however, moves forward without hesitation. It takes me only a moment to realize that he's angling toward the large wooden towers at the midpoint of the field. "You fight well with the staff and cudgel, but only against opponents of shadow and men of straw," he says, referring to my practice dummies behind the manor house. He watched me far more than I realized. "You have no experience with the sword. You cut and defend well with the knife, but this isn't a battle of defense that you face."

I stay close to him but offer no response as he continues. "The way of strategy is long, it's said, and your time is short. But that's not a true statement. What is true is that the way of strategy is neither short nor long. It's exactly the time it must be to the open heart and mind. This is what I would teach you."

Nazar speaks with a fluid cadence, almost offhandedly, as if he's discussing the morning's meal. But his words strike me with an intensity I don't expect. "I don't understand."

"The way is not understanding." The priest stops and lifts his gaze to the structures where the two warriors fought. "It is knowing." Turning to me, he drives his staff into the ground with a force I wouldn't have expected. Then he folds his arms over his chest. "Summon your Divh. We must know what we have to work with."

"I—"

He waves away my protest. "You are Merritt, warrior knight of the Tenth House. You've set foot upon the Lighted Path and cannot leave it. The way of the warrior is to reach the end of that path, which is death. There are no other options."

My gaze snaps to his. "Warriors don't die in tournaments, Nazar. They're not supposed to die at all."

He watches me with flat eyes. "All warriors die, if they are true. They also don't deviate from their chosen path until the goal is reached and their house is honored. Would you so quickly bring dishonor upon yourself and your house?"

I shift uneasily. "I have no house, Nazar. Not really."

"Then act as if you do. Again, the way is not about understanding." He plants his feet in a wide stance.

I gesture nervously. "There's no room here. You saw how big Gent was. It'll trample the platforms here, and someone—" I drop my voice low, trying to cover the hysteria in it. "Someone will see. Or hear, certainly." I dimly remember how Gent's bellows shook the mountains. Someone will *definitely* hear.

"The plane of the Divhs is always ready for warriors. You'll fight there."

"The plane of the... What are you talking about?" I stare at Nazar, wholly lost.

The priest reaches out and clasps my shoulder, the shock of his contact startling me. As a noble daughter whose only worth to my house was as a virgin bride, I'd never been touched by any man before this week. Here, it's happening every time I turn around. Something else to get used to, and there's already been so much I've needed to learn. Too much.

"It's time," Nazar says. "I'll remain here in prayer, but you'll hear me. Summon your Divh."

Sweat runs between my shoulder blades, but there's no denying the priest's command. I reach up with my right hand and tentatively wrap my fingers around the living band that encircles my left bicep. Even through the thickness of my shirt, its heat nearly sears my fingers as I grasp it, a sudden pulse of fire leaping along my fingers and down my arm.

"Fix your mind on an open field hung with blue mist." Nazar's words pound painfully in my head, but I do as he asks. A breath later, I can picture it: an enormous yard opening up before me, towering stone walls surrounding me in a long oval. I turn, then turn again.

"Open your eyes, warrior," Nazar murmurs, but his isn't the only sound that reaches me. Another draws my attention, a short, huffing breath high above me… Far too high.

I open my eyes. There are walls surrounding me, not coliseum stands. There is the yard I had imagined, not the tournament ground filled with fighting platforms. The blue mist that hangs in the air is thick enough to cut through, blanketing everything with a distorting haze. And there's that huffing sound again…the sound of a heavy breeze whistling through thick, wet columns.

I look up—and up still farther.

A monster stares back at me.

CHAPTER 15

"**G**ent." I say the name without thinking and manage not to scream as a shadow drops down next to me in the near darkness. Thick, fleshy walls close around me, and I'm scooped up in a cradle of warm hide, then lifted with sickening speed. This...this is the Divh's *paw*. Shock silences me, and a moment later, I am face to eyeball—what I assume is an eyeball—a dark gelatinous mass that seems close enough to fall into.

I don't think that would end well for me.

"Say your name, Talia. Your name. Not Merritt's." Nazar's voice whispers in my ear, but my mind cannot comprehend him being here and not here—and he's definitely not here, standing in this, this...

I swallow and sway against the thick, warm skin, instantly shrinking away from it, but there's nowhere to go. Panic builds again.

"Your *name*," Nazar snaps in my mind.

"Tal—Talia," I whisper at the enormous eye, anger and shame suffusing me. I'm not Merritt, the rightful warrior for this Divh. I should have protected him better, should have—

The eyeball shifts in the moonlight, the lid hovering above me, and all other thoughts flee as I realize my Divh has *eyelashes*.

Eyelashes! That seems so preposterous that a laugh rolls up from my belly, and I grab the sides of the Divh's palm as my shoulders shake.

"Again, Talia," Nazar urges from—wherever he is—breaking in on my hysteria.

"Talia!" I shout on the heels of a hiccupping laugh, the sound seeming far too loud next to an eyeball.

Gent, apparently, thinks the same thing. Its head jerks back, and its paw closes convulsively around my body, my laughter instantly choking into a terrified yelp. At the last second before it completely crushes me, the Divh freezes. For a long, sickening moment, so slowly that it has to be deliberate, it peels its fingers back until it can see my face again.

We stare at each other, and I realize something else.

Gent is not an it.

It's a he.

I don't know how I know this, but this long-eyelashed beast breathing in short, huffing gasps so as not to blow me off his own palm is male—a sire and a son, a creature with a family and community. I can't fathom it, but I know with a blasting certainty that this Divh—*all* Divhs—are connected in a way I'd never possibly imagined. Connected to their warriors, certainly, but also...connected to each other, even if they've never before met.

There's something important about that, more important than I can fully grasp, but I don't have time to think on it further, because now Gent is staring at me—his own eyes wide as if he's struggling to comprehend me as well.

Perched in his hand, I'm now far enough away that I can see the whole of his face too. It's the face of a horned demon, ringed with spikes that glisten in the blueish light, his two eyes on either side of his immense central horn beetle black and sharp with intelligence. Those eyes are set slightly to the front, like a horse's eyes, not a fish, but enough to the side that his peripheral vision has got to be better than mine. That and the fact that he can probably see for miles in any direction, with eyes so large.

Gent snorts again, a powerful blast of breath that fortunately is directed beneath me. It blows against my tunic and breeches anyway, and I stabilize myself against his palm as I frown up at him.

"Can he hear my thoughts?" I ask into thin air, though Nazar isn't here. I know he isn't here. And I know this question would only annoy him.

Sure enough, I receive only silence to my question.

I try again.

"Um, can you…" I shake my head at the ridiculousness of talking to a monster. How could this enormous creature even know my language?

The Divh simply stares back at me, his face placid for all that his gaze is direct. I think of the men on the stage, even of Merritt. He'd shouted to his Divh, sometimes cursing at it, but was all that even necessary? Or was simply Merritt's *thought* of leaping into the air all that was needed to show his Divh his intentions. Surely the men on the platforms hadn't shouted to their Divhs—they couldn't have. They were too far away. So there must be some sort of mental connection…right?

I picture myself turning around in Gent's hand as if we are in the middle of the coliseum. I fling my arms out, seeing all there is to see, imagining myself focusing intently on the smallest rock at the top of the stands, or the farthest wooden tower, or the far-distant campfires dotting the hills beyond Trilion. Then in my mind's eye, I imagine Gent looking around the same way.

My eyes suddenly cloud over, then clear, and I blink in amazement.

I'm looking at the coliseum from a great height. I can see the stadium and the mass of fighting platforms far below, but I can't tell if anyone stands atop them. I can see the myriad campfires stretching into the night, but I cannot make out fine details. And beyond the edge of the wasteland to the other side of the coliseum, where I know the mighty castle of the First House stands, I can see nothing but an indistinct blur.

Gent isn't *blind*, exactly, but he can't see as well as I would have thought for something whose eyes are the size of a waterwheel.

"That's okay," I say, patting his meaty paw. "You can still see farther than I can. That's good enough."

I blink again, and once more we're surrounded with the heavy blue mists of Gent's plane. The Divh's chuffing breath blows across my face, smelling of grass and rich earth. I peer around, trying to understand.

"It's night here?" I ask him. Another huff, and I sense the answer is yes. Probably just as well. If I could see too much more, I'm not sure my nerves could take it.

Instead, I imagine Gent putting me back down on the ground. His paw moves, more slowly this time as well, as if he thinks I might break. Which, of course, I might.

When I stumble out of his paw and back onto the yard, however, my knees suddenly give way beneath me. I sink to the dirt—

A resounding crash sounds beside me.

My teeth bounce off each other and I turn, scrambling up again.

In mirror fashion, Gent leaps to his feet and backs away, covering the distance of five hundred ordinary paces in a few short steps. Despite the mist, I can see him more clearly now. His snout is stretched into an outsized grin, and his arms are flailing wildly…

I freeze my own arms, forcing them back down to my sides. "He just…mimics me?"

"That's the most simplistic way of explaining it, yes." Nazar's voice is in my ear once more, as clearly as if he's with me in this plane. "You are bonded. What you do—he does."

"But, he's giant. I'm not. Shouldn't this be the other way around?"

Nazar pauses for a long moment, then continues as if I hadn't spoken. "You must learn to fight with your mind, not your fists, Talia. Otherwise, your Divh fights with its fists and not its mind. And you will fail if that happens."

"He," I grumble. "It's a *he*, Nazar. His name is Gent."

Nazar's chuckle reassures me that he was already aware of this distinction. "And Gent is no longer linked to Merritt, but to you. He has changed."

I flush. "He was forced to change. He needed to be stronger." Irritation wars with my embarrassment. "To make up for *me*. That I'm weaker, our connection forbidden. His role is to take care of me and, well, I guess he will."

Nazar doesn't speak for a long moment, but I don't need him to confirm what I know to be true. "Then given all that," he finally says, "what are Gent's strengths?"

I stand back and look at the monster, who takes a similarly long stride backward. "Size." That's certainly true. Gent stands far taller than the coliseum—as tall as the two monsters that fought in the exhibition match, I'm certain. Maybe even taller. "Big legs, big arms, big hands." I tilt my head, considering him. The Divh tilts his and considers me back. "He can run fast I bet, faster than most."

Gent chuffs a happy breath.

"He can hit and—because he's sort of built like me, with, uh... arms, I understand how he hits." Sort of.

"That's a good observation. What are his weaknesses?"

"He doesn't have a lot of wide mass—so stability. He can't fly. He can't..." I frown at Gent. "Do you breathe fire or anything?"

Gent scowls at me. He blows out a long breath and cocks his head as if to see the results.

"No fire. But he's got a sense of humor."

Nazar's voice becomes a little more strained. "How would he fight the purple fire lizard of the Sixth House? Or the pale lion of the Fourth?"

"I..." I try to imagine Gent against either of those creatures. The images that tumble into my head so quickly make me gasp. "He would rush into the lizard, get beneath her wings. Her belly is her weakness. The lion..." I frown. "He wouldn't fight him."

"That's not an option."

"I know, but..." In my mind's eye, I see Gent circling the lion, who keeps equal pace, turning in a tight rotation. Gent seems confused but not upset, more curious at the size and mass of his competitor. It's bigger than Gent by a fair margin, though Gent is taller. Gent can't get close enough to wrap his hands around the lion's neck. Eventually, he sits. He waits.

I flap my hands nervously. I don't know what to do. "He's not moving. He imagines himself just sitting there."

"Don't mistake patience with inactivity." Nazar's words whisper in my mind. I shrug, the image clearing away. I know what I saw. Gent isn't able to fight the lion, and so he'll give up if we ever face the Fourth House's Divh. Something to keep in mind.

Across the field, Gent looks at me, grinning again. Or, perhaps not truly grinning. His wide mouth can't really assume any other shape, I suspect. I lift an arm, and one of his mighty paws goes up. I kneel on one knee, and he genuflects in front of me, like a mountain bowing down to an ant. I turn slowly, and he turns with me.

"But the men on the platforms didn't move, not really. They shifted position only in reaction, after their Divhs had been wounded or knocked off-balance."

Nazar's voice is back again. "They've trained for many years, those men. It will take you time to have their comfort level in a battle of your own. Your challenge is to focus on stillness. Your Divh's challenge is to understand you."

I tilt my head, and Gent does so again, like a dog mimicking his master's move—and yet not. His move is more playful, almost teasing. As if he's already learned that trick and is waiting for me to catch up.

"I will be very still and imagine only in my head," I say to him now. He stops, his eyes alight with energy.

Run, Gent. Run fast.

Without warning, Gent throws his head back and roars, a sound so loud, it seems to shake the very walls surrounding this sacred field. Then he turns and bounds away from me, leaning into the run, only it's not a run like anything I've seen him do before. He allows his arms to flow backward, like the trailing tail of a horse or a fluttering cape, and bends forward almost double, his enormous legs churning as his feet pound heavily on the ground. In fifteen impossibly long strides, he's reached the far edge of this field, and he runs yet farther, whooping with joy as he bursts through an enormous arch I didn't notice before and into the mists beyond. I step backward, once more at a loss. I hadn't been specific with my orders to Gent.

What if he keeps running and never comes back?

Nazar seems to share my concern. "Talia..."

"Shh." I hear Gent's cries of pure, untroubled joy as they float back to me on the mists. When, at length, the sound grows louder again, I imagine him turning in a wide, happy arc. I send out another call, this time imagining him with me, near me. Picturing him running back to stand with me, to fight with me, to—

Gent erupts out of the thin air directly in front of me, a large paw sweeping forward to scoop me off my feet. He howls again in total elation, and I can't help but laugh, exhilarated and frightened and more alive than I've ever been. All at once, I see the world not through my eyes but *his*. The small person in his grasp shining like the brightest star imaginable for all that it is a tiny, fragile thing. The fierceness of his connection to the tiny creature, a connection forged of time and strength and loyalty to elders.

I don't understand all of it. I don't need to. Gent lifts his arms high and runs with me through the mists—and his strange eyes can pierce these mists easily, I realize, whereas his sight is simply not as fine in my plane.

At length, he slows and stops, his lungs blowing, his heavy, chuffing breath sounding almost like laughter as he gently sets me down on the ground once more. As I take one shaky step, he reaches out with a finger. I lift my arms high to protect my face and he pokes me, sending me sprawling. At once, he falls on his own back, and his laughter booms above us in the silence of the training yard.

When I stagger to my feet once more, though, it's not Gent who laughs beside me, it's Nazar. And he's not exactly laughing.

"What happened?" he snaps, and I wheel around to stare at him. I'm back—back in my own plane, in the heart of the coliseum. Everything feels damp, I realize suddenly—my face, my hands, my hair.

"What...why am I wet?" I hold out my hands as far as I can, but my cloak is stuck to me.

"You looked as if you were running—head down, arms back, legs straining, though you didn't move." Nazar peers at me. "And though you didn't move, it was as if a cloud had burst open upon you."

"The mist—we were moving through mist. That's what did it. And Gent was running hard, working hard." I peel my tunic away from my chest, grimacing. "This is sort of slimy."

"It's also unprecedented."

I turn to peer at Nazar, only now he's leaning on his staff, looking like the ancient man I've always thought him to be. His words are thoughtful, almost confused. "I don't know of a connection such as this."

All my questions from before crowd forth. "How do you know of any connection at all? You're a priest from the Exalted Imperium. How is it you know *anything* about fighting or the Divhs?"

Nazar flashes his teeth, but when he answers, I get the sense that he's withholding far more than he reveals. "I'm a priest of the Light," he says, as if that explains everything. "Stories of Divhs aren't difficult to come by. The bards who visited the Tenth House were always quick with a tale, and your father had stories as well, told to him by his father, and his grandfather before that. Stories handed down as a legacy from one generation of warriors to the next."

My lips twist. "I don't know those tales."

"You're female, and your father was brought up to honor the ways of his father. There was no need for you to know. Your father knew me as a priest of the Imperium, however, not Protectorate born. There was no harm in awing me. And I took the opportunity for what it was, to learn of your world and its customs."

I shrug. "Your world too."

"No." He shakes his head. "There are no longer any Divhs outside the Protectorate, Talia. Not in the Exalted Imperium, nor in the vast nations beyond. Not for more than fifty years."

Vast nations? I've never given any thought to what might lie outside the borders of the Imperium. That nation itself is a mystery to me, a land of gold and jewels and riches beyond imagining.

I put those thoughts out of my head. "What did you learn, then, from the tales of the bards? How can they help me?"

Nazar grimaces. "Now that I've seen you with the Divh, they can't, I suspect. Not completely. And I thought my information was quite good. Certainly nothing I saw in the battle here the other day was unexpected. But those men didn't laugh with joy as they connected with their Divhs, and they didn't drench themselves in the mist of the Divh's realm. They didn't immerse themselves so fully in its..." he nods, correcting himself, "...in *his* world. You did. You did so naturally, without needing instruction. From your words and your reactions, your Divh followed your lead without question. You thought a thing, and it followed."

"He," I say, offhandedly.

"He," Nazar agrees.

"You're right, though," I continue. "Gent didn't know my words, but he knew my thoughts, instantly. And when he was running, I knew his. I could see what he saw, feel what he felt. But that's no different from the warriors of the Fourth and Sixth Houses. They guided their Divhs with their minds too."

"They did," Nazar says gravely. "But such guidance improves over time. Much time. Years' worth of time. Not mere minutes. It will bear watching."

I drop my arms to my side, resigning myself to being clammy for the near future. "Then I did something wrong, you're saying. Everyone will know I'm an imposter."

"An imposter? No." Nazar turns and begins making his way once more across the wide tournament field. "You have no history with these warriors, and they haven't seen your Divh. Merritt has been bonded for several years now to his creature."

"Gent," I mumble. "His name is Gent." I don't know why it's important, but I say it anyway. "Who is beautiful."

"To Gent," Nazar says, with a trace of amusement in his voice now. "Who is powerful and fierce." I can feel his gaze upon me again, but I keep my head down, focusing on the way before us. My wet tunic makes me unreasonably chilled, and I fold my arms over my chest, my right hand covering the spot where my tunic clings tight against my band. It's warm beneath the wet cloth, but I still shiver.

"As long as you don't draw any undue attention to yourself and fare well enough in the early rounds of the tournament—you won't be seeded in the tournament proper against a seasoned warrior," he says. "You'll gain a few critical wins and slip through the middle of the tournament unharmed."

I nod. "And when I do have to fight a warrior who knows his Divh and how to use him...or her? What do I do then?"

Nazar's solemn words float back to me on the breeze. "Then you will follow the way of the warrior. You will win, or you will die."

"Not really die, though, right?" I mumble. "No one dies in the tournament. Not really."

Nazar, however, says nothing more.

CHAPTER 16

Caleb has the horses ready by dawn the following morning, but the camp still needs to be broken down. I stay huddled in my blankets as the sun clambers over the top of the spectator stands. I cannot get warm. Though I changed out of my tunic and breeches into clothes Nazar had at the ready when we returned to camp last night—even richer garments than before, soft and thick against my skin—my heart races and my teeth chatter, my fingers wrapped tight in the blankets.

"Are you sick?" Caleb murmurs to me as he walks by.

I try to shake my head, but my whole body convulses. "I don't know," I say miserably.

"You do know." Nazar's words are calm and matter of fact. "Caleb is your squire. He must know too."

I blink up at Nazar, his form wavering in the morning sun. That's part of the problem too, I think. My vision has never quite recovered from seeing through Gent's eyes. And Gent is damned near blind in this plane, it appears.

Caleb is staring at me now, and I sigh. "I trained with Gent last night in, ah, secret. It went differently than I expected it to go."

"You trained?" Caleb's gaze swings from me to Nazar. "But you didn't wake me?"

"You needed your sleep," I begin, but he's already on to his next objection.

"You *couldn't* have trained, though. Not in secret. You would've been seen."

"We weren't here." I pull an arm out to wave vaguely. "We were on the Divh's plane. Out there, somewhere."

He gapes at me. "But you can't *do* that."

The panic in his voice brings me up short. Here once again is something I don't understand. I stifle a groan. I am *absolutely* going to be caught before I even attempt my first tournament battle.

"He can't do that," Caleb says again, this time turning to Nazar. Even in his surprise, Caleb refers to me as a 'he.' A tiny knot of worry I hadn't realized I'd been weaving together unravels in my gut.

Caleb pushes on. "No warrior sets foot upon the Divh's plane except when they're first banded. No one ever returns from that plane other than fathers who bring their sons. And begging your pardon, but you don't look like Merritt's father."

I frown into my blankets, the knot of my nerves now snarling back together. How little I know about this time-honored practice of the Protectorate. In truth, there's been no reason for me to know, yet I draw my cloak around me more tightly, more for protection than warmth. *I'm never going to pull this off,* I think miserably. Never.

Nazar, however, is unperturbed.

"The Tenth House is on the doorstep of the Exalted Imperium. Its ways are different. Its warrior is different."

Oh. Well, that sounds good.

Caleb snorts wryly as his gaze swings back to me, and I straighten despite the sick whirring in my stomach. "And its Divh is different," I say with a confidence I don't feel. I throw off the cloak and stand. Surprisingly, the sun on my head and bare shoulders proves an instant balm, and I sigh beneath its healing rays, grateful for the heat that seems to blossom on my skin everywhere the sun reaches it. Even my eyesight is starting to clear, now that I'm standing.

"Exalted *lord*," Caleb stutters, and he stumbles back. I turn to him, but he isn't staring at my face, but my arm—an arm uncovered, my tunic's sleeves still at my side, waiting to be stitched on. I glance down.

The sentient band gleams in the sunlight, dark as onyx. But the flesh both above and beneath the band is no longer scorched. Instead, it's ringed round with ink flowing in an intricate pattern. There are birds lifting away above the band, and a roiling sea beneath.

"That design wasn't there yesterday," he insists. "I know it wasn't. But it looks like it was etched into your skin two summers ago, not two hours."

He blinks up at me. "Did going to the Divhs' plane do that to you? Because I have to tell you—I've never seen any of the younger warrior knights with a tattoo like that. The older ones..." he scrunches up his face. "Some have them, I think. But nothing that intricate, I'm sure of it."

I study the ink with a curious detachment. It wasn't there yesterday, of course. Caleb is right. Before, the skin around my warrior band had simply been a ruined mass of scars. But yesterday, I hadn't truly met Gent. I hadn't run with him, like a fish jumping through the water or a bird soaring high. I hadn't felt his mind touch mine, hadn't looked into that large and impenetrable eye.

I turn and face Caleb fully. "I'm a warrior from the borderlands of the Imperium," I say evenly. "I'm *different*."

He shuts his mouth with a snap, but a second later, he grins widely. "That you are," he says, his eyes once more alight as he grapples with the change in my appearance.

He moves forward and picks up one of my sleeves, gathering the length of thick thread to attach it to my tunic. "Did it hurt? It looks like it hurt. Is that why you were sick?"

I sigh. "I don't remember it, honestly. I was sick most of the night, after working with Gent. Maybe that's when it happened." I hold out my arm, and Caleb stitches the sleeve in place, weaving the twine through the premade holes. "Maybe it's his excitement about the tournament."

"Who?" Caleb shoots me a funny glance. "The Divh? It's an it, not a 'he.'"

I shrug and extend my other arm, glad to have my band covered. "Mine's a 'he.'" I waggle my brows at him. "And some of the others? *Shes*."

"No *way*," he protests, looking mortified. But he says nothing further, and at length, I'm fully dressed. At this point, I'm useless for doing anything but riding in a parade, what with my festooned tunic and heavy breeches and ground-dragging cloak. I try not to collect dust as my squire and Nazar break down the rest of the camp.

By the time Caleb saddles Darkwing and helps me up, it's high morning, which I suspect Nazar has timed deliberately. We move through the crowd with a single-minded purpose, and there's a smattering of cheers as we do so. Men, women, and even a few children—their faces turning up to see the warrior knight pass.

I don't miss the exchange of money bags either, bright flashes of color catching the light.

There are even a few dark green tunics in the crowd, and I blink in surprise as I recognize the men from the coliseum the day before, the soldiers we hired, whose time is their own until we leave for the Tenth House. They grin fiercely at me, raising their hands in support, and I wave back at them. *My men*, I realize, trying the idea on for size. Men who would fight for me. Support me. Defend me.

Men who would hand me over for execution in a blink if they knew what I was.

Then I see a boy I remember well. He looks up at me with eyes blackened, but his mouth isn't mutinous, merely resigned. His family stands with him, but he seems to hold himself apart anyway, cloaked in shame and disappointment. This is the boy who'd won his bout in the fighting pits, not one day earlier, by smashing his opponent's nose...and then who'd lost when that opponent had rushed him after the fight should have been called. His competition in the tournament is done, I know instantly.

He could have been Merritt, a few years ago.

Without considering anything more than the child's hollow eyes and grim expression, I extend a hand. "You," I say, surprised at how far my voice carries across the suddenly hushed crowd. "In the brown tunic. Stand forth."

I half turn, but Nazar is already riding up beside me, and in his hands, he carries a simple green tunic, the smallest of those remaining from my search for soldiers. It will fit this boy, I suspect. It may not mean anything to him, but he deserves to know he earned it.

And to make this moment memorable, I need to sound like someone I'm totally, woefully not. The fiercely proud warrior knight of the Tenth House, first-blooded and firstborn. I take the shirt from Nazar and straighten my shoulders, pitching my rough voice even lower.

"You fought admirably and well, by the rules as you knew them. You fought with the spirit of a warrior." I toss the shirt down to him and he catches it, for all that he stares gape-mouthed at me. He believes me to be what I appear to be; I know it in my bones. And so, in this moment, I am what he believes me to be. Nazar offers me a second bag, and I weigh it in my hand. Bronzes, I think. Not a large amount, but enough coin to make a difference here. "Should *I* fight well and win in this tournament, I'll need squires. Squires who might one day become banded soldiers. I'd be honored to count you among my men, if it comes to that."

The boy clutches the tunic to his chest and bows to me once, twice, three times in rapid succession. I nod to him as well, then to his father, whose face is now split in a wide grin.

I turn Darkwing away as the buzz of the crowd starts and point the horse toward the First House.

The journey takes longer than I expect. Once past the coliseum, the land turns into an uneven patchwork of field grass and mud, broken by dozens of small streams that pool into ponds and marsh. The path is clear, at least. A large, broad road has been cut into the marshland. But I peer to either side, confused. "Where does all the water go? Marshes such as these are usually close to great water, and the sea is nowhere close."

"Remember, there used to be great water here, and there's still a grand lake beyond those trees," Caleb says, pointing into the far distance. "Not deep but fed by the winter snows from the mountains. See the falls?"

He points, but I can barely make out what he's trying to show me, rocks and trees crowding round a geyser of mist. Something shifts in that mist, and I squint. "Are those horses?"

Caleb peers more closely too. "Marauders, most likely," he says, disdain thick in his voice. "I told you; they've been worse this tournament than ever before, worrying at the edges of the encampments like a plague. Rihad's going to have to do something about them, if he wants to keep the spectators happy."

"They're stealing money?"

"You'd think so, but it's whatever they can get their hands on, really. Silver, food, weapons. Even clothing." He makes a face. "Filthy bastards."

I glance again to the mist, but the shadow horses are gone.

Caleb continues on, "It's pretty out there, but believe me—be glad you're not here in the spring. The bugs out there settle around you like a net." He gestures next to the towers of the First House. "There's a reason why they built the castle so high. It wasn't just for the view."

Nazar remains quiet, and we travel on with only occasional conversation, Caleb filling me in on everything I should already know about the First House. Though I'm grateful for the information, a second emotion wells with each new detail of the great house's might, its glory, its honor.

What is the use of honor when one of these exalted houses is so bold as to strike down the firstborn son of the Tenth House? How can the First be so consumed with pageants and poetry when warrior knights are being slaughtered in its very shadow?

Surely, my brother isn't the only son who's been targeted... surely, he couldn't be. The Tenth House is no threat—no threat at all!

None of this makes any sense.

Anger twists and spins within me, and I swallow it whole, struggling to maintain my composure. We aren't alone on the road, but most of the travelers we encounter are coming *from* the First House, not heading toward it; a trickling stream of farmers and merchants, their smiles broad as they greet us, their voices carrying above the clanking of what's left in their packs.

"It's a good time to have something to sell," Caleb observes after a string of horses pass, led by a tall, slender man and woman in a cart pulled by another team. "Those are pack horses. The First House is preparing for a series of great banquets, and it's ever generous to its suppliers."

"So, the Lord Protector is fair to his people?"

"Fair?" Caleb tilts his head at that, considering. In that moment, he reminds me of Gent, and I stifle a laugh. "Generous, as I say. Not fair, exactly. He can turn on you as easily as embrace you. As long as he's in a giving mood, he gives. But you can't ever expect it. That's where you'll fail."

I nod. It's sage counsel, and Caleb's first hint that the Lord Protector isn't as honorable and glorious as he might wish to be perceived. It's also the advice of an insider. "How do you know so much?" I ask quietly. "Who did you serve?"

We're well ahead of Nazar by this time, but Caleb still stiffens, glancing around. "I served no one. I simply hear things." He hikes his left shoulder, his missing arm almost indiscernible given the artful hanging of the Tenth House tunic. "People talk freely around me, as if it's my ears that are gone, not my arm."

I don't believe him, but I can see the blush flagging his cheekbones. My gut tightens with chagrin. His secrets are his own to keep. I certainly have mine.

"Well, however you heard it, I'm grateful. I don't even know how little I know until you say something like this. I'll be lost in the halls of the First House."

"No, you won't be." Caleb turns to me, his gaze fervent once more. "You're a warrior knight. You'll be recognized as such. Maybe in the mountains you didn't realize the importance of what that means, being the only warrior of the Tenth House, but here, you'll see. Your position is one of great honor. There are men who live their entire lives dreaming of fighting alongside a Divh, and they die still dreaming. You've been banded. You're already elite."

I grimace, shaking my head. "I'm not elite, Caleb."

"You are." He smirks and looks forward again. "You just don't know it yet."

The sun crawls across the sky as we ride. We stop once to rest the horses at the base of the great mountain, where the road has been cut into the sheer rock.

Caleb notes my stare. "It took workers a generation to cut it, another to complete the great castle above. Until then, the First House ruled from this rise." He waves across the open space. Roiling vines have taken over most of the terrain, and the trees grow tall. "No stone remained once the mountain tower was completed, by order of the Lord Protector of that time. He wanted no memory of any stronghold save the one that ruled from on high."

"Seems a waste." I squint up, but the mountain crowds around me, sheer cliff walls that hide the rich estate above. "Surely he could have housed someone in this secondary building?"

"A tower isn't built for efficiency." Nazar's voice startles us from the side. He leans against the base of a stone wall, smoking his pipe. "A tower is built for might and war. To awe the approaching army, or quail the lone rider. The Lord Protector was wise in his choice."

"I guess," I mutter. I accept Caleb's help in remounting Darkwing, and the warhorse snorts and stamps with anticipation. He too can feel the power of this place.

Power. My lip curls with irritation. What use is power in the center of the Protectorate, when treachery lurks at its borders?

Slowly, we pass through the great gates at the base of the mountain. Beyond the first turn of the castle road, we reach a checkpoint of guards. Nazar gives my name as Merritt of the Tenth House, and they stand aside—if not with deference, then with speed. Caleb straightens his shoulders and stares dead ahead, but I don't think the men recognize him. Still, he doesn't waver in his stance until we're well around the turn, and we hairpin our way up the mountain at a pace slow enough to move forward but not tire the horses. There remains a steady stream of merchants coming down the mountain, but I pay less attention to them the closer we get to the main gates of the First House.

Then Darkwing noses around the last turn, and the fortress rises above us.

It's *nothing* like the Tenth House.

Tall and slender, built in line with the mountain, the First House castle surges toward the sky in pinnacles and spikes, a mass of narrow rose-stone towers. Its foundation boulders are massive, and three large gates open at its base, with a drawbridge over a frothing moat. It looks most like a bird about to set flight from the mountain, and I sense the tension of its coiled strength.

The mountain trail opens out onto a wide plateau, and the castle dominates that space, surrounded by what looks to be a thriving village. There are people everywhere, rushing around as if it's market day, and the air is filled with the smell of cooked meat and heavy spices, wine and ale. Beyond the castle, a waterfall crashes into what I assume is a small lake, which then feeds the moat and presumably the second waterfall whose mist I'd witnessed along the side of the mountain, pouring toward the wetlands below. Above the falls, the mountain surges up and up still higher, and I shudder to imagine winter in this place.

Now, however, the quaint village before the imposing castle is overflowing with laughter and cheer, and as we ride forth, the villagers take note of my warhorse. Many of them are children, and they rush closer with wide eyes and ready smiles. Beside me, Caleb sits almost painfully still, but no one points and laughs at him, no one seems to notice his missing arm. Instead, the current of their talk lifts and falls on the breeze, reaching my ears.

"Merritt of the Tenth House!"

I blink, looking down, surprised to see a line of young women ahead of us. Young women who smile and flutter, waving to me as if I...as if I...

"Merritt." Nazar's word is all the admonition I need, and I belatedly lift a hand in return greeting, bowing to the girls as I pass. Some of them are older than I am, and they all beam at me as I wave. It's...unnerving.

Caleb snorts beside me. "You're blushing so hard, I'm getting a suntan. Act like you've done this before."

"I..." I shut my mouth, knowing he's right. Nevertheless, I'm deeply grateful to leave the village behind us minutes later. Ahead of us, the wide moat of the First House roils, fed by the mountain waterfall. The main gate is open, however, and no guards stand at attention at its mouth. As we cross over the drawbridge, I look up at the archway—the sharp metal teeth of the interior gates held fast by a tight rope—and force myself not to shiver.

The courtyard of the First House is nearly empty, a shock after the chaos of the village beyond. The building is immensely tall—its entry stairway alone nearly as big as the manor house I've known all my life.

But the person who stands at the base of those wide steps is familiar enough, even surrounded by a cadre of guards liveried in shades of gold and black.

"Merritt of the Tenth House, hear our words," Fortiss calls out, his voice rocking me with unexpected strength. "The Lord Protector of the First House welcomes you to the fight."

CHAPTER 17

Almost before the echoes of his grand welcome die out, Fortiss launches into a treatise of what we're supposed to do next, offering a million and one instructions as I try to look both intelligent and relaxed.

I'm completely unnerved to be talking to him again. *This* is why I wanted to leave the tournament early, I remember now—but it's far too late for that. Fortiss thinks I'm Merritt, a warrior, a fighter. How would a fighter act?

Like he belongs, I decide. Like he's always belonged.

My stomach churns, though I do my best to project an air of easy confidence as Nazar leaves with a servant to find shelter for the horses and prepare our lodgings. Though we'll take our meals in the First House, all warriors and their personnel are apparently housed in the barracks beneath the castle, large cells built beneath huge stone arches that have been cut into the mountain.

"Lord Rihad awaits you, Merritt of the Tenth," Fortiss announces far too loudly, and I sense he's finally done with his recitation. Instead, he grins at me across the courtyard then gestures me to approach. "You and your squire, since he's chosen not to leave you."

"I won't, either," Caleb assures me, and I swallow my shaky laugh.

"Thank the Light."

I stride with shoulders back, remembering to swagger as I approach Fortiss, but I feel his gaze on me too keenly. When I reach the base of the stairs, he lifts a hand.

"Your sister," he asks, with an interest that makes my guts twist. "She is safely on her way back to the Tenth House? I enjoyed talking with her, did she tell you?"

"She did, but she didn't share much else," I say, too quickly. "She was—overwhelmed, I think. Embarrassed? She wouldn't say much more. Caleb here..."

"Embarrassed, to be sure," my squire pipes up, as guileless as spring flowers after a long and blustery winter. "She giggled a lot."

"Giggled," Fortiss echoes as I shoot Caleb a vicious glare. Then I swing my gaze forward again.

"I think she enjoyed speaking with you, Lord Fortiss, but well —she's not used to so many people. She prefers the safety of the mountains. She's a quiet and docile sort."

"Your sister," Fortiss clarifies. "That's who we're talking about?"

"Yes, of course." I give him a stare full of dim-witted innocence as the next warrior knight enters the courtyard behind me. I bow gravely to him then straighten. "Well met, Lord Fortiss."

Caleb and I mount the stairs as quickly as possible, stifled snickers between us. But as we enter the shadowy foyer, both our moods dampen quickly. A pair of guards await us and turn to move ahead, escorting us deeper into the castle. The moment they draw far enough away for discretion, Caleb begins whispering to me about the number of guards, warriors, nobles, and staff in the castle, how to greet them all and where I'd find them.

Once again, irritation flares in my gut. All these careful rituals! All these polite displays of manners and grace. How many of the men who've entered these halls and stood before the Lord Protector are capable of murdering their own? Only one, in all of the Protectorate? I don't believe it. Instead, I feel the very walls of the First House press down on me, as if longing to share the truth of the treacherous villains who've passed before me.

Caleb gestures to the stone passageway ahead.

"This leads to the throne room, though the Lord Protector doesn't want it called that. It's what it is, though," he murmurs as we walk down the long corridor, silent guards flanking us. "You'll be presented, and you should bow at the waist like you did with Fortiss. Don't kneel. Kneeling means you've pledged your allegiance to this house."

He snaps his mouth shut as the guards stop sharply and turn to face each other, creating a wall of men for us to walk between. When we step into the "throne" room, however, I can't help but gasp. Caleb is right, there's no other way to describe the opulence of this chamber.

The room is filled with gold.

Rich enameled flooring extends from the base of the central throne to the far walls, and great gilded tapestries hang against every wall. Where there isn't cloth, there's artwork, richly framed and lushly painted scenes of war and glory—one of which depicts the enormous castle at the center of the Exalted Imperium's capital. I stare in wonder. The Tenth House has a similar painting, but a fraction of the size. *To each according to their merit*, runs the inscription beneath. I never realized how meaningful that phrase was until now.

"Keep going," hisses Caleb, and as I stride forward, one hand on my belt as both Nazar and Caleb have instructed me, my booted feet ring out on the floor. My other hand holds my cloak wide, to display the fact that I'm carrying a sword but also to assure that I have no intention of grabbing it.

As if I'd attempt to wield a sword in a place with so many warriors primed for battle.

Caleb falls into position behind me. Eventually, he too, stops, but I move forward with another guard until I reach the base of the short staircase that leads up to the Lord Protector on his throne.

I saw him on his stone platform at the coliseum, so I knew he was tall—but I don't realize how tall until now. Thin and sharply angled, with an aquiline nose and strong jaw, Lord Rihad gazes down at us. His most compelling feature is his eyes, I decide. They appear nearly black at this distance and pick me apart like a carcass worked over by vultures.

I stare back, my expression flat. This is no time to let my true emotions show.

The Lord Protector's long fingers grip the edge of his gilded armrests—not in concern or dismay or even great emotion, I think. It seems almost as if it's merely his habit, to remind himself that the throne is there in his grasp. He's a pale man, the kind whose emotion would easily be seen in the flush upon his skin. His hair is black, peppered with gray and swept back from his forehead, and his lips and nose seem pinched, for all that he smiles.

The guard beside me halts and announces my name again. As instructed, I bow at the waist, then stand straight beneath the gaze of the Lord Protector.

"We have not had a warrior of the Tenth House take part in the Tournament of Gold since Lemille last tried his hand, long years ago," Rihad says, leaning forward to place his elbows upon his knees. When he looks at me that way, I've no choice but to stare back at him, though I can sense others standing behind the throne. Not more soldiers, but priests in long robes, all of them eyeing me with scant interest. How many fighters have they seen cross this great hall, how many tournaments?

How many murderers?

But the Lord Protector's next words jerk me to attention. "How does your father fare?"

"Well, Lord Protector Rihad." I nod. My voice is a rough rasp, but it's loud enough in this cavernous hall. "His foot pains him, but he's in good spirits and rides whenever he's able. The crops in the mountain fields have fared better than expected these past few seasons."

"Good." The Lord Protector's arched eyebrows lift. "And yet he hasn't petitioned for more banded soldiers. If he is thriving, it is his due."

I didn't know this, but it makes a certain sort of sense. Beyond its secondary warrior knights, the First House has so many banded soldiers because the First House is large and robust, and probably has been that way since its earliest days. If any of the subsidiary houses thrive, then they would be granted more soldiers as well.

With the Lord Protector waiting, however, I manage a grim smile. "Perhaps I will do him the honor of faring well enough in the Tournament of Gold that we'll be granted soldiers from my efforts."

"Indeed." The Lord Protector claps his hands together, the sound loud enough to echo off the far walls. "You'll be in good company. Fully fifty-one warrior knights are committed thus far, and we receive more every day. The Tenth House is a welcome addition; perhaps the remaining houses will offer their warriors as well."

He speaks without guile, and I peer at him, accusations regarding the murder of my brother leaping within me. But what words can I speak? I have nothing—not a name, not a face. Only a knowledge that I shouldn't have, except that I was traveling with my brother when he was killed...on my way to my own *wedding*. As a *girl*.

If I share that, I'll lose everything.

"It's an honor for every warrior to have his chance upon the battlefield," I say instead, reciting the words Caleb fed me on the long ride up. The Lord Protector is as much a traditionalist as my father, it would appear. To him, everything is about honor.

"Your men are settled in the barracks?" He directs the question not to me, but to a figure behind me. I assume it's Caleb, but then Fortiss's clear voice responds. I jolt with the awareness that he's so close.

"They are, my lord," he says, his voice rich and smooth. "We also expect warriors from the Eighth and Ninth houses yet this day. It will be a grand celebration."

"Good." The Lord Protector pounds his armrests and stands, and I am struck again by his height. "Tonight, we feast, and soon we fight. For the honor of the Protectorate!"

I hear the sound from all around me, the crunch of knees upon the ornate floor. I bend at the waist as I've been instructed, but when I straighten again, the cruel, pale face of the Lord Protector is fixed on me, like a hawk on its kill.

"Soon," he says again. "We fight."

I should be unnerved, I know. I should quail and shrink. But I don't. Partly because I know I can't show fear. But partly because the barely banked rage I carry within me is stoked by the challenge in Lord Rihad's eyes. I am here for my house; I am here for my brother.

But now that I'm here, I resolve, I will *not* go quietly.

I will not.

Another warrior is announced, and I move to the side, turning to see guards dressed in the flamboyantly orange livery that marks the Eighth House flow into the room. The men of the westernmost House of the Protectorate are dark-skinned, tanned almost ebony, and I don't have to feign my interest as they step forward to be introduced to the Lord Protector.

"The Eighth House wasn't expected this year." Caleb stands beside me once more, murmuring in my ear. "Though their house is small, their Divhs are said to be unbeatable."

Three men, not one, stride forward, each bowing at the waist as the Lord Protector addresses them. "We are honored to welcome you to the Tournament of Gold."

"And we are honored to win it for the greater glory of the Protectorate."

The tallest warrior speaks in a loud, resonant voice that seems to carry great weight. I'm watching the Lord Protector, not the men in orange, but what catches my eye this time isn't the tall, slender leader of the First House, but the dozen men gathered behind him, each garbed in gold and black like their leader. These men aren't powerfully built guards or even quick-eyed warriors.

Instead, they wear their age like a mantle, gray hair flat against their heads, wrinkles mapping their years upon their faces. To a one, they tense at the Eighth House warrior's bold words, and one clutches the chain of gold at his neck. I can't tell if they're amused or frightened by the baseless claim, but something in their look unsettles me.

"And we will be pleased to watch you try," announces the Lord Protector. I keep my focus on the collection of his priests and advisors with their pinched and worn faces.

Then the First House company shifts, and I notice something else. Caleb was right. They aren't all men.

I stare, fascinated, as a slender, white-haired female turns to the man beside her to murmur something in his ear. Her hair is short, her face as equally lined as her counterparts', and she wears no paint upon her skin to augment her looks—no kohl at her eyes nor salve on her lips. Her gown is long and gray beneath her gold and black cloak, like those of her fellows, belted at the waist to display a thin, unfeminine body. Is that how she's able to get the other advisors to listen to her? By dressing and looking more like them? I tug at my own tunic, aware of the irony.

Around the room, there are no women who stand as proud warriors, and only the one who stands as an advisor. The remaining handful of women in the chamber are huddled off to the side, dressed in court finery, their sacred hair coiled around their shoulders in elaborate braids and cascading down their backs. They watch with intelligent eyes and smiles that range from shrewd to excited, but they might as well be figures in a menagerie, collected for display.

I sense a gaze upon me, and I flick my glance back to the throne, suddenly afraid that the Lord Protector is watching me ogle the women of the First House. Only it isn't Lord Rihad but the female advisor. Her gaze is clear and untroubled, and it spears me across the wide room with a power I wouldn't have thought possible. I keep myself from jerking back, but only because Caleb is right beside me. I hold the woman's gaze for a long moment, but I'm glad when she moves her glance from me and takes in Caleb. He's fairly bouncing on his toes, and a smile twitches at her lips.

Good. Focus on my squire, not on me.

I shift my gaze to the Lord Protector as he claps his hands together again. He's still on his feet, and he spreads his long arms wide once the attention of the entire room is upon him. "Tonight, we feast," he declares once more. "But soon we fight!"

The rest of the day passes in a blur of activity. I'm officially added to the rolls for the tournament, a laborious process involving a scroll-bearing scribe who painstakingly enters my name and my house, the name of my father and mother, and my intent to compete. I grow increasingly nervous as the questions continue, wishing I had Nazar by my side. Instead, I have Caleb, who nevertheless stands with me staunchly, his slender body seeming several times wider than I know it to be, a barrier between me and the clutch of warriors behind me.

In addition to the Eighth and Ninth Houses, the Second House has sent more delegates that they want entered in the rolls. Not every warrior of every House is expected to participate, but rumors are traveling quickly throughout most of the Protectorate. Anyone within easy passage of the traveling bards heard the first call to arms, and now the closer houses are learning of the boon of fifty banded soldiers to be parceled out among the winners and are sending more to improve their chances. The First House will soon be full to bursting.

In truth, the great hall is already teeming with people by the time Nazar, Caleb, and I set foot in the space for the great feast. Unlike the warrior feasts once the tournament is underway, this is a more informal meal, for all that it is immense. Warriors can sit with their own houses, or with friends. Many of them are doing so, and I watch their broad smiles and back clapping with growing dread.

"This isn't my place," I mutter to Nazar. "I know no one, and no one knows me. I'm an outsider."

"Everyone is an outsider when they arrive," he says. "You have merely to look like you belong, and you begin to create the expectation in others that you do belong."

Easy words for him. He's a *priest*. People don't even see beyond his white hair and ceremonial robes, just scurry out of his way bowing and muttering swift hosannas to the Light. Whereas I'm supposed to look like a swaggering warrior knight with no care in the world except when my next chance will be to impress everyone.

I look around, stretching my face to mimic the entitled smirks of my fellow warriors, and Caleb and I jostle forward to find a set of seats at one of the long tables. My dark-green tunic proclaims me as a warrior of worth, and people bow and smile, which helps keep me from feeling like a fraud. I don't have the luxury to hide in the shadows, not anymore. Now I must stand for my house.

We press on and at last, there's a shout and a raised hand. I turn toward it eagerly, then stiffen as I realize who it is.

"Go," orders Caleb, his voice low. "That's the greatest honor you can hope for this night."

"I'm not here for honor."

"Then go for Merritt. Because *he* wouldn't be such an idiot as to give up such a chance."

I shoot Caleb a glare as Fortiss waves us forward.

"Join us," Fortiss calls out, and his table of nobles shifts easily to make the space. "You have the smallest entourage of any of the houses; you're easy to dine with." He grins at his own joke, and I grimace—then catch the faces of other men, in the table beyond them. Warriors of the Second House, also enjoying Fortiss's joke… maybe a little too much?

My jaw sets as anger and suspicion knife through me, but either way, Caleb is right. Dining with Fortiss is the highest honor I can have this night, and I should make the most of it. Never mind that my hands are shaking, and my mouth is dry.

"Well met," I say, gesturing to Nazar and Caleb. "We prefer to travel light."

A man sitting next to Fortiss, dressed in the gold and black of the First House, snorts a laugh. "Light enough to be missing an arm is light indeed."

This newest, well-thrown barb would have felled a lesser man or caused awkwardness in a lesser group. But Caleb knows his role here as well—and he can act even better than I can. He grins and rests his right elbow on the table as we seat ourselves. "I never knew how lazy I was until I was forced to use one hand to do the work of two. Trust me on this—one-handed is harder."

His rejoinder merits a laugh, and the moment passes. The servants flood the hall to bring in the first course, and we bump and shove until we're all seated—leaving me directly opposite Fortiss.

I watch him turn to greet another man and fix my gaze on his profile. There's no way he was the one who shot the arrow at Merritt, I decide. He couldn't have, surely. Not and be so easy with me, so *noble*. He can't be acting that well.

But...had he ordered my brother's murder?

Even as I think the accusation, everything within me argues against it. The First House has so much strength—why would they be behind the murder of any house's warrior son? It has to be a lesser house. Plus, Fortiss is too relaxed with me, too open. There's no way he would be, if he'd sent one of his soldiers to assassinate me.

I don't want Fortiss to be involved, if I'm honest with myself. And not because he's so handsome. I just...I want Merritt's murderer to be a seasoned warrior, not someone my own age. I want him to have the cool self-possession of a killer, not the laughing, gamboling manner of a knight. And I don't want him to be so... alive, I decide. So confident. So—

As Fortiss turns back to me and catches my eye, I hunch my shoulders and focus on my food, so he can't see the flare of embarrassment that rides up my neck.

It's easy to stay distracted with a meal such as this. The feast the First House has prepared for us makes the finest banquet ever hosted by the Tenth House look like the meanest leftovers. I've never even seen some of the dishes we are served, savory meat pies and dripping sweetbreads laden with thick syrup. Whole pigs roasted and spitted for each table, mounded over with candied fruits and roasted vegetables. An entire herd of fatted calves must have been killed for this meal, and from the looks and sounds of those around me, they weren't slaughtered in vain. The chamber is filled with mostly men, and they fall upon the meal as if they haven't eaten in days—some of them, possibly, haven't.

The men of the Eighth House have traveled over the great plains of the west to reach us, and the soldiers from the Third and Ninth look as if they might never scrub the dust of their sandy home from their faces. The revelry of these warriors is unforced but also tinged with desperation, and I wonder at that. The Tenth is a small House at the far edge of the Protectorate, cut off from allies. Marauders are an issue for us, certainly, bandits and brigands pouring in from the Exalted Imperium.

But are there worse threats that my fellow houses face?

Is their fear so great that they would turn against another, smaller house to gain some kind of advantage?

If so, then why the Tenth? We're not the smallest house, but we're certainly one of the farthest away. Beyond our position on the very border of the Exalted Imperium, we offer no threat or appreciable benefit. So, why...

The questions chase their own tails in my mind, making me dizzy.

"Merritt." Nazar's voice is quiet, but it instantly recalls me, and I fix a bright smile on my face as I glance at him. He's eating sparingly, but he is eating, playing his own role to perfection. Priests of the Light aren't kept separate from the masses, but they are expected to maintain their sense of decorum at all times. I suspect Nazar has never suffered from a lack of decorum in his life.

To my right, Caleb chatters on, and with each new round of laughter, my stomach knots anew. My new squire won't hurt me, I remind myself. Not on purpose, anyway. And yet...

"How was the journey over the Eastern Mountains?"

The question comes so quickly, so fluidly, it feels like an attack. My pulse leaps, and I turn sharply to Fortiss, the heat coming to my face well-earned, for all that my words are too quickly blurted out.

"You of all people know it was not a smooth one," I reply coldly. "The attack on the Tenth was an abomination. It will be avenged."

My intensity surprises everyone, even me. I don't look at Nazar but sense his careful gaze. Fortiss, however, commands my complete attention—and that of all the men around us.

"I, of all people...?" he asks, letting the question linger.

I let it hang there too. For no other reason than I have absolutely no idea what to say to walk back my accusation. *What was I thinking? Why can't I hold my tongue?*

Fortunately, Fortiss assumes my continued silence is embarrassment. His eyes flash with earnest comradery.

"Lord Merritt, if the Tenth House has been wronged, then we will do all we can to strike down who is responsible," he declares. "You have my bond."

Seeing my chance, I nod quickly, praying I can end this conversation that I've so rashly blundered into. "As you say, Lord Fortiss," I reply with credible force.

"As I *do* say," Fortiss insists. "House protects house. And the First House protects all."

A low, resounding tide of agreement rises around us. Flagons are lifted, toasts given to the First House. Through it all, Fortiss eyes me intently, as if trying to convince me of what he says. Once again, I feel my heart quickening to hear his words, wanting so much to believe them.

Fool.

I don't want Fortiss to have anything to do with the death of Merritt for reasons both practical and stupid. I know this. But for Fortiss to be emphasizing the First House's protection so stridently, means there must be others besides me who don't trust that protection.

Pondering that, I settle back in my seat. I reach for a cup of wine and take a long draught.

"House protects house!" Fortiss cries aloud.

I join the warrior knights in another brash cheer, but no drink can wash away my growing uneasiness.

There's something not quite right threading through the gilded corridors of the First House. Something that may lead me to Merritt's murderer? Possibly. But there's more to it, I think. A darkness that lies coiled at the heart of the Protectorate, waiting to strike.

CHAPTER 18

The banquet continues on for a solid hour of food and drink. There are no more difficult questions, though I don't miss the furtive glances I receive from both the First and Second House warriors. I follow Nazar's lead and not Caleb's in conducting myself at Fortiss's table. The priest eats little and drinks less, though his hands are most usually holding his fork and knife, and he's lifted his cup to his mouth countless times. Caleb, for his part, both drinks and eats as if he might never be fed again.

Through it all, I do my level best to ignore Fortiss sitting opposite me. I don't care that he laughs, smiles, and tries to stimulate conversation with men up and down the table. I don't care when he speaks about art or war or falconry. I especially don't notice when he catches the eye of one of the women sitting at the master table, lifting his cup to her. I'm the warrior of the Tenth House, and I know better than to pay attention to such foolishness and guile.

"Say, will there be music tonight?" asks Caleb brightly, looking around as if he half expects it. "Seems a fine night for music."

Fortiss bows to him, acknowledging the question is a sound one. "Not this night, squire Caleb. We've a better entertainment planned. Bards have arrived from the western borders."

That does sound better than music. "The western borders?" I ask, unable to restrain my interest. "What news do they bring?"

"Ah! At last something to draw the Tenth House warrior out of his shell." Fortiss grins, but there's a sharpness to his tone that makes me uneasy. "I wager their news will entertain us all. And in any case, they've been gone a long while. They've traveled farther than I ever have, and I've been to almost every border of the Protectorate."

Something cold knots in my gut. "You have?" I ask gruffly. "Recently?" In my mind's eye, I see the dead gray arrow winging toward Merritt, loosed by a skilled hand.

"Recently enough. The First House succeeds because it takes an interest in every inch of the Protectorate, as we all should," Fortiss says. I notice he hasn't answered my question. "We've sent out men to every corner to strengthen ties. You can never be too careful."

I shift uncomfortably on my bench and try to keep him talking. "To the southern sects as well?" I ask. "I see the Third House is here. Were you who summoned them?"

"Not likely." Fortiss snorts. "The southern houses are built on sands that would as soon burn your boots right through as support you. It takes a hardier man than me to tread so heavily for so long." He waves his hand. "But you can be sure messengers of the First House went to summon them all, and we are assured by the Eighth House that all the western warriors will venture forth, for the glory of their houses and the Protectorate."

Another thread of wrongness curls through me, and even Nazar stirs restlessly. But at that moment a single horn blows, cutting across our conversation.

We all turn in our chairs as the Lord Protector of the First House stands. "Tonight, we shall hear tales of the Western Realms —believe me when I tell you, these stories aren't to be missed," he announces. "We'll clear away the food and keep the wine, the better to enjoy ourselves. While they are assembling, please— meet merry and well."

That seems to be a signal for the tables to empty and the crush of people to converge, one group on the other. I lose Caleb and Nazar in the shuffle and find myself carried forward, closer to the high table than I truly wanted to be.

"Lord Merritt, is it? Of the Tenth House."

I turn to see the female advisor of the First House striding toward me. She pays no mind to the other diners as they hasten out of her way. Up close, I can see she's not as thin as I'd first thought. There's no hint of curves to her, but she's sturdy and well-built, nearly as tall as I am.

"Well?" She positions herself in front of me. "Speak, warrior. Do you have no tongue?" She peers closely at me. "How old are you?"

"Seventeen," I say, instantly wary. How much does she know? If the First House has sent runners out to all the houses—even ours, as Fortiss has said—there'd be information on who lived in the manor house, and who didn't. This was precisely why my father insisted I hide myself away during the whole of any outsiders' visit. It was too dangerous for me to be seen, even dressed as the second child. Anyone could be looking.

Rihad's advisor simply nods. "Young, but not too young. It's no small task to stand tall against the hulking brutes we're assembling here. You do your father honor."

She flashes me a knowing smile, and I try to mask my dismay.

"I'm Councilor Miriam." She nods in the half bow of the nobility, and I follow suit. "I like your aspect. You were not an expected addition to the Tournament, and Lord Rihad enjoys surprises that set his own warriors on edge. He'll make an example of you."

I grimace. "I've no desire to be an example to anyone."

"Which is why you've no choice in the matter." She pivots abruptly, crossing her arms as she surveys the assembled throng. "So tell me, Merritt of the Tenth House, what do you think of our gathering here?"

"It's..." I hesitate, choosing my words with care. "It does the job it's intended to do," I say at length. "The warriors from the far houses, especially the smaller ones such as mine, will be awed and humbled, as they're meant to be. The warriors from the nearer houses, the Second and Fourth and Seventh, they won't be awed, but they will be reminded of who holds the power in this area of the Protectorate. And that reminder is by design."

She flicks me a glance. "You're awed and humbled?"

"Awed, certainly." I raise a hand to take in the sweep of the room. "You could fit most of the Tenth House in this room alone. The food I've seen falling from these tables would feed our retainers and their families for a month. That too, I think, is intentional."

"You think we waste food for a purpose?"

"The illusion of waste." I point to the servants gathering up the leftover breads and cheeses and platters of meat. "The illusion of excess. The warriors who leave this place will believe that Lord Protector Rihad and the First House have more wealth than they could ever spend, so much wealth that they become the arbiters of what true abundance even means. It solidifies their position twice over."

"It does at that." Miriam's voice is steady, and I've no way of knowing if I've offended her in some way by being so candid. "You're more than you appear to be."

I blink, wary once more, but Miriam's gaze sharpens over my shoulder. "Some of your fellow warriors are less, it would seem."

She clasps her hands behind her as I turn to see what she's looking at. The women of the high table have now completely surrounded the few warriors of the Eighth House who've not escaped to higher ground.

Miriam sends me a sidelong glance. "You don't seem to be drawing your share of admirers yet."

I shake my head, not having to feign my discomfort. "That's not why I'm here."

"True," she says. "But I wouldn't dismiss the fairer sex so easily as that. They often have eyes in places you might want to see."

I frown at her, but she no longer looks at me. Instead, she keeps her attention trained on the women across the room. "Rihad is no fool, for all that he appears to be a beneficent lord, smiling indulgently as the young women of his court simper and preen before this robust crop of young men. This house is run by a man, not a woman. And that can mean one of two things. Women are either oppressed or they are used, each according to their merits. Rihad prefers the latter approach, which I generally appreciate."

I nod then glance again at the beautifully dressed women of the court. They're paying equal attention to each of the men, be they handsome or homely. There's one young woman talking to Caleb too, and I grin to see it, even as I register Miriam's subtle warning. *Spies*, I think. She's warning me against not just spies, but *female* spies. Should I trust her? Dare I? I don't know this councilor, don't know any of these people.

More importantly, why is she telling me this? I resolve to watch her, to make sure she visits with each of the warriors, that she isn't singling me out.

"How long have you served as advisor to the Lord Protector?" I ask, turning the conversation's focus back to her. "It would seem a challenging role to manage a house this large."

"For twenty years," she says. I can hear the pride in her voice. "My father served before me, and I was at his side constantly. It was a seamless transition."

Seamless. I suspect she's lying, but I can't gainsay her. "Lord Rihad is wise to seek counsel from many different sources."

"It's his most valuable trait." Miriam's voice has grown clipped again. "The bards assemble."

Dread pulses in my stomach, but I angle my gaze to take in the bards lining up before the high table, their manner easy and laughing. Why did they bother me so?

The first man stands forth, and I frown. He seems strangely familiar, and yet...

Then I have it—I *have* seen him before, and recently. This man had been kneeling to the Lord Protector earlier this day, when we were all in the great hall. Kneeling, not bowing, an act of allegiance to his house's leader, according to Caleb. These men—bards all—are not supposed to be affiliated with any house. They earn their living as merchants of tales and information, taking money equally from every house and giving equally as well.

"Behold, I bring you news of the Western Realms!" declares the bard, but my mind is churning. Miriam departs my side and takes up her station next to another warrior knight, so at least that question is answered. I'm not reassured, however. I move my gaze from the bright and flashy bard to the equally glittering women, now arranged at various tables of warrior knights, clearly ready to be delighted by a diverting tale. It's all I can do not to stare at them. These are the daughters of the First House's lesser noble families, and we have no secondary nobility at the Tenth. But even if I hadn't been relegated to the shadows at the Tenth House, there's no way my father would have allowed such a display of wealth and pride by me—or anyone—with the exception of my wedding regalia. My own mother dressed as simply as a servant, even at the high festivals. To see these women dressed so luxuriously, moving so freely...

I shake myself hard, forcing my gaze away. The bard is joined by a second man and a third, men I don't know, haven't seen, but somehow, I suspect they've also knelt in subjugation to the Lord Protector. And if they are dedicated to him and him alone—if all these men are so dedicated...

My memory conjures up the last bard to our home, some two months earlier. Merritt had been so taken with the man, he'd followed him around, begging for stories in exchange for coin or bread or wine. The man had given him far more time than I would've expected, but he'd not been the only one talking, I realize now.

What had Merritt told him about the Tenth House?

Not about me, surely. I'm a blot, a stain on the household. But how easy would it be for a man of wiles and guile to ease out of an unsuspecting boy the strength of the Tenth House—how many warriors we have, how many mere guards. What our strengths are, and our weaknesses. If that bard secretly reported to the First House...

"And there are monsters there the likes of which you've never yet imagined. Larger than the tallest Divhs our bold warriors command."

That statement brings me back to the moment. The bard's now strutting in front of the crowd, soaking up the attention. "They stood as tall as this mountain, I tell you plain, sentinels to the Western Realms."

"Surely you jest, Bard Andris." The Lord Protector's voice rings out over the crowd, and predictably, all eyes turn to him. "Or perhaps you haven't seen the Divhs our warriors now control. You should stay for the Tournament of Gold."

"I would be honored," the bard says gravely. "But I assure you, I don't jest. The monsters were dormant, almost sleeping, but you got the sense that they could be brought to life with a single word from the right mouth. When we saw them, I and my small company of men hastened away, back through the Pass of Naught, but we were not followed. There appeared to be no life within the Western Realms—just these two enormous monsters, and doubtless more besides, locked in eternal slumber. Slumber...but not death"

He turns, his gaze traveling around the room. "Behold, the truth of the Western Realms, and why the Exalted Imperium stopped pressing further against its immense and mighty borders. I tell you there is *living* evil there."

At that statement, a burst of conversation surges up around the room, the women fanning themselves nervously, the men squaring off as if against an unseen attacker. Living evil lurking among emptiness and dirt may sound a bit dire, but it also sounds... interesting.

And I'm not the only one who thinks so, it appears, judging from the hard grins of the warriors. After three hundred years waiting for an attack that never came, interesting is new.

Interesting is, potentially, dangerous.

The first line of houses have known the truth about the Western Realms for the past centuries—that there was a threat so immense, so dire, that the imperial army left the Protectorate behind to face it alone. The emperor's army had returned two hundred years later, only to flee a second time.

That's what we know. But no one ever talks about the exact form of that threat, or at least I've never heard of it. And if it's simply terrible raging creatures who strike fear into the hearts of their opponents, well, we have Divhs. Dozens of them. And plenty of warriors itching for a meaningful fight.

I can sense the energy in the room building further. These men, these warriors, are here without the guiding hand of their own House Lord. Is that why Rihad has chosen this moment for his bards to share such tantalizing news?

A second bard jumps to his feet. "My news is from the south," he cries. "For a full six months, I traversed the coast of the Dark-'ning Sea, weaving through rock and hill and endless rolling sand. I came upon the greatest House of all in the southern climes, the Third!"

A cheer goes up from the table housing the warriors of the Third House, and I watch the women with them as they refill the cups of the warriors from the flagons lining the table. Their actions are smooth, arch, and flirtatious, but are they also shrewd and focused, each acting according to a plan?

"So too do we find the Seventh House, and finally the Ninth at the very mouth of the southern citadels. Rich houses, both of them, but none so great as the Third, with their ferocious warriors who stare down the truth of their fiery borders."

"There are no monsters to the south, bard," rumbles a man from the center of the Third House Warriors. "There is only sand."

"And the sand is monster enough, I know. I've heard it stated so often, my ears would fall off." The bard turns around, laughing. "But you who live in the north, in these lands of water and trees and earth, let me paint the picture of the world of the southern warriors, that you might understand their fire."

The bard spools on, regaling the wide-eyed listeners with stories of the sun's merciless heat and the dryness of the air, the freezing cold of the nights under the open sky. The rich lands to either side of the few major rivers in the area, and the thriving sea industry controlled almost exclusively by the Third House.

Unsurprisingly, the warriors of the Third sponge all the tales up with pleasure, their grins growing wider and their eyes brighter as the wine pours more quickly into their cups and down their throats. By the time the bard is finished, the men are almost reeling.

"But we aren't only graced with the bards to the west and south this night—nor only their warriors!" Another man I hadn't noticed strides forth out of the crowd to take his place near the high table, and I quail back.

It's Blackmoor, the bard who visited the Tenth House not two months earlier.

CHAPTER 19

"Merritt. I wondered where you'd gone to ground."

I turn as Fortiss's bold voice cuts across my nerves but seeing him here doesn't make me any happier. I'm arguably the least of the warriors in this room, and the First House's number one knight is tracking me down? That's dangerous interest to court.

"Fortiss." I nod, holding my ground as the First House knight and his gaggle of companions stride closer. Without hesitation, Fortiss hands one of the women toward me. I experience another excruciating moment of embarrassment as I grapple with her hand, finally succeeding in placing it on my arm. She's as delicate as an orchid, and just as beautiful, and she stares up at me with wide, trusting eyes.

Councilor Miriam's warning still rings in my ears, and I still almost fall for the act.

"This is Gemma," Fortiss says, nodding to the fair-skinned brunette. Her eyes have the same dark intensity as Nazar's, but she's petite where he is rangy, and soft where he's as weathered as an old tree. "And Elise. They both wanted to meet you."

He grins broadly, but the woman on his arm doesn't look at me when she smiles, but at Fortiss. Her eyes are even sharper than

Gemma's, and she tilts her head up with a careful precision, maximizing the beauty of her profile.

Heavy with beads and sparkling crystals, Elise's blonde hair drops in thick coils over her shoulders and down to the hem of her fine dress.

Gemma, in contrast, has nothing in her hair but a delicate spray of white flowers at her crown. Her hair isn't coiled either, but hangs in a straight dark fall down her back. She's not as highly ranked among First House families as Elise, I think, but she's lovely all the same.

I straighten, thinking of my own hair. I don't regret lopping it off. The burdens of men are less tangled by far than those women must bear.

Gemma squeezes my arm. "You know this man who speaks of the eastern borders?" she asks, and her voice is as ethereal as the rest of her.

I send a look across the hall to Blackmoor. It's a risk to disavow him, but I have no choice. "Not well," I say. "And I've been traveling. There's much to keep us busy at the Tenth, even when the bards come calling."

The mysteriousness of my answer isn't lost on her, and I see it again, the hint of shrewdness before it's masked in dewy-eyed interest. "Travel is good," she says softly. "I traveled long and far before arriving in this house."

"Shh," Elise says from Fortiss's side. "He's starting."

My heart in my throat, I turn toward the bard.

"The eastern borders, I'm here to say, are far worse than the western, and even the south, though there is neither monster nor sand nor brutal heat and savage cold. But they run thick with forest and mountains, ridgelines cutting through your path in a thousand different places. You can pass a settlement like the Tenth House and never know you missed it." He shakes his head. "It was luck alone that got me there. The storms were torrential, and the skies seemed especially dark that fell eve, taking me deep into the mountain hold."

I keep my face placid, though it takes some doing. When Blackmoor visited us, it had been the very edge of spring into summer. The mountains were in blossom and the breezes light, the days growing long, and the cloudless nights filled with stars.

"It sounds very grim," Gemma murmurs, and I pat her hand.

"It's home."

"The generosity of the Tenth House was great, for all that their holding is small," the bard continues, the backhanded compliment earning him a round of laughter. With Gemma pressed tightly to my side, I dare not stiffen. Blackmoor, emboldened by the response, presses his advantage.

"It would have to be great, else no one would ever venture so deep into the mountains to find them. They boasted only one warrior, too, the son of Lord Lemille. And he was no warrior such as we have in this grand hall."

I stiffen. What on the blighted path is this? How dare he speak of Merritt this way?

As if feeling the weight of my stare upon him, Blackmoor turns toward me. I try to press back into the shadows without moving, glad the bard is all the way across the hall. My disguise cannot fail here as it failed with Caleb. Instead, I pray that Blackmoor only registers the façade I've worked so carefully to create. I'm wearing Merritt's clothes, my hair is cut like him, my face similar enough... for me not to be Merritt would be unthinkable, impossible. *See what I want you to see, Blackmoor,* I silently beg.

The bard's eyes go wide, his face a comic show of surprise, and my heart shrivels for a half-second more before he speaks.

"Why, Lord Merritt!" he cries, falsely aghast. Clearly, he's already marked my presence. "You're here!"

A raucous round of laughter surges forth, and the bard suddenly grins. I nod my head graciously toward him, acknowledging the joke and hoping desperately he doesn't seek to prolong it.

I call out my response, pitching my voice as close to Merritt's as I can. "The houses of the eastern border don't host grand tournaments, Bard Blackmoor—or any tournaments at all, as you've seen for yourself. I've had no chance to try my skills against my peers. As luck would have it, I'm here to do just that."

I look around the room, trying to read the faces watching our exchange. Some are eager, some sated, some interested, some bored. None look like the face of a killer. My gaze finally reaches the warriors of the First House, standing at their ease before the high table. I swallow then force myself to remember that Merritt would be brash, bold. Even foolhardy—and he *had* lost good men on the road to this tournament.

I plunge on. "In the Tenth House, we are born to honor and raised to battle. May the warrior knights at every house always prove to be so noble."

Not all the men, but some, give the slightest glance my way, too sharply to be idle curiosity. Beside me, Fortiss has gone as still as stone. My heart hardens in my chest as Blackmoor's gaze intensifies. He's another spy for Lord Rihad, has to be. He took our food and money, drank our wine, entertained my father and Merritt with talk of exploits and even this cursed tournament. Yet all the while, he'd been gathering information for Rihad. Information for what, I have no idea. Had he shared our family's wedding plans with some other house? Do I have him to thank for feeding this conspiracy of murder?

"It will be a tournament that we'll sing about for generations to come." The bard turns quickly round, as if this is part of his standard performance, his arms wide. But the movement serves to break our eye contact, and I allow myself the smallest satisfaction that he sought to do it first.

"In that, you're certainly correct." Lord Rihad's voice draws everyone's attention once more. "We have a great fire here already, and we would do well to build the blaze yet higher. The men in the fighting pits have labored long this week to vie for a place among the most elite warriors in the land. We should give them more of an understanding of what they are aspiring to!"

Lord Rihad turns and considers me, and I feel the trap closing in. But I can't run, I can barely move as Gemma's fingers clutch me like iron claws, and Fortiss hems me in on the other side. I don't know where Miriam has gone, but now I understand her calling out to me, stringing me along with her talk of spies, when I should have quit this room for air and peace. I'm part of their trap, without question. And now that trap is about to spring.

"I propose a new exhibition to entertain the crowds thronging in the coliseum, for demonstration only, a chance for our warriors to show what sets apart the truly great from those who merely fight," Rihad continues. "And you, Merritt of the Tenth House, you will have the honor of being a combatant in that exhibition."

I stand frozen, knowing I have no recourse. I'm at the mercy of a man bent on entertaining the masses and, perhaps, on making an example of those who dare speak out of turn.

But I've barely connected with Gent, and that's a problem. I'm no more his master than I am Rihad's. Now, if Rihad has his way, Gent will be lining up at the edge of a battleground, expecting me to guide him during a fight—a fight that's happening far too early! Gent, who seems more at home with his arms flying in the wind than he is attacking something else, is about to be tested. And so, it appears, am I.

"And who shall we pit against the new blood from the Tenth House, I wonder?" Rihad stares around the room, clearly relishing his role. There's a shift in the crowd, and I see Caleb again. He's no longer laughing with his new friend but watching me proudly. Nazar stands beside him, smoking a long pipe. I watch the pattern of smoke curl and eddy around his face, and lose myself in the wisping curls, even as Rihad's voice shouts on.

"Kheris, I think, of the Third House."

"Challenge accepted." An enormous warrior from the center of the Third House gathering pounds the table and stands, grinning at me across the space. "You'll see how we fight in the Southern Realms, boy. A lesson you won't soon forget."

The room erupts into cheers, and suddenly my back is being clapped hard, and I'm congratulated from all sides. Even Fortiss grasps my shoulder above my warrior band. The bolt of awareness that shoots through me at his touch startles me from my reverie.

"It's an honor to fight in an exhibition," he says, tightening his hand briefly. His face seems sincere, but everything is turning around on itself. There's no way I know who to trust, or how much weight to give to their words. "Though I'm well past the age to claim my own Divh, I've not yet been granted that boon."

I nod, trying desperately not to betray that I already know this information. It's even more difficult to hide my pity. Fortiss is the favored warrior of the Lord Protector, and his nephew in form if not by blood, which makes him as close to first-blooded and first-born as the First House has, since Lord Rihad has no offspring. Why *hasn't* he been granted a Divh?

Fortiss doesn't seem to notice my silence. His face is set beneath his cheerful grin, and his eyes are a shade harder. Clearly, there's some dark reason Rihad has not allowed him to claim his own Divh, but that's not for me to prize out of him. All I know is, I don't want the "honor," he seems to value so highly. But I say nothing. I understand an order when it's given, and I understand a punishment when it's meted out, even if it seems a blessing.

The crowd quiets at last, and the next bard strides forth, a young man freshly returned from the northern frontier. There's naught to the north, however, but snow and steadily worsening weather, and the bard's only saving grace is that he makes the crowd laugh with the tales of his travels.

Meanwhile, I disengage myself from a curious-eyed Gemma as soon as I'm able and bid my leave of Fortiss. As I weave my way back to Caleb and Nazar, I sense I'm being watched—and not just by random members of the crowd either. With experience born of my time in the shadows, hiding from my father's sharp gaze, I sense the attention at the side of the great hall, from the small knots of warriors and from the high table itself. Rihad and Miriam are tracking me. I deliberately loosen my stride and square my shoulders, a young warrior eager for the chance to show the world what he's made of.

In my case, however, I know I'm made of lies.

I reach Nazar and Caleb, and the priest continues to smoke his pipe, indicating for me to stand at his side as if at my leisure. I do this, breathing in the soothing smoke as I turn to watch the farce of the final bard. Nazar pauses in his draw only briefly, long enough to pull the pipe from his mouth and murmur to me, "Consider what you have learned tonight. The right man, with the right sword, can be as ten thousand men if he follows the way of the warrior."

He goes back to smoking his pipe, and I scowl into the empty air before me, hoping that my expression isn't being taken for the blind panic that it is.

Consider what I've learned tonight? I've learned that I have no allies outside this room. Councilor Miriam had seemed to seek me out...but only to hold me in place long enough for Fortiss to intercept me. Fortiss appeared likable, even friendly—yet had served to hem me in when the bard began speaking of the eastern borders and, far worse, when Rihad announced the next day's battle. The women of the First House were beautiful, sure, and yet they trapped me as effectively as Fortiss had. And warriors of multiple houses had seemed visibly uneasy about my participation in the Tournament of Gold. Especially those from the Second House.

Is it because they're the ones who slaughtered the Tenth House retainers, and who then witnessed a much larger Gent rise up in outrage against them? Are these the men who thought they'd killed Merritt and now don't know what to think about his return from the dead with an even more powerful Divh? And if those murderers are from the Second House, not the First, why was Fortiss so close by?

Too many thoughts race through my mind, twisting around on themselves.

I've also learned that I'll be pitted against the largest man I'd ever seen. Rough skinned, beefy, and dressed in heavy sand-colored silk, the warrior Kheris has a broad, open face and a booming laugh. He's laughing again now, gathering the women close as they simper and fawn over him and his men. Watching him, I realize I've made a tactical error in abandoning my own female companion.

Just then, as if reading my mind, Gemma sways into my vision. "It's tradition for a favor to be granted from a warrior to his favorite of the court," she says, dimpling. "I would be honored to receive your favor."

Nazar's quick brush against my hand is the only warning I have, and then I'm lifting the sash, as surprised as Gemma, who stares at it, then me, as if I'd just conjured the cloth into being. It's a long slender strip of green silk, painted with a thin silver tree branch. At the top of the tree branch is a fat little bird, nestled into its own feathers.

I cock a glance at Nazar but can only spare a moment before I have to start apologizing. Gemma stands stock-still, gaping at the cloth as tears pooled in her eyes.

"Gemma—I am sorry," I stammer quickly. "Forgive a fool who doesn't know the ways of such a large house."

"No—no—" She looks up at me, and her eyes are mirror bright, the smile blooming on her face as fresh as a new flower. "It's *beautiful*. It reminds me of a long-ago time. You could not—" She shakes her head. "You couldn't have known. Forgive me."

She holds the cloth to her breast. "I'm grateful for the honor," she says, and her voice has a strange aspect to it as well, the same as her smile. This is the same girl I'd watched smile archly at me across the room, clearly targeting me, but now her face is open, her lashes blinking too quickly. She bows once, then again, and she turns away from me slightly, then whirls back to kiss me on the cheek. The movement is so fast, I can barely track it, and her words in my ear are equally rapid, as rushed as a moth's wings.

"You will *win*," she says urgently.

I smile wryly as she pulls away. She has to know by looking at me that I'm a long shot against the powerful Kheris. But Gemma's face is resolute, her eyes shining. She bows again, and I bow in return.

I watch bemusedly as she turns and flees back across the room, clutching her favor close.

"So, can you explain what that was—" I stop as I turn to the side. Nazar is gone.

"That was *unexpected*, is what that was," Caleb says instead, snapping his fingers in front of my eyes to refocus me. I scowl, batting his hands away. "But I'll tell you what I saw—that priest had three different sashes at the ready and pulled out the silk one only after it was clear which girl had latched on to you. He's a sly one."

I stare at him. "Three?"

"Three," Caleb nearly crows, bouncing on his toes. "And I hope you've gotten caught up on your sleep, because you'll have precious little tonight. Nazar told me you'll have to practice in the barracks for tomorrow's fight, where no one can see."

"The barracks." I blow out a breath. "That won't be enough, Caleb. That can't replace practice on a real open field."

He shrugs. "It'll have to be enough. You've already given Gemma your favor." He grins at my glare. "You don't want to make the girl cry twice."

I open my mouth to offer my thoughts on the subject, but the flicker of Caleb's attention stops me, and I stiffen as his eyes go wide and urgent. I don't have to turn to know who's approaching us with his long-legged stride.

I turn anyway and greet Fortiss with my best, most confident —and hopefully most Merritt-like smile.

"I thought we could talk at last, Lord Merritt." He nods to Caleb, then me. "Alone."

He turns on his heel and keeps walking. I meet Caleb's wide-eyed stare, then follow.

Here we go.

CHAPTER 20

Fortiss leads me along the outer wall of the feasting hall and through a set of double doors that empty out onto a wide terrace. He stops only long enough to pick up two goblets of the-Light-only-knows-what, some kind of drunken brew. I accept it when he offers and down a sip with him. I'm glad to have something to do with my hands.

He finally pauses at the far end of the terrace, setting down his goblet on the thick, waist-high wall. It's all that keeps an unwary reveler from pitching over into open sky. This terrace is oriented to look out over the same empty marshland we'd ridden through to wind our way toward the castle. Ostentatious preening or not, there's no denying how well positioned the First House is against attack.

"So, how do you find the First House?" Fortiss asks abruptly, as if he's having as hard a time as I am coming up with conversation. He stares out over the nearly empty marshland while he speaks. "Are your accommodations adequate? Your men have all they need?"

I remember to keep my voice low and graveled. "They are and we do. We don't require much, and they knew our status coming in. We're a small house in the mountains."

"So I keep hearing. Yet I suspect you'll surprise us in the tournament. I suspect your entire goal is to surprise us, no? To advance as far as you might into the Tournament of Gold and win more men than you bought? Maybe even take your seat in the Court of Talons and wear the winged crown?"

When I tried to formulate a protest, he waves it away. "You don't need to stand on ceremony with me, Lord Merritt. We need strong warriors who are willing to fight for what they want. It's why I've sought you out. Why I'll continue to seek you out."

Fortiss's words are light, but his tone brooks no opposition. He's the celebrated son of the First House, for all that he isn't a true warrior knight, and he's used to getting what he wants. If he wishes to show favoritism to the least of the warriors in the tournament, a symbol of his generosity of spirit, I'm honor bound to let him.

An ember of anger flares to life within me. *Honor* like this can't stand much longer. Either it will fall, or I will.

I blow out a short breath. "I'm here to fight, and to win, if it pleases the Light. But then I'll be off again to the mountains as well. It has more need of me than the First."

"Mmm, as you say. So, again, what are your impressions of our tournament?" Fortiss sounds falsely cheerful as he redirects me, and his words clang in my ears. I glance around to ensure we're not being quietly surrounded by his men in some sort of ambush.

Fortiss doesn't say anything more, so I've got no other choice than to respond. "It's not the first time I've seen battle." I try to keep the irritation from my voice as too many emotions surge to the fore. Anger for the warriors who have already been wounded, for the boys and men cheated in the pits. Outrage that Merritt's killer still walks free. "I won't shrink from it tomorrow, if that's your fear."

"Not at all. But you hold yourself apart from the other men, and you shouldn't."

I snort, but Fortiss keeps going. "You're part of a larger family now. A family of warriors that knows no house, but who works for the greater glory of the Protectorate."

His words draw me up short. *Warriors who know no house? The greater glory of the Protectorate?* My surprise serves to calm my nerves. This time, when I respond, it's with far greater care. This is the nephew of the Lord Protector. Something I should never forget. "I don't want glory, Fortiss. I want to protect my house. My house and the borderlands until the Exalted Imperium returns. That's what our charge is—our only charge."

"The Exalted...seriously? You can't truly believe that."

I blink at his sudden disavowal, and Fortiss laughs. "Merritt, come *on*. It's been nearly a hundred years since the Imperium left us to manage on our own. You really think they're coming back?"

I can only stare now. "What do you mean?"

"You tell me. Your house stands at one of the easternmost points of the Protectorate. When is the last time you saw a messenger or even a bard from the Imperium who was planning to actually return to the capital and not just escape it?"

I open my mouth, then shut it again. "I don't know."

"You do know. You're what, seventeen years old? The answer is *never*. Not in all your seventeen years. Do you think the experience at the Twelfth House is any different?"

"The Imperium doesn't require tithes. There's no reason for them to come to us," I say mutinously. "Our service as protectors is enough."

"The Imperium has *forgotten* us. The capital is corrupt with the power struggles that leave the troubles of the Protectorate a far distant memory." He laughs at my expression. "Think on it, Merritt. Do you truly believe Lord Protector Rihad would leave our future to chance? While the Imperium hasn't sent emissaries, he's not been so lax. He's dedicated himself to learning all he can about our land, our worth, our magic with our mighty Divhs...and why we've been abandoned. He's sent bards all the way to Hakkir to watch and report, while never betraying who they are or where they're from."

Hakkir. Nazar's home, for all that it seems a world away. The beating heart of the Exalted Imperium. Reluctantly, I curb my anger. "It would seem he's very wise, then, if what you say is true."

"Wise and farseeing." Fortiss moves closer to me, and I cannot resist the small step back, ever mindful of the sheer drop to the rocks below, just over the terrace wall. I don't shift enough for rudeness, but for the space I need to keep from breathing in his scent—or him, mine. I don't know how intuitive he is, and I can't risk him wondering where he might have sensed my presence before. I've done a good job keeping my distance from Fortiss as Merritt, despite Talia not being so wise. But I don't want to push my luck.

"Your sister believes your attacker lies in wait among the warriors who do battle here," Fortiss challenges me abruptly.

"My sister." I scowl with all the brotherly censure I can manage. "Such thoughts are not hers to have, and certainly not hers to comment upon. My apologies."

"Well, at least one of you is well taught." Fortiss laughs, and I curl my hand into a fist despite my best efforts. Then his next words catch me up short. "She's a fierce one, though. I'm surprised she's been promised in marriage to Orlof's son. It's such a waste. The boy's barely tall enough to wield a sword. Surely there could have been a better match."

"Tell me she did not complain of it," I groan, though my head is spinning. A waste. He's used that term before. Where is he going with this?

"Oh, no," Fortiss assures me. "But Lady Talia's nearly of an age as you, well older than the boy. And Orlof is a hard man, with hard ways against his soldiers and servants alike. Did you not know this?"

I shrug. "Such matters are for my father to decide, not me." And I have no doubt my father knew of Orlof's cruelty. It would've been a soothing balm to his long-held outrage to imagine I'd be treated poorly. "Talia has learned to take care of herself."

He snorts. "Now that, I can believe. Orlof had better make sure she's been relieved of her blades before he tries to bed her himself."

The barb was so expertly thrown, I never saw it coming. I jerk up my chin, face flushing with horror and fury at the suggestion, only to find Fortiss staring at me full on. "Strange, there'd be no reason for you to know of my sister's knife skills, unless she'd had a chance to practice on you. Is there something I should know?"

Whatever he expected me to say, this wasn't it. He blinks, then smiles at me, long and slow.

"Not at all," he smirks. "If Talia held the secrets shared between us close to her breast, I can only do the same. But there's something here you're not telling me, something you both aren't. With her having run away, I find myself wondering what secrets *you're* hiding, Lord Merritt, and when we'll all learn the truth."

With that, he offers me a short bow then strides away, leaving me to look out over the dark, murky marshland. The desolate landscape stretches out in silent testimony to the truth of how poorly I've played my hand this night.

Fortiss knows something is wrong. He may know a little—or a lot—but he knows the Tenth House warrior is hiding something dire.

And when he finds out?

I'm as good as dead.

CHAPTER 21

My night doesn't improve.

It's another hour before I make it back to the barracks, and another still before the castle quiets down enough for me to follow Nazar's instruction to reach out for Gent.

The moment I call for him, Gent mentally draws me into the training yard of his own plane. But though he mimics my movements and eventually follows the lead of my thoughts, I have nothing really to prepare him for. I've never fought a Divh. I've herded animals and occasionally fended off a guard too drunk for sense, but that's not the same, no matter how Nazar insists I should pay attention to such trifles as these.

At my side, murmuring into my ear, judging my experience as I share it in fits and starts, the priest seems unusually content—too content, given the fool I'm about to make of myself. It's too soon for me to fight—far too soon. I'd thought I would have *days* yet to practice.

Eventually, I sleep, only to be plagued by nightmares of the tournament field. I wake into an early dawn weighed down by exhaustion—which perversely seems to please Nazar as well. He dresses me in yet another heavy tunic and cloak, thick breeches and boots. Hanging from my belt are more green sashes, along with my sword and a pouch for a ceremonial warrior's knife.

"I'll swelter in all of this," I grumble, trying to stifle a yawn.

"But with any luck, you won't bleed through it," comes the unhelpful response.

I peer at the priest to see if he's joking, but can't read the expression on his face. Instead, he continues talking. "All warriors bleed. In time, all fall. Timing, in truth, is how you will win this battle."

"Nazar," I groan. "I *won't* win this battle." I thought of Gemma's words the night before, the first time I've thought of her again in my panic to prepare. Now, with no more preparation possible, I frown. "That favor you gave me to present to Gemma. What was it? She recognized it, I think."

"She recognized the bird, nothing more. A mourning dove. A fitting gift for a young woman so beautiful."

"But how did you—" I groan as Nazar's eyes brighten, and I hold up a hand. "Stop, no. I can't bear it. The way of the warrior is timing, I know. You're going to tell me you somehow anticipated this. Anticipated it and came to my aid before I even realized I needed help." I shake my head. "Thank you, Nazar."

Nazar stands back from me, but amusement is still evident in his face. "It's not unreasonable to believe that you would be plied for gifts in advance of the tournament."

"This isn't the tournament, though. Not yet."

"Isn't it?" Nazar asks mildly.

The guards arrive, and there's no talking for a long while. Darkwing is restless and eager, and I think again of Merritt, so proud to sit atop this warhorse and charge into the Tournament of Gold.

I will do all I can to not fail either my brother or his beautiful horse.

"Merritt." Nazar's prompt floats to me, and I straighten, knowing the rebuke for what it is. There are too many people around us. I can't show weakness, even to myself. My mind thrums with Nazar's words as he'd stood beside me through the long night. The warrior Kheris of the Third House has fought at previous tournaments, Nazar has learned. And so his Divh is well known—known and feared among the other combatants, known and adored among the battle-lusting crowd. It's a long, sinuous serpent, as thick as Gent is wide, and more than five times as long. Though a snake would normally not seem interesting to watch, this one can leap in such a way to seem like flying, and it prefers to squeeze its opponents to death, or to lock its jaws tight around a shoulder or leg or arm.

None of that sounds terribly appealing.

I'm still contemplating how best to protect Gent when we clear the lower gates of the First House, and Nazar rides up to keep pace with me. Caleb falls in behind. The guards along the route stretch the distance between us, giving us privacy to speak and strategize. The same respect is allowed Kheris, who follows me at a distance of a half mile. Runners have been sent ahead to assemble the populace. It is to be a grand, unexpected spectacle, we've been told.

"You are holding yourself in a grip of iron," Nazar says now. "Be as a river, flowing from one movement into the other. To be tight is to let your enemy see that you aren't prepared."

I glare at him. "I'm *not* prepared."

"You must believe that you are. Think of Kheris, laughing boldly at the feasting hall. He does not know you or your Divh. However, he has been a warrior long enough to know that the gifts of the Divh can be awe-inspiring. He may worry on this, but he won't show his worry. He will know he is prepared and be certain that you know this as well. And that gives him the advantage. He is as the river."

"The river," I grumble, but Nazar's words spark through me. I ease the tension in my brow and straighten my back, and he nods in approval.

"Good. You must hold yourself with your head erect, your gaze neither low nor high nor off to the side. Your brow shall be calm, your stare unblinking. Your shoulders shouldn't hike above your ears but remain low and at the ready. Your belt shall remain tight, not slack, your sword wedged in."

I nod, but my lips twist. "No swords, Nazar." He'd done this often in the night, speaking of swords. Caleb had been staring at me through most of it, but I'd been too tired to challenge any of the priest's teachings, even that coming from a man who spent his lifetime not fighting, but praying to the gods who dance between the Light and the Darkness.

"When you see, there is both the far and the near. The two are equally important. The near view will ensure you remain protected, the far that you will win. Focus on the far, on the slightest move of your enemy's shoulders. You must see without moving your eyes."

"Oh, is that all." Still, I allow Nazar to continue, his words a soothing cadence in my mind as the trail rolls on.

Before we're anywhere close to the coliseum, I can hear the crowd. My stomach knots and my hands clench the reins.

"Merritt." This time it isn't Nazar beside me, but Caleb. He's remained silent for most of the long night, charged with keeping watch at the door to our quarters, that we might practice unmolested. He's remained quiet during the morning preparations as well, listening to Nazar as if he's absorbing the words of a master. Now he rides up beside me and keeps his smaller horse at a quickened step to match mine.

He says nothing further, though, and we ride like that for a long minute more before he speaks again, his eyes on the far horizon. "You've never actually fought with your Divh, have you? Not against another Divh. You haven't had time since..." He pauses, shifting his glance to me. "You haven't had time."

My lips twist, but there's no reason to deny it. "I haven't."

He nods then turns his gaze away again. "Well, you need to know that despite all that, you *can* win this. In any tournament battle, there's always that possibility. You have to believe it."

Irritation knifes through me, but Caleb takes my clear skepticism the wrong way. "I know the advice of a cripple is tough to swallow. But even now, I know I can win any battle I find myself in. It's why I enter so many. And you're more reckless than I am."

I snort, but he continues, "In time, I can teach you how I can handle a sword with one hand, when the balance is all off. I'll teach you how to pin your opponent when they don't expect to, because you slip beneath their defenses. Nazar can teach you—"

"Nazar is a priest," I growl, real fear beginning to claw at my eyes. For all that I've listened to the old man the whole night through, the truth is still there, mocking me. "A priest, Caleb. He knows the Light, nothing more."

"No." Caleb leans close, though I can sense that he wants to check on Nazar's position behind us. "That man may *be* a priest, but he's not *only* a priest. Surely you know that as well."

"He came to us—"

"We all come to places we don't expect," Caleb cuts me off. "You listen to him, yet you still doubt him. Well, don't. He's not only a keeper of the Light. He's a master of the sword and of strategy. I know it as sure as I'm born."

I start to protest then stop. Nazar is a priest—and an old man—but he was also the only other survivor of the attack on the Tenth House caravan in the mountains. I...I'd never really thought about that, until now.

Caleb continues, "It's not important how, though, not now. What's important is that there are many things he can teach you. Everything but one. He can't teach you heart. I can't give you heart either, though *I'd* sacrifice another limb if I had one to spare, to enter into the Tournament of Gold as a banded warrior. To feel what you feel and see what you see when your Divh takes the field."

Caleb's voice is so caught up in enthusiasm that it tugs at me, lifting me slightly from the mire of my own dread. "It'll be good to see Gent here, out in the open," I say reluctantly.

The smile my squire turns on me is almost radiant. "Good? It'll be a moment to savor for a lifetime! I haven't seen your Divh, and I cannot wait. No one has seen it—him—up close." He eyes me knowingly. "Kheris hasn't seen him either. Remember that."

"Kheris." I frown. Perhaps...perhaps I do have an advantage, after all. Though Caleb's wrong, of course. Fortiss has seen my family's Divh. Fortiss and whoever killed Merritt.

I pray they're not one and the same person.

At that moment, the horns of the tournament sound. The distant roar of the crowd flows over us like a surging tide. Caleb falls back with Nazar as I ride forward, surrounded by a battery of guards. As the challenger, my task is to enter on the far side of the fighting field. I feel my shoulders relax, my brow ease as a stiff wind kicks up. My long, dark-green cloak flows out behind me, and I and a few outriders break off from the main line of guards to take the secondary path to the tournament field.

Less than a quarter hour later, we're in position at the far end of the field. The coliseum is even fuller than it was earlier this week —has it only been a few days since I saw the men of the Fourth and Sixth House in battle? It already seems like a season has passed. The horns down the far end of the field blare but distantly, and Darkwing blows and champs, held too long in check from the gallop he craves.

"Soon." I pat his shoulder. "Then you'll show them all."

One of the guards looks at me, startled, and I give him a half shrug.

"He was meant for the race, I suspect, not for the battle. But he's got a good heart."

The second guard flanking me gives a grudging laugh. "Better hope he's got strong legs too, to get you out of here."

"If he gets that chance, you'll be well ahead of the game." A third guard saves the words from being a sneer, but only by a hair. "Kheris wasn't chosen lightly. You're a lamb being brought to the slaughter."

"Probably." The guards chuckle darkly, perhaps surprised that I know the fate that lies before me. Meanwhile, I face forward again, tightening my knees against the horse's sides.

I do know the fate before me, I realize. That fate is the way of the warrior, to hear Nazar tell the tale. And the way of the warrior is to be prepared to face death at every turn.

This day won't bring me death, I think. Not yet.

But it *will* bring me Gent. Here in the bright sunshine, where I can truly see him with my own eyes, on my own plane. And for that, I am grateful.

The far horns sound again, and the guards urge me on, their cheers more heartfelt than I would have expected. Beneath me, Darkwing races across the field in a blissful bounding gallop, and I feel the warrior band on my left arm burn in sudden awareness of the animal's fervor. Unexpected laughter surges up within me, suffusing my entire body with its light. Gent will be coming, I think, and Gent loves nothing more than to run and feel the land fall away beneath his feet. He'll enter this world a hero and he'll leave it as such, I vow. All of Nazar's words coalesce in my head, and I bend forward over the horse's withers, urging him on.

Darkwing needs no more encouragement than that. He surges forward, easily beating Kheris's mount to the center of the field, and dances as the crowd roars with delight and laughter. He's won *his* race this day. The rest is up to me.

Kheris clearly wasn't expecting that move, and though he lifts his arm in acceptance of the enormous rolling cheer, his face is already dark with annoyance. "You so quickly want to die, boy?" he shouts at me. The weight of his anger slams into me like a malevolent fist. "I can help you with that, if so."

"I'm honored to fight you, Kheris," I shoot back, "Nothing more."

He blinks, but he can't find the insult in my words, nor any challenge.

"Then you'll be equally honored to lose." He turns his steed sharply, pulling hard at the bridle as the horse fights against it.

I turn as well with a squeeze of my legs, but Darkwing knows his duty. He pivots and trots up to the two wooden towers. It suddenly occurs to me that the towers are all that remain of what

I'd seen when I was last on this field, at this place. There are no fighting pits surrounding us, nothing but bare ground.

The attendants help both Kheris and me dismount, and we turn to our respective towers amid more raging cheers from the crowd. Two of my guards stand at the door to my tower, and they nod at me grimly. I give them a rueful smile. "Go easy on my horse. He just wanted to run it out."

Once again, they start in surprise, and I pass by them, also grateful for my horse's need to run. It seems to have cleared my head. The guard at my back speaks up. "A moment, Merritt of the Tenth. I'll take your cloak. To keep you from tripping." I wait until he pulls the heavy garment from my shoulders and feel lighter still. Bounding up the stairs, I round the series of tight corners and all too quickly find myself at the final door at the top of the platform. The light breaks in around it, and the guard comes up the stairs behind me. He speaks again. "You haven't been in a tournament before."

I grimace. It must be obvious to everyone. "I haven't."

"You'll exit and acknowledge the crowd, then stand at attention, facing the Lord Protector while Kheris does the same. When the Lord Protector gives the signal—he'll lift his arm—you'll lift your left arm high and cross your heart with your right. When he drops his arm, summon your Divh."

Hearing these instructions settles my nerves yet further. "Thank you," I say, turning around to meet his gaze. "You may only be doing your job, but there are many ways to do one's work. Yours is appreciated."

He might have said something in return, but the door is opening now. I face forward and step into the sunlight.

CHAPTER 22

The crowd's roar jangles my ears, and I follow the guard's directions exactly, nearly blown back by the second roar when Kheris takes his position. I hadn't realized how well I'd be able to see him, but he strides confidently onto the platform, taking the exultation of the crowd as his due. When he turns to honor the Lord Protector, his gaze sears me across the open space between us. I find myself suddenly glad that warriors don't fight with their fists, as Nazar keeps saying, but with their minds.

The Lord Protector says something, and I rivet my gaze to the top platform, though in truth I can't focus only on Rihad. Fortiss stands there as well, his face placid as he stares out at the crowd. He doesn't look down at me, and I suppose that's a blessing. He probably also expects me to lose.

Irritation sears through my gut, turning that river I'm supposed to be flowing along into fire.

Lord Rihad lifts his left arm high into his air, and mine shoots up as well. I can feel the fiery band clenching tighter around my arm. I curl my right hand into a fist and lay it against my heart. I can suddenly hear the pounding of my blood in my own ears, but unexpectedly, it isn't rushed. It's slow, like water falling over rocks.

Gent, I think in my mind, feeling the wind in my hair as we raced through the blue mists of the training field. *Gent.*

A far distant roar of joy greets my words.

Lord Rihad drops his arm.

The first thing I see is the coliseum, but not with my own eyes. Instead, I am far above it, staring down, the people screaming like so many field mice in their strange—

I shake my head, hard, and am once more back in my body. I yearn to turn and see Gent in the sunlight, but my feet stay rooted to the platform, my breath hitching in my throat. *Focus.*

Kheris faces me now, his hands lifted in preparation for a strike. And then I look behind him with my human eyes to see the monster roiling at the far end of the field.

I blink.

Kheris's serpent is everything Nazar had warned me of and more. Broader than the Tenth House manor, it's impossible to tell how long it is because it hovers and darts and retracts and hisses all at once. Its hood is flared wide, and I see how it seems to leap up far enough to fly—it has hooded sacs all down its body, like flaring gills meant to catch the wind. It eyes the far end of the field with interest. Behind me, Gent lets out an almighty roar that drives the crowd's cheers to a fever pitch.

But I know Gent a little already, if not his roars. As I shift back to his view, I feel the confusion in his mind. He's never faced a monster like this. He surely didn't expect to be attacking it when he came here today. He merely wants to run.

The serpent shoots forward. It moves with blinding speed, and my thoughts flow into command as clearly as I can make them. *Run, Gent,* I urge. *Run fast!*

In my mind's eye Gent surges forward, but I don't have to rely on a mental picture of him for long. I feel the shuddering of the earth and hear the pounding of his feet on the tournament field. As he shoots by me, I gasp at the sight of him—so much taller than I'd imagined, his long arms flowing behind him as he bends forward. Not only because he wants to make them into wings, with his silver hair flowing over dark green hide, but because his hands are bristling with long claws that click together heavily, a dead weight. Another claw sprouts from his elbow in a thick gnarl of bone, and his body seems bulkier now as well than when I'd seen him in his own plane.

His keening wail rends open the sky as he surges forward. His head is larger than I remember it too, made imposing by the thick ridge of bone that rises up from his shoulders and flares into horns. Now those horns are targeting the serpent, who, despite its greater speed, is apparently not used to monsters running straight at it. Some of Nazar's words seep into my mind, a way of strategic timing that counseled to close in fast and hit the enemy quickly and directly, before the enemy has decided to withdraw, break, or hit back.

Even as I think the words, Gent shifts his body and angles more tightly toward the serpent, who hesitates the split second needed for Gent to propel his arms forward and wrap them around the beast, flipping it over onto its back.

The crowd roars but I can't hear it, can't hear anything except the crash of Gent's blood in my ears, the rasp of his throat. Gent grunts as he flings himself away from the creature, and I mimic his actions, shaking my arms slightly as I straighten on the platform.

All at once, I see Kheris across the space between us. The giant warrior holds his body in the forward pose of attack, his face a mask of fury. I pull Gent around with a twitch of my torso and the Divh swings, reluctantly, his arms still spread wide. Everything that isn't bone stings in a light, zipping fury, and I realize the skin of the serpent must be secreting some sort of poison. Not enough to cause serious harm, I suspect, but enough to make a combatant think twice about grappling with it.

Gent hadn't known about that. I hadn't known. And so we'd rushed in and done what apparently no one had done before.

It takes the serpent another long moment to flip around, but its belly has been exposed. A more experienced fighter or one going for the cut that springs to my mind—a cut that follows the body with the long sword or in this case, Gent's brutal claws—would have attacked that belly, I suddenly know instinctively. Even a poor cut would be better than withdrawing and circling around, as Gent is now doing.

But the moment is lost.

The serpent recoils and follows Gent with his eyes, its hood flaring ominously, its mouth open in a long, protracted hiss. No fire flows from its mouth, and I'm grateful for that. Gent's arms still sizzle where the poison has hit him. The snake darts out, and Gent twists to the side, but the two hold their détente for nearly a minute, Gent circling and the snake watching.

The crowd rustles with shouts of encouragement, and there's even some laughter at Gent's taunting feints, but I hold my Divh close—on his feet, poised—knowing that the danger is only growing. The snake is longer than him by several dozen paces. And if it touches Gent, the memory of its poison is strong. Close combat isn't the answer with this creature.

I'm in Gent's eyes again, seeing what he sees. The billowing sacs along the serpent's body are aspirating like the gills of a fish, their rhythm almost mesmerizing as they gape and withdraw, gape and withdraw. A kernel of an idea forms in my mind as my gaze sweeps the open, dusty field. If I can only—

I don't have the chance to finish the thought.

On the other platform, Kheris shouts something in a language I don't understand, and as I blink my focus back to him, torn between what Gent sees and what I see, he punches his hand into the air several inches.

In the center of the field, the snake shoots upward too, propelled by the intensely tight coils of its tail. For one incredible moment, it soars straight up, and even Gent flings back his head, staggering in wonder to see it move that way. Then the serpent comes down again, all mouth, and plows its full weight into Gent's left shoulder.

Pain blasts through me as teeth bear down on Gent's tough hide. The snake wrenches its iron jaws hard to the right, and Gent screams as flesh tears and muscles split. I clench my hand into a tight ball and shift it up, more out of instinct than any true knowledge. At the center of the field, Gent wraps his massive hand into a fist, rendering it a spiky ball of bone, and drives it into the base of the snake's jaw. But though Kheris staggers back a step on the opposite platform, the searing pain in my shoulder does not give way. The snake holds on, clamping down, as Gent pounds at its head both above and below.

A hot sluice of liquid pours down my chest and I glance toward it, startled to see a small patch of blood blooming on my shoulder. Fury ratchets through me that's not wholly my own. On the field, Gent screams anew, this sound an awful mix of rage and fear—not for himself, I realize on some level, but for me. With another mighty punch, he manages to loosen the serpent's jaws, then screams again as the vile creature slides bodily along his arms and legs again as he attempts to fling it from him, the poison of its scales setting fire to every inch of skin.

I stumble to the side as the horns blow above my head, and the roar of the stadium is deafening. The battle is over, but my eyes are still Gent's, my skin his as well. Everything burns like fire, and he turns, then turns again, finally finding the tiny platform at the center of the coliseum. He takes a step forward, only stopping as I raise a hand.

No, no, I implore, though my mind is his mind, his fury and pain and outrage mine as well. Gent reaches his paw to me, pointing across the giant field, and I lift my hand toward him. The warrior knights who battled on this field before hadn't done this, but I feel as if I cannot help but reach out to this Divh who is my Divh, even as he reaches out to me who am his bond. We hold that connection for a long, impossible moment, and I see more—so much more, as pain washes through me. The sunlit hillsides of his homeland, strewn with dark blue and white flowers, overlooking a windswept sea. The deep rich purplish green of the far mountains that he calls his home, the—

With another blast of trumpets, Kheris's mighty war snake

disappears, shaking me back to the tournament grounds. I focus my mind on Gent returning back to that mountain home he imagines, running through those flowering fields.

Go. Heal, I think, and Gent vanishes as well. His presence in my mind lingers, however, as the door to the wooden tower opens beside me—those flowers, that windy vista, the smell of something fresh and clean—the image swamps all my senses and I smile, feeling Gent's touch of healing all the way down my spine.

Thank you, I think, though Gent is long gone.

Then there's someone at my shoulder, the guard from the staircase. "Bow at the waist," he instructs tersely, though his words aren't harsh, exactly. More scared.

"Oh, right. Sorry." I curl my fist to my heart and bow across the open space to the triumphant Kheris, then again to the Lord Protector, who stares down at me from his lofty perch. Everyone up there is staring at me, I realize. I straighten as I accept the heavy pad the guard is pressing to my shoulder, and glance his way. "Did I do something wrong? Besides the obvious?"

He snorts. "Not so anyone could see, or nearly anyone. Otherwise Kheris would be over here demanding blood for drawing any attention from his victory. We'll get the platform cleared quick enough." He nods to other men as he turns me toward the door, and I frown as they all converge around me.

And then I see it.

Flowers.

Midnight-blue and white petals lie scattered over the platform, stirring in the wind. Across from me, Kheris is being led through his own door, and I duck inside as the men sweep and push the mound of flowers in behind me. "How..."

"Get these bagged and hauled out of here, or it's our heads," snaps the guard to the other men. To me, he nods toward the stair. "You can manage?"

My stomach pitches queasily, but I duck my head. "I can manage."

"Good. I'll go down ahead. You fall, I'll catch you."

We make it around two tight corners before he speaks again, his voice low. "You be careful. The Lord Protector doesn't like surprises he doesn't engineer. Those flowers that showed up at your feet qualify as a surprise."

"But I—" I shake my head. I have no idea how they'd appeared. "That's not...usual?"

He coughs a short laugh. "No. That's not usual. And you'll want a believable excuse if you're asked. Say they were sewn into your tunic, and the force of the serpent's attack loosed the seams."

"Oh!" I turn to him as we make our way down the stairs. "That's good. Thank you for—for this. For your kindness. I'll repay you for it, I swear."

That's clearly the wrong thing to say, as the guard stares back at me, the color in his face too high. "You must be living under a rock, you and your house. You have nothing to repay. I'll be asked as well, and the better my story and yours, the more likely we'll both escape Lord Rihad's wrath. Right now, he finds you a curiosity, not a threat. Best to keep it that way."

I grimace as we reach the bottom floor. "I think I've amply proved I'm no threat."

"And I think you're wrong." He peers at the door and sighs, listening to the sound of trumpets above. "We wait," he says simply and then, a minute later, he cocks his head, listening to the ebb and flow of noise outside.

"Kheris is off the platform," he says, nodding sharply. He raises his voice. "Open the door!"

The door swings away, and I hear the cheer of the crowd, clenching my jaw tight as the guard roughly shoves me out and into the arms of one of his fellows. The two of them push me up on my warhorse so quickly, I wrench my shoulder again, but as my vision swims, I manage to hear the guard's orders to his mate. "Get 'im out of here fast. Full gallop, down to a walk after he enters the central passage. Don't let anyone look too close."

Panic fills me as I look down at my tunic, my breeches—has my costume failed me? Have I done something wrong? But nothing looks out of place, save for a few stray blossoms on my tunic. I frown but hold on to the pommel of the ornate saddle, grateful for something to focus on as my warhorse surges forward. The animal doesn't need me to tell him to run fast and hard; it's how he's made. Still, as we make our way to the central passage, cut into the middle of the spectator stands, the applause finally breaks through my pain. I lift my head, and a roar of cheers go up in the stands closest to me, none louder than one young boy near the central passage.

"Merritt! Merritt!" he shouts, then he disappears down the corridor, shoving his way through the crowd.

My stomach twists. It's the boy from the fighting pits, who even now is wearing my tunic, I suspect. I've failed him, after all he's already endured.

Are the other men I purchased watching as well, I wonder? Are they reconsidering their decision to ally with the Tenth?

I grimace as another surge of pain rips through my shoulder, then the warhorse slows to a trot, turning into the cutaway passage through the coliseum walls. We'll pass beneath the seats and onto the open ground beyond, and then this will be done.

But I am not finished yet. The boy from the fighting pits suddenly appears above me, leaning above the railing. "Merritt!" he shouts again as he drops something over the edge.

Instinctively, I flinch, angling the horse away from the thrown rock or garbage or even my balled-up tunic. But as I blink, my eyes focus on the flashes of midnight blue and white that are falling softly down over my head and shoulders, drifting over my horse's thick mane.

Flower petals.

The roar of the crowd pounds through my ears as we flee the coliseum.

CHAPTER 23

The long ride back to the First House starts out in a throng of people, all of them shouting at once, cheering on the warriors of the tournament. My pulse pounding in my ears, I stare straight ahead, desperately hoping that no stray flower petals remain on my livery or on Darkwing's tack. My gaze flicks down as the road curves, raking across the horse's mane. It's clear, thank the Light.

As we move slowly through the crowd, I try to keep from openly flinching every time Darkwing jerks the reins. My shoulder throbs, and I'm convinced the wound will bleed through my clothes at any moment, though a quick glance down confirms my tunic is still pristine. I haven't had a chance to speak with Nazar—I can't even see him yet, in fact. I assume the retainers will join our procession out on the open plains once we break free of Trilion.

Darkwing tosses his head, and I gasp with sudden pain, blinking quickly at the unwanted tears that spark behind my eyes. I have to *focus*. I am Merritt, warrior knight...

I set my jaw against a fresh wave of pain, this one having nothing to do with my shoulder. *Merritt...*

We pass a wide space that separates the main road from one of the dozens of spectators' encampments, a warren of carts and tents and makeshift wooden walls. Even at this distance, I can see it's teeming with people. It seems to have grown a third larger since the scant day I last rode past it, its proximity to the tournament coliseum apparently making it a prized location.

But even as I gaze across the open space, I can tell something's wrong. A commotion is unfurling deep in the heart of the encampment, walls swaying, the peaked tops of the tents shuddering back and forth, as if a stampede of horses is passing through the crowded maze. For the barest moment the disturbance is silent, then screams of outrage and fear swell up as if on the wind, strange shouts of "Hai! Hai!" ringing out. A whoosh of fire erupts on the heels of those shouts, a tent clearly having caught ablaze in a sudden and shocking inferno.

"Marauders!" someone yells close to me. Our procession abruptly falters, men and horses falling out of line—some to the left toward our own crowd and safety...some surging to the right, toward the conflagration.

"For the glory of the First House!" A rush of guards sweeps by me, but it's not only guards that are charging across the open field. Kheris has wheeled his mighty warhorse and so have half a dozen other warriors—warriors! Charging their ornately decorated steeds into the deathtrap of narrow passages and too many people. I stare in amazement for another breath. What are they *doing*? All this to rout out a handful of thieves?

But where they go, I have to follow, I know instantly, as the crowd around me bursts into excited cheers. I'm a warrior knight, a descendent of the ancient protectors of the Exalted Imperium. If I don't race pell-mell into the same chaos the other warrior knights have entered, it will be noticed. Remarked upon.

I can't afford that.

And more than that...what if Nazar and I have been wrong all along? Even now I am almost certain it was a warrior knight, but what if it *was* marauders who killed Merritt, with their despicable gray arrow? Though surely it can't be an archer from this same group, the idea of hunting down any outlaws who would dare attack so boldly, and in broad daylight, fills me with renewed determination. The pain in my shoulder is staunched by fury and even hope, that someone—*anyone* will be made to pay for everything my brother suffered, everything he didn't live to see.

The throng is now overrunning our procession to press close enough to the encampment to see the hated marauders get cut down. Swallowing my own panic, I turn Darkwing into a run across the open field behind the others, leaning close over the stallion's mane. Silently I pray that no child or stray dog is foolish enough to cross my path—I won't be able to stop. Light, with the smoke from the fire now spreading over the encampment, I can barely see as I plunge down the same wide track the other horses have taken.

The moment I breach the edge of the encampment though, I'm out of my depth. The temporary walls are flimsy enough, meant for privacy more than protection. But they've been thrown up without any rhyme or reason. Together, they create a labyrinth of passageways that all drive deeper into the heart of the encampment before suddenly opening into a roiling mass of humanity. Everyone scatters like rats under lamplight as we burst into the middle of them.

A knot of warriors head left, guards thundering behind them, but I'm pushed back by the sudden tide of humanity. I wheel Darkwing around, heading right into a particularly grisly knot of tents and walls that smell of cook stoves and roasted meat.

One of these tents is the one that caught fire, and a desperate ring of men and women are heaping everything they can onto it—water, dirt and heavy mats, others using the mats to beat the worst of the blaze into submission.

I glance back at their efforts a second too long, totally missing the wooden crossbeam of a large cart-like structure that suddenly appears in my path. I'm ripped from the saddle and thrown from Darkwing, who plunges on, blind with the smoke and screams of too many people crowding close.

Despite my padded tournament gear, I land with an agonizing crunch, the wind knocked out of me by the crossbeam, and the wound in my shoulder wrenching with a sickening rip. The jolt shocks me to sudden clarity, and I scramble to my feet, yanking my short knife from my belt and sweeping the area with my gaze as I whirl around.

Where would I go if I was a marauder? We had enough of them at the Tenth House, Light knew, but we were surrounded by forest, not open ground. Still, if this had been an attack at the Tenth, the marauders would be heading for anywhere away from all these people, that much was for sure. With no clear sense of direction, I spy light—precious daylight!—through a break in the tents, and bolt toward it, well away from the main track through the encampment.

Pressing through the crowds, one turn, then another twists me further toward the far edge of the tents and walls, the smell steadily getting worse, and the number of people dwindling. Then I wheel around a final corner and dash into the middle of what looks like an abandoned watering yard, complete with a dry well that stands several paces distant from the last set of dilapidated walls.

The stench of rotting meat is strong here, and I realize this is where the carcasses of boar and chickens and goats have been thrown: the garbage heap of the encampment. I've gone the wrong way.

I turn back—and see him.

A man is crawling in the dirt directly through the worst of the mounds of refuse. I'd never have noticed him if I'd merely glanced into the opening of this foul space. The marauder's entire body is wrapped in rags, and he's bleeding heavily as he tries to drag himself toward—to where? The well?

I stare in horror as he scrapes his feet along the dust to cover his trail, but he's doing a good job of it, I have to admit. In one hand, he's grabbed some recently gutted animal and is dragging it along, leaning into its bloated belly every few paces, the blood spoor also covering his tracks. His tunic has been sliced open from collar to waist, and as he stretches to haul himself another few paces, I nearly drop my knife in shock.

The marauder is a *woman*.

I can only stare, and in that moment the marauder seems to realize I've spotted her. She lifts her head and glares at me, and her eyes flay me from all the way across the carrion ground.

"Are you just going to stand there, boy?" she barks. "Help me or kill me, but don't waste my time."

The order jerks me to attention, and several things hit me at once. *This* is a woman. *This* is a fighter, and *this*—for all that she's a criminal, for all that she perhaps even set the encampment tent on fire...this is someone I cannot let fall into the hands of the First House's guards. They're all men, and to them—this woman would be an abomination and a creature to be used. Just like me.

For the moment, nothing else matters but that.

I rush forward, belatedly remembering my knife. She sees it as I raise it high, and her face flashes with a new emotion. Resolve, determination, and a sense of acceptance I'd only ever seen in old women whose time it was to die. But this woman isn't old. Her face is weathered and darkly tanned, but her eyes are bright, the skin bared by her torn tunic far paler and soft.

"Where?" I demand as I reach her, pocketing my knife then yanking the dead and oozing carcass away from her. She's lucky she hasn't poisoned herself already with its gore. "Where are the others? Your people?"

She grunts in pain as I push her back to assess her wounds, and her head lolls forward for a moment before I shake her back to consciousness. I catch a glimpse of a wrapped packet tucked against her belly and wonder if whatever that packet contains is worth the woman's life.

"You can't close your eyes," I tell her. "You sleep, you die. Understand?" I've seen too many wounded men who have lost far less blood than this fall into a slumber from which they never waken. I pull one of my sashes from my breeches. "Your leg wound is the worst. You've got to stop the bleeding there or it won't do you any good to crawl away."

As I talk, I wind the long sash around her thigh. She's cut deep, but not as deep as I'd at first feared, and though her heart is racing, the blood that seeps from the wound doesn't pulse with its pressure. She can survive this, if she can get away.

Another surge of shouts erupts from the encampment, louder now, closer. I grit my teeth, tying off the sash. "You've got to get out of here."

The woman's eyes are still open, and she seems lucid enough. Then she says something that makes no sense. "The well," she gasps.

I glance across the litter-strewn space. The cover of the empty well has been shoved aside, but there's no telling how far down the stone structure goes. Does she think she can hide there? Maybe she's not so lucid after all.

"That won't work. You won't be able to crawl back out."

"The well," she insists, and her hands start to flutter, new sweat streaming down her brow. She'll exhaust herself trying to move her own body, and that won't do either of us any good.

"Okay, okay, I'll get you to the well." I shove my hands beneath the woman's shoulders and stagger to my feet. She's heavier than she looks, but I manage to pull her several paces toward the well when I stumble and go down hard, jolting her. She cries out, but the sound is a mere murmur. She's far more disciplined than I would have ever expected, given her injuries.

I haul her back upright, twisting around again—and find myself staring at the edge of a ragged blade.

"Drop her."

The voice is clear and cold—and also feminine. I freeze for only a moment, then do as I'm ordered, easing the wounded marauder to the ground. Suddenly, two other figures appear from the well, scurrying out and running low, looking more like rag-covered dogs than humans. They reach out and snatch up their comrade, and I note their hands in a kind of stupefied wonder—also small, with long and slender fingers—as they drag the wounded marauder toward the well.

My curiosity gets the better of me. "You're all women?" I ask gruffly, turning to the marauder whose knife still hovers above me. Her face is completely wrapped in rags, and only her eyes are bared—eyes that stare at me with sharp cunning.

Too late, I realize my mistake. Another pair of marauders have emerged from the encampment and are edging between the piles of trash to my back. I'm trapped here, dressed in tournament finery but without my horse, without my guards, too low to the ground to pull a sword I have no hope of wielding.

"*Warrior*," the marauder sneers, and she shifts her hold on the knife to slash down hard at me from above. At the well, the wounded woman says a word I can't make out, making my attacker pause.

She glances back. "He'll identify us," she practically snarls. "I shouldn't kill him?"

Only one word floats toward us in response. "Her."

The marauder whips her gaze once more to me, but by now I've gotten my wits together. I spring to my feet, swiping fast enough with my knife that the marauder wheels back, giving me the space I need to yank my sword free. They don't know I can't fight with the thing. They only know what they see.

Even if they've already seen too much.

I take three steps to the side, turning so the others are no longer at my back, and face down my ragged opponents. Still, I wait for their attack—I have to be able to use their momentum against them, I know that much. "What, are you just going to stand there?" I demand, echoing the wounded woman's taunt.

A cry of fury sounds from the encampment behind me, and a shrill whistle goes up from somewhere to the right and high—a lookout on a distant wall, has to be. The marauder lowers her knife, her gaze raking over me, my clothes, my sword.

"Her," she grunts. She's no less startled than I am.

There's another shout, men roaring with bloodlust, and the

two ragged women to my left shift urgently, their eyes on their leader, but their confidence clearly faltering. The marauder with the knife, however, continues to stare at me, defiantly. She won't back down first.

I sheathe my sword, then point to the well, where the other women have disappeared. "Go," I order with a strength I don't truly feel. "I'll keep your secret."

She pauses the barest moment longer, then twists her mouth into a snarl. She flees.

I do as well, only I turn and run pell-mell back through the field of rotting carrion, toward the nearest commotion, hoping like the Light that I can blend in with the rioting crowd long enough to get back out in the open and find Darkwing. I'll be bloody and covered in smoke and grit, but no one will know what I saw. No one will know what I know. I've kept my own secret so long, keeping another is no hardship.

I don't understand it, can barely believe it—but I will keep the marauders' secret...from *everyone*, I vow.

I suspect I won't live long enough to worry about them keeping mine.

CHAPTER 24

Most of the warriors are already back in the procession by the time I stagger free of the encampment, and the crowd is alive with shouts of outrage that there was no marauder blood spilled. The villains had gotten away cleanly—and apparently, this isn't the first time. Anger rumbles and rolls about the outlaws, though at least this day, they were interrupted. Rumors of a tent filled with pallets of gold rush along the breeze with whipped-up furor—a tent and holding that remained safe because of the intercession of the tournament's warrior knights.

Caleb is there with Darkwing and helps me mount up, making no comment about my disheveled state. A cheer goes up all around us as we reform our procession, and now shouts of thanks drown out the grumbled protests. No one seems to know yet if anything was stolen, but at least no Light-honoring tournament attendees were harmed.

There's no further opportunity for true conversation as we ride, though there's plenty of murmuring about the attack. The guard nearest to me holds forth long and earnestly that these unusually bold marauders are some scourge from the west, possessed by the demons that live beyond the Protectorate's borders. A grim smile teases across my face as I listen. How much more horrified would they be to know that on top of their apparent magical powers...these fell attackers were women?

Eventually, their talk dies away as we plod back to the First House. Unlike the morning's journey to the coliseum, I'm now surrounded at all times by guards. I don't know if they're protecting me from further marauder attacks or ensuring I don't flee, but the pain in my shoulder grows with every stride. By the time we wind our way back up the mountain passage to the First House, I'm drooping in my saddle.

At Nazar's insistence, we don't stop to rest until we're back in the barracks of the First House, beneath the immense central tower. The priest sends Caleb to stand guard at the open door and to alert us if any should draw near. Then he moves quickly, slicing through the lacings of my sleeves and down the delicately picked-out embroidery stitches of my tunic.

"Should another guard care for you, he can take off your tunic in pieces," he says, making no mention of the dirt and smoke that are now ground into the material.

I groan, leaning against the wall as he works. "If another guard cares for me, I'm already dead, Nazar. You know that."

He purses his lips and pulls the last of the material away. The burst of blood on the outer tunic is nothing compared to what lies beneath it. The thick padding covering my breasts is soaked, and deep slashes mar my skin where the snake bit Gent. I frown down at it, despite my skin pulling taut at the movement. "Do people normally get hurt this badly?"

"People don't get hurt at all. Warriors do. It is the way. In this battle, the serpent maintained the hold longer than prescribed, and that's why the wound reached you. It's a mark against Kheris that he allowed that to happen."

"Or a mark against me that I couldn't get it off Gent more quickly." Disgusted, I sag back against the wall. "I thought—for one moment there, I thought we had a chance."

"You completed your strike in one timing," Nazar says. The salve he puts on the wounds instantly cools my skin. "You then should have hit with the cut of no design, no conception, but that takes much training. Training of the mind and of the spirit as well as the body." He glances at me. "Gent's arm is as a long stave or sword. The way is close to your understanding."

"None of this is close to my understanding." I sigh as Nazar finishes wrapping my shoulder. "There were flower petals at my feet when it was done, did you see that?"

He hesitates then motions me to lean forward. He drops a new tunic over my neck, standing back to review his handiwork. Then he nods. "Caleb," he calls, and I look over as our squire ducks inside our quarters.

Caleb grins at me. "Not one fight but two!" he announces. "Did you even see the marauders you all were after? I heard they went to ground almost immediately, but they smuggled out a stash of gold from one of the richest tents in the camp. Did you see any of them, anywhere? I can't believe we were all so close!"

I let his words wash over me without responding, and as usual, Caleb leaps in to fill the gap. "But forget all that—you did so well in your fight today! That first hit took everyone by surprise where we were standing. Apparently, no one has ever gotten so close to Kheris's Divh before."

"For good reason. Its skin is toxic." I hold my arms out, but there's no trace of the poison on me as Nazar works to reattach the sleeves of my tunic. On my left arm, the tattoo remains fixed into the skin, but other than appearing darker to me, it's unchanged. "Don't ever let it touch you. You can tell that to everyone you know too."

"But you got in close and threw it down, exposing its belly. There were some who thought you'd win at that point, but the serpent Divh is one of the most difficult to defeat in single combat. Most didn't think you had a chance."

I smile grimly. "Well, then at least I didn't cost the bettors too much money." My eyelids are suddenly heavy, and I fight to keep awake. But there's something—something I want to know. Something I'd asked Nazar already, but it's already slipped my mind...

"Show her what you found in your pockets, Caleb."

"Oh!" Caleb says with such force that my eyes flare open. "These—here."

He sticks his hands in the pockets of his breeches and pulls forth a fistful of flower petals, the deep midnight and white of the mountain flowers Gent showed me. "Nazar says they were at your feet as well, but I couldn't see, and he told me to stop asking about them almost as soon as I started." He looks down at the petals, then strides over and dumps them beside me on the pallet. "They just appeared."

"When?" I pick up a delicate petal and turn it over in my hand. It's dark blue from the tip to almost the base, with a burst of white leading down to the stem. Others are white with a burst of blue, and I paw through the small pile absently, wondering at their silken touch against my fingers.

"At the end, when you and Gent reached for each other. I felt something brush against my legs, and I swiped at my pockets out of habit, thinking they were being picked. Instead, these were there."

"They appeared in my belted pouch as well," Nazar says. He's retired to the other side of the room, his long pipe now glowing in the dim light. Smoke wafts around him, thick and redolent. "Not too many. A handful."

"The boy..." I murmur sleepily. "The boy in the stands. He had them too."

"Well, no one else did," Caleb says emphatically. "Otherwise, there would have been a stampede. That's some kind of *magic*."

"Well, obviously." I quirk a brow at him. "The Divh are magic."

"But that's magic we know. This..." He points to the flower petals. "This is something else. Something different."

I smile a bit, thinking of the picture in Gent's mind, in my mind, of the flowers silhouetted against the sun-brightened sea. "I think they were intended to make me feel better, is all. Gent will heal, but he was surprised I was hurt."

"Rest, Merritt." Nazar stands abruptly, as if eager to be away.

"There is a victory feast for Kheris tonight, and we should be present to do him honor. No one will expect you to make an appearance so soon." He gestures. "Drink the water before you become thirsty. You'll heal more quickly."

"I'm really—"

"Rest." Then he and Caleb are gone.

I drift for several hours, and when I wake, it's full dark outside. I'm still alone in the barracks. The courtyard of the First House isn't silent, though, as the sound of high-pitched laughter carries to me on the breeze. I sit up, testing my balance, and find my head clear. Even my shoulder no longer aches, for which I give up a prayer of thanks to the Light.

Sitting in the darkened room, my mind immediately returns to the marauder attack, the wounded woman, the well. What was beneath that well, that she wanted—that all of them wanted to escape there? Some sort of ancient, unused aqueduct, heading out into the marsh? And there were four—no, six women in that one place alone, coming out of the encampment. Was their entire group female? How had they survived without being found out?

With a wry smile, I recognize the irony of this last question, given that I am masquerading as a warrior in a far more public arena. But I can't stay focused on the mysterious women for long. I stand and pull on one of Nazar's long robes, belting it in place to keep it from dragging the ground. The idea of fresh air and the sound of laughter tugs at me, and I move down the silent corridor, all the cubbies empty of warrior knights and their retainers. When I enter the courtyard, I glance up at the lit-up windows of the First House. I can hear the music filtering through them, but the laughter I heard was much closer, and I swing around to see where it came from.

Women stand at a small well with large stone jars. One by one, they lower the jars into the well. These are the house servants, tasked with replenishing the carafes and jugs throughout the castle, and they don't notice me as I sidle closer. Their laughter heals a part of me I'd not thought injured. How long has it been since I've eavesdropped on the casual conversation of my peers? It feels like forever.

And these women *are* my peers, as much as the nobles are above. Far more so, even, given the life I've led. Certainly more so than the fierce women I encountered on the edge of Trilion, at least for the moment.

For the moment...but not for long, I resolve.

I edge closer to where the servants have shed their outer wraps in the warm night air. Within the castle, they will always be hidden in those hooded wraps, their hair tucked back from their faces, their bodies covered from their necks to their toes. The wraps aren't shapeless sacks, but they're modest and distinctive, patterned in bold gold and black, with a fringe of delicate gold chains falling from the crowns of their deep hoods. Beneath them, the women wear long kirtles over their shifts, their sleeves rolled up to free their hands for their work.

"He was sweet and shy, he was," insists one of them now. "Stumbled all over himself, shocked I was there to bathe him."

Another snorts. "I'll take him next, then. The Third House warriors took my presence as their due, and they're all bigger'n the monsters they're banded to, you ask me. Twice as rude too."

That brings more laughter, and the talk runs round the group—most all of it about the men. Who's handsome, who's not, who's cruel or frightening. As I'm beginning to fear I'll be discussed next, one woman pokes her mate. "The Lord Protector had you in his chambers for longer than any of us, this morning. Are you hurt?"

The woman shrugs. She's older, her face lined in the moonlight, her mouth thin. "It was nothing as bad as you're thinking. He wanted me to take on the care of the beast below."

The other women's gasps were audible, and my brows climb. None of the Divhs remain corporeal in this world long enough to eat...otherwise, they'd ravage the countryside. So what sort of beast could Rihad be keeping, and where was "below"?

"You be safe—it could *eat* you—why you, what did you do

wrong?" The servants' words tumble over on themselves, and the older woman holds up her hands.

"It's all right, it's all right. The guards have been called away to handle the incoming warriors, is all. The Second House is sending others. After today, we should expect more from the Third as well."

I freeze. *After today?* Why? Because of the exhibition battle at the coliseum? The marauder attack? The other women titter knowingly but don't speak anything aloud. I clench my hands and strive for patience. There's still too much I don't know!

"But who'll care for the councilors, then?" asks a quiet voice, a woman off to the left of the group. She can't be much older than I am, and her hair's pulled back, revealing a harsh scar beneath her eye. I wince, my own scars at my father's hand beginning to throb as my cheeks flush. Who's harmed this girl so boldly?

The older woman waves a dismissive hand. "They barely eat as it is, and I'm glad to be shut of that job for a while. They ask without asking about all that goes on in the lord's private chambers, but I tell them nothing. What goes on there isn't fit for any eyes that aren't wise or ears that aren't cagey."

"Well, your eyes have seen it all," another servant jokes. "And Light *knows* what your ears have heard."

"My eyes and ears know how to detach from my mouth. It's why I'm still alive, with my tongue still working." The older woman stares around at the others. "You ever find yourself in Lord Rihad's chambers, remember that. He's asked the whole of the council to attend him after the feast tonight, what with that warrior of the Ninth House dead on the ivory road."

I go rigid. The Ninth House?

"Oh no," sighs another. "Not another attack, with the tournament so close. No wonder the councilors have been in a huddle."

I press my lips tight together. There's too much going on in the hidden rooms of the First House that I don't understand, too much I need to know. But I can't swagger into hidden spaces looking for secrets as bold warrior Merritt. He draws the eye wherever he goes. For this work, I need to be invisible.

A loud splash at the well draws all their attention. Almost before I know what I'm doing, my hand darts out as they all turn away. I grab one of their overwraps from the pile and ball it up as best as I can against Nazar's robe. I step quickly backward on kitten feet until I reach the arched barracks entry. Then I turn and flee to our chambers.

Caleb and Nazar aren't there, and I move quickly to our packs, rifling through them to find what I need. A long tunic of dull gray replaces my dark green warrior's garb, and I switch out my heavy breeches for thinner ones I'd worn as I traveled to the tournament. Then I pull out my wig of Lady Talia hair and set it aside. Sure enough, beneath it in the burlap sack, lies a second wig of simply braided hair, this one far more suitable to a young girl—or a servant.

I pull it on, then drag the servant's hooded cloak over my head, arranging the fall of thin gold chains that hang from its crown, smoothing my hair along my neck to hide my scar as best as I can.

I rub my hands down my face. Had the servants worn kohl around their eyes and salve on their lips? I hadn't noticed, and I don't have a glass to apply either with any sort of skill. At least my face isn't too beat up from the day. I slap my palms to my cheeks to give them color and move back outside as silently as possible. Striding quickly, I cross the courtyard and enter the First House. The other serving women would recognize me as an outsider, but I hope in the great celebration that's still carrying on, I might have better luck blending in. Rihad must employ temporary servants from the village, surely. Especially with additional warriors coming in.

Warriors. Like the newly deceased warrior from the Ninth House.

I screw my face up in concentration as I enter the great hall. Unlike the night before, there are no bards holding the attention of the revelers, but several bands of musicians are playing a discordant clash of music in every corner. I see Lord Protector Rihad immediately, and as always, he's attended by a dozen servants, all of them female, all of them dressed like I am. If he doesn't see me directly, I can make it work, I think. I need to get closer, but I could—

"Wine!" A woman jostles into me and would have sent me sprawling had I not had all those years of training in the shadows, hiding from my father's attention. As it is, I hop sideways, banging my hip against the nearest table. I turn and see graceful long fingers tipping a cup precariously toward me. I hastily pull it from the woman's hand.

As yesterday, flagons of wine line every table. I grab the nearest one—it's empty. So's the second and third. By the time I find a flagon and turn around again, the woman is no longer holding her hand out for her cup. Instead, she's pulling down the face of the nearest warrior to kiss him full on the lips.

I stand there, staring dumbly, my eyes impossibly round as I watch Fortiss return the kiss.

The woman is beautiful. Not Elise, but every bit as stunning, she's petite, fair, and dressed in richly embroidered silk. Her golden hair is styled in ornate coils that pour down her back like a frothy avalanche. When she pulls her mouth from Fortiss and laughs, I can see the detailed kohl-work around her eyes, and the soft pink of her lips, still touched with salve despite the wine and kissing. She moves in for another embrace, and I duck my head, keeping my eyes trained on the floor, never mind that they are sparking with rough, angry tears. I hold the cup up and am startled a moment later to hear her laugh.

"Well, then. An even trade."

Instead of merely plucking the cup from my fingers, however, she grabs my wrist as she frees the vessel, turning me smartly to the left. I go pliantly so as not to hurt her, only to realize that she's thrust me into Fortiss's arms—*Fortiss*, who stinks of wine and something sharper, his eyes unfocused and his manner loose.

"A trade I've clearly won," he laughs, before his arm snakes around my back and he pulls me in for a kiss.

A kiss!

I've *never* been kissed before, not like this. Fortiss's mouth is hot, his lips both soft and demanding at once. Something bright and fizzy explodes in my stomach, warming every inch of me, and for one blessed instant, I press back, touching and tasting of a fruit so forbidden that it can only mean my death. My hands reach up of their own accord, and dimly I'm aware that beneath Fortiss's tunic, there is no telltale band wrapped round his bicep—as Caleb's said, he's yet to be awarded a Divh.

Then my brain catches up with my body, and I jerk hard away.

Fortiss looks equally thunderstruck. He blinks and tries to stare at me, but his eyes keep sliding away from my face, still half-hidden by my thick hood. I'm glad of it as I struggle in his arms belatedly, and he opens them to allow me to escape. The blonde girl giggles as I stumble back, then wraps herself expertly around Fortiss's outstretched arm.

"Your service is fully appreciated. Thank you." She dimples at me.

I bow deeply from the waist, still backing away. By some miracle, I don't knock anyone over, and by the time I look up, Fortiss and his woman are gone.

I swing my gaze to the high table.

Unfortunately, so are the Lord Protector and his councilors.

CHAPTER 25

I hurry though the feasting hall, my gaze fixed on the high table. I have to get close to the Lord Protector and his advisors—to learn something, *anything* about this newest death. I know in my gut whatever I discover will shed light on Merritt's killing, and that certainty spurs me on.

They've all disappeared too quickly to have left by traversing the whole hall and exiting its front doors, though. That means there must be some sort of rear exit to the great hall.

I squint as I plow ahead, encumbered by the decorative chains draping down from my hood but not daring to push them out of the way to see more clearly. I think I see the long robe of Councilor Miriam there—no, there!

She moves past a large column, and I glance around, then pick up a large ceramic jar still half-full of water. What I'm going to do with this jar, I can't guess, but I stride forward confidently, balancing it on my hip as I angle through the crowds. I mount the steps to the high table and skirt it, rounding the large column—only to see three archways.

"Perfect," I mutter. I close my eyes and try to calm my mind, Nazar's words coming back to me in sudden clarity. *"The way of the warrior is to blend the body with the spirit and the void."*

My eyes pop open as the sound of metal upon stone grates up from somewhere below, flowing through the third door—at least I think it's the third. The noise doesn't repeat. Hefting the large jar, I angle for that door, slipping into a dark corridor that immediately dampens the sound of the feast behind me.

I blink, becoming accustomed to the gloom as I make my way forward. The shadows are broken by first one torch, then another, the pathway leading down a long corridor and then a winding stair.

Each step makes me surer this isn't the right direction. The Lord Protector would position himself on high, I feel in my bones, not bury himself in the heart of the mountain. Then again, what safer spot could there be for him to seek his councilors' wisdom than holed up in some cave?

Either way, I'm committed to following the stair until it dead ends. As long as I don't leave the staircase, I can't get lost...or so I assure myself.

I trot down more steps, grateful for the occasional torches lit in their sconces. Someone clearly uses this pathway often enough.

The farther I go, however, the faster I move. I need to reach the end of this wrong turn then discover the true path. The path of the warrior.

I grimace. How is Nazar so intimately familiar with that path, anyway, for someone who's never done battle? The priest's words had come through clearly to me while I was practicing with Gent, and his instructions resonated once more in my mind while I'd been fighting. Both times, I'd felt their rightness.

I'd insisted to Caleb that Nazar was only a priest, but...well, he must've watched warriors train at some point, or...or something. Had he been conscripted into the army of the Exalted Imperium as a young man? He says there are no longer any Divhs in the empire outside of the Protectorate, but I can't imagine that's true. As powerful as our Divhs are, surely the Imperial army would have brought some back to defend the emperor, handed down generation to generation until this present day.

But Nazar remains a puzzle. The first time I'd ever seen the priest handle a sword was in the forest clearing after Merritt's death. At the Tenth House, he'd take long walks in the forest with only his walking stick, but he'd never attacked any animal and certainly no person for as long as I'd known him. How can a man be so skilled in a thing yet never speak of it or seek to practice?

It *can't* be that he just had learned about fighting, somewhere in the distant past, part of his role as a priest of the Light. That he was merely a teacher and not one truly skilled. It can't. Can it?

My mind rushes on in time with my feet, and eventually, the fiery sconces grow farther apart. I find myself hurrying forward to reach the glow of the next one, until finally...there isn't a next one.

I slow as a wide apron of stone spreads out from the base of the stairs. Here, the space smells cool and damp, and several water jars are lined against the wall, exactly like my own. With the clatter of my feet stilled, however, I can hear the rush of water falling in the distance.

I frown, looking down at my heavy jar. If there's water falling close by, why would anyone carry more down?

I lean down and settle the jar on the floor next to the wall and wait another few moments while my eyes adjust to the dim light. It's clear this isn't the Lord Protector's private rooms, yet someone has been down here recently. The cobblestones have been swept free of dust, and there are no cobwebs hanging in the space. No creatures at all that I can hear, in fact, and in a sheltered space such as this, there's always something trying to wedge in.

Eventually, another vat becomes visible in the gloom, a wide, well-like container, also made of stone. I tiptoe up to it as if it'll bite me. When it doesn't, I reach out, my fingers skimming over a thin lid of stone. It's the work of a moment to shove that lid free a bit. Immediately, I'm overcome with the scent of ginseng, bloodroot, and sage, plus the heavier, exotic notes of jasmine. I frown. A healing salve? I reach down and feel the thick paste, scooping up a thick dollop. I know what the water is for now—it's to thin this muck.

But thin it for whom?

Something shifts in the darkness up ahead, and I freeze. My warrior band heats, and I rub my arm, my gaze pinning on the deeper gloom. It doesn't seem wise to shout "who's there?" yet it's almost impossible not to. Still, I haven't come down all these stairs for nothing. I want to know what's in those shadows—need to know.

I peer into the gloom and step forward. With each stride away from the last flickering sconce, the space grows darker, the shadows blending together. I reach my hands out in front of me, my steps short and cautious. In another five paces, my fingers brush against something smooth and metallic before I ever see it. Bars.

I frown. Bars?

Reaching high, I feel where the metal poles have been driven into the ceiling, then I follow the line all the way to the floor. But they're not meant to hamper an average-sized person's movement, it appears. Each of the bars is over two handspans distant from its neighbor, but they're as thick as a man's leg. In tracing their vertical length, I realize the roof of the cavern has dropped low while the floor has risen up, narrowing the space where I'm standing. I'm on the edge of a precipice. As I peer through the bars, I realize something else.

There *is* light, after all. It's so dim as to seem unreal, but it casts a soft blue haze over the space beyond the bars. At once, I'm reminded of Gent's home plane, but I chase the thought from my mind. In another moment, I realize that the apron of rock extends farther about ten paces. Beyond that, there is a fathomless pool of darkness. Some sort of cave, I think, a great open center in the heart of the mountain.

I slip between the bars and drop to my knees, not trusting myself to walk. Crawling, though, I can manage. I edge toward the dark abyss and know immediately when the overhang above me opens up—the light is distinctly brighter here. I look up, and up still farther, and see it.

An oculus set high above seems slightly less black than the surrounding space. It's full night now, so there's nowhere near enough light to see by, but just knowing that light had been here, at one point, and that it would be again, is enough to slow the hammering of my heart.

I inch forward to peer over the edge of the precipice.

An enormous cavern stretches before me, as broad as the tournament field and as deep as the coliseum is tall. Beneath me, down the side of the rocky cliff, something glistens thickly—and the scent is clear. Salve. The salve from that large vat is being poured over the side of this precipice, to coat the rock wall. There must be a reason for that...

A noise, a scrape, and I freeze in place. There's something down there.

At that moment, a flash of light scores across the oculus, then another. I yelp and stagger back, lunging for the nearest bar, before the sound of explosions peppering the sky registers in my mind. *Fireworks.* Lord Rihad is setting off fireworks. Bursts of white and red and yellow are illuminating the sky visible through the oculus in quick bursts.

Something shifts again in the cavern over the edge of my rocky cliff, and despite my hammering heart, I creep forward, once more on my hands and knees, until I can barely peek over the lip of the precipice. Another burst of fireworks erupts, and I glance up instinctively.

When I drop my gaze again...I'm staring into an enormous eye.

With a choked-off scream, I flop on my back, but it's as if my arms and legs can no longer move correctly. I sprawl like a bug, trying to gain purchase as I watch a long, vicious head angle to the side and crane up, stretching toward the oculus. The sound of metal scraping on stone rattles through the cavern, and the head snaps down again, rearing back with a slide of creaking scales to focus on me.

By this time and by mere luck, I've managed to scuttle my way back to the bars, and I lurch through them as the creature's muzzle peels back from tree-trunk teeth to snap at me. The sound makes my ears ring, but I can't speak, can't move.

Another burst of fireworks lights up the space beyond, and the head twitches back skyward. I sense more than see the eye focusing on the ceiling, straining toward the distant lights.

Then, in the beam of another soaring stream of fire, that eye fixes on me.

It's a lizard, I realize. A lizard with *wings*. A dragon like those in the sandy desert of the south, I think, though a hundred times larger than any of those dragons should be. Its head is deep bluish-black. Its snout is lined with burnished gold, and it has not one pair of eyes but two, angled in a sharp slant, each of them gold with black pupils and more than half my height. Sharp, vicious horns spike up from its temples. The dragon's neck is thick and sinuous, the better to balance its head, but that's all I can see of the creature. It doesn't lift its wings, though I can only imagine how broad its span must reach. Even what I can see of the lizard is achingly beautiful, its predatory profile magnificent in another flash of fireworks, its eyes furious and intelligent. All four of them.

My mind suddenly flares to life again.

"You're a *Divh*," I whisper. The truth of it is obvious, but I can't reconcile what my eyes are showing me with what I believe—know—to be truth. "But Divhs don't stay here, they can't... they don't stay here. They go home."

The dragon simply watches me with two of its massive eyes, head cocked, as if it can understand my words.

Despite the danger, I slip through the bars again, approaching the great cavern on wobbly legs. The creature shuffles back—whether to lure me out or give me space, I don't know. When I reach the edge of the precipice, another flash of fireworks overhead throws the entire basin into bright light for an extended moment, and I see the great iron shackle holding the enormous dragon in place. The chain is long, and the cavern immense, so the creature could...possibly...fly. It just can't leave.

Then the light flashes again, and I see something else.

"Your *wing*," I gasp—for I see it now. The right wing of this enormous, majestic dragon looks like it's been slashed to shreds, its delicate leather torn and scarred. The wing hangs awkwardly from its body, and as I stare, the creature huffs a warning, with a trickle of sulphury smoke streaming up from its muzzle.

A second later, it lunges at me, and I bleat, scrambling backward from the snapping teeth, barely missing being made the creature's next meal.

"I'm sorry!" I manage, trying to stuff my heart back down my throat. The snap was a warning I know, a warning not to get too close, not to stare too hard.

A warning I'm happy to heed.

And yet... "How is it you're here?" Unreasoning sorrow touches my voice. The dragon shuffles a few short steps below me, hauling the heavy chain with it, but the chain doesn't look so sturdy as that. It's not what's holding the dragon still. The bird's damaged wing is doing that. Or...something even worse.

"Who did this to you?" I whisper, and in the darkness, my hiss seems to carry deeper into the cavern. But the creature doesn't turn again at my voice, doesn't react to me at all. It's not bonded to me, like Gent. It's not my place to know its secrets or its—

Her.

The thought is so clear in my mind that I fall back again against the stone precipice, trembling like a bug once more. I stare straight up into the far-off oculus, wondering what just happened, if anything just happened. Wondering if I've been given the precious right to know a new Divh's thoughts—a right that's not possible, like this Divh was not possible, this bold and mighty dragon, lifting its wings below—

Her wings.

The words cascade through me, blasting every other thought away. And as I stare, I see an image of the dragon in her full glory, soaring toward the sun, her great wings pumping with razor-sharp spikes at the tips, each of them a separate spear, her neck outstretched, her breast as blue as raw sapphires shot through with ebony fire.

The image disappears again. I can sense nothing more from the creature, the Divh, the immense dragon in the cavern below me. I don't know why she's here, but something very wrong is happening in the underbelly of the First House for this to be possible. Something wrong and dark. I know so little about the mighty, extraordinary Divhs, but I do know this: you can't keep them in this world. It's not their world. They will die if they stay too long... or they *should* die.

I creep once more to the edge of the stony outcropping, staring down. Though the fireworks still explode overhead, I can no longer see the Divh, can no longer hear the snap of her teeth. I should go, and yet, a sudden aching maw of loneliness opens up within me.

Forgettable, forgotten.

How can I leave her here?

"I'll come back," I whisper. "As soon as I am able. I'll come back, and we can..." I break off, feeling foolish. This creature doesn't know me, won't care if I come back. I am as nameless to her as to whomever brings the large jars of salve to coat the rock wall, no doubt to allow her to soothe the pain of her broken wing. She won't miss me.

But still, I'll definitely return for her. Somehow.

No Divh should be held captive like this.

There's no further sound from the cavern below, and at length, I retreat back through the bars. I've no intention of picking up my half-filled jar of water and lugging it up the stairs again, but perhaps there's another one that's not so heavy. As soon as I can see by the far-off torchlight again, I go to the jars lining the walls. I lift the lid of the nearest one and stop.

The jar is filled with small metallic balls. I pick one up, feeling the weight of it. It's lead. I half turn. The bars are made of lead as well. Did lead have some sort of effect on the Divh? Is that what her shackles are made of? I think about her face next to mine, staring at me with her huge eyeballs. If I'd lined my pockets with lead, maybe thrown some down to bounce off the sloping rock wall, would she have left me alone completely? If they were sending down servants to ladle the salve over the cliff, that made sense.

But forget about the salve. What do you feed a dragon whose *foot* is chained to the floor? The very thought is preposterous. Dragons are made to hunt, to fly. Not to eat leavings tossed over a cliff.

How long has she been here?

The other jars are empty, and I realize I can't leave mine here, not half-full like this. It might be noticed. I also don't want to dump its contents over the side like so much garbage.

I sigh, suddenly wanting to be free of this place, these bars, the extraordinarily beautiful Divh tied up like a cow in the cavern below. Something is desperately wrong in the First House. Something that has led to the death of the Ninth House warrior...the death of my own brother. And I have a feeling that the truth of it all lies in one of the other two doors off the great hall. Doors I must enter, if I ever want to learn the truth.

Reluctantly, I pick up my heavy jar of water and trudge back up the long staircase.

CHAPTER 26

For a scant moment as I emerge from the dragon's lair, I entertain the possibility of exploring another passageway. A quick glance around advises against that strategy. Guards now stand at the entrances of all three doors, including mine. Grateful that I've lugged the jar all the way back up, I duck and hurry past the guards like a scuttling beetle. They don't spare me the slightest glance, but I only breathe easier when I've cleared the high table once more and set down my jar next to several others.

The Feast Hall is nearly empty, the revelers apparently having taken themselves outside to enjoy the fireworks. Servants swarm the tables and floors, cleaning away the leftovers into large burlap sacks. I don't know if these scraps will go to feed animals or people, or if they're intended for the glorious dragon below. Anger burns in my gut—no Divh should be so constrained.

I lift the hem of my overwrap to hasten out of the feast hall just as a knot of guards stride in. All of them are First House men in gold-and-black livery.

"Wine!" barks the man in the lead, and my heart stops in my throat. *Fortiss*, no longer appearing anywhere close to drunk. He jabs a finger at me and two of the closest servants, both women. "Wine and whatever is left of the bread and sweetfruits. Quickly."

He sharpens his glance on me, and I lean down to scoop up a large mason jar that stinks of red wine. The other women grab platters of untouched bread and fruit, and we follow in the wake of the guards. As far as I can see, Fortiss is the only nobleman among them, but I don't recognize the guards as his personal attendants. Has he been summoned by Lord Rihad?

Perhaps this night's work hasn't been in vain after all.

Once more we traverse the steps and pass the high table, but instead of angling right, toward the door that leads to the dragon's cavern, we move beneath the leftmost arch. Fortiss's pace is a long-legged, angry stride, and the women and I have to trot to keep up, no small feat with our long cloaks. The other two women are ahead of me and don't speak, nor do they look at me sidelong. I get the sense they don't know each other either, which is a blessing. The castle must be teeming with villagers to assist the First House with these enormous feasts. For Fortiss to have summoned us so carelessly means that we might not see anything interesting, but at least I can discover one thing of value: where this doorway leads.

We encounter more stairs, several short flights curling up into the mountain, finally leading to a long corridor. I stare, shocked to see that the corridor empties out into open sky at the far end—some sort of observation deck that clearly looks out over the marshlands. A breeze flows in from the deck, and as we turn away from the open doorway, I see that the airflow continues through a set of high windows at the opposite end of the hall.

"Faster," grunts one of the guards, and I stiffen, realizing I'd fallen behind as I stared gape-mouthed at the open deck. I hasten forward, falling in line with the women ahead of me, and we soon cut to the right into another archway. Two guards stand on either side of the arch, and my stomach knots anew. If I'm caught...

But I can't be caught. I won't.

The arched corridor angles around, opening into several small antechambers, until it empties into a room dominated by a large fireplace. The flames within roar, and smoke licks up a slender chimney despite the warmth of the night. Rihad is surrounded by his councilors, everyone standing except Rihad himself. They turn to observe Fortiss striding in, then their eyes fall on us as we slow.

"Put the food and drink on the table and leave." The voice is authoritative, crisp and certain...and female. Miriam. We all rush to comply, and I sweep the room hurriedly with my gaze, trying to glean any secrets from its very walls.

I'm almost to the door again when I glance back a final time toward the fire.

And then I see it.

Two great urns stand on either side of the fire, stone cylinders fashioned like quivers for arrows. But while the vases are of stone—the arrows that fill them aren't. Their feathers stand out stiffly from slender shafts—all of them the same color. A dead, flat gray. Identical to the broken arrow still hidden in my bags.

My gaze darts from the left urn, which bristles with arrows, to the right, which appears to be only half-full. *Half-full.*

I blink, staring at the urn as if it holds the key to everything... and yet—how? How could that be possible? Only one arrow was loosed to take down Merritt, one deadly arrow of gray, but it seems like there are several missing here. Is that the case, or were they always arranged so haphazardly? My eyesight dims, as if to ward off what I'm seeing, what I'm clearly seeing, and my heart seems to curl up into a hard little stone in my chest. Could this be? Could the First House be behind the death of Merritt after all—and not a lesser house?

They're just arrows, I remind myself sternly. Gray arrows made with care but gray all the same. Unhoused. Anonymous. They could be used for anything.

But why are they here?

The girl behind me nearly knocks me over in her haste, and I hustle out of the room as quickly as we've come, past the guards and down the many flights of stairs. When we reemerge into the great hall, however, I dally at the high table as the other girls flee, then grab another jar of wine.

Resolutely, I turn back.

The race back up the steps is short, and the guards at the archway don't block my path, not when I'm merely carrying another jar of wine. As far as they know, I've been ordered to do it. But after I pass them and turn the first corner, I slow my steps to a crawl. As I creep forward, I can hear Fortiss speaking. He's making a report, I think. I keep the jar with me in case I'm caught and hold its cool stone against my chest to quiet my heart's thundering.

I'm all the way up to the final archway when Fortiss's words finally reach me. "All the First House warriors have reported their tallies. The Tournament of Gold will see five more entrants in the coming days, and that's all. As you have foreseen, Lord Protector, the doomed warriors from the Ninth and Eleventh Houses are dead. The newer delegations from the Fourth and Fifth have been plagued as well. Those houses are down to six warriors apiece."

I jolt, momentarily frozen in wonder. Foreseen, not commanded? What is this? And, worse...the Eleventh has been struck as well?

I set the wine jug down carefully, silently, deep in the shadowed alcove. Inside Rihad's chambers, the council erupts in indignation, peppering Fortiss with questions. *How can there be these attacks on so many warriors? How have the marauders grown so bold, so quickly?*

I edge forward, emboldened by the councilors' distraction as Rihad lets their outrage swell. A second later, I can peek into the private chamber once more. My attention fixes immediately on the grand fireplace. The flames leap in the grate, and in their flickering light, I see once more the two stout urns of arrows.

And though I can't be wholly sure, can't say without a doubt that these truly are arrows in those urns and not simply decorative shafts, in my heart, I know the truth. Rihad is to blame for my brother's death. Rihad pulled those arrows free and handed them to one of his warrior knights, signing my brother's death writ as surely as if he'd wielded quill and ink. My brother and apparently other innocent warriors as well.

I stare at the urn half-filled with arrows. Who else will bleed by Rihad's decree, I wonder...who else will die?

Fortiss continues, "No further damage has been caused to the southern delegations so far, though we're watching the Third House's newest company carefully as you've requested. I should be out there with them."

"You had your chance to track down the marauders, Fortiss," Rihad says dismissively. "Your place is here."

My brows shoot up at that, but Fortiss doesn't falter. "Very well, Lord Protector. The bards have confirmed that the Ninth has no additional warrior to send. They'll retain one warrior alone in the Tournament. The Eleventh, none."

"Lord Beryl is too old to have another son, and too stupid to bend the old ways." Rihad leans back in his chair. "The Twelfth?"

"The bard assigned to scout the Twelfth hasn't yet returned." Fortiss lifts a hand, drops it. "Lord Orlof's son is only fourteen, though. He won't venture forth. There will be no further entrants beyond the southern parties, and they are expected tomorrow, plus the five remaining warriors from the northern houses. The tallies are complete. The north is now fielding thirty warriors, the south twenty-five. We're lucky that the Tenth survived the attack you feared for them and that I should have stopped, but..." He hesitates, and Rihad narrows his eyes.

"But what?" the Lord Protector demands, and I wonder the same. And more to the point, *should have stopped*?

Fortiss remains resolute. "Lord Merritt still harbors deep anger over the attack his house sustained. He believes there's retribution to be had."

I watch as Rihad's eyes narrow. "Against whom?"

"He doesn't say, but he refuses to accept the idea that it was marauders who made the attempt on his life."

I pin my gaze to Rihad as he considers Fortiss's words. The Lord Protector's face is an impenetrable mask, but I can see the fury hidden there. He has the same look my father always wears when he looks at me, a rage too cold to boil over, but nevertheless resting just below the surface. "And what did you say to him when he raised these doubts?"

"I told him he was wrong," Fortiss says flatly, and my brows shoot up. He did no such thing...did he? I try to remember everything I said and all of Fortiss's careful words—both to me and to me-as-Merritt, but my mind is a jumble.

"Good." Rihad nods. "You've done well. You're nearing your redemption."

If anything, Fortiss's body seems to stiffen further. "I'm honored to serve."

He says more, but the roaring in my mind is finally strong enough to drown out anything else. I know the truth of what I'm seeing, finally. The Lord Protector of the First House won't offer me justice for the death of my brother after all. Because he's done more than *foresee* such death, no matter what Fortiss says, what he believes.

Lord Rihad had *commanded* the attack on Merritt. Possibly even commanded his death. Not the Second House, not marauders. It doesn't matter what soldier loosed that arrow, it was shot from Rihad's bow, as sure as if he'd drawn the string back himself. I have no doubt of it anymore.

And not my brother alone, but warriors from other houses as well, some with no more than one warrior to offer, like the Eleventh. What is the point of it? The worst hit seemed to be those houses bordering the Exalted Imperium, but we are buried deep in the mountains, difficult to reach. Our warriors would have posed no threat in the tournament; far from it. The Divhs of the Ninth, Tenth, Eleventh, and Twelfth Houses are smaller, and our training nonexistent. The threat to the Protectorate was never so great from the Exalted Imperium, after all. It was the right place for the smallest Houses to be stationed.

So why would Rihad have taken such a path...?

My head continues to spin, but some tiny ember of self-protection flares to life as movement stirs in the room beyond. Fortiss is leaving, the councilors all beginning to mill about as well. They're leaving! I have no time to flee ahead of them. I dart into one of the small antechambers off the corridor, pressing against the wall as the lot of them passes. First Fortiss with his phalanx of guards in attendance. Then, more slowly, achingly slowly, the councilors.

They leave by ones and twos, and I wedge myself more thoroughly into the crevice in the antechamber, grateful for the darkness. Outrage and grief surges up within me at equal turns, until I'm wrung out.

Someone's still in the room beyond, however, so I can't leave. The conversation remains animated, Rihad talking to someone I can't discern. I dare not venture forth, not when I have no idea where the guards are. Better to wait until everything falls silent and the Lord Protector himself has gone. Then, with any luck, the guards will be gone as well, and I can exit safely.

I close my eyes and steady my breathing, trying to put everything in its own separate box. Lord Rihad has commanded the killing of warriors—but the houses he has chosen don't make sense. Targeting weak houses such as the Ninth, Tenth and Eleventh cannot help him...can it?

My hands clench as I force myself to the next subject. Was Merritt killed to prevent him from coming to the tournament—or to prevent him from buying more soldiers? Either way, such a murder was wholly unnecessary. Gent as he originally appeared was a rabbit compared to the wolves I've seen so far. If my brother had been foolish enough to enter, he and his Divh would have been defeated within the first round of the tournament, at no time a threat or a risk to the outcome.

A pang of misery rings through me. Merritt would have caused no harm...no harm!

There must be a reason, though. Such a horrific offense could not have been an act of random brutality. I need to *think*.

Despite my scowl, wetness scores my cheeks, and I press my fingers to the swollen skin beneath my eyes, willing the unwanted tears to stop. My brother had been so filled with joy at the idea of seeing the First House and competing with his equals amid all the pomp and finery of the tournament. For him to have been shot down so needlessly...

Move on, I command myself. But the inconvenience of grief won't listen. I lean back in the darkness and let the tears stream down my face. Tears for a boy who would never see the coliseum of the Tournament of Gold. Tears for warriors I have never met, ripped from this life and their families, their Divhs dying as they took their last breaths, disappearing into the mists.

I wait and wait, and gradually, all goes still. And still I wait more. I cannot be found, I know. I cannot be found. Far better to stay here all night than allow myself to be taken, discovered, when I've already learned so much. I will simply rest here, in my quiet nook. Rest my eyes but briefly, my breathing soft and still, my body heavy, silent...hidden...

An unfamiliar sound jerks me awake. I nearly gasp then snap my mouth shut. I'm trapped in the antechamber, still wedged in the darkness. *How long have I been sleeping?*

Hastily, I wipe my hands over my face, patting my robes back in place, and ease forward out of my corner. The roar of the fire still sounds from the other room, but there is no other sound. It's never wise to leave a fire unattended, but Rihad's blaze was contained in a deep and generous fireplace, so perhaps he's gone as well.

I poke my head out of my hiding place and peer into the darkness. There's silence all around me, the only light coming from the flickering shadows in the other room, and I breathe a tiny sigh of relief.

Then Lord Rihad's voice echoes through the silence. "It is done," he says.

I freeze.

Another voice sounds then. Its words twist and curl around on themselves, some language I cannot hope to guess at. Almost against my will, I find my body turning toward Rihad's private council chamber. I bite my lip to quiet the chattering of my teeth as

I move through the shadows. Finally, I reach the edge of the last archway and realize there are no guards there anymore.

There's no one except Rihad, standing, hands clasped behind his back, staring into the fire.

Only, it's not a normal fire anymore.

The flames that leap from the blaze are stained a deep crimson, throwing the entire chamber into shades of red and black. And in the center of the fire is a twisting, roiling column of smoke, with something slithering and hissing at its base. It's a figure, I realize with surprise, who turns to face Rihad as I watch. It wears a cloak of fire, its head shrouded in darkness. Then it speaks in a raspy voice not unlike my own, its words picking out through the feral muttering of the creatures at its feet.

"The way must be made clear," the voice breathes, and the foreignness of it arrows through me, making my bones ache. "Speed is of the essence."

What way, speed for what?

Rihad merely nods, as if he's expected this. His words are placating. "The entire eastern border is already opened. The tournament calls all the warriors from every corner of the Protectorate, and when they assemble, those already controlled by my house will far outnumber the rest. We will be ready to aid you in your time of need."

Aid *who?* Questions crowd into my mind as the thing inside the fire changes aspect. It lengthens, still cloaked in fire, but now with arms that reach out wide as if in exultation. A face emerges from the hood for only a moment—a face? Or a reptilian maw? Then it retreats again, too quickly for me to get a fix on its features. Before the creature, Rihad falls to his knees, his arms also outstretched.

"See that you—" The fire demon stops midsentence and lifts its hooded head, staring out beyond Rihad...toward *me*. Unconsciously, I take a step back, deeper into the shadows, but the damage has been done.

"There's no one," Rihad begins, but he's back on his feet again, and I know his half-hearted protests won't last. "No one—"

"A female!" spits the creature. "I can smell the stink of her."

I turn, hiking up my dress as I run. My sight is still dazzled by the firelight, and I smack off one side of the archway, the sound unmistakable as Rihad roars in anger behind me. No guards come running, though—there's only a single set of footsteps.

I turn down the long corridor and flee headlong toward the open doors at its end. I glimpse night sky beyond. As I run, I bend forward at the waist as Gent has done, the awkward position possible only because my right hand has knotted up my skirts to my waist.

My legs pump, eating up the distance. I hear Rihad's sharp command behind me, but he's too far—too far! He cannot catch me; he won't catch me.

I burst out onto the wide veranda and the empty dark sky glares down at me, neither moon nor star evident in the inky blackness. Chairs and tables attest to the veranda's use as an observation point, and in another three strides, I am almost at its edge.

Without thinking, without even breathing, I leap up onto one of the chairs, then onto a large table, gaining speed as I hurtle toward the brink of the overlook, my left arm outstretched, my hand reaching, straining, so much like Merritt had done for so many years that I once again see his face, hear his laughing cry.

I catapult over the edge and then I'm completely flailing, my legs suddenly churning though there's nowhere else for me to run but onto the air itself. The word on my lips is torn from me in a ragged gasp as I plummet toward the marshy ground far, far below.

Gent!

CHAPTER 27

As I hurtle toward the open plain, I sense the air around me snap in the dark, the impact lifting me on an invisible current that has me soaring *up*, not down, *up* for a precious moment more. Then an enormous hand snatches me out of the sky and Gent's body curls around me, the two of us now a heavy stone tossed off a cliff.

Instantly, I realize my mistake. Gent is no longer the giant he was with Merritt—he's three times larger now. The moment he lands, the entire valley will quake with a crash loud enough to stretch to the Sounding Sea.

But Gent continues to soar up, not down, somehow gaining speed instead of losing it, and when he does finally hit the ground running, there is no rumble and roar but merely the sound of his full-throated laughter. I peel my eyes open and realize we're no longer in the darkness of the mountain and marsh, but on the side of a rolling hill, racing through a midnight-and-white patch of flowers.

Run! Gent cries in my mind. He's racing and I'm racing with him, his hand cradled around me. I feel twin flames of sorrow and joy coursing through him. He *caught* me, I think his thoughts, bracing myself in his grip. He did—he finally did.

He couldn't catch Merritt, but he caught *me*.

He saved me.

Gent races into the night until even he tires, wide looping turns over endless hills bathed in summer sunlight. I don't want to leave, but know I have to get back to the First House, to tell Nazar what I've learned, to warn...

My mind is a jumble, all the events of the day crashing together, especially my encounter with the female marauders on the outskirts of Trilion. Who were they? Was it truly only gold they'd stolen from the encampment? Could they be attached to that...that *thing* that Rihad was talking to, in the center of the fire? Were there more of them, fighting in the shadows, all of them women?

Before I can form the words to ask Gent to return me to the First House, my glorious Divh is swooping his arm down, down, dropping me once more to the cool meadow grass. I stand, so dizzy I can barely breathe, and his finger nudges me with what I suspect he believes is a gentle push—

I sprawl face-first into the mist-dampened dirt.

Dirt. Not grass. Not flowers. Dirt.

The world around me suddenly prickles with humidity, warmer and so much louder than Gent's meadow with the sounds of insects and chirping birds.

I'm not in the First House courtyard, I know immediately. I'm not anywhere near the First House. I struggle against the urge to rise quickly to my knees and instead lie still, breathing shallowly, smelling the mist in the air, feeling the cool, broken earth beneath my fingers.

As my senses gradually acknowledge the world around me, I hear the crash and rumble of falling water, and experience a wave of sick certainty about where I am: the falls that Caleb had pointed out to me, when we'd approached the First House gates. I'm nearly *two miles* from those gates, I think in sudden horror. Gent has dropped me in the middle of *nowhere*. How am I going to get back to the castle before dawn, before the next fight, before...

Then, over the mutter of insects and the crash of water and the pounding of my own pulse in my ears, I hear something else. Laughter. Voices.

Women's voices.

Slowly now, with infinite care, I lift my body from the damp earth. I stand, getting my bearings. The voices are coming from a thick knot of trees ahead of me, but there's no flickering fire to light my way. Instead they float, disembodied on the lifting mist, at times so quietly I think I must have imagined them. But no—no. There they are again. I take a slow step forward then another.

Cautiously, painstakingly, I inch forward, pausing every time the voices fall away. I can't see much of anything, and my clothes are already sodden from the mist in the air, but I decide not to shuck the heavy servant's robe, contenting myself only with pushing my hood back to clear the infernal chains from my eyes. If these are the women from the marauders' camp, and they almost certainly are, then being dressed as a woman will serve me far better than—

The sharp chill of a blade presses against my temple, and I stop short as a voice hisses in my ear. A female voice. "Not a word, girl, you understand?"

I nod quickly, remaining entirely still as I'm searched with quick, efficient hands. I have no weapons on me, for which I give silent thanks, but then the dissatisfied grunt of my captor chases even that small relief away. Did women typically approach this campsite armed? And why would they approach it at all?

With a second grunt, the woman reaches for my arm and tugs me forward. She appears to have no need for light and walks quickly and confidently through the thick trees. The sound of crashing water grows stronger at first, then dies away, and I realize it was only by chance that I landed in the place where I could hear anyone talking. Chance, or more likely, Gent—who read the uppermost questions in my mind and put me in the exact place I could resolve those questions, instead of the safety of the First House courtyard.

Clearly, I need to think more careful thoughts with my Divh going forward. Assuming I get the opportunity.

We step into a clearing, but by the time we do, all is silent. I squint, trying to see in the gloom, but there is no campfire, no shadows of women huddled together. My captor also stands quietly beside me, so still that if my arm wasn't being held by her, I'd doubt she was there at all.

Then something shifts in the darkness behind us, and a soft whistle breaks the stillness. An eerie voice floats out of the gloom, thick with an accent I can't place, but an accent I'm certain I've heard in recent days. "She wasn't followed?"

"She was not," confirms the woman beside me. Her voice is flat, with notes of Trilion's broad accent, very different from the other's.

"You're dressed as a servant of the First House. Why are you here?"

The question is bold, abrupt, and I scramble for a moment, thinking how best to answer. But I am too disoriented, too exhausted, really, to do anything other than speak my truth. It's been so long since I was able to do it. And here in this disembodied forest, with darkness all around, I find the words come more easily.

"I am Talia of the Tenth House," I say simply.

The next command is spoken in a language I don't know, but what's left of my hair is pulled back, a hand clapped over my mouth. "Careful now," the woman beside me hisses in my ear, her anger as cold as the blade of her knife. "You'll march, you'll not say a word, and maybe you'll live."

I don't give the woman the benefit of another nod, but she pulls her hand away from my mouth and our trek begins anew, this time toward the falls. We make it there in a matter of minutes, and as we step into the clearing near the rocks, I finally can see. The line of women is still almost invisible, wraiths disappearing behind the falling water to what I now realize is a cavern of some sort. We don't walk for long, though, once under the cover of stone. After a few turns deeper into the cave, a flame is struck.

That sudden light blinds me after so many minutes in the dark. I flinch away briefly before my captor pushes me forward.

The flame lights a small fire in the center of the cavern, and there rests a familiar figure, the injured marauder from the attack in Trilion. Her leg is no longer bandaged by my green sash, though I notice that sash is now wrapped around her wrist. She's wearing a fresh robe, cut down the middle, and I can see the bandages at her shoulder as well.

She's not the only woman at the fire, though. Another one reclines an arm's length away, beside a large earthenware bowl that steams with a smell I don't recognize. Soup? Medicine? Either way, it's not the bowl that captures my attention most fully about this woman—but three entirely different details.

First, she's wearing a large scabbard strapped to her back, the hilt of a longsword protruding up from it, even in the relative safety of the cavern. Second, her face is marked with lines of war paint, the likes of which I have only seen on male warriors—warriors represented in paintings of the far distant past, celebrating the battles of the Western Realms.

And third, the woman's belly is swollen heavy with child.

I know what it is to be gaped at, and I don't wish to do the marauder any dishonor. Instead, I take all these truths into account at a glance then return my gaze to the woman I'd helped by the well. She stares steadily back at me. Unlike the pregnant woman, she's not merely a warrior of these people, I decide. She's their leader.

"You'll heal," I say simply, my words so calm and assured they bring a smile to her face.

"I'll heal," she agrees. "Thanks in no small part to you. You could have brought the others back to that well, easily and quickly enough. It was built at a time when far more water rushed over these lands. The chute that leads away from it is straight and offers no place to make a stand until it empties out into a far ravine. We would have been killed well before we ever reached the surface."

I don't move, don't nod, as if of course I wouldn't have

betrayed her and her people in such a way. In truth, it never occurred to me to bring the force of the guards and warriors back to that well. Were this woman my true enemy, I would have failed my house beyond redemption.

But this woman, I sense, is anything but my enemy.

She continues, "Instead, we ran free, and you returned to your exalted procession, riding all the way to the First House. Not as Talia of the Tenth House, we've learned, but as the warrior son Merritt. A warrior son bonded to a Divh, by all accounts."

The woman beside me hisses in derision. "Gods in service to fools."

"Yet here is a woman claiming her place among them." The leader gestures, and the woman beside me claps her hand to my left arm, below my shoulder, searching but not squeezing tight. For once, there's no pain, no bolt of agony at the sentient band being touched. Still, even through the heavy servant's robe, there's also no mistaking that I do, in fact, wear the band. The marauder gives a tight nod to her leader, who smiles with satisfaction. "And not an idle claim, it would seem. Stranger still."

I keep my voice even. "No stranger than a group of women without a single man to protect them, harrying the edges of the greatest tournament in Protectorate. No stranger than a band of marauders who, if the stories are true, are possessed of demons from the Western Realms, a harbinger of even greater evil that's to come."

That revelation sparks grim laughter in group. I glance around, my vision sharper now that my eyes have adjusted to the gloom. There are maybe twenty women in this cavern...and not only women. I see girls, too, some not even as old as I am. Their eyes are wide and searching as they stare at me, as if they can't believe what they're seeing, can't believe that someone like me exists.

I know the feeling.

Before me, the leader of these women and girls tilts her head, eyeing me shrewdly.

"It seems we are at an impasse then, Talia of the Tenth. But we hold the strength here. We could kill you and drop your body at the gates of the First House, a testament to our demons' strength, and none would be the wiser. Why shouldn't we?"

I take in these words, but without the fear that should attend them. Because these women are hiding out in secret, brandishing long swords, their faces streaked with war paint. They're terrorizing the encampments at the edges of the grandest tournament in the Protectorate, hiding beneath a roaring waterfall, and living free without the protection or aid of men. This isn't merely unheard of in the Protectorate, it's heresy. Blasphemy. Sacrilege.

And it's not all that different from what I am doing.

"You could kill me," I agree. "And dump my body to cause panic and unrest. But there wouldn't be so much unrest as you maybe expect. Warriors are dying on the road to the Tournament of Gold, more every day. Darkness flows from the west on the whispers of bards and the slithering tongues of creatures in the fire."

Someone shifts in the back of the room. "What's this you've heard?" comes the sharp demand, but I ignore it, my eyes only for the leader.

"And so, instead of killing me, you can tell me why *you've* come to Trilion, where all the eyes of the Protectorate are focused. You're healthy, strong. Well fed." Once again, I cast my gaze around the stone chamber, taking in each of them, their fierce expressions and set jaws. Then I nod to the pregnant warrior. "Safe enough in your center that you choose to bring life into this world. There's no need for you to cause disruption at the Tournament of Gold, merely for the sport of looting. I don't care if it was gold in that packet you smuggled out or something far more valuable. You don't need it. Why are you here?"

The woman besides me grunts with appreciation. "Not completely an idiot, then," she observes drily.

"My name is Syril," the leader says, and I can finally place her unique accent. It's the same resonant inflection that the tall warriors of the Eighth house used. This woman is from the western borders of the Protectorate. "Marta, beside you, is my second."

She gestures around the cavern. "These women who live and hunt with me, we are the Savasci. Some of us came to this life by choice, eager to hunt and fight and stand beneath a sun that doesn't seek to keep us in shadow. Some were pushed into the fold by the blows of our supposed betters and the damning silence of our own kind. But all of us value our lives, and we value the soul of this land. There are battles and then there are wars. We choose both carefully and with purpose."

She leans forward, staring intently "How did you come to choose yours, Talia of the Tenth?"

Clearly, I wasn't going to get any answers until I gave a few of my own.

For the second time since coming to Trilion, I tell the tale of my journey to the Tournament of Gold—or most of it. I speak of Gent, and Merritt, and the push for soldiers, honor, and even vengeance. But I don't share the shame of being firstborn and female, not even to these women. They might guess my shame—might even understand it, living as they do. But that disgrace is still a guttering heap within me, and it will do me no good to stir those ashes here.

When I finish, the marauder at my side, Marta, murmurs something in a language I don't know. The word is harsh and guttural, a curse.

By the fire, Syril nods. "You'll be killed if they discover you," she says, her tone contemplative. "Or if they discover that you're female, anyway."

A now familiar fear worms through me, the same sour apprehension I still feel every time I think of Caleb knowing the truth about me. Because the squire had the right of it. Treason of the level I'm committing would be worth a lot of money, to the right person.

And now a friend—an enemy—and more than a score of outcast marauders know my secret.

"I'll be killed immediately," I agree. "But my brother's already dead. My house is broken, though no one knows it yet. If I don't stand and fight for what is left of my family, my home—who will?"

Something in the woman's eyes flashes, and she shifts forward, making to stand despite her injury. Another woman steps forward quickly to help her then remains with an arm at her leader's back, holding her steady.

"Who will indeed," Syril says quietly, and in that moment, I begin to see why these women follow her. It's more than simple strength, it's conviction...conviction that what she's doing matters more than anything in the world.

In her, I see what I could become, if I survive this night, this tournament.

What I must become, if I truly want to make my house strong.

"Our territory is along the western border of the Protectorate, and we thrive there most of all. We're still within reach of the Third House, though not clutched within its tight grasp. Truth to tell, we thrive anywhere money and goods are needed, and where those who need them aren't picky about who brings such items to their door. We've lived our lives in the shadows, many of us for years, doing what we must. As I said, some of our number wished to run from this world the Lord Protector has created, some simply longed for a life they could claim as their own. But all of us are willing to fight for what we love."

I nod, but she isn't finished. "Still, it's not enough. You talk of the whispers of demon possession, stories of creatures in the night. But those tales aren't solely limited to our small tribe. They bubble up all along the western border. There are...things across those borders that not even the bards dare to speak of. Close enough to howl in the night, chittering with excitement, filling all who hear them with despair. Because there are more of them with each passing season...and more in the past few months than twenty seasons before combined."

I stare at her. "What are they?"

"No one knows, and the history books have all been wiped of any trace." She curls her lip. "Or, more likely, rewritten to fit the boundless vanity of people like Lord Rihad and Lord Gamon of the Third. They want to remember nothing but the victory, not the threat that still twists and writhes at our very doorstep. That, no one seems to want to talk about."

Twists and writhes. I can't help but think of the creature in Lord Rihad's fire, the snakes coiling at its feet. What unholy alliances is the Lord Protector forging, even now? And what would happen to the Protectorate because of it?

Syril's soft words bring me back to the moment.

"You ask why we came from all the way from the western border to Trilion—we came for information. For supplies. Even, of course, for gold. All those things, we've found here." She leans forward, her face harsh and intent in the flickering firelight. "But one thing we *didn't* come for, was hope. We'd long since given up on that. Yet here you are. A woman who stands and fights in the sunlight, not the shadows. A woman warrior to champion the soul of the land."

I grimace, lifting my hands. "I'm no champion," I say quickly. "The Divhs fight. Warriors guide the Divhs. I'm a warrior—but by chance, as much as anything else. By mistake."

At my side, Marta moves so quickly, I don't have time to defend myself. She once more grabs hold of my band and squeezes—hard. This time, fire does erupt along my arm, but I don't flinch away from the heat…she does.

"You're a banded warrior," she says, her words absolute. "Call it what you want, but that is no mistake."

Then Syril lifts her hand to me, and I see my green sash wrapped around her wrist. "Neither is this. You helped us live another day, Talia of the Tenth. For that, we owe you a debt of honor. And the Savasci always repays its debts."

I swallow, sensing the importance of this moment and wanting to honor it, even as I feel the peril of my immediate predicament clawing at me once again. There's so much I need to understand about these women, about their challenges and hopes, about what really drew them to Trilion. But I know instinctively that that information won't be shared on the basis of one meeting. And there's no time for anything more than this meeting. Not now. Not when the night is rushing so quickly toward dawn, and I'm still miles from where I should be.

"Right now I need to get back to the castle," I finally say. "I'll be missed. I want to speak with you, all of you, and learn your story and your truths. But if I'm missed and caught outside the gates… none of this will matter."

"Then you must not be missed," Syril says, resolutely, but a smile flickers at the corner of her mouth at my obvious worry, the smile of a woman who no longer lives by anyone's rules but her own. "We'll get you back."

CHAPTER 28

In the end, my return to the First House is far less complicated than I expect it to be. A fast horse's gallop takes us to the ragged edge of Trilion. From there it only takes a quick exchange of money to get me aboard a bread cart destined for the First House before dawn breaks. For enough money, the driver has no problem hauling along a servant girl whose master's entourage had stranded her in the city. For even more money, he said, he'd agree to keep his hands off me.

Given that he was negotiating with a member of the Savasci, he'll likely never know how close he came to dying for his idle joke. Instead, more money crossed his palm. There are battles and then there are wars, as Syril said.

True to his word, the baker keeps silent about my presence all the way through the gates of the First House and up the long and twisting road into the castle itself. I slip away before he even stops his cart, though it's all I can do not to steal a few loaves of his fragrant wares.

Moving quickly, I dash away from the carts and enter the pedestrian courtyard. At the far edge of the courtyard rises a buzz of voices at the well, servants all. I give them wide berth, angling along the shadowed outer wall until I step into one of the enormous archways that leads the-Light-only-knows-where. Still, there's no one around, so as my eyes adjust to the gloom, I pull back my hood and pat at my hair, amazed at Nazar's handiwork. I never would've believed his wig would have lasted through all the indignities of this night, but it has.

But now I need to sneak back into the barracks as Merritt. If I can just ball up my wig and robe together, shove both of them under my tunic, no one will pay me any mind. Besides, I can't leave this servant's robe laying around. I can't risk it being found and linked to—

"Hello, Talia."

I freeze in place, not moving a muscle as Fortiss steps out of the shadows. He strolls up to me, his golden eyes intense, his face alight with interest in the half-shadows of the archway. He says nothing, but stares at me with a heat that makes my heart skitter like rocks thrown down the mountain.

"My...lord," I manage, sweeping into a curtsey, if only to give my racing mind some precious few seconds to think, to think! I could run, I could faint, I could cry out, I could—

I straighten and glance up, and Fortiss takes the choice from me.

"It *is* you," he hisses. Without another word, he moves closer and reaches for me, cradling my face in both his hands. His mouth comes down over mine, our lips connecting in a kiss so fierce I'm surprised it doesn't light my skin on fire. My heart leaps, my blood races, and for one long, glorious, dizzying moment, I give myself over to that kiss, to everything it means and cannot mean, to everything I want and cannot have. With some belated sense of self preservation, I curl my left shoulder towards him, arch my neck, giving him ready access to my right shoulder and arm but not my left. Not my left!

Only I would be swept into a kiss by the most beautiful, dangerous man I've ever met, and be more worried about my disguise than in reveling in the moment.

He follows my lead eagerly enough, using a free hand to hold me close, all the while deepening the kiss, drifting his mouth across my face, along my jaw. With each new area plundered, a piece of my control falls away and is burned up into cinders.

And why—*why* am I so dazed by him? I may be unused to the touch of a man, but I questioned Adriana endlessly. She told me everything she thought I'd need to know...and a fair amount I never wanted to know, if I'm being honest.

But I never expected to be kissed like this, by a man of nobility and strength. I never imagined what it might feel like to be held in the arms of someone whose touch is so fierce and passionate at once. I never truly believed a warrior's fire might burn for me.

And Fortiss is a warrior, Divh or no Divh. A warrior I would do well to tear myself away from...if only I could force myself to do so.

"I knew you were here, knew you were close. I couldn't believe you ran away as Merritt said you did. I felt you everywhere. I couldn't think but imagine you, I couldn't sleep but dream of you. I couldn't breathe but sense you there, just out of reach."

"What?" I manage, sounding stupid to my own ears, but my mind slips and shimmies along the current of his words. Each new admission is punctuated by lick, a nip, a shuddering sigh, until at last, Fortiss wrenches himself away from me to stare at me, wild-eyed.

"*Talia*," he gasps, as if he's only now seeing me clearly. "What in the blighted path are you wearing?"

"Oh." I'd much rather him continue kissing me, but words tumble out of my mouth too fast for my brain to catch up. "Fortiss, you can't tell anyone. You can't. I know that Merritt believes and so do you that all is well, that he is safe. But I saw the arrow that brought him down, I felt the agony of him in my arms when I thought he was murdered. I couldn't leave him here, alone, and dance my way back to the Tenth House to wait for his return."

"Again, I knew it." Fortiss grins, his hands pinning my elbows to my sides. "I knew you wouldn't flee, no matter what your people said. There's nothing about you that would make me believe you'd run back to your father or to your child husband.

You're stronger than that, Talia. Fiercer. And you couldn't stay away."

"I couldn't," I agree breathlessly. His hands tighten on my elbows—my *elbows*, thank the Light, but it's still too close! I have to distract him. No matter how my blush stains my cheeks, I part my lips and stare at him with what I hope are wide and needy eyes. "I couldn't stay away from you either. I had to see you again, I just thought it would be from a distance."

"I felt you watching me," he says, his words losing their urgency, drifting into teasing, even tempting. "I have felt you all around me. Is that your ploy Talia? Do they teach you witchcraft up in the mountains, that you've preyed so on my mind?"

"No…I…" I swallow, desperately trying to remember that this is all an act. "You've thought of me?"

My voice sounds so tremulous, I'd be proud of myself if I was doing any of it on purpose. But Fortiss's eyes fire with interest.

"I've *burned* for you," he breathes out, and when his hands slide higher on my arms, I do the only thing a warrior can when faced with certain ruin.

I misdirect him.

I shift and take his hands in mine, bringing them both to my mouth. Kissing first one palm than the other, then brushing my lips along the fingertips. I lay my cheek into his left palm, while his right I guide unerringly to the swell of my breast beneath my servant's cloak.

I don't expect my groan of absolute pleasure when his hand cups the curve of that breast, kneads it, but there's no mistaking the catch in Fortiss's breath as well, the urgency of his hold as the moment snaps between us.

"Where are you staying?" he hisses. "You're dressed as a servant. Are you in the barracks? No woman is allowed there."

"I'm hiding in the servants' quarters. There are so many brought in for the banquets, it's easy to lose myself among them." I glance up, acting as if I hear far-off conversations. "But the others…They're heading back to their chambers. I have to move with them, stay in the crowd. I need to leave, Fortiss—to blend in."

"You could never blend in so well if I were looking for you," he counters, but he straightens, looking down at me. At least he seems to realize that dragging me off into the shadows isn't a viable option, not with so many people around. "And I *will* be looking for you Talia. When I find you next, you won't escape so easily."

"I won't want to escape," I assure him, but at this moment, I would say literally anything to get away. And besides all that, it's true. "Don't say anything to Nazar, I beg you! He'll tie me up himself and send me packing if he finds out. He couldn't bear for me to be in danger."

Fortiss's lips twitch. "But you are in danger, Talia," her murmurs. "Everything about you is danger. So beautiful, so fierce."

He bends to me again, capturing my lips, and I feel the skitter of power that leaps from him to me, igniting my warrior blood. Because like it or not, I am a warrior, and he was born to be one. How fierce those who fight with the Divh would be if unions such as these were common? How powerful?

The sacrilege of the thought takes my breath away, or at least I tell myself that's why I swoon in Fortiss's arms, praying that my cloak will serve to hide my band from his questing touch as I lean into his kiss. Need opens up deep within me, a wet and licking fire, and for half a second I forget about my plans, my worries, my strategy.

The way of the warrior may be death. But right now I just wish it could lead to Fortiss's bed—my precious virginity be damned.

"Go," he manages finally, pushing me away mere seconds before I'm reduced to begging for his body. I rock back on my heels, dazed. "Go. But make no mistake, Talia—this isn't done between us."

A cry goes up among the servants around the well.

I wheel away from Fortiss and flee back into the light.

CHAPTER 29

"Where have you *been*?"

Caleb yanks me into our cell then sticks his head out the door, ensuring that no one is following me. Having torn off the servant's cloak, I look perfectly normal, normal and boy-like, but his panic unnerves me even more than my racing heart and kiss-bruised lips.

"Why? What's happened?" I ask.

"A servant fell to her death this night," he spits. "Her *death*. We thought...I mean it could have been you. It could have." He runs his hands through his hair, standing it up on end. "It wasn't, but it could have."

"I..." I don't have anything to say to that, the events of the night crashing together in my mind. Nazar turns and regards me curiously as well. My priest and my squire, I suddenly think. If there's another attempt on my life, they both may just as easily be caught by an arrow or fist. I swallow, feeling the weight of the obligation to protect them. I need to tell them about Rihad. About the fallen warriors. I won't tell them about the marauders, though. Not yet. Not until we're well away from Trilion, reminding ourselves how very close we came to death.

"The attempt on Merritt's life was ordered by Rihad," I say to Nazar, and Caleb goes rigid beside us. "And it's not the only one. A warrior of the Ninth House has also fallen, and one from the Eleventh. The Fourth and the Fifth too. A warrior of the Third House may yet fall."

"What are you saying?" Real fear lifts Caleb's voice to a quavery yelp. Nazar merely watches me.

"Fortiss apparently went out to the borderlands to try and—I don't know, stop it somehow, though he clearly failed." I add this last as coldly as I can, forcing away his earnest face and his sweet apology from my mind. "He believes his uncle has merely *foretold* the deaths, but they're coming too quickly. The hardest hit are the eastern border houses."

"Fortiss used the word foretelling?" Nazar's question is quiet, and I frown at him. Surely this is the least of the concerns before us, but there's so much I don't know about the priest that I can't let my ignorance stand in the way of our safety. He's proven himself both wise and knowledgeable several times over.

"He did," I say. "And you can bet he's likely to *foretell* a few more killings before he's done. The Tenth House is at risk, Nazar. We should go now with the men we have."

"What, you mean leave? *Now*?" Caleb's mouth opens and shuts several times as he tries to work through what I'm saying.

"You're certain," Nazar says. It isn't a question.

I nod. There's more, so much more. But that will have to wait until Nazar and I are alone. As it is, my squire's doing his level best not to explode with panic.

"You *spied* on the Lord Protector and found all this out?" he seems to finally realize. "You could have been *killed*. Arrested."

I squint at him. "How is that different than any other day within these walls?"

"But—"

"Squire Caleb," Nazar says quietly. "I fear the warrior of the Tenth House may have indeed been noticed, having seen so much.

Could you..." He pauses, letting Caleb see the worry on his face. "Could you use the skills you've amply displayed to make sure his name isn't on anyone's tongues? You must have a care not to be noticed."

Caleb straightens with pride and purpose, his fear no match for his eagerness to please Nazar. "Consider it done," he says staunchly. "No one will see me, I assure you. No one ever does."

My heart twists at the simple, frank admission, then Caleb is gone.

The moment he clears the doorway, I pull Nazar's tunic off my body in one rough movement.

"You'll strain the stitches in your shoulder," Nazar comments mildly.

"That's the least of my problems." I blow out a long breath, thinking again of the Savasci. The women who pledged to help me in my hour of need, but they hadn't seen what I'd seen. They didn't truly know what we were facing.

But what we had to fight...

I close my eyes and steady myself, and my words, when they finally come, seem to take far more effort than they should. "Nazar, I...I saw something. Someone. In Rihad's chamber. A creature that stood in the fire."

Nazar's eyes flash with an emotion I can't discern, but his voice is calm. "What did you see, specifically?" he asks. "What words were spoken?"

I try to recount the entire horrible scene. By the end, Nazar's face has grown more pinched, his gaze now hard and flat. "I don't know this creature—and I would, were it ever to have attacked the Exalted Imperium. It isn't in any of my teachings of the Light."

"Maybe because it's from the Wes—"

"Don't say it," Nazar snaps. "Such treason..." He draws a deep breath, his eyes taking on a faraway cast. "The Imperium must be told of this. And it's you who must tell them. As Merritt. The Tenth House is the closest to the border—the last defense. It must be you who carries this tale."

I make a face. "First, let's see if I survive this week." The idea of traveling to the heart of the *Exalted Imperium* as my *brother* is so ridiculous it doesn't even spark panic in my heart.

Much.

We talk more, until I've begun to doubt what I saw with my own eyes, heard with my own ears. Surely, Rihad couldn't be planning anything so dire as an attack on the Protectorate—or, so much worse, the Imperium. Surely, I somehow misunderstood...

I'm midway through another round of rationalization when Caleb finally returns.

"There's a good number of men out there," he says. "Laughing and talking—but not about you. Still, it's most of the warriors from the tournament."

I know he's implying I should join them, but I refuse to leave our chambers right away. Instead, Caleb and I practice our skills of not looking at each other for a while, each of us occupied with our own thoughts. At length, however, I venture out to the bonfire in the central courtyard. I'm surprised when Caleb joins me shortly after, but I can't deny how glad I am for his company. He hands me a cup as he hefts a flagon of wine.

"Stolen," he says with a shrug, and I lift my brows.

"They made the stealing easy I take it?"

"They practically forced it on every warrior and squire in the castle. If you'd stayed on your pallet where you should have been, you'd have probably found a girl in your bed." He grins at me. "Not that you would've known what to do with her."

I snort as he pours the wine into my cup. He's not entirely wrong...or right. Not anymore.

We stand watching the fire for a long while as we drink, and I welcome the warmth that flows through me, both from the fire and the spirits. My mind buzzes from all I've learned this night, all I still don't understand.

Caleb finally speaks, under the murmur of conversation. "The servants are still talking about that girl who fell to her death."

"They saw her fall?" So I *had* been spotted by more than Rihad.

Blessings to the Light for a disguise over a disguise of a disguise. Twice the blessing to Gent for saving me.

He nods. "Enough did. She leapt straight out a window and was gone. They predict her body will be eaten by wolves before it's ever found."

I grimace, imagining that fate. "Who do they think she was?"

He shrugs one shoulder, shooting me a glance. "No one knows—they assume a day worker from the village, like I said, but so far no one is talking. Of course, it's not yet dawn." He turns his face toward the castle walls. "If she did fall from that height, though, she'd surely die."

I follow his gaze. There's a light blazing from the high windows of what I now know is the Lord Protector's rooms. Does he truly think a mere servant girl had been spying on him, I wonder? Better for me if he does.

Caleb blows out a long breath. "So, Gent was there to catch you?"

I stare into the leaping fire, but I can't stop the grin as I recall the Divh's sudden appearance and all that came after. "He was," I say simply.

"But—how?" He pauses, his throat working. "Bad enough that you dressed as a servant and *spied* on the Lord Protector. Then what? You were discovered, you ran, and you *jumped*? How'd you know he'd be there?"

I think about that, my headlong dash with my arm extended. Caleb's guess is accurate enough to bring it all back in vivid detail. "Because I heard him laughing. In my mind. He was that close and...and then he was there."

Caleb looks at me then shakes his head, returning his gaze to the fire. "You jumped into empty air and expected him to catch you."

"Yes." Once again, I see Merritt's face, hear his laughter. My heart twists in pain.

Because Merritt was right...Merritt had always been right. If he jumped, his Divh would do all he could to catch him. If he called, his Divh would always answer.

Just as he answered me this night.

Caleb and I stand together for a long while, our talk eventually turning back to the feast. Caleb speaks of Fortiss making a speech to honor Kheris, and the bold southern warrior taking it all as his due, the clear favorite to win the tournament after he so soundly defeated the strange boy from the eastern border.

That catches me. "Strange?" I ask. Strange is bad, very bad. If the way of the warrior was to stick out like a squash in a field of roses, I'd have already won the tournament by now. Speaking of roses... "They don't mean the flower petals, do they?"

Caleb huffs a laugh. "No. That escaped much attention, as far as I can tell. But the moment when you stretched your arm toward your Divh before he disappeared? That was noticed and remarked upon. Rihad made a joke at your expense, about how living in the mountains made friends hard to come by, and everyone laughed."

"But for everyone to laugh, that meant they'd noticed it too. The connection." I frown, turning the problem over in my head. "I thought that's what everyone did."

"And it's being presented as simply a lack of experience, so you're good," Caleb says. "You're from the Tenth House, after all. You're closest to the Exalted Imperium, hemmed in by rocks and trees. Who's to say what odd customs you've developed?"

"Right." I nod. "What other talk was there tonight?" I ask, as casually as I can. "Were they able to catch the marauders in the camp?"

"Oh that," Caleb scoffs. "You won't believe this. Rihad is blaming malcontents from the western borders, stirring up trouble. Says the Divhs and warriors fighting in the tournament will remind them all of why we won the battles of the Western Realms, and that they'll quail in fear once more."

I think of the women I'd just met this night, women coming to seek the source of darkness leaching into the Protectorate. "How'd that go over?"

"A lot of cheering, knocking of mugs, stamping of feet," Caleb says, shrugging. "Rihad knows his audience."

We work our way back to the barracks then, and Caleb goes to look in on our horses as I rejoin Nazar. As expected, the old man is smoking his pipe. Beside him, laid out on a rack, is the servant's overwrap.

"I need to return that."

"Perhaps, perhaps not," Nazar says mildly. "A servant's garb is soiled easily and often. Extras are equally easy to come by, I expect. Keep it awhile yet." He watches me over a curl of smoke. "The first round of the tournament has been charted. The warriors selected for battle. We have less than a week before it begins."

I wince, moving my arm. "Am I in the first round?"

He shakes his head. "The second, and you are against a minor foe, one of the Ninth House warriors."

"The Ninth." That can't be right. "They had their second warrior killed. There's only the one left."

"And you command arguably one of the stronger Divhs in recent memory." Nazar nods. "You are expected to advance."

"What about the other southern houses?" I ask. "Who are they slated against?"

"The lesser warriors of the northern, to a man. The strongest fighting the least strong, winnowing down the field quickly." He pauses. "But Rihad has added a new element. At the close of the tournament, there will be a melee, pitting the Divhs against each other on the open ground between the First House and the spectator stands."

I stare. In the deepest pit of my gut, I know that's very wrong. "A melee of Divhs? But how—"

"The details are scant, except this one: Every warrior knight still standing must participate. The entire Protectorate is anticipated to flow toward the First House for the event at the close of the tournament. Great honor goes to the First House for creating a battle that will go down in history."

"But multiple Divhs against others? That's never been done

before, surely. Not in a tournament. Not even in open battle since —well, since the borders were closed to the Western Realms, right?"

Nazar takes a long draw on his pipe, and we stare at each other, the knowledge of tonight's discoveries weighing down the air between us. "Then it would seem that the First House wishes to create a new tradition."

"So it would seem."

Caleb returns then. We make our pallets, but my mind refuses to rest. The entire night, I turn in my half sleep, dreaming of Gent's laughter, his bounding strides and his leap into the darkness to catch me, the race along the mountainside. How had I summoned him so quickly and so well? Even now, it seems as if his enormous hand is close enough to touch, his glassy eye with its long, thick eyelashes barely a breath away.

I tumble into deep slumber at last, dreaming of blue mountains. And of all the monsters of the Divh lined up against each other, blowing and huffing like bulls about to charge.

One of those monsters I recognize too, smaller than many of her peers, but no less fierce.

The dragon trapped in the cavernous hollows of the First House's dungeon hold.

Only now, the dragon is free and forced upon the battlefield, her broken wing flopping oddly against her body. The other Divhs watch her with a curious mix of anger and fear, and when the horns finally blow to signal the start of the melee, the monsters don't turn on each other, they turn on the dragon in their midst, arms and paws outstretched, jaws open wide, all of them rushing, jumping, thrashing—

I jolt awake. Nazar stands above me.

"We go to train," he says.

In the shadows, Caleb also stands watching me, his eyes wide.

"What?" I ask him as I shoulder on my cloak. Nazar moves ahead into the barracks corridor, motioning me to follow. But I can't ignore the horror on Caleb's face. "What?"

"You were *screaming*," he whispers. "You weren't making a sound but—your throat, your face..." He shakes his head. "Whatever you saw...bad things are coming, aren't they?"

It isn't a question.

A sudden chill clamps my stomach. "I hope not."

CHAPTER 30

The week passes in a blur of pageants and rumors, and two more hurried, breathless training sessions under heavy cover of night. I make no attempt to re-dress myself as a servant girl and do my level best to be seen by Fortiss on a daily basis as Merritt...but only at a distance. With more warrior knights coming every day, I manage to avoid both Rihad and Fortiss easily—and eventually stop replaying my memories over and over again: the shock of the creature in the fire, my gut-wrenching leap into darkness, and my foolish lapse with Fortiss.

I even try to convince myself the last bit never happened...yet I can't. When all this is done, and I am dying on some field, I will have the taste of Fortiss's kiss on my lips to savor, the feel of his long hard body pressed up against mine. I wouldn't give that up for anything.

The marauders on the outskirts of Trilion seem to have stopped their looting for the moment, and the townspeople hail the might of Rihad for this reprieve. No one speaks further of the servant girl who jumped to her death, and no one has come looking for the robe I stole. I know I should burn it, but I can't bring myself to do so, wondering if—as Nazar seems to think—I might use it again. Wondering if there's something I can learn as a female that is barred to me as a warrior knight. With Nazar's help, I refashion the robe with heavier, reinforced sleeves—so thick from shoulder to elbow that no one could guess the real size of the arm that lies beneath the fabric. The arm...or what might be circling it.

Unfortunately, I must attend tonight's final feast as Merritt before the tournament officially begins tomorrow, a two-day event of, well, massive proportions. Nazar sends Caleb to fetch me while the sun is still high in the sky. He presents me with a new tunic he's had sewn in Trilion, made of cloth the deepest forest green shot and with silver in a fine spray over my left shoulder.

"This seems...elaborate," I muse as Caleb stitches it on.

"It's expected," Caleb says. Nazar doesn't comment. "There will be the official calling of the rolls, plus some special announcements that Rihad has been hinting at all week. If you miss it, you'll be noticed. And you don't want to be noticed for anything but how magnificent you look."

"But why the silver? That's not the Tenth House color."

Caleb looks at me oddly. "Because it suits you," he says, as if it's the most obvious answer in the world. "Believe me, you'll want to put on a strong showing this night."

When we reach the great hall, I understand what he means. The First House isn't entertaining the masses—that's left for the tournament to follow. This fete is for the warriors and their entourages, allowing all to see who they might face in the days to come. Caleb, Nazar, and I take our seats at the table assigned to us—not the best by far, but there are no bad positions in the hall this night. The only table slightly raised on a small dais is the high table, with the warriors of the First House seated to either side of Lord Protector Rihad.

Food and drink overflow each of the tables, and I grab bread and begin tearing it into small pieces, if only to give myself something to do, until Nazar frowns at me.

"Relax." Caleb leans close and pats my arm. "I've made the rounds once already and will do so again. No one's talking about anything but the tournament to come, not about the jumper, and definitely not about you, other than rumors and supposition about your Divh. There's a few mutterings about warriors attacked on the way to the tournament, but those are squelched almost as soon as they start. There will be nothing to mar the glory of Rihad's hour, I suspect."

"Good." I can't look at Rihad for longer than a moment. Our gazes meet when he toasts each of the tables, but I slide mine away as quickly as propriety allows. He doesn't look my way again.

The same can't be said for Fortiss. He stares avidly at each of the tables, mine as well, as if memorizing not only the details of the warriors but our attendants. Unreasoning fear clutches at my throat. He's looking for me, but I'm hiding in plain sight.

"You're sure no one's talking about the missing servant?" I ask Caleb quietly.

"Not a word. That night was dark as pitch, most everyone drunk following the fireworks display. Besides, no one wants to think of scavengers eating dead bodies when we should be celebrating."

"Well, that's...reassuring."

He grins. "I figured."

Dinner is well underway but nowhere near finished when Rihad stands. The hall hushes with impressive speed.

"Friends and warriors, the First House salutes you!" the Lord Protector calls out, raising his glass. "You represent the best of our men. Men who will stand and fight when the need is great, and men who will gladly give their lives to serve the Protectorate. This Tournament of Gold we host will bring you honor no matter how you fare and could enrich you and your house beyond your greatest expectations."

A cheer follows that, along with much scraping of boots and cups and benches. The men are restless to get back to their wine. The fiercest battles of the tournament begin tomorrow, so drink and women are heavy on their minds, not speeches from Rihad about the Protectorate.

But Rihad's next words focus us all. "However, we have a more pressing reason to apply ourselves to winning this tournament with skills and strategy," he says, and his voice has taken on a note of somber dread. I sit up straighter, wondering if Nazar is paying closer attention too.

"There is betrayal afoot in our own lands, coming from we know not where. Who among us has not heard the rumors of ambush on the roads and byways of the Protectorate? Who among us has not wondered if the rumors were true? Or known, to their greater sadness, the truth of those rumors through the loss of a warrior and the great Divhs we are bound to? And then there is this talk of marauders, marauders possessed of the very ancient demons from the west we're sworn to guard against—marauders our own strong men have protected us from. Well, I'm here to remind you that we shall *not* let fear grab us by the throat. Fortiss!"

Rihad turns, and Fortiss quickly masks his surprise at being called. He rises. To be singled out in such a way by the Lord Protector is clearly a great honor. Fortiss stands tall and straight, ready to be bathed in glory or to have his head lopped off.

My fingers clench into fists below the table, because I don't know which it will be. I shouldn't care, but I do.

"Give the report that we have learned from those loyal to the First House and spare no detail. The warriors of the Tournament of Gold deserve to know what they are fighting for."

All our heads swivel toward Fortiss—even mine, and I at least suspect what he's about to say. But as he speaks, detailing the deaths on the roads of the Protectorate, warriors killed in cold blood, I scan the faces of the men assembled. The older the face, the greater the outrage—and something else too. Not fear. These men have reached their majority with a mighty monster at their command. Fear is something with which they have no true experience. But there is a sense of wrongness in their countenances, as if the world is falling away from their feet, and they cannot quite keep their balance.

The names of those killed, when they come, are chilling in their finality.

Marcus of the Ninth House.

Bertrand of the Eleventh.

The party—but not the warrior—of Merritt of the Tenth House

And on they go. The Fourth, the Fifth...and rumors of the Third. So Rihad's final prophecy came true, it seems. Convenient.

During Fortiss's recitation, Rihad stands with his mouth drawn down, his brow furrowed, as if this travesty is something not of his doing, but an atrocity and a curse.

When Fortiss finishes, Rihad steps forth again. "So now you see, there's more to fight for than the simple honor of reaching the Court of Talons or being granted new warriors to strengthen and sustain us. We must fight to hone our skills. We must better ourselves so we can protect our holdings and people. We must strive to present a united front against any that should stand in the way of the Protectorate!"

Anger and fear crash together in the room, and the cheer the warriors give this second time is louder and bolder than that which came before. Fists and cups pound on the tables, boots stamp on the floor. All are in agreement with the First House.

After a long moment, Rihad lifts a hand to quiet the men. "I'm too old to fight," he says, placing a modest hand on his chest. "And too vain to lose to warriors who are my betters." Laughter crackles through the room, but curiosity too. "But I would make an example to all House lords, that they might follow my lead. Bards!"

Always at the ready, the bards jump to their feet and stare at Rihad eagerly, each striking exaggerated poses. More laughter sounds at their antics, but I don't mistake the bards' actions for simple artifice. There are eleven of them present—a number that's clearly not accidental. One for each of the remaining houses present in the Tournament of Gold. Rihad means for his pronouncement to be shared with all the land.

His words bear me out. "Travel fast and well and give my news to all who would hear it. In the Tournament of Gold, Lord Protector Rihad of the First House pledges the finest warrior of my house to fight in my place...and with Akrep, the most deadly Divh in all of the Protectorate!"

Fortiss's head comes up, but his face shutters instantly into a mask of obedience. Still, murmurs spring up throughout the hall at the idea of this Akrep Divh taking the field—some excited, some aghast, some curious.

Rihad allows the rumble of words to ebb and flow before plunging on again. "Those who know the great Divh I command also know its might and cunning. But its obedience is its greatest asset. Obedience to my mind, and to my will. It will fight for Fortiss, and I challenge every lord unwilling or unable to take up the fight himself, who yet remains unwilling to give up the Divhs which are our destiny either to make way for a son or a chosen warrior, to heed my words. Your Divhs are an asset to the *Protectorate*, not your personal right."

His words pierce me like a sword. I've been a warrior for only a few days, but I do know this—my bond with my Divh is my own. Not the Protectorate's. And certainly not Rihad's.

The Lord Protector, however, barrels on. "By my example, you shall see the truth of my words. Through the force of my mighty connection with my Divh, Fortiss will take the field with Akrep—a Divh banded to me, where none is yet banded to Fortiss." His grin is almost feral. "And I'm not going to lie. My money is on Fortiss. Who will take me in this bet?"

Another rousing cheer goes up. Such a wager is something the men understand. Even Caleb leans over and starts jawing with one of the pale-green-garbed soldiers of the Fifth House who already has a money bag out on the table and is protesting loud and long that it can't be done, a warrior knight being able to guide a Divh who isn't his own. It simply can't.

But my gaze isn't on any of them. It's fixed on Fortiss, standing in the full light of scrutiny of Rihad and the councilors, not to mention the warriors of the Tournament of Gold. He'll be allowed to fight, it appears, but with a Divh not his own. I didn't even know it was possible for a warrior to command his Divh to fight with another—and one who bears no band, at that. Rihad is positioning it as an honor, but knowing what I know now, it's totally not. Merely another breadcrumb to a warrior who has yet to be granted the right to bond with his own Divh.

And Fortiss can't deny Rihad's command, can't oppose him. He can only fight in whatever way his lord commands, and hope that —one day—it will be enough.

There's no *need* for him to wait, though. There's a perfectly powerful Divh in this very fortress who needs a warrior. And he's practically standing on top of her.

"The rolls for the Tournament of Gold are set. Tomorrow we shall honor the victors from the fighting pits—the future banded soldiers of the Protectorate. They will have a stadium-side view for the contests to come, so they might see more closely than ever what their strength and cunning has brought them. And then the true competition will begin. Every hour, we will delight those who have traveled from all corners of the Protectorate to bear witness to the powerful creatures and men who stand between the people of the Protectorate and all that would attack us. Our role here isn't merely to test each other's mettle—but to awe our audience. To inspire in those watching, the belief that all is safe, that they are protected, and that the Protectorate is a powerful force in its own right." By now, Rihad is practically roaring. "No one shall make the best and the boldest of our houses cower in fear—instead, they shall feel our wrath!"

I keep my face carefully neutral as Rihad finishes, and all the men around me chant and howl their approval. This isn't the whipping up of nationalistic fervor, this is the goading of men to battle—*true* battle, not merely the sleight of hand that the Tournament of Gold has become over the last few centuries. What is Rihad's game? And how much of it does Fortiss know?

I can't forget the creature I saw in the fire in Rihad's private chambers. A hooded figure with a face buried in darkness, heavily cloaked in a robe of fire, snakes roiling at his feet, twice as tall as Rihad and as broad as an oak.

I know the barest details of the Exalted Imperium's attempt to breach the Western Realms, of course. But I have never heard stories of a creature such as what I saw in Rihad's chambers—not even from the lands of the southern houses, and they have snakes to spare. That Nazar hadn't seemed to recognize it either merely adds to my horror. *Had I really seen what I thought I had?*

As the crashing of the feast begins again and more wine flows, I bid my leave of Caleb and Nazar, claiming fatigue. My attention flicks to the forced merriment animating the unluckiest of all warriors in this hall, Fortiss. There are deep shadows in his already pale eyes as he drains his tankard.

Fortiss might be too proud to talk to Merritt about his pain, but I am a warrior who follows the way of strategy. According to the teaching of that way, I should look at Fortiss not as my enemy but as one of my own troops, someone I can guide and push and harry into whatever position I need, allowing me to make my attack.

And in this case, an attack against Fortiss in his moment of weakness is one against Rihad. The only attack I can make right now. The only way I can learn more of what is truly going on in the First House.

I slip out of the feasting hall and run to the barracks. It doesn't take me long to do what I need to do.

When I return to the feasting hall, I am once again wrapped in a servant's robes and golden chains...and this time, ready for war.

CHAPTER 31

The flowing wine and ale is having its intended effect, and the warriors have gotten louder, if anything, and certainly freer with their hands. Dressed in my serving robes but with my eyes now heavily outlined in kohl and red salve on my lips, I put myself to work fetching more wine almost as soon as I reenter the great hall. Cups and flagons change hands across each table, and the demands grow brasher and more boisterous by turns.

It takes only a few trips back and forth from the kitchens to position myself in front of Fortiss. When I lean forward, he looks up with a jolt. "You..."

I bow and step back, awaiting his instruction like the servant I am.

"More wine," he finishes, as the giddy laugh of the girl beside him breaks his concentration long enough for me to slip away from his glare. I don't mind. I've done what I wanted to do. After that, I sense Fortiss's gaze upon me constantly as I weave my way through the crowd. I don't make his task difficult. I set up position near his table, eventually dragging a water jar over to rest against the wall. I'll have need of it soon enough.

Fortunately, no one disturbs the vessel or pays undue attention to me. By the time the women and men begin pairing off to leave and the rafts of retainers file out of the feasting hall, leaving the servants to clean, I'm not surprised that Fortiss remains behind. He stays as the councilors take their leave, and Rihad as well, who looks very content with the evening's work. Eventually, even the pouting blonde leaves Fortiss behind, though she's clearly reluctant to do so. He turns to stare at me.

I roll my eyes, fixing my attention on the table I'm clearing. How many girls have made that offer to Fortiss this week alone? Probably too many to count.

"You've done a good job hiding from me this week," he murmurs.

"Hiding is sometimes the way," I return easily as I survey the room. It's nearly empty now, and the guards are paying little attention. I suspect I won't get a better opportunity.

"Before we can, ah, do anything else, a moment, sir." I half curtsey as timidly as I can manage and gesture to the water jars along the wall. "This won't take long."

Fortiss frowns, watching me curiously as I move the short distance to the large water jar. I squat down to pick it up—and don't have to feign staggering under its weight. The jar is nearly full.

"Here." He strides over to me and lifts the jar from my arms as if it weighs nothing. "Where are you taking this?"

"To the beast below," I say, as if that's perfectly obvious. I turn away from him, heading toward the high table.

"*What?*" He hastens after me, then slips around and positions himself before the door that leads down to the cavern when I try to enter. "Talia," he bites off under his breath. "It's forbidden for you to do such work."

I shrug. *Interesting.* "Well, I'm playing a role, here. I was given these orders from the head cook. She says to take this jar down by this door, adding to the supplies where the beast rests."

"I don't care what the cook instructed you to do." Fortiss works his jaw, and I think for a moment that perhaps he does know what resides in the caverns of the First House, the glorious Divh held captive. Then he shakes his head. "Lord Rihad has his own servants to attend to...that."

"You've seen yourself how busy the house staff is. Here." I hold out my arms impatiently to take the jar again. "Caring for the creature is the work of servants, not warriors. In this, I am happy to serve."

His lips twist, and he turns stiffly away. "It's not right."

Without another word, he strides into the archway.

As I recall from before, the stairs are long and winding, and at some point, Fortiss slows enough that I can step in front of him, trotting quickly ahead. "Thank you, sir, I'm in your debt, sir," I keep murmuring just to needle him, but I get only grumbled responses for my efforts.

At last, we reach the lowest level, where the wide apron of stone spreads out toward the metal bars. Fortiss is barely moving now, and I pull the jar from him, wobbling a little under its weight. I go to the great vat at the side of the room and shove the lid free, spilling the water into it and stirring.

"What're you doing now?" Fortiss demands. "You've done this before? I've never been down here."

"Then all the better that you're with me."

When the salve is prepared, I scoop several portions of it into one of the smaller jars next to the vat and move toward the bars. I'm almost through them when Fortiss seems to come to life.

"No," he says urgently. "I can't go in there. I've given my word. It's forbidden for any warrior knight to enter this section of the dungeons. But I won't have you get hurt."

I blink at him as another layer of Rihad's damnable deception slips away. If Fortiss knows only that there is *something* in this dungeon that he has pledged not to explore, but not what it is—then clearly his level of personal honor is far higher than I ever expected. In my father's house, I would have gone exploring straight away.

Either way, I can't completely let this moment pass. He may be constrained by his sense of loyalty to Rihad...but I'm not. "Shh. You'll wake her."

"Her?" His voice is strangled, and he doesn't speak as I move to the edge of the precipice and kneel, dumping the oil mixture over the side.

Despite himself, Fortiss approaches. I hear him slide between the bars. "What are you..."

"She likes it." I sit back on my heels, waiting. I hear his soft footfalls on the stone even as a scraping in the cavern beyond begins. "See?"

"I can't see anything. I'm surprised you can."

Fortiss reaches me and, with a hand on my shoulder, sinks down to the stone ledge. "I shouldn't be here. And it's too dangerous for you."

"Right." I shrug. "But I'm here to perform a service to the beast that roams these caverns, nothing more. And she's chained." I nudge him with an elbow. "You can't tell me you've never been down here before."

"I...it's forbidden to me." A curious non-answer. "I serve the Lord Protector."

"Well, yes. But not in the same way as a servant, right?" I find myself tired of this misdirection. It's time someone told me the truth about what's chained Fortiss to this place as much as the beast below us. "I mean, you're a warrior. Why don't you have a Divh?"

I can sense his withdrawal, but in the darkness, it seems that secrets are easier to share. At length, he speaks, with the tone of a man confessing to a crime. "Because I'm not worthy. When my father died, I wasn't with him. The band was supposed to transfer to me. I was his only son. Only...it didn't. I wasn't worthy, then or... or later."

The scratching beneath us has stopped, and I can almost imagine the dragon's graceful head twitching to the side, her cruel teeth gleaming in the half-light as Fortiss speaks. But the creature comes no closer, doesn't lift her mighty head.

"My father was the greatest warrior in the land," Fortiss continues. "Toma the dragon—they called him dragon in honor of his Divh. It was the most fearsome creature in the Protectorate, some said, swift and lithe. There were hundreds of bardic tales written to honor both my father and his Divh."

Szonja. The word is whispered in my mind. *Szonja.*

"She," I murmur. My eyes are wide beneath my hood, my breath practically choking in my throat. So this Divh *does* by rights belong to Fortiss—she does.

Fortiss pauses. "What?"

"The Divh, your father's Divh. The dragon. She's a she, not an it." The word forms again in my mind, quick and absolute, *Szonja.* A more beautiful name I've never heard, and one that fits this mighty Divh perfectly. I open my mouth to speak it but catch myself just in time. As Merritt, I could share this name. As Talia, I can't.

I can sense Fortiss's scowl even though I can't see it. "How would you know? He never told me its name."

The snap of gnashing teeth is so loud, I jerk back, and Fortiss reaches out and clasps my arm, pulling me farther away from the abyss. "What was that?"

"I don't know," I lie. "What else do you know of your father's Divh?"

"Well...I only saw it once. My father went out one morning with me to the marshlands and lifted his arm and it—"

"She."

"*She* appeared in the near-dawn light and, well, she was glorious. Ebony and sapphire with spears of gold glistening along her skin. Her wings full and proud, her expression fierce, her..." He frowns. "Why am I calling it a 'her' again?"

"Because it's her truth." I pause. "She sounds like a worthy Divh for the greatest warrior in all the land."

"Yes," he sighs. "And Rihad told me I'd surely merit it—her—when the time came. But he was wrong. I was only twelve, but...my father died before the transfer could be completed. Rihad wears the band himself, now, in sorrow for my father's death. He..." He swallows. "He's supposedly truly banded to the Divh, double banded and all, though I've never seen it...her...I've never seen her again. What's more, the Lord Protector has never awarded me my own Divh either. I haven't been worthy."

I stare at Fortiss as rage and sorrow waft up from the cavern, and more than that—I know how he feels. Know the burden of a shame you can never release, no matter how hard you try. In that moment, I also sense another truth. Fortiss is first-blooded and firstborn, and for him, that means something. It means honor, discipline. Adherence to the old ways, and to a path that shines in the Light. He would never have intentionally killed Merritt, and he didn't loose that arrow. But that doesn't mean he is innocent of being his uncle's pawn.

"You're going to fight with his Divh, though, aren't you? I heard the others talking. That would be a feat of worth."

He blows out a long breath. "I don't want to fight with a borrowed Divh. I've never heard of a bond that allows such a transfer of allegiance, and it feels...it feels like a lie, somehow. I wish to fight honorably. With my own Divh."

I nod. "What if your Divh was injured, somehow, and not the glorious creature like—like your father's Divh? What if she...or he... was weaker? Smaller? What would you do, then?"

He thinks for a moment. "Size is no replacement for heart. That's something my father once said. If my Divh is small or hurt, but it—"

SHE.

This time, I don't have to remind Fortiss. It's as if he can hear the Divh in his own mind, even if he can't understand it. "—but if she still chose me, then..." He shrugs. "That's all I'd need. It'd be the same as if she was the mightiest creature in all the land."

There's a sound of rippling hide, and Fortiss jerks his head toward the cool darkness. "Did you hear that?" he asks, a frown in his voice.

I feel the quick, hurried touch of Szonja in my mind, urging me away. "I think we can probably go now." I stand and pull up the jar, now empty, but he takes it from me without leaving the edge.

"Have you seen it?" he asks. "The beast Rihad keeps here?"

"I have," I allow. "But not often. Maybe only once before." I suddenly don't want him to see Szonja this way, and I wonder...are these my own thoughts, or something the Divh is impressing on me, asking me to leave? Does she not want to reveal herself to Fortiss in her current state, broken and chained? Either way, I feel I must honor the sense that we should step away from this dank cavern.

Fortiss seems to agree, and we turn toward the bars. Once we are safely through, he sets down the salve jar again. I hesitate, frowning at him as he hesitates. The shadows shroud him in gloom, and I can barely make out the features of his face. "Are you all right?"

He stares at the bars another long moment then back at me.

"I don't want you to go," he murmurs. "Not yet. No one will bother us here. There's danger, but...my rooms are on the other side of the castle. We might be seen trying to reach them."

I swallow, but he's right. There's no way I could make my way across the castle in Fortiss's company without drawing the interest of idle eyes. And interested eyes could recognize me—even if they don't quite know why. We can't stray far from the shadows...and we shouldn't be lingering in the shadows at all.

As soon as I think that last thought, I reject it. Instead, I step closer to Fortiss and stare up into his beautiful face.

"No," I agree softly, taking his hand. "No one will bother us here."

CHAPTER 32

I lift his hand to my face, turn it, and plant a soft kiss upon his palm. He hisses out a breath.

"There's something different about you, Talia," he murmurs. "Something I can't figure out—but I will. You have to know I will."

Apprehension slithers through me at that, but when I step away, Fortiss follows, not letting me retreat. Somehow, in the space of just a breath, I've lost power and position here—given it up willingly, in fact. It occurs to me that Fortiss is attacking me all in one timing, as the way of the warrior dictates, yet I can't gain the upper hand.

"Do you want to know what I see in you?" he continues, his words a murmured tease.

"No." My response is emphatic, but it only makes him smile. He curls my fingers into his and tugs on my hand. As if my head is attached to some sort of string, I find myself leaning toward him. He lifts his other hand to ease the veil of chains back from my face, then brushes his lips against mine. Once again, heat suffuses my entire body, yet I'm so cold, I shiver.

Which, of course, makes him draw me closer.

Which, of course, I let happen.

He deepens the kiss and with a faint, strangled moan, I press into him for one glorious moment, savoring the strength of him around me, the taste of his lips on mine, the sound of our hearts beating together. It's as if sharp rays of light are billowing forth in my mind, and I hear and see and feel everything at once. The wide-open sky on a sunny day, the sound of Gent's chuffing laugh, the chill of a swollen brook on my bare skin, a burst of midnight-blue-and-white magic, swirling and whirling around me.

I revel in that magic, gathering it all to hold in my heart. I'll keep it there forever, to box and re-box and bury it in the rich, fertile soil of my memory, one day to unearth, one day to savor anew. One day to...

No! Another flare of warning trills in my mind, forcing me to focus. *This isn't real.* This isn't mine to take. I'm a cheat, a lie—I *know* this. And if I'm not careful, Fortiss will know it too.

So I'll just need to be very, very careful.

Fortiss has no such concern but is peering at my servant's robe. "First we need to get you out of this—"

"No," I say, with enough force that Fortiss freezes, his hands hovering over my shoulders.

"Um, I'm not sure how they do things in the mountains, but..."

"I'm serious, no." I grasp his hands and press them together. "If I've learned nothing else in my time as a servant here, it's that I can't afford to be caught unawares. The bodice and sleeves of this garment take a full quarter hour to tie into place. I can move it around a little, but I can't take that part off—I just can't. If I'm summoned, or if someone comes down those stairs, you will recover from the embarrassment quickly enough, but I won't."

"That's ridiculous," he protests, but something shifts in his gaze when I don't back down. "Talia, no one will hurt you here."

I snort. "Fortiss, everyone wants to hurt me."

I don't mean to say it with so much fervor, and I grimace as his mouth tightens. "It's not so bad, really. You get used to it."

Still looking dubious, he takes a step back from me, then watches me with heated eyes as I lift my skirts and kick off my slippers. I slide out of my leggings, rolling them up neatly for ready access, lift the hem of my servant's gown and knot it high—

Then I realize Fortiss hasn't moved from the spot he retreated to. In fact, he's doing little more than stare at me. "Don't let me stop you," I say with a grin. He laughs but makes no move to disrobe, appearing transfixed by my legs as they emerge from their covering.

"What, you've never seen bare legs before?" I glance down and grimace. "Oh."

"By the Light, Talia," Fortiss whispers. "Who treated you this way?"

I blow out a long breath, not sure precisely what he's talking about, though I can guess. The scars that slash my legs hearken from the same time as the scar that graces my neck beneath its fall of hair, the summer of my seventh year. I've blocked most of those days from my mind, and of course anyone from my own holding wouldn't be surprised to see such proof of my father's wrath. But I didn't pause to think…

"I'm sorry," I groan as my hands twitch to unknot my skirts again. "I've embarrassed you and myself, I—"

"No." Fortiss practically lunges for me, grabbing my wrists to keep me from moving my gown back into place.

"Stop, Talia. Listen to me." He stares hard at me, golden eyes flashing, and the intensity of his gaze arrows all the way to my heart, making it pound in awkward thumps, as if it's forgotten its place as much as I have. "You're *beautiful*."

I choke out a cough. "I'm hardly—"

"You are. And so much more than that. You're fierce. True. Your light shines so sharp and pure, I want to swallow it whole for the hope that it may live within me for just a moment. Here, sit."

His hands still gripping my wrists like a vice, he edges me down to the stone floor on a cushion of my own robe, then steps back to wrench off his own tunic and breeches, baring his gorgeous, well-formed legs, his powerful arms and chest. I blink, realizing again how differently they make warriors in the plains.

I've never seen skin so smooth and clean, muscles so sharply defined, or limbs without scars.

Fortiss doesn't stop, but kneels down next to me, bunching up his breeches to form a pillow on the stone. Then he lays me back so gently, I have to smile.

"Fortiss, you have to know by now I won't break." I gesture to my battered legs. "You have ample evidence."

"Shut up, Talia," he mutters, and his lips come down on mine.

Once more, the light bursts within me, a kindling fire that starts in my core and surges up as strong as my connection to my Divh. I hear Fortiss gasp and wonder if he feels it too, here in this place so close to the Divh I know in my heart is his birthright. I hear her distant cry, the echo of her sigh, and he shudders, groaning as my hand snakes around and cups the smooth hard planes of his buttocks. It's like grabbing silk over granite, and I glory in the feel of his tensing, flexing muscles.

He pulls away, his gaze once more raking down my body—the part he can see, anyway.

"Let me," he murmurs, and I stare as he shifts down. He drops his head to the top of my left thigh, where the worst of the scars remain, a faded reminder of a far unhappier time. He follows one cruel slash over my thigh, raining light kisses where once there was only pain. I tip my chin up, sighing with need as he slides silkily along my skin. His hot breath offers ample warning of his change in direction, yet the touch of his tongue against my sex is so surprising I nearly shove him off me. But he holds fast as I shiver, he doesn't budge.

"Let me," he implores again, and when I whimper my consent, he whispers kisses along my quivering skin, now damp with want. After a few more, dizzying moments of this glorious torture, I know I can no sooner stop him than I could push back a racing storm. His tongue slides along the most intimate part of me with exquisite precision, seeking out every lick of fire, every shiver of joy. Excitement, pleasure, and a swirling, whirling power expands to fill me then overflows, replaced by a twisting, winding need that builds so fast—too fast!

I suck in unsteady breaths, giving myself over to the sensations, unhooking all the ties that bind me to this earth to be lifted up, up—before I jerk in a sudden, ferocious convulsion, a soft cry ripping out of me like lightning chasing across the summer sky.

"Oh, *Light*!" I gasp, in sheer, delirious pleasure. "Nobody ever told me *that* was possible."

As soon as the words are out of my mouth, I know I'm doomed.

Fortis freezes. Totally freezes, somehow managing to suspend himself above my legs for a long, soul-breaking moment, like a shadow turned to stone. Then slowly…so slowly…he levers himself up my body until his face is even with mine, his muscular arms caging me, his fists pinning both me and my tangled gown to the stone ledge. He stares down at me with eyes so wide and horrified he might as well be upending a bucket of snow on my head.

"Talia," he grits out in a low, strangled voice. "Are you untouched?"

He doesn't wait for me to respond, of course. He doesn't need to. The answer is plain on my face. Anger and dismay twists his beautiful mouth as he glares down at me. "Why didn't you *tell* me?"

I stare right back at him. "You didn't ask."

"I didn't—*hey*," he protests as I finally have the presence of mind to push him off me, scooting back in my unwieldy gown until I reach my discarded leggings. "How was I supposed to…I mean how could I have…"

His words die off as fast as my own withering desire. Because of course, he should have known. If he understands anything about the practices of the noble houses of the Protectorate—especially those noble houses in the backwards mountains of the eastern borderlands—he would know exactly how much we hew to the old ways. Despite the fact that my cheeks are burning, I spare him the trouble of having to say it aloud.

"That's right, Fortiss. That day we met on the forest road? I was heading to my wedding as a jewel-draped *virgin sacrifice*." I huff and strain, shimmying my leggings up my thighs as best as I can with my shaking hands. "It was my only worth to my father, and he made sure I understood that fact every moment he could. And now, when I finally have a chance to grab something—*anything*—one brief moment of pleasure for myself, I ruin it. Ruin it! Because of my ignorance and stupid chatter! I will regret this night for the rest of my *life*."

He jolts at my vehemence, still clearly not tracking well. "But you...I mean, you remain untouched, Talia. Nothing happened. Not really."

"Blood and *stone*, Fortiss, I understand that." I roll to my feet, yanking my gown into place and stomping across the ledge to find my slippers. Humiliation sours my stomach and makes my fingers twitch, and all I want to do is cry. "I'm fine. You're fine. You didn't do anything to harm my bride price, just my pride. You're safe."

My words hang harshly in the still air, bitter and raw. Fortiss doesn't respond to my rant, which is some small mercy.

In truth, I know I should be grateful. How I ever thought I was going to be able to have *sex* with Fortiss while *wearing a disguise*, I have no idea. Besides, what even happens when two banded warriors make love? Do the skies open up? Do their Divhs appear to stomp and roar? And why hadn't I thought even *one tiny bit* about the potential chaos I was blithely walking us both into?

Fortiss isn't the only one not thinking clearly tonight, but he has far less to lose. *Fool!*

"Talia—" he begins, but I can no longer bear to breathe the same air he does. Nothing is right, nothing will ever be right again. I am neither woman nor man, daughter nor son. Now, I'm only a banded warrior, and even that future teeters on the edge of a razor-sharp talon.

I lift up my long skirts before he can say anything more, and race up the stairs.

CHAPTER 33

The two-day climax to the Tournament of Gold begins like a forced march to an execution—but with better music.

The trumpeters of the Lord Protector are stationed all along the roadway between the base of the First House's gates and the coliseum. Every warrior in the tournament is dressed for competition, even those not scheduled today, because we all process in as a great parade, with Rihad at our head.

I think about the symbolism of that, the symbolism that has taken up so much of the tournament so far. Rihad's sponsored battles in the fighting pits, with the promise of these newly created warrior-Divh partners to be shared among the winning houses of the warrior-knight competition. Fortiss, charged with commanding a Divh that isn't his own. The novelty of the warriors from the southern realms, many of whom have never fought in the Tournament of Gold. And over all of it, the haunting threat of marauders, both those here at the tournament, and those targeting our best and brightest warrior knights.

Marauders. I *know* Rihad has ordered the assassinations of the warriors enroute to the tournament. I simply don't fully understand why. To leave the south, north and the east exposed while he builds up his own strength in the heart of the Protectorate? To put new Divhs in place in those border houses? What could be the advantage there?

Unless...unless he knows how weak we are at the border, and he seeks to reinforce us. I think of my father, walled up in the Tenth, desperately clinging to the old ways. Father would never allow Lord Rihad to usurp his authority in his own house. But without Merritt...without our Div...

I narrow my gaze on Fortiss, well ahead of me at the leading edge of the procession. My stomach knots in equal parts delirium and doubt as I think of what we shared last night.

If he ever discovers who I really am...

But he can't. No one can. I've come to this tournament to seek protection for my family and honor for my house. That remains my primary charge.

Though perhaps, no longer my only charge.

Whether it's the way of the warrior or not, I *want* revenge. Justice. I don't know who killed Merritt among these warriors, but at Lord Rihad's request, one of the men or boys riding in this procession loosed the arrow that buried itself in my brother's back. There can be no forgiveness for that.

I hope I'll be able to fight every last one of the First House warriors until I find my brother's murderer. If I look across that open space and see the truth in his eyes, know *this* warrior is the one who killed Merritt, I won't stand down from my attack, no matter how the horns blow.

And I *will* win, I resolve. Especially if what I saw in Rihad's chambers lies in wait for the Protectorate. Especially if the dark tales of the Savasci have any basis in truth. I will win warriors for the Tenth House and for the Ninth and Eleventh, the Fourth and Fifth, to replace their fallen sons. I will win warriors for the Twelfth House too, so they aren't caught unawares.

I frown, considering the reality of what I seek to accomplish. But Rihad has promised a brace of twenty warrior knights to the winner, and the Tenth House doesn't need twenty men. We need two. Perhaps three. More than that and we'd need to build a second manor house.

I snort as Nazar rides up beside me.

"Your manner is dark, and your thoughts take you away from the path you must tread," he says conversationally, as if the words he speaks are of no import. "That's the way to destruction, both for you and your lord."

I narrow my eyes at him. He *cannot* mean Fortiss. The man isn't a mind-reader. "I have no lord, Nazar."

"Then all the more reason for you to follow the way of strategy, that you might serve as the lord of yourself and your troops. That you might push yourself nobly to the actions you seek to achieve."

"It's one of them, ahead of us, who killed him." I stare stonily up the long procession, unable to let the thought go. "I can't tell which one. With them all dressed alike, they're all the enemy."

Nazar falls quiet for a moment. "You must think hard on what you say," he tells me gravely. "Your words contain more answers than you realize." He waves off my retort. "Your opponents in the coming rounds know precisely what you have shown them, and only what you've shown them. What have they seen?"

I sigh. I've given this a great deal of thought too. "That I attack quickly, but allow my opponent to regain his feet, so I can be taken down with equal speed." I shift uncomfortably. "I've given them much to work with."

"Now you must give them something else," Nazar says. "Something that is most important, given the line of First House warriors you have emblazoned in your mind as your due. They will come at you, in ones and twos or all at once, but you must make your body into rock as well as water, such that no one can touch you, no one can harm you."

I frown at him as he leans over, fussing with the thick gullet of Darkwing's saddle. "Harm me or harm my spirit? I thought warriors fight with their minds."

Nazar straightens, and his face is so intense that I cannot look to see what he's done to my tack; I can only stare into his hard, gray eyes. "What is the spirit of a warrior worth if there is no body of the warrior for others to see? If you learn to make your body like rock, your thoughts like water, all who see you will know what you do, and will wish to follow a warrior and a lord who can master such an act. You must think hard on this truth and make it your own."

Nazar peels away from me, and something flutters in the wind as he falls back. I glance down at my saddle. Now, hanging from the saddle in a tight knot is a spray of long, delicate sashes, each stained a deep forest green, painted over with slender silver bands. I know what they are: favors. I reflect on what Nazar has told me. As we near the coliseum, there'll be more people—people all around, both those waiting to enter the stands and those who cannot afford to enter, the masses of spectators who can still see much of the battle of warrior Divhs simply by looking up to the sky.

They've come to be entertained. They've come to be awed.

I fan my fingers through the sashes. I don't think they've come to be led, though. Not by me. Perhaps by Rihad...

I frown, peering ahead. Rihad has almost reached the coliseum, where he will honor the fifty-odd soldiers and villagers who've fought and earned the right to become banded soldiers.

He will be their sponsor, and...

I blink. He will be their *sponsor*. Their sponsor and patron, in the end, much like he is to the bards. For all that he is to release these men to far-flung houses, how is there any way to ensure that their loyalty would be to their new lords? None. Not when Rihad is the benefactor who made it all possible in the first place. Not when Rihad has the power to grant men the opportunity to become warriors. There's no more potent bond of loyalty than when you've lifted a man into a new station.

My lips settle into a thin line. *I am a fool. A thousand times a fool.*

Fighting in the tournament won't bring back Merritt, and it won't bring the Tenth House honor. Even if I discover the identity of Merritt's killer, there will be no justice for my brother.

Winning the tournament won't even truly bring the warriors we now lack at the Tenth House. It will merely bring spies and minions for Rihad into our home.

I glance sidelong at the armed guards lining the path to the coliseum. They're here to keep the crowd from us, true enough. But they're also here to ensure we don't break ranks. Rihad has carefully orchestrated this day, and he's certain of its outcome. Just as he's certain that the bards are in his employ and the warriors of his house will do his bidding without fail. He's certain of a lot of things.

At last, the coliseum looms high overhead, and in its shadows teem the crowds of Trilion. I gape, startled at how many more spectators seem to be in attendance than even a week earlier. They spill deep into the marshlands, spreading out from the coliseum, and as the first of our line reaches them, the cheers start loud and long, growing with each new warrior that passes by them.

Even though the cheers for Lord Rihad are great and there are many streamers thrown in celebration, the crowd's shouts boom even higher as the final First House warriors pass. And then come the Second House warriors, well recognized in this place. More streamers and flowers fly through the air along with shouts of encouragement. And on it goes, until finally the Eighth House passes into the crowd, and I eventually pace Darkwing forward close behind the stallion carrying the lone warrior for the Ninth House. My face burns as I worry there will be no one to cheer these smaller houses.

I'm mistaken.

The cheers rise up with what sounds like even greater abandon, urging the smaller houses on to impossible victory—or perhaps the spectators are simply grateful that the procession is drawing to a close. But as I ride, I begin to see makeshift flags, dark green slashes among all the gold and black, orange, sand, and blue.

From my saddle, eager hands pull away the favors that Nazar has given me as well. I stare, trying to make out faces in the crowd. There is more than just the boy from the fighting pits or even his family, there are easily a dozen—a small pittance compared to the rolling swath of gold and black, or even the fiery flurry of the orange...but there *are* a dozen, definitely.

A dozen souls who hold up a flag for a warrior knight to whom they have no allegiance, who failed in his first trial. A dozen brave bettors who, for at least this moment, think I can progress through the tournament. Think I can battle proudly. Think—possibly—I can win.

Or maybe they just feel sorry for me.

I laugh aloud at the traitorous thought, and several of the crowd nearest me turn and add more gusto to their cheers. All the warriors before me have been taciturn, stoic. Theirs is a sacred trust, and they'll be returning to their proud houses as victors no matter their efforts here.

I have no proud house, no trust. I have only this: a doomed battle against a stacked field, where the greatest warriors in the land are but the puppets of a larger hand, turning and twirling us for his own dark reasons.

And yet, there are those few green flags...

We make the final turn into the mouth of the coliseum, and if I was surprised at the overflow crowd, I'm completely overwhelmed now. Everyone is on their feet, stamping and chanting, and again, the flags fly at the tips of outstretched hands. Men and even women crane forth, holding up children to see, to experience the glory of this procession of the Protectorate's finest combatants. These are men charged with highest honor from the Exalted Imperium itself, and handed into service generation over generation, divinely blessed with the obligation to protect and defend.

As we march, the procession splits off, and I pivot to see the outriders shunt away to a cordoned area, to dismount and wait until they are needed. For this, the real tournament, First House guards won't be required to minister to every combatant, especially those who are injured in battle. No, each warrior will be cared for by his own men, which means Nazar and Caleb can stay close, both to help and to protect me from unwanted attention should I fall.

The procession finally stops in front of a grand new platform that has been constructed before the wooden towers, upon which stand all the councilors and Lord Protector Rihad. We dismount and are escorted one by one to the stage, where we stand in front of the councilors but behind Rihad, looking for all the world like we are foot soldiers to his general.

Rihad holds up his hand, and the crowd stills as criers before each section hold up their hands as well. As impossible as it is for me to believe that mere criers can hold such sway over this enormous throng, I squint more closely and see the guards lining the field to either side of the criers, apparently ready to enforce silence on the tips of their blades.

Rihad drops his hands and shouts out, "Welcome to the Tournament of Gold!"

As the criers repeat the statement, a roar loud enough to be heard in the Imperium capital sails forth. He lets it continue for a time. Then he speaks again, pausing so that the criers can echo his words in an ever-expanding wave.

"First, we honor the winners of the fighting pits. Fifty brave men and boys who have earned the right to fight as banded soldiers. At the end of this tournament, you are the ones who will be feasting in the First House. You are the ones who will bow down beside the priests of the Light, to receive your sacred warrior bands."

Another deafening roar accompanies this pronouncement. I gaze down over the men and boys assembled before Rihad. The cheater from the first round isn't among them, and I lift my chin higher at noticing that, sweeping the group with an assessing gaze.

They stare back boldly—some a little awed, some intense, all of them proud and exhausted at once, with the look of souls who've been cast one too many times upon the shoals of a distant shore. Their efforts will be rewarded, however. With Rihad as their sponsor, they will get their Divhs. One by one they will be granted a fearsome creature—to the size and manner they deserve.

I look over to Fortiss, standing stoically by Rihad's side. He, too, deserves a Divh, and not to be simply swept along by circumstances he cannot control. Perhaps his father had died too swiftly, perhaps in great pain. Perhaps he'd thought he would recover...

"Your thoughts betray you, Merritt of the Tenth House."

Beneath the roaring of the crowds, the voice close to my ear is almost intimate. I stiffen, turning slightly to the side. "Councilor Miriam."

"You feel pity for Fortiss." The words aren't said as a rebuke, but I harden my jaw all the same.

"I have no need to feel pity for the exalted warrior of the First House. He'll fight nobly and well with Rihad's Divh. The Tournament is graced by their alliance."

"He'll fight nobly and well." Miriam breaks off as Rihad speaks again, but she doesn't flow back into the crowd as I so desperately want her to. "But their alliance is no act of grace."

I can't help but gape at her then dart my gaze to those around us. But I am the last warrior on the platform, with the Eleventh and Twelfth Houses absent, and Miriam stands between me and the rest of the half circle of men. She turns forward, smiling as Rihad speaks again. Then her words float to me as the men on the field below depart, swamped in a roaring tide of honor and adulation.

"You forget, I have lived long among the council. I have known generations of warriors of the First House, and all the great men as well. Fortiss's father was both. He was as honorable as his father before him."

"His loss was keenly felt, I am sure."

"By most." She nods. "Not by all." She slides her glance to me again. "You have great anger within you, Merritt of the Tenth. It surrounds you in a corona of fierce light. Protects you, even. I cannot pierce it as easily as I would like."

All the saliva dries in my mouth. "You're a sensitive."

Even in the backward mountains of the east, I've heard of people like her. Not mystics, exactly. Not priests or priestesses of the Light either. But they are highly intuitive, keenly discerning, their skills almost—not quite, but almost—magical. No wonder Rihad has allowed Miriam on the council. Not because he's so advanced, but because he cannot allow himself to miss out on her insights. And he's already proven he's no stranger to magical incantations and premonitions.

What other secrets is he hiding?

More to the point, how is it that Miriam hasn't already outed me as a woman? Surely, she can intuit that most basic of truths, unless...

I frown. Unless her sight is blinded by the warrior's band she can sense on my arm? Is she truly so entrenched in the doctrine of the Protectorate that she cannot imagine a woman connected to a Divh? And is that why Fortiss, too, hasn't seen my truth—when he, more than anyone, should?

If so, this warrior band has been blessed a thousand times by the Light. I will bow to wherever it leads me.

But Miriam recalls my focus. "Such anger as yours leaves a residue wherever you go—not for long, and your anger is so bright that it flares and is quickly gone, like a shadow in the heat of the sun. But it rests long enough for those who know how to look."

Caution pricks at the hairs upon my nape as she regards me more fully. "You were in the caverns of the First House, weren't you?" she asks, her words sounding like a death knell. "You saw what lies trapped within our very walls. And you must have asked yourself why. But 'why' isn't the right question."

I stare at her, my mouth set, my face a winter's sky. How does she know these things—and what else does she know? I've no idea, but I won't give her the honor of ensnaring me further in her web.

At least now I know why she hasn't betrayed me, though. She has her own agenda here, her own goal. One that leaves no room for a consideration so banal as my gender, not when the warrior's band around my bicep fairly radiates with its own sentient energy.

She leans forward and taps my arm where the band cuts into my flesh. "The right question is 'who' and then 'how.' Who had a Divh and then didn't...and who should have been chosen by one, and was not? And, more importantly, how was such a deed done?"

The cheering ends, and now Miriam does retreat, leaving me to stare ahead at Rihad—and at Fortiss. The truth I had already suspected now laid bare to me, the cruel deception I had shuddered to imagine brought to light...and brought to light by Rihad's own councilor. Why?

But as Miriam herself said, why isn't the question here. But who...and then how.

Fortiss is the son of Toma, once the greatest warrior in the land. Toma's awesomely fleet and powerful Divh, Szonja—the Divh of a generation, the Divh of a hundred bardic tales—should have died with him or been passed on to his son.

Instead, a creature who is a shadow of that former Divh lies chained in the bowels of the First House, held fast by the Lord Protector, while Rihad wears two bands.

He holds that Divh, without question, through abilities that are not of the Light. Rihad has trapped the most glorious Divh in a century, binding her up in ever-tightening coils of darkness.

He has trapped her, and he has trapped us all.

CHAPTER 34

The first day's battles are cruel, but brief.

Each of the great warrior battles takes place at the top of the hour and lasts no more than a few minutes of actual fighting—some far less—from the moment the Divhs appear until they're banished from the tournament field, in triumph or defeat. Then the crowds shift and eddy as spectators abandon their seats for food and drink, and new ones flow in to take their spaces.

But when the Divhs fight, no one moves—not in the stands, nor in the grounds beyond, I suspect. I've now seen Divhs both great and small upon the battlefield, and victory doesn't always go to the mightiest in form. More often it is the sharpest of strategy that prevails—or, as Nazar's words echo in my mind—those whose instinct is strong enough to border on strategy. Fast wins except when slow and measured takes the upper hand. Big wins except where nimble and cutting works better. The warriors atop the wooden towers seem driven to a frenzy by the time each battle is finished, sweat darkening their tournament clothes, blood seeping from wounds gartered by their tight garments.

Divhs are summoned, they fight, and then they are dispatched back to their cool, quiet plane, while we remain surrounded in chaos. People throng the central platform where the warriors wait, calling out names and waving flags, sending up great cheers when a new set of combatants is called to fight. Money changes hands at every turn, whether warriors are battling or not—wagers appearing to be made on the way a man stands and turns, if he smiles or growls, even on the length of his stride.

I've seen two warriors of the Southern Realms carried out on stretchers, their faces a mask of pain. This is the first tournament of any merit for most of them, the whispers surge. Perhaps the line on the houses of yellow, sand, and umber was too quickly made? Flags gather and scatter like flocks of birds, and by the day's end, I see no more of the dark-green-hued banners. The battle doesn't come to me this day, however. I have to wait.

But now I perch on my tiptoes along with every other person in the stadium, be they warrior, squire, or freeman. Because Fortiss has taken his position on one of the wooden towers, here to fight as a warrior knight, though he has yet to receive his own band or his Divh.

Instead, Fortiss's rightful band still circles the left arm of Rihad. The more I think of that outrage, the less I can stomach it. Fortiss would have been banded to his Divh long ago were it not for Rihad and his twisted games.

Fortiss's opponent is a warrior from the Fifth House, a grizzled veteran twice Fortiss's age. The older man shows no fear as he curls his right hand to his heart and lifts his left arm high, but I feel fear for him.

The Fifth House warrior's Divh appears first. It's large—easily one of the largest of the day, and I slant my glance toward the Lord Protector. Not surprisingly, Rihad is leaning forward from his perch upon the stone ledge, his smile wide with anticipation. He peers eagerly at the monstrous Divh and nods. It is a worthy foe.

Worthy is right. This Divh is apelike, its large, thick arms hanging down heavily to the ground, ending in barrel-shaped fists that knuckle under as the creature uses its arms as a second pair of legs. Its haunches are equally powerful, and those end in viciously clawed paws that scrape at the ground, gaining purchase in the hard-packed dirt. Its head seems unreasonably small for its body—except for the tusks which sprout from either side of its tightly drawn mouth. Its beady eyes—all eight of them—sweep the stands and the grounds before him, waiting for its combatant to appear.

Fortiss curls his right hand to his heart and raises his left arm.

The entire coliseum goes quiet for a long, harrowing moment.

Nothing appears at the far end of the tournament field; nothing appears in front of the wooden towers. I shoot my gaze toward Rihad again, but his grin remains intact. At this distance, I can't tell if he's surprised or angered or—

The air around me snaps tight, like a sheet whipped by a gale.

A roar of an entirely different kind booms over the tournament grounds.

The crowds might be screaming, or they might have fallen silent. I can't hear anything above the torrent of sound rushing through my brain as I turn to witness the creature that Fortiss and Rihad have now summoned forth.

It's the hugest monster I have ever seen. Nearly as tall as the coliseum is long, the creature looks closest to a scorpion, but with the head of a lizard and two sets of arms—one with clawed hands at its ends, the other tipped with the cruel pincers a scorpion would typically employ. Its body is covered with a glistening carapace all the way down to its viciously barbed tail, and four sets of slender legs brace its immense body. It rears upright and spreads its wings, its mouth opening horrifyingly wide to utter an enraged hiss.

My gaze leaps to Fortiss as he turns around to see the creature himself, but he shows no surprise. Instead, the two stare at each other a long moment, taking each other's measure. Then the apelike Divh of the Fifth House screams, whether in annoyance or anger, I can't tell. But that apparently is all the encouragement that the Lord Protector's Divh needs.

The creature's wings snap wide, and it launches toward the center of the stadium. The apelike Divh follows suit, only that beast's gait is a loping, full-bodied lurch that looks like it's throwing himself forward on the ground versus truly running. I focus on the center of the tournament field and only then notice that Fortiss and Rihad hold almost identical stances—Fortiss moving forward on the warrior's platform and Rihad locked in place on his stage, their bodies taut, their expressions focused. Their eyes seeing something other than what is right in front of their faces. They're both looking through the eyes of the enormous, winged scorpion, and they both grow wholly still as the two Divhs crash together in the center of the field. The fighting between the monsters is frenzied, and though the minutes stretch, both Rihad and Fortiss never move.

In fact, it's the grizzled veteran of the Fifth House who finally breaks the spell. With a sudden shudder, he twists to the side, and I find my gaze jumping back toward the fight, where I see, to my horror, that the razor-sharp scorpion's claws haven't merely grabbed the Fifth House Divh—they've gouged the chest of the ape wide open. The wound is deep and vicious, and on the platform, the veteran warrior knight drops to one knee, blood blossoming below his neck.

My gaze shifts to Rihad, but his hand is out, staying the trumpeters who even now are pressing the horns to their lips. Instead, he watches, his face wreathed in feral glee as his monster swipes forward, its blow clearly aimed for the ape's unprotected throat. At the last moment, the Divh jerks its pincer up instead, clipping its victim in the jaw and spinning the ape in a wide, tumbling arc.

I watch Rihad as he drops his gaze to Fortiss and see the fury in his countenance for a moment as the two stare each other down. Then the Lord Protector drops his hand and the tournament horns finally sound. Guards scuttle out to both men. Fortiss raises his arms in triumph even as the other man swoons on the stage, then both of them lift their left hands again to release their Divhs.

Huge, rollicking cheers roll through the coliseum as a new round of trumpets blare, signaling the end of the day's competition. Rihad's monster disappears immediately, but the other warrior's Divh doesn't. It moans pitiably, trying to scratch its way forward, only to see his warrior turn and slash his arm out a second time. Then it winks out, no one the wiser of its momentary defection from the rules...a defection born of trying to reach the very warrior who hadn't been able to protect it.

I stand stock-still as the trumpets crash around me. Everyone is moving, pushing, shouting. The Fifth House Divh is mortally wounded—there's no way it can survive that hit, no way that its warrior can either, I know it in my bones. I look up at the platforms, but I can't see anyone standing there. The men have been cleared away like the evening meal.

Fortiss emerges moments later at the bottom of his tower, but the warrior from the Fifth House doesn't appear. And when the guards come to take us to our horses and escort us to the makeshift tent camp outside the stadium grounds, the Fifth House's horse remains with his people outside the tower. They all look determinedly cheerful.

I watch for him the rest of the day. The warrior doesn't return.

"He's probably been taken back to the First House for rest and doctors." Caleb leans over our table that evening at the open-air feast on the tournament grounds, his hands around a fat loaf of fruited bread, a steaming meat pie at his elbow. "No one wants to see injury in a tournament, least of all Rihad. And in this case, he *literally* doesn't want to see it. Or, alternatively, they've spirited away the fellow and his entourage and horse entirely, and he's getting patched up somewhere in Trilion. It's not like he's going to be able to fight any more in the tournament."

"I don't think he's going to be able to fight anymore, period," I say, staring into my own cup of wine. "He was hurt—badly. So was his Divh."

"Divhs heal." Caleb waves his hand.

"That one won't."

A burst of chatter and cheers sounds at the far end of the tent camp, and I squint that way. Fortiss has arrived, amid much back-slapping and shoulder thumping. He accepts it all graciously, but his manner seems different somehow, reserved.

"He doesn't look as happy as he might, for someone who just pulled off the impossible," I observe.

"Who?" Caleb cranes his neck around until he sees Fortiss. "Oh, him. He was ordered to speak to Rihad after the day's closing ceremonies, and I didn't get the idea it was for a fatherly hug. Rihad looked seriously angry."

"He did?" I keep my tone light. "You mean because of the fight?"

"Not the fight." Caleb laughs. "Are you mad? The fight made Rihad the talk of the Tournament. *Rihad*, not Fortiss. Everyone knew that Rihad's Divh would be showing up today, but people had...forgotten, I guess, how big it was. I know I sure had."

"How long ago did you see it last?"

He screws up his face in thought. "Well, I was pretty young, so I don't remember much except the beast itself—and that it scared the stuffing out of me. Later, I learned the details of the battle. Believe me, the bards wouldn't shut up about it. Rihad wasn't fighting. Like this one, he was running the show, not participating. So that would have made it maybe..." He blew out a long breath. "Ten years ago, easily."

"He would've still been in his prime, able to fight alongside the other warriors."

"Well, he didn't. But it's not as if he didn't try." Caleb grins. "I remember the story now. It wasn't the tournament proper, but right before. He summoned his Divh for an exhibition match. The other warrior fainted dead away."

I stare at him. "He didn't."

"He did. But anyway, he's not upset about the fight, he's upset that Fortiss pulled his Divh off the Fifth House's beast so quickly.

He wanted more blood. But! I'm out of wine. And what sort of competent squire would I be if I didn't keep us well stocked with wine?"

He pushes back from the table and stands, a little wobbly.

"I think we might be good without the wine." I glance around, but Nazar still hasn't joined us. The priest isn't my servant, of course, despite the charade we're carrying on. He doesn't have to inform me of his actions.

Still, I find I miss the old man and his counsel as I look around the lavishly decorated grounds.

Once again, Rihad has spared no expense...or someone hasn't. I can't fathom how much coin such an encampment costs. Great flowing tents of thick cloth drape the grounds outside the coliseum, one for each house, even all the way down to the lowly Tenth. Unlike in the procession, however, we aren't segregated by size. That means I've been sandwiched in between the Third and First Houses. Now I stare again at the warriors who eat and drink with abandon, welcoming Fortiss back into their midst. There are a dozen of them, ranging from a boy barely older than Merritt to dark-eyed, dark-scowled men in their thirties. I drink from my cup, regarding them all more carefully.

Think of yourself as the enemy, Nazar told me, and I allow my gaze to swing from man to boy and back again. Who would I choose to kill a first-blooded and firstborn warrior knight? Who would I trust among my own company to not only be able to shoot with flawless accuracy over a great distance, but to be able to pull the longbow taut in the first place?

Not a boy.

One by one I rule out the younger members of the First House's warrior knight base—those who seem too small or weak, or too wide-eyed. Neither bodes well to carry out a murder, especially murder by loosed arrow. And while I never caught sight of the archer who killed my brother, I believe without question that it would be someone who could be trusted implicitly. Someone who has served long and well. That means someone older. Experienced.

Comfortable with the idea of taking a man's life in cold blood, and with following whatever order I give. Someone who understands how to keep his mouth shut.

I sip my wine and gaze out over my enemies. They are many, I realize—the members of the shooter's caravan who fled when Gent appeared behind me during the attack in the mountains, even the soldiers who were sent out to kill the other warrior knights beyond Merritt of the Tenth. But for now, I cannot think of anyone but the man who was directly responsible for my brother's death.

It must be one of the three older warrior knights of the First House, I decide. There is no other possibility. I could be facing one of these men across the tournament field tomorrow, looking into the face of a killer. Not just a killer, but a cowardly one. A weak, slinking snake who slithered through the forest on a mission to sacrifice a boy—and would have sacrificed more, I was certain, if he'd waited around to see me hold Merritt in my arms. But he hadn't waited around. He'd assumed there was no more threat from the Tenth House.

He'd assumed wrong.

Still, to shoot an arrow that far—it had been close to a quarter of a mile—would have taken tremendous strength. That leaves two of the men. Both of those warriors watch everyone around them, especially Fortiss, but they don't drink. Both of them have food upon their plates, but they don't eat. Idly, I push my own dish away, my appetite curdling even as I realize that the time for vengeance is not yet here. I will meet them on the battlefield, or I will meet them in the shadows. But I cannot stomach seeing them unharmed and unpunished across the luxurious tent camp.

I step away from the table. I need to breathe the sharp, crisp air of open grounds. Even in this outdoor camp, I feel confined.

No one tries to stop me as I stride quickly between the large tents. I don't actively try to avoid anyone, be they councilor, warrior, or hired man. But I don't seek anyone out either. My mind is too full of possibilities, my thoughts too full of poison. I picture the two men of the First House in my mind. Which one killed Merritt? One tall and thin but with deceptively broad shoulders, one built like an ox, his neck as thick as a tree trunk. Which?

I've almost reached the outer perimeter when I hear a familiar voice calling to me from behind.

"Merritt! A moment, let me catch up."

My heart skips three beats, maybe four.

It's Fortiss.

CHAPTER 35

"Well met, Merritt! How goes the day now that the tournament has begun in earnest?"

Fortiss is practically bursting with good cheer, but all I want to do is get away from him. How can he not know…how can he not recognize me? We were wrapped in each other's arms less than a full day ago!

The band, I remind myself, straightening with spine-cracking severity as I smile grimly at Fortiss. The band protects me. Now I just need to protect myself. "Well enough," I grunt, trying to damp down his exuberance. "I've never seen battles such as these."

Fortiss doesn't seem to notice my sour tone. "Of course you haven't. Rihad is constantly seeking to improve the Tournament of Gold, Merritt. He seeks to make us stronger, to challenge our abilities."

"He's allowing warriors to *die* here. How is that making any of us strong?"

Fortiss's expression flickers, but he sets his mouth in a hard line. "The Tournament of Gold is a sacred charge, but not all houses answer its call. As tragic as these deaths are, they do show that not all the legacy lines have maintained their dedication to their calling. Divhs are awarded each to the strength of their warrior. You see your own Divh—its size, its strength. All the men here are those that should be here."

Anger stirs anew, but I snap my mouth shut. I can't convince Fortiss of my position—I shouldn't try. Because, despite his words of Protectorate glory, that's not why I'm here. I'm here to protect my house...and my people.

"Perhaps you're right," I say at length. "It's hard to accept, especially when you also consider the death of the warriors from the Ninth and Eleventh Houses. They were young and untested, with families and houses to protect."

"I know." Fortiss lifts a hand to my arm. "But Rihad won't leave the houses unprotected. He has structured the Tournament of Gold this year to install warriors where they would not have been accepted otherwise, whether for pride or honor or vanity. Think of the Twelfth House, where a lord has not allowed his son to take his place. I cannot think Lord Orlof is battle-ready any longer, yet his pride holds his son from his position."

I grunt. The Twelfth House's son is fourteen years old, and Fortiss has already told me his father is a brute. The boy can wait a few years more. Still, I cannot gainsay Fortiss's words. I don't know much about Lord Orlof other than what my mother instructed me years ago in how I should act as the wife of his son. And that, of course, doesn't recommend the old man. He seems to be cut from the same bolt of cloth as my own father, which would make him everything that Fortiss has said: prideful, vain, and stuck in moldering tradition.

But I'm grateful for that, anyway. Orlof's vanity has kept his son safe from Rihad's arrows. Not even the Lord Protector will attack a sitting lord in his own house, it seems. So Rihad still has some restraint.

For how long, though?

"Merritt?" Fortiss is frowning at me again, and I shake my head.

"Sorry. A lot to take in."

"I understand." He manages a crooked smile, and I wonder if

he's thinking of me—of Talia—of our night together. You'd never know it from his manner. "You should look sharp, though. Your first real battle tomorrow is against Hantor of the Second House. To hear him talk, his Divh will crush yours before yours draws its first breath on the tournament field."

"Hantor?" I squint at the sky. "That's not right. I was against—"

"There's been a change. That's why I was coming to find you, actually. I saw you that first day, when you mounted the platform. It seemed you and the Second House already had bad blood between you. I wanted you to know."

"But why the change?"

"Councilor Miriam meddling again." Fortiss says the words so off-handedly, I think I misunderstand.

"Miriam?" My heart skips a beat. "But how—"

"She's a sensitive. Can pick up moods and attitudes in a blink."

I nod. So it's no secret. "I thought as much. But how can that matter in the tournament?"

Fortiss grimaces. "Rihad has been running the Tournament of Gold since before I was born. No matter what he says, his primary goal above all things is to entertain. The greater the challenge between warriors, the better the entertainment. As you no doubt saw today."

"You managed Rihad's Divh well." I don't mention the Fifth House's warrior knight again. Or that he's likely dead.

Fortiss shakes his head. "I—" He catches himself, then begins again. "Thank you. But Rihad had instructed me before the battle on how the old man I fought had disdained his choice to allow me to fight in his stead. He believed it was against the old ways. Rihad wanted a lesson to be made of him."

I think about the empty tent of the Fifth House, and now I do push the point. "Did he die?"

Fortiss hesitates. "Not yet. But it's expected sometime later this night. And even if he hasn't..."

I nod. "The message has been delivered."

"Yes. It was Miriam who provided the information to Rihad that changed his mind about the tenor of the battle. She also moved through the lot of us today, talking randomly. But she listened and absorbed more than she talked."

I think of Miriam and struggle to remember what she'd said to me as we'd stood on the platform, protected, I'd thought, from the thundering roar around us. I hadn't suspected that I'd need to protect myself from her, even as she'd spoken her twisting words about Fortiss.

Fortiss and I turn and move back toward the camps. I don't miss the deferential glances sent his way. These men saw him command a Divh that was not his own, and they have to suspect that the Fifth House warrior knight is dead. Now here Fortiss is, walking with me through the camp on the eve of my next battle.

I eye him. "What are you doing, talking to me? You didn't have to warn me."

He stops, and the glance he sends me is hurried and even a little embarrassed. "I didn't. I probably shouldn't have. The announcement will be made tomorrow at the tournament platform. Have the grace to look surprised."

I nod but am even more confused. "I have no standing in this tournament. In this place. You'll be noticed, talking to me. As you are noticed talking to anyone."

"True." He offers me a small smile, and the moment feels even more awkward. "Maybe I don't care."

"Fair enough." I don't push the point, but I haven't seen him speaking with the men from the southern houses, or even with those from the west. I feel a strange emotion prick the nerves in my neck. "And I appreciate the warning. I can prepare for what I know, not for what I don't."

"Good." He smiles again, and I feel it anew, the tiny shiver of awareness that could be friendship among men, comradeship...but given what happened between us last night, it's something different, something dangerous, despite the protection of my band. Fortiss is a leader under a man who's murdered for the greater glory of his house. Fortiss hasn't killed for Rihad—but he would. I must remember that.

Instead, I force myself not to startle as he claps me on the shoulder. "Tomorrow, we shall fight, warrior." He grins. "And glory will be ours."

By the time I return to the Tenth House encampment, both Caleb and Nazar are there. Caleb's curled in slumber, his hand clasped around Nazar's seeing glass, which now hangs from a long chain around his neck. I eye the priest with surprise, and he shrugs, his lined face at peace in the trailing wisps of his pipe smoke.

"He has a need to see far, and I would help him do so," Nazar says, as if that's reason enough to give up the delicate instrument.

I find myself smiling, looking down at Caleb, but when I glance again to Nazar, the priest's face seems unusually set. Drawn, almost. He gestures me closer, and I step near, into the protecting cover of the thick canvas walls of our tent.

"What is it?" I ask when I'm close enough that none might overhear our words. "What have you learned?"

"It's not what I've learned, but what you have," Nazar says. He takes another pull on his pipe. "You've endured much in this tournament already, and a warrior deserves to know the truth of those with whom he fights."

I frown at him. The priest seems older than he should, suddenly, his face lined with new sorrows. "I don't understand."

He offers me the pipe, and my brows shoot up. I get the sense this isn't an idle offering, but I've never drawn pipe smoke and suspect I'll choke to death if I try.

Still, he doesn't speak, merely lifts the pipe higher. I take it, and as Nazar's eyes crinkle with the faintest amusement, I fit the mouthpiece to my lips.

"Draw soft and don't swallow, bringing the smoke to the mind but not the heart."

I don't know if Nazar is speaking those words aloud or not, but I take a shallow, cautious breath, not trusting myself to do more.

The taste of the smoke is curiously sweet, heady, and I blow it as quickly, waiting as long as I dare to take another shallow breath of fresh air. My eyes water, but I manage only the slightest cough.

Nazar nods as I blink away the moisture, but he doesn't take the pipe back at first.

Instead, he unshoulders part of his cloak, leaving his left arm bare.

"Know the truth, Warrior Talia," he says.

I blink again hard, then a second time, but the horror of what's in front of me doesn't flow away like smoke and tears.

"*Nazar*," I gasp.

The priest who stands before me has been horribly, grievously wounded. Scars rip and rend their way in a ragged scream down his left arm, making the once-muscular length of it a shredded waste, deformed and twisted. The bones appear to have been broken and poorly reset, and the devastation continues all the way to the base of the priest's hand—where, unmistakably, a thick scrap of leather is still buried in his wrist, like some forsaken relic. The skin around that knot is white with scars, clear proof of the attempt to fully remove it...an attempt that apparently had been stopped before Nazar lost his hand entirely.

"What..." I begin to ask the question, then realize I don't need to. The answer has been waiting for me to see it from the very first day. "*You* were that banded soldier you told me about, from all those years ago." All Nazar's training, his guidance, and his knowledge make sudden, irrefutable sense. "You have a *Divh*."

Nazar's mouth creases into a tired smile, his eyes suddenly as old as the Sounding Sea. "Had," he says, his voice sounding very far away. "Wrath. He was the mightiest creature in the capital—in all of the Imperium, perhaps. Noble, strong, and true."

"But what..."

My words seem to bring Nazar back to the moment. "The Imperium, in its weakness, forbade the connection of warrior and Divh outside the Protectorate many, many years ago. But that's not the truth you must know now, merely the test of that truth. In my privation, I sought the Light, and I learned that such weakness as I encountered in the Imperium takes many forms. Each equally damning."

Whether it's the heaviness of the smoke still in the air or the lulling cadence of Nazar's voice, I find myself riveted to attention as he continues.

"In the waning days of the Imperial Wars, entire households had been established in the western frontier. Once those warriors understood what lay outside our borders in the Western Realms, both men and women fought to turn back the threat. In that time of dire need, the emperor discovered the unlikely ally of the Divh, and a contract of protection between our races was struck. The Imperium to lead, the Divh to follow, and the Protectorate was formed."

I nod, my gaze still fixed on Nazar's shattered arm. How had he...*why* had he been unbanded so gruesomely? What did he mean by the Imperium's weakness?

Then his next words command my undivided focus.

"But that contract was not—could not—have been made by men," the priest says quietly. "Instead, it was proven that the first-born *daughters* of the imperial warlords fought with the fiercest strength and greatest connection to the Divhs, and that only they could broker this agreement with the mighty foreign race. Accordingly, they were granted the mightiest of the beasts. Those women became the true first line of warriors."

I gape at him. "The...daughters?" Unbidden, the image of the Savasci springs to my mind. It's not so difficult to imagine those women as warriors, having seen their faces, their eyes.

"This is why the law is so harsh in the Protectorate, Talia. Because once upon a time, women were the mightiest warriors in the land. Eventually, men could no longer stomach that truth. But the truth, it still remains." He fixes me with a hard gaze. "It's why Gent evolved to match the strength he saw in you, Talia—*not* because you were weak, but because you were stronger than any son of the Tenth House had been for generations. It's also why you have taken both to the band and to the way of the warrior with instinctive truth. And why you can succeed now."

I flinch back, immediately rejecting his words out of habit and yet...and yet...I *want* to believe him. I want to think that maybe one day I'll be worthy of the enormous, beautiful Divh who has pledged his bond to me. I want to be the warrior knight both Gent and Nazar believe me to be—someday.

I'm definitely not there yet.

"But it's not enough. *I'm* not enough. I'm not trained," I protest, still staring as the priest slowly reshoulders his cloak, hiding his ruined arm from view. "There's still so much I don't know."

"That's true," Nazar says gravely, reclaiming his pipe from my frozen fingers. "But what is also true is that you are Talia of the Tenth House, first-blooded and firstborn. As such, you will fight with power and with honor, and with the strength your blood has given you. And you will *always* be enough."

CHAPTER 36

The next day, standing on the platform of warriors as Rihad reads the assignments of the new combatants, I don't feel like I'll be enough, despite the roaring of the crowd. Dutifully, I jolt in momentary dismay as Rihad announces Hantor's name, holding my startled expression long enough that the Lord Protector gets his moment of preening. *Unmitigated ass.*

The moment he glances away I wipe all emotion from my face.

Hantor, of course, leers at me, clearly delighted at the opportunity of our coming battle. My mind still swimming with Nazar's revelation, I stare at Miriam. She gazes back solemnly the whole while, and I try not to squirm beneath her scrutiny. Has she guessed I'm not really Merritt, at long last? Surely she would have alerted Rihad if so, and yet—how can she not know?

Or does she know...and she's merely holding her tongue, for reasons of her own? Is she also acting the part of the warrior, in the only way she can?

Once again, I think about the women of the marauder tribe, angry and independent and strong. Once again, I can see them as warriors, for all that they aren't nobly born. In another setting, any one of them could have worn the band.

Suddenly, there's a guard at my side. I step out as another wave of cheers soars through the air. I follow silently as the guard threads his way through the remaining warriors, then we enter the narrow tower—the same one I'd entered to fight Kheris and his serpent. According to Nazar, Hantor's Divh is less imposing, but I still hear his follow-up admonition in my mind. A warrior does not prejudge an opponent, neither to fear nor to discredit him.

Nazar's gentle words are scattered, however, as the guard's sharp voice cuts across my thoughts. "Hold a moment. Lord Protector Rihad bade me give you this news."

I halt, turning around in surprise. The guard is new to me, and his face is impassive, his eyes hard. When he sees I am listening, he continues, "Hantor, the warrior you fight, is responsible for your squire's injury."

Of all the things that could come out of his mouth, that's the last thing I expect. "What?"

"It happened two summers ago. The squire Caleb beat Hantor in a mock combat with rods and boasted that he should be the highest warrior knight of the Second House, despite the bloodline that made Hantor eligible at birth. Hantor paid men to attack the squire, to sever his arm with an axe."

I stare, but there is something about this tale that makes it eminently believable. I can see Caleb taunting Hantor in this way, never realizing the danger he was courting. I can see Hantor working to ensure Caleb paid for the slight.

"Why are you telling me this?" I barely hear my own voice, but the guard's expression doesn't change.

"Lord Protector Rihad bade me give you this news," he says again. "And this as well: The standing guard of warriors for the Protectorate must be made of those both strong and noble."

He turns and resumes climbing.

I don't take note of any of the risers beneath my feet, and it's only by some miracle that I don't fall down the stair entirely, into the arms of the trailing guard. I step out on the fighting platform. My mind fights against the impossibility of the images racing before my eyes. I perform the motions of my station by rote as the horns blast high above me. A shouted command penetrates my fog, and I look up to find Rihad staring down at me. He's close enough for me to see him nod, as if confirming the words of the guard. Then another horn sounds. I lower my gaze to Hantor.

The boy grins at me, all teeth, as his hand shoots into the air, his right fist curled at his heart. I mimic the movement more slowly, barely able to hear the trumpet blast.

This is no man, I remind myself. This is a boy who acted in petulant fury to silence a threat he couldn't quell with his strength alone.

And yet he has a Divh. That makes him a dangerous warrior... and he shouldn't be a warrior. He's nothing more than a weak and spiteful coward.

Lord Rihad's words pound through my mind. *"The standing guard of warriors for the Protectorate must be made of those both strong and noble."*

Hantor doesn't look noble or strong. He looks almost feral as he pumps his left fist. Now beginning to burn with a leading surge of anger, I summon Gent.

As I do, I look beyond the boy to the monster at the far end of the tournament field.

Hantor's Divh is a worthy opponent for most, but he's no match for Gent, I know in an instant. My anger grows in size and stature like Gent behind me, snuffling with interest at his combatant. This will be no fight.

Hantor's Divh is smaller, for one, but also wide and thick, a four-legged creature with a bony outer shell that I suspect betrays a soft underbelly. His head and back is covered with spikes, and the thick ridge on his brow bone no doubt serves as a battering ram to any creature or object unfortunate enough to find itself in the Divh's way. Even now, he swings his head back and forth, and I realize his eyes are on either side of his head, set too far back. I frown. For all his ferocious stature, this is a creature of defense, not offense.

A good army has all sorts of warriors, attackers and defenders alike. But while Hantor's Divh can survive deep into a tournament by bravado and speed, he can't fight ably against a Divh the size of Gent. And Rihad *must* know that.

Rihad, who bade his guard to tell me...

Hantor's bone monster launches itself forward, faster than I would have thought possible for its stumpy size. I turn my hand, and Gent releases a huge, almost happy roar, the world around me suddenly swept over with the sound of his loping, pounding feet. I gaze at Hantor, but I can't see through Gent's eyes. I can only see Hantor, laughing at Caleb as his stump hung uselessly at his side, a stump where once had been a sturdy, powerful arm. Fury sweeps through me, and I lift my hand further a few degrees, then Gent is past me and launching himself at Hantor's Divh. Gent's right paw sails high, and the bone creature's eyes follow it, missing the cutting swipe of Gent's left fist until the very last minute.

The bone creature surprises us both by leaping straight up, missing the bulk of Gent's blow but doing something that causes Gent to jerk back in surprise. A stinging pain erupts in my hand—not debilitating but unexpected. A flare of panic knifes through me, effectively slicing through my anger. *Stupid!* I shouldn't have underestimated Hantor or his Divh.

Gent shoves out again, sending the bone creature spinning end over end over end as Gent straightens, clearly confused.

Hantor's laugh startles through my consciousness. I refocus on the runt, and he sneers at me, jubilant at making the first cut. Suddenly, I flash back to myself just days before, standing in this very spot, startled and excited and foolish in my flush of momentary victory against Kheris's serpent. I hadn't pressed my advantage then, but I won't be so foolish this time.

Hantor's bone creature has no advantage. Even now I flicker back to viewing through Gent's eyes and take in the lumbering beast. Its trick of gathering all four legs beneath it, then bounding straight up with the strength of all four, will take some work to get around. The spikes on its back and head are formidable, and as

Gent has shown me and experienced himself, those spikes can detach easily from the creature to embed in paw or arm.

The two monsters circle, the bone creature dodging and weaving, almost dizzying in its dance. And that's part of its strategy too, I realize. Feint and deception, until its opponent is off guard—then zeroing in for the kill.

I level my gaze again at Hantor. He's too far away to hear me, so even if I want to rail against him, hurling accusations about his cowardly acts, I can't. I can only lift my hand, angle my head, and stare daggers at him across the open space.

Gent moves closer to the bone creature, and I dimly hear the responding roar of the crowd. They want blood. And, I realize with no little amount of horror, *I* want blood. The blood of Hantor in exchange for the blood he'd spilled of Caleb's—blood, bone, and sinew.

What am I becoming?

Gent roars, and his mighty paw swings in a wide arc, apparently poised to miss high again as last time. Instead, he widens his thick claws and jams them inward at the last moment, making the bone creature hiss and gather his legs beneath him, ready to jump to the side.

But Gent is too fast this time. Nazar's words ring in my head, and Gent fights down the sword as Nazar has instructed, pressing in further, further, until he's practically on top of the bone creature when it surges up. It springs higher into the sky than I would have thought possible, but Gent is right there with it and catches the trailing edge of its hind foot as it leaps away, turning it hard. The creature screams, and across from me, Hantor stumbles, his left ankle giving way.

The crowd stamps and howls, bloodlust raging in their cries. Gent moves forward to hold down the head of the opponent Divh like a pillow, keeping the bone creature on its back, its head and neck exposed. Its foot shakes violently, the creature in clear torment. Gent holds it still as I watch, his great head coming up as if he wishes to meet my gaze across the beaten creature.

Another curl of horror snakes through me...Hantor's Divh is down—down! I can't cause it more pain. I lift my hands slightly, and Gent shifts as well, easing his pressure on the beast. It can't move; there's no need to drive it to greater levels of agony. There's no gain in it.

Even the redness has now cleared from the edges of my vision, and I realize the battle for what it is. Hantor is beaten, but there's no honor in destroying the bone creature or damaging it beyond aid. Just as there is no honor in hurting the creature more, simply to hurt its warrior.

I shift my gaze to Hantor, seeing him tremble with the effort of trying to get his Divh to leap up and fight again. He's frenzied for all his apparent stillness. He's panicked too, and his eyes and mouth are rimmed with white. What must he have done to gain power, I suddenly wonder? What must he have been driven to, inferior by his very nature, yet thrust into the greatest position a boy could want?

What would it be like to be unable to rise to the demands the world made of you? Would it drive you to kill—to maim to ensure the safety of your position? I hold Hantor's gaze with mine, but let no pity mar my expression. He doesn't deserve it, and he wouldn't welcome it.

Neither does Rihad, whose glare fairly sets my face aflame.

Gent holds the bone creature still for another breath—then it's over.

The horns sound in one long, clear blast. Gent has won this contest.

As I watch, my beautiful Divh pulls his shoulders back, tensing as he moves to stand away from the bone creature, to allow it to rise. He even lifts a great paw as if to steady the other Divh then shifts it gently away as the bone creature gets its feet beneath him. A curious buzzing starts in the crowd around us, but I hold my position, watching the bone creature test its injured leg.

At that moment, a movement in the corner of my eye catches my attention, and I step back as Hantor suddenly surges forward on his platform, his hands splayed wide no matter that the match has already been called. I turn my hands back, and Gent steps half in front of the bone creature, looming over it as it crouches down despite Hantor's flapping arms. The injured Divh can't do otherwise—Gent now has its good back paw trapped beneath his own clawed foot, and the broken paw can't gain any purchase. The horns blast again, longer this time, and Gent wheels toward the platforms. Taking his paw off the bone creature, he swings his head up and down and lifts both his arms high into the air, then screams in outraged fury at...

Well, at Hantor.

My Divh's roar is filled with anger and disdain and a cold wash of pain that I am sure Hantor can't understand, won't ever understand. He understands being rebuked, however, and he seems to be able to reason out why. His Divh is in clear agony, shuddering beneath Gent, and Gent even more clearly wants the Divh sent back to its own plane.

Hantor raises his arm, now obviously dizzy with his own injuries. The bone creature finally disappears.

Gent stops roaring and resettles his own feet, now that he no longer needs to trap Hantor's Divh. He drops one of his mighty arms.

The other one he lifts toward me. As he had before when we'd fought on this tournament field. Fought and lost, even as now we'd fought and won.

I lift mine as well, the two of us moving as if to touch fingertips across the wide-open tournament grounds. We hold that pose for a moment where there is no breath, no true sight even, and I stagger beneath the onslaught of thoughts that Gent pours into me. Rage and loss, pain and fright. On some level, he'd felt more than just the power of my suggestion or command during the battle.

He'd *felt* all the emotions I'd experienced—indignation and horror, panic and fury—in the wake of Rihad's message about the true nature of the warrior I was fighting. He'd felt it, and he sought to ease that pain, to make right what had been wronged, and finally to accept—as I was forced to accept—that some things could never be right again.

A breath later, my beautiful Divh disappears.

Silence blankets the tournament field for a heartbeat, then another.

Then pandemonium breaks out.

The roar of the crowd is so loud, it shakes the tower on which I stand. I barely hear the trumpet blast—can't hear Rihad saying something high above me—but I throw up my other arm in a mimicry of what I saw from Kheris in his first battle at the tournament. I am the victor of this contest, the first of many that will be fought this day. Sound rushes over me, and I steady myself against the torrential wind that blows through the now-empty tournament field as if it had held its breath during the whole of our combat.

I've won this battle.

A guard pushes out onto the platform, and I turn to him, confused at his slow progress. And then I see something else.

Petals.

A pile of blue and white petals roils around my feet like a storm and blows off the platform into the field beyond. As I turn, horrified at the sight, I see that more petals are being thrown into the sky—or have been blown there, soaring over the assembled crowd. There's more cheering and then the hands of the guard are on me, half pulling me to the door.

"Are you injured?" one of them demands.

"No—no," I gasp as the door shuts behind me on the raging sound outside. "The petals—I didn't mean for that to happen. I didn't mean it!"

"Too late now." The guard standing at the top of the stairs is the one who had given me Rihad's news about Hantor. "He expected you to kill the boy, you know that."

That stops me short. "Hantor? But this is a tournament."

"And people die in tournaments. You had every right to avenge your squire." I feel the sanction in his words and swallow hard, thinking of Caleb's grin, his irreverent words, his pride. The guard continues as he stomps down the stairs, "I served awhile in the Second House. The boy Caleb wanted nothing more than to be a banded soldier, and failing that, a regular soldier. He was good, he fought hard and well, and he would have done anything for his house. Hantor took that away from him."

I stare at the man's back and can feel the other guard's glare behind me, no less chilling in his censure. Rihad might have expected me to kill Hantor, but so had these men. How many others thought that as well?

Any words I would offer die in my throat. I should say something, I know—defend myself, my actions. But what would it matter to this man, who's already made up his mind about what is right and good? More to the point, how will Rihad choose to repay me for—unwittingly or not—ignoring his demand for blood?

Suddenly, I feel weaker than ever. I just want to be gone from this tower, this coliseum, this Tournament of Gold. There's a darkness here that is leaching into my very soul, drowning out the Light.

CHAPTER 37

The remaining battles pass in a haze of enormous monsters and screaming crowds. Everywhere, people are reveling, and there are no more disruptions by marauders. Perhaps they have left after all, as Rihad announces at every opportunity.

I'm called upon to fight twice more, but there are no further messages from Rihad, no personal connections in the battles. One is a warrior from the Third House, like Kheris, but unlike Kheris, he only recently became a warrior. He and his lizard Divh move slightly out of sync with each other—one too fast, the other too slow. Gent beats the great lizard by toppling it over, using his long arms and bony claws to protect himself from the lizard's skin.

The second combat is with a warrior from the Eighth House and a creature with both wings and furred haunches, his face like that of a great cat. It takes Gent and me several passes to defeat it, and I'm weak with fatigue at its end. But not so weak that I can't raise my arm to my own beautiful Divh as the world roars around us.

Thankfully, after the first battle, the platform is never again blanketed with petals, and I pray that my misstep has somehow escaped detection. As beautiful as they are, they are yet another marker of how different I am...a marker I can ill afford.

There are no more deaths, but several injuries, and the field of more than fifty men is winnowed down to eight by the end of the day. Tomorrow, these eight warriors will fight as two-man teams, leaving four who will fight each other again in teams, then two for the final match—two men who've just fought and won twice by each other's side, asked to turn on each other and do battle to receive the ultimate prize of the Tournament of Gold.

And then there will be the melee, a mock battle for the ages, where monsters will line up against their fellows and wage brief and brutal war. This is to be the extraordinary capstone to the tournament, and bards are already spinning tales around it to last another quarter century and more.

My mouth tastes like ash.

Whatever Rihad has planned holds no more interest to me. I only want to win whatever I am able, transfer the men and their Divhs to my house, then face the fury of my father. There will be no justice for Merritt and no vengeance for me.

The only regret I harbor is that my time with Gent will be cut short, but there's nothing for it. He's carried me through this tournament, yes, but no matter how bravely and fiercely women used to fight alongside Divhs in the wars of three hundred years ago...no woman can fight now. Not with people like Rihad and my father ruling the houses. And Gent deserves an honorable warrior to fight with and for. He'll get that warrior if it's the last thing I do.

It *will* be the last thing I do, I suspect.

At length, the battles are done and we turn toward the warrior's stage, waiting as our warhorses are ceremoniously walked back out to us. I see Caleb holding Darkwing's bridle, his face not stoic like his counterparts. Instead, he's grinning from ear to ear.

Something seems wrong about Darkwing's tack, however. I frown, trying to place it. Then the horses reach us, and the procession begins anew, each of the warriors walking down to their mounts, to be assisted by their squires.

"You did it." Caleb speaks gleefully as Darkwing fusses and stomps, and I miss placing my foot in the stirrup the first time.

"Did what? I can't even get on my own horse by myself."

"You won the day, at least as far as the public polls are concerned. You're the one they're talking most about, never mind Kheris and his great serpent or Baltor and his fire ape. You're the crowd favorite."

"And you're insane. The battles I fought were no greater than any of the others, and quite a bit lesser, in some cases. Did you see the Seventh House death worm when it burrowed under the tournament floor, only to emerge behind the Fourth House warrior's Divh? I didn't even know that was possible."

Caleb snorts. "The Fourth House's man didn't either." He seats me in Darkwing's saddle, then pats the horse's shoulder. "But you *are* the favorite, make no mistake. Helps that no one knows you, that you're from such a small house. You're the one everyone wants to know everything about."

That doesn't sound good, but I suddenly realize what's wrong with Darkwing's fine tournament gear. "Where are the remaining sashes?" I point to the spot on the saddle where the long strips of green and silver had hung. "What did you do with them?"

"Oh! Those. Nazar told me to give them out to anyone in the crowd who wanted them." He grins up at me. "There were a lot of people who wanted them. I ended up having to go back to him for more."

"For more?" There's no more time for talking, however, as the great procession of warriors turns to stream out of the tournament grounds. As before, I'm the last of the men, the final warrior from the smallest remaining house, the Tenth. But I don't mind, I'm glad to finally be shut of this place, at least for another day.

As we ride, I look up and around. There are brightly colored flags for every house—but now there are banners as well, hundreds of banners it seems, and as we ride through the cut in the stands toward the wide-open marshlands beyond, I can see those with the green-and-silver sashes rushing through the crowds toward the stands above the exit tunnel, a school of desperate fish swimming upstream against an impossible current. Shouts of "Lord Merritt! Merritt of the Tenth House!" ring through the air, and I raise a hand as we turn into the corridor leading to escape—

The sky is filled with petals.

Another resounding cheer crashes around me as everyone with a green sash seems to unearth great handfuls of petals and sends them scattering through the stiff breeze pouring through the tunnel. The breeze surges up and out, carrying the petals with it, but as I am the last warrior through the passage, there's fortunately no one behind me to catch a faceful of the things, other than the unfortunate guards. I wince at what they might be thinking but still hold my hand high, my fingers tight in a fist. The roar lasts long after I've escaped into the relative stillness of the dark passage, focusing on the waning light beyond.

We empty out onto the broad marshlands. There are more people there, as before, chanting and singing and dancing in great celebration. Trilion will be reeling tonight, Caleb has told me, and I can well believe it.

Finally, the processional line stretches out, and the outriders are allowed to join their men. I watch with a rueful smile as the great entourages of the Second and Third Houses flow into line with the warriors. Every House has a brace of a half-dozen men or more, but I'm grateful beyond measure when my small honor guard rides up behind me, Caleb on his gelding and Nazar on his trusty mare.

"You fought well and admirably," Nazar says, and I blush at his compliment. It's perhaps the first he's given me. But I have other concerns now.

"How many other people have you given sashes to, Nazar? Like the ones you affixed to my saddle? Because I saw literally *dozens*."

He shrugs. "The seamstresses of Trilion had idle hands and

need of coin. With Caleb's wagering, we were amply supplied with the latter."

"Still, those petals," I groan. "They were everywhere in the first battle, but I thought that would be the end of them. Then the procession happened, and those people—all those running people, coming to drop those petals into the corridor. Rihad can't have missed that."

"Rihad was a league ahead of you at that time," Caleb puts in. "It's not like he was looking back."

"The guards could see it, though—at least for a few moments. Thank the Light for the wind that blew up, that nothing was left behind."

Nazar doesn't turn to me as he rides but keeps his gaze steady on the mountain home of the First House, looming larger with every step. "There is always something left behind," he says.

We weave our way through the scrubby, marsh-ridden plain, and I think again of the worm of the southern realms. "I thought I'd seen everything before this day. That worm..."

"That was the first time I'd seen it too," Caleb pipes up. "Makes sense, though, right? The southern realms are buried in sand. Of course they'd have Divhs who'd be able to fight well in it."

"I..." I hadn't thought of that. Before he'd bonded to me, Merritt's Divh had seemed much like Father's before it, rangy, tough, and comparatively small, now that I've seen these other Divhs. But then, we are tucked into a tiny corner of the Protectorate, surrounded by mountains and forests. A Divh in those lands would need to be able to move through forests and streams without trampling everything beneath its feet. Here, in this wide plain, the terrain is different. The needs of the warrior are different.

I consider the problem aloud. "The First House Divhs are large—very large. Suited for barren mountains and plains. The northern Divhs are smaller but with thicker hides and fur."

"The southern Divhs are covered in lizard skin or poison, and sometimes both." Caleb's eyes are wide as he turns to me. "Do you think...I mean, it's so obvious. But is that part of the warrior-Divh connection? Not only the strength of a warrior's blood but where his house is, what his needs are, what role he plays in the Protectorate?"

I've never been so weary, thinking of this. I sigh. "I have no idea. Such knowledge was forbidden to me."

The honesty of my own words shocks me, but Caleb merely nods. "I know what that's like. I was little more than a squire even before I lost my arm, so no one gave me any information," he says. "You're expected to figure it out on your own."

Nazar is silent on the other side of us, and the guards bringing up the end of the procession are far distant, talking among themselves. It's as good a time as ever to tell Caleb the truth. At least this truth, anyway.

"Rihad...sent a message to me, before my battle with Hantor."

Caleb turns to me with wide eyes. "He did! That's unexpected. I'd have bet differently had I known that. I mean, I thought you were going to win, but to have the sponsorship of the Lord Protector, that's impressive!"

"That's not the kind of message it was," I say, waving him to silence. "He told me that Hantor... He told me what happened to your arm. That Hantor was behind it."

"Oh..." Caleb looks away, shifting his body so that his shoulder isn't so easily seen by me, and my heart twists anew. "I didn't know he knew about that. Seems odd that he would."

I think again of Miriam, and all the deception of the First House, but I push on. "I'm sorry, Caleb. If you'd wanted me to kill Hantor, I'm sorry that I disappointed you. You deserve vengeance. Any warrior who's wronged deserves as much."

Nazar still rides in silence on my other side, but Caleb's laugh, when it comes, is wry.

"No, I don't want vengeance, not like that, anyway. Hantor—I should have been smarter. About my position and about his." He lifts his head and stares into the shadow of the mountain. We're only a quarter hour from the gates, and I can already feel the whispered secrets of the First House closing around us as Caleb continues.

"Hantor is a warrior knight, but not a very good one. He was given the band too early. His father was lazy and wanted to focus on his gold and his feasts, but he was cruel as well. Hantor wanted both to appease *and* please him. I can't say I would have been different." He sighs. "When I bested him in the fighting pit, it wasn't the first time, only the most public. It was also in front of his father. I'd thought to gain glory, because the father often ridiculed Hantor in front of—well, everyone. But I'd miscalculated on both sides. Hantor's need for redemption, and his father's need for Hantor to be feared. Hantor recruited Jank to help him, and another warrior knight—a good man who didn't realize what was happening until it was too late—stood watch."

I think of the Second House warrior knight on the stage in the tournament grounds, the one who'd looked down at Caleb with guilt and pain, but I say nothing.

Caleb shrugs the stump of his arm. "What happened next was the natural outcome of that."

"What happened next has forced you to hone the skills of a warrior." Nazar's quiet words flow over us, and Caleb's face flushes in surprise that the old man has been listening so closely. "What happened next has improved your speed, your stealth, and your ability to manage the weight of the sword and stave with only one hand. It has also improved your strategy." Nazar pauses. "Which clearly needed improving."

I can't help my bark of laughter, and Caleb laughs as well, even as the great gates open to draw us once more into the twisting, turning road to the First House. Our progress is further delayed by the cheers of the villagers who've been stationed along the way, and as we wind our way up the mountain, the cries get even louder —for all the warriors, but especially for me. Perhaps because I am the last one, or perhaps once again in anticipation of the coming feast.

There will be two feasts, in fact, according to Caleb.

"The villagers' one tomorrow is better, you ask me, because then the feasting will all be out on the main plains between the First House and the coliseum. Another swarm of tents and food for all. But the journey back to the First House tonight is specifically to gather all the warriors here and keep them safe and celebrated."

I grimace, looking at the high walls on either side of us. "Or to keep them corralled, anyway. This has been the worst day yet," I say, almost more to myself than anyone else. "One man and his Divh nearly died today, and so many more were injured. If I were given my preference, I'd leave tonight, and I didn't fare so poorly."

Nazar leans forward on his horse, peering ahead. "Rihad is a man of great strategy and guile. There's nothing he does that isn't carefully thought out."

Whatever he sees on the far horizon seems to sober him, however, and we ride the rest of the way in silence. We don't lack for noise as we enter into the hamlet leading up to the gates of the great fortress of the First House. Once more it has all the laughter and activity of market day, and the savory smells and crackling fire remind me how hungry I am. But we can't stop—not yet. The procession continues to the very doors of the First House, and by the time we flow in at the rear, Rihad is already off his horse and standing on the steps, ordering us to make haste to the great hall for the feast he has prepared.

We move quickly then, driven both by hunger and an interest in appeasing Rihad, who has not yet set the rolls for tomorrow's paired-off battles. Caleb and Nazar bully me into another tunic and breeches, and I think with grim amusement about the servant's overwrap I have stashed in my bags. How much I'd rather leave the feast hall behind and secret myself in the caverns with the great dragon Szonja buried below. This may be my last time to see her. After the end of tomorrow's battles, the First House will be barred to me once more.

Perhaps...

"Merritt." Nazar stands in front of me, straightening my half cloak over my tunic. "What is the way of the warrior? "

I frown at him, but the answer he's insisted upon so many times comes instantly to my mind, and I speak it before I can think. "Death," I say simply.

"And what does that mean?"

"That the warrior must fight when death is certain, and accept that death may be the end, and even welcome that death, versus not taking up the fight at all."

The priest smiles then, a tired, determined smile. His words are quieter, too. "Then go, and face this night as only a warrior can, Talia of the Tenth House."

He turns away from me before I can ask him what he's talking about. Caleb bounds up to me, laughing and happy and eager more than anything for the food and drink promised in the great hall. We join the throng of warriors pouring into the room, and I look around, noting the layout of tables is much as it had been the first night. Several small tables scattered around, and one high table, set upon the pedestal, for Rihad, his family, and honored guests.

Now Rihad stands, and I sense the wrongness in the air, the danger, though I can't understand it, can hardly breathe as we're jostled and pushed into the wide space, everyone heading for a table overladen with food, wine, and ale.

But I can't keep my eyes off Rihad. Especially when the crowd before him clears and I can see the man standing to his right. I freeze.

"Tonight, we honor the warriors of today—and yesterday—who fight with pride for the glory of the Protectorate," the Lord Protector announces. "And as part of that honor I present to you Lord Lemille, master of the Tenth House!"

CHAPTER 38

The cheer of the warriors is heartfelt and loud. I hide behind the shoulders of taller men and watch my father flush with pride. What is he *doing* here?

Rihad's next words solve that dilemma. "Lord Lemille has traveled hard and fast to witness the tournament's end. When he learned from the bards of his son's presence in the early battles of this tournament, of the marauder attack that warrior knight Merritt survived to even compete, he knew he must come. He'll be granted a brace of soldiers from the tournament's finest competitors, to protect his home and rebuild its glory."

My gaze narrows to a pinprick. I don't know how to act, how to breathe. Is that all it takes, then, to replace Merritt—a handful of soldiers? But Father doesn't know Merritt has died, that a usurper fights in his stead. He certainly doesn't know that it's by Rihad's own hand that Merritt was killed. In accepting soldiers from the First House, he's playing right into the trap the Lord Protector has set for him.

I watch my father stare haughtily around the gathered men. He makes no attempt to find his son in the group. It's not appropriate for him to do so—as Merritt, I'm officially as much my father's lackey as the meanest servant. But still...shouldn't he at least try to look for his son? I know I would have.

Now I wonder: Had Father even loved Merritt at all, or was his son simply an extension of himself? I'd thought his affection for Merritt genuine, deep and true. He had certainly loathed me well enough. My fingers trace the proof of his hatred forever scored along my neck.

He'll learn soon enough that Merritt is dead, though. And when he does...

My head swims. My hands go cold and clammy. When that happens, I definitely want to be gone from this place.

I try to remember Nazar's words from the barracks. The old priest must have known. *This* is what he'd seen as we'd climbed the long path up to the First House, my father's entourage. He must have seen, understood what I would be facing.

He's also not here, I realize with a start.

"Where's Nazar?" I'm surprised I can even form words, my throat's so tight.

Caleb looks around, his mouth grim. "Hopefully praying to the Light that we get out of this in one piece. But look, here's a spot. Let's sit here. Maybe it won't be so bad."

"Maybe," I say, though neither one of us believes that.

Rihad calls for the feast to commence, and there's great jostling and scraping as the warriors plow into the food. Caleb has made friends with the squires of the Fourth and Sixth Houses, it seems, and we're now seated in their midst. I'm glad of it. I need to hide.

I don't touch the food.

Looking around the room, hunkering down low so as not to be seen by my father, I survey the warriors—both those who triumphed today and those who failed. There's still no sign of the fallen Fifth House warrior's cadre of men—they've flowed away like ebbing water. While their remaining men must stay for the final melee tomorrow, they no longer have any warriors in contention for top tournament honors. The final eight combatants include two of the Third House, including Kheris, two from the

First House, and one each from the Second, Fourth, Seventh...and the Tenth. Fortiss remains as well, of course, but he hasn't fought, except in the exhibition match with Rihad's Divh. I don't expect him to fight again.

I grab a small loaf of bread as I think on that, and my gaze swings to the high table. By now, Father has surely stolen a look my way. He'll instantly know something is wrong. I don't look so much like Merritt that a father would be fooled. If he asks to see me, will he challenge me in public? Will he betray me to everyone here?

A deep, sour pain swirls in my stomach. I should never have vied for a seat at the Court of Talons. This world of politics and warriors and deceit is too complex for me to navigate. This tournament is a foolish game thought up by men to fill their ever-emptying cups of pride. There's no honor in this.

"Stop scowling, Merritt, you're frightening Gemma. And she's been trying to catch your eye since we entered the room."

"Gemma?"

Caleb's admonition bumps me out of my dark thoughts, and I look again toward the high table, thankful that the women have been segregated to the far end, well away from Rihad and my father.

Sure enough, Gemma's looking my way. Her beautiful dress is the rich gold and ebony of the First House, but in her hair, she's artfully tied the long green-and-silver sash of the Tenth House. My favor.

I manage a smile, but my queasiness worsens as I see the altered colors of the Tenth House—Father will *definitely* notice that. How can I escape this room? I can't breathe again, and I pick up a cup of wine, forcing myself not to drain it with one gulp.

Perhaps—perhaps I can remain anonymous. Perhaps my father won't ask to see me until after tomorrow's battles. It's only one more day, after all. Surely I can manage to avoid him for one day. I've already come so far.

Panic swamps me, scattering my thoughts. All I have to do is escape the tournament with my life. Not win, not even close. When the close of the tournament sweeps down and everything is chaos, I can run. I *will* run. Far to the north or even, possibly, to the wilderness of the west. I think of the Savasci. Would they accept me among them, a warrior and her Divh? They would, I think. I know they would.

In fact, I've already put in an appearance this night. I've paid my dues. I can claim illness and retire, maybe—

Nazar's words burst into my mind again, unwanted. *You are Talia of the Tenth House, first-blooded and firstborn. As such, you will fight with power and with honor, and with the strength your blood has given you.*

I can't run, I realize. I can't hide. I can only walk the warrior's path.

A trill of horns brings the room to silence. Rihad stands again, his face wreathed in smiles. "It's time to honor the men who will represent us in the final day's battle—before we all go to war in the grand melee."

My heart goes numb. One by one, Rihad announces the winning warriors, and they stand and stride into the center of the room, grinning widely, accepting the approval and cheers of their fellow warriors as their due. At last, when he speaks my name, I rise as well. The way of the warrior might be death, but right now, death seems preferable to this.

I lift my head high, forcing a smile to my face, an easy looseness to my walk as I stride to the center of the room. Gemma applauds fervently from her spot at the high table. I nod to her, causing more laughter and cheers to rise up as I take my spot at the center of the room.

Rihad says something else, and there's another round of shouting, but I feel more than see the wiry figure of my father rising to his feet at the far end of the table, leaning forward to scowl at the eight of us.

My father's face goes stony cold, morphing into the mask of fury I learned to fear so greatly as a child; a mask I counted myself lucky to have never seen at all past the age of ten, when I'd finally learned how to stay out of his way. Now that mask—a frozen expression of hauteur pierced through by eyes so fiery they could almost be red—is leveled at me.

He knows.

To my utter shock, however, he stays silent. Have I been granted some reprieve? I don't know, but I don't feel any better. My feet are heavy, my heart filled with tears, my skin too hot, and my breath thick in my throat. Fear like I've never known presses in on me, making me gasp.

Rihad dismisses us to our tables and orders the feast to continue, but I haven't made it five steps before a guard appears at my side. "You are summoned to the high table, Merritt of the Tenth. By special request of Lord Protector Rihad and Lord Lemille."

I nod. In the distance, at the table of the Fourth and Sixth Houses, I see Caleb laughing and drinking with his new friends. He'll be an outcast again—far worse this time—unless I think of something. The crowd shifts, and I finally see Nazar as well. Unlike Caleb, he's not in the thick of the feast but standing just inside the shadows, hidden and still. Watching me. His gaze meets mine across the room. He *did* know of this trial awaiting me. He sent me in here unprepared, but he knew.

He's betrayed me.

I blow out a long breath, immediately acknowledging the wrongness of my thinking. If Nazar had breathed one word of my father's presence to me, I wouldn't have come at all. That would have been the coward's way, not the warrior's.

Which leaves me, irrevocably, on this path toward death. Of one kind or another.

Think! My father hasn't looked at me intently for the past several years. I seemed to disgust him more deeply the more my body grew and changed, the evidence of my femininity impossible to hide.

Still, he must know I'm not Merritt. He spent morning, noon, and night with my brother.

Then all at once, the guard and I reach the table, and Rihad watches with keen interest as my father pulls himself to his feet again.

"Merritt, my *son*. Well met," my father says, and his words are low and filled with such malice, my bones fairly turn to milk. His smile, however, never wavers. "Walk with me and tell me of your success. You have made quite a name for yourself and our house."

"My lord." Somehow, I manage the strength to bow to him without throwing up. I turn and bow to Rihad then, grateful that he's the one staring at me and not Councilor Miriam. As we turn, though, there's little gain in that. Miriam blocks our way, not ten steps distant.

"That's Councilor Miriam, Father," I say, ducking my head toward him even as he stiffens with revulsion at my nearness. "She's a sensitive, a good one. Have a care."

My father may be a brute, but he isn't a fool. He strides ahead of me with three long steps, his face no doubt as open as his arms as he greets Councilor Miriam with such a wash of goodwill, I suspect the woman is reeling. Their greeting allows me to step past the councilor and move several strides ahead, a guard between us now, before my father breaks free. I wait deferentially as the two exchange more pleasantries, then my father joins me once more.

By now, we're behind the high table, facing the three doors. I long to take the portal that leads to the chained Divh Szonja, but instead we move toward the center archway. I now realize what lies beyond it is a wide antechamber, not a corridor at all. My father steps quickly into it.

Then he turns on me.

His hand shoots out so quickly, and I'm so used to cowering before him, that I barely even flinch when he pulls me onto my toes by what's left of my hair, exposing the long scar he inflicted upon me more than a decade ago. But I know enough to step back from the openhanded smack that follows.

I might be executed by this man, but I'm not going to be struck by him—not anymore.

Father doesn't pause. "Where is Merritt?"

I blink at him, stunned. Surely he's heard of the attack, surely he knows. "There—there was an attack."

"Where is your *brother*?" He fairly spits the words, though he keeps his voice low. Even now, he has no desire to draw the attention of Rihad.

"He died," I snap, the words releasing a swell of grief I have no place to feel now. "There was an arrow—he jumped—you know how he jumps with his Divh and—"

Before I can react, Father reaches out again. This time he grabs my shoulder, wrapping his hand around my bicep where the warrior's band has embedded itself in my skin. Clearly, he can feel the cuff through my tunic sleeve, and his face reddens with hatred, his eyes going nearly black in their intensity as the pain of his grip sends bolts of wrenching agony through my arm.

"You shameful *whore*," he breathes. "You *dog*. I thought myself well rid of you when I sent you to that swine Orlof, yet not only do you not have the grace to die on the road, but you allowed your brother to die—your *brother*—" The mention of Merritt seems to pull him out of his anger and plunges him down another waterwheel of emotions, shock and horror and grief. "*He* is the warrior of the Tenth. You aren't. I should have killed you before you took your first breath. Rihad will never forgive this—"

"Father! *Listen* to me."

He's so startled at my voice that he steps back, but I have not been Talia the meek and serving for more than two weeks now, and it feels like so much longer. I've been a warrior, fighting for my house's safety—a safety that is now more at risk than ever. "Rihad is no true protector of our house. He knew you were sending Merritt out on that mountain road. He knew it because the bards told him as much. He sent—men. To kill Merritt and destroy his Divh. I have the arrow that took Merritt's life."

"You dare—!" he grates out.

I plow on. "I didn't come to the tournament to fight. I came here to buy us soldiers for protection and then beg for restitution, for vengeance. For Merritt and the Tenth House. Only after I got here, I learned that Rihad had struck not one but *three* border houses. Probably more. He seeks to shore up the strength of the Protectorate with his own men, Father. Men *he* controls, not you. The warriors he sends you won't be beholden to you. They will bow to you, while to him, they kneel."

To my surprise, my father seems to actually consider my words. "You have the arrow that killed Merritt?" he asks, his voice low and ominous.

"I'd planned to present it to Rihad. It's a gray arrow, nondescript though well made. The arrow of someone hiding who he really is. A *warrior's* arrow."

His face turns mutinous, and I rush on. "I...was with Merritt when he died. I couldn't reach him in time."

"You *failed* him." Father's words are so matter of fact, I jerk back again. "He was your lord. Your life was forfeit to his. Instead, he is dead and *you*, you who have no right to even still breathe, you *walk* while he is consigned to the Light."

"I sought only—"

"*You*." He reaches out again and clamps his hand around my arm, squeezing even harder. I nearly faint from the pain. "You stole his band."

"I did *not*," I say hotly, wrenching from his grasp. "It—it moved. Toward me, and—"

"*No.*" Father's words are so intense, he's almost hoarse with anger. "You are *lying*. It is forbidden!"

Rage surges up within me and overflows, my words stupid and desperate and coming far, far too quickly. "Forbidden or not, it happened. And I have *won*, Father. I've won battle after battle. Not the first, no, but since then, I've learned, and I've succeeded. I have brought honor to your house, not shame!"

Something shifts in my father then, deep and ugly, that seems to suck all the air from the chamber. He stares at me with flat, cunning eyes. "You have brought something, yes. At long last. From the moment you came squalling into this world, I have cursed the Light for its cruelty. Shaming my family, my house. The Protectorate. The very Exalted Imperium. A firstborn daughter is an *abomination*. I should have killed you a dozen times over already."

In the face of such fury, I can only stare. Stare and stammer words that don't make it past my throat. "I won't fight anymore," I try to say, all my newfound strength buried in a lifetime of shame. *I'll run. I'll hide. I'll stay far, far away.*

But my father isn't finished. "Even in my despair, I prayed that there would be some use to your slovenly, disgusting life, some payment for my years of torture in suffering you to live. And now there will be."

I rear back, but he lunges at me, and this time, his hand catches my wrist, not my shoulder. "Rihad will know the traitor he has in his midst. Guards!"

CHAPTER 39

Since we're already behind the high table, there's no disruption to the feast as the guards swoop into the room. Clearly, my father knew they were following us. When they hear the word "traitor," they stomp to either side of me.

My father gloats as he takes in my confusion. "You forget I wasn't always deep in the mountains," he says. "I fought in tournaments as well, long before you ever saw your first accursed sunrise." He seems poised to say something else, then changes his mind. "I've asked Rihad for an audience. Show me to him."

We emerge from the antechamber and immediately enter the archway that I know leads to Rihad's chambers, and my guts wind tighter with each passing step. I don't have a strategy for this. This isn't war, not in the way I know it. I sense there is a strategy to be had, for war isn't only fought on the tournament grounds or at the tip of a sword, but my mind is filled with wind and rushing words, nothing clear to me. The guards hasten me along at a fast clip, their long legs sturdier than mine, and all too quickly I find myself once more in Rihad's private sanctuary. There's the enormous fireplace, crackling despite the heat of the day, and there is Miriam.

Once again, she stands perfectly composed, beaming as Father strides toward her.

"It's worse than I imagined," he says stiffly, and she extends a comforting hand but says nothing more as her cool, unreadable gaze slides over me.

"Rihad will join us presently," she says. "He'll be honored that you have alerted us to this danger."

"It's a disgrace and an atrocity," my father snarls. "And to think this creature carried forth in such a manner in front of the entire Protectorate. The shame is agonizing."

"What's this?"

Rihad steps into the room, still in full flush from the triumph of the feast and the long day before it. He claps his hands together. "Lemille! You've only just arrived, and you've already found something to complain about? It truly feels as if we were both twenty years younger, and you were still fighting in the tournament yourself. I must say, though, I am surprised that Merritt is some sort of traitor. He's conducted himself as—"

"He is *not*—!" Father sounds as if he is choking on his own words, but he catches himself in time, then straightens. "It would be better if we had complete privacy, Lord Protector Rihad." He gestures to the guards. "I don't wish to offend..."

"Not at all." Rihad seems to be enjoying himself far too much. I remain stiff and unyielding as I watch my father pace back and forth, waiting for the guards to clear the room. Rihad even has them check to ensure that there are no other hidden ears in the rooms off the narrow corridor. He's wise to check, given what I'd seen from that space just a few days earlier.

Still, even as Rihad reenters the grand chamber and my father squares his shoulders, I can't believe that Father will betray me in the end. I can see him outing me as a charlatan, yes. That I'm not Merritt. But to reveal me as a female would be to sign my death warrant. Surely, he will stop short of that.

"Very well, Lemille," Rihad says, watching my father keenly. "State your case."

"The creature you see standing before you is *not* Merritt of the Tenth House as you've been led to believe," my father betrays me without hesitation, refusing to even glance my way. "*She* is Talia, a servant of my own house. And a female."

I gape at him, more shocked at his refusal to name me as his daughter than at the revelation of my sex.

Rihad is clearly stunned, however, as is Miriam. Or is she? I frown at the woman, who maintains an expression of incredulity. I assumed she'd already guessed my subterfuge with her gift. Then again, she's stood in front of me only twice, surrounded by crowds of men. And of course, I am a banded warrior. Her mind apparently couldn't process a female in that role. If so, then Miriam's gift is mighty, but it's also grievously flawed.

Rihad recovers first. "Councilor Miriam," he snaps. "Verify—"

Light and fire, *no*. I won't be stripped in front of these people unless I am truly incapacitated first. "There's no need for that, Lord Protector," I say sharply. "I'm female. I came to seek retribution for…Merritt of the Tenth. I was in his party when he traveled the mountain road. I was with him when he was murdered." I glare at Rihad. "Which makes him yet another warrior knight cut down on the road to the Tournament of Gold. The list has grown long."

"But you're a woman." Strangely, it's Miriam whose voice cuts across the room, not Rihad, who merely watches me with undisguised curiosity. "A woman…wearing the band of the Divh."

"The penalty for a female attempting to band with a Divh is *death*," growls my father. "Immediate. Let it be known that I exposed this traitor to you, Rihad. A traitor under your nose that you didn't sniff out in all the days that she was here."

"She is of your house." Rihad slides his glance to my father, and I catch the danger in that gaze.

My father doesn't. "Was," the old fool says succinctly. "And I myself would not have believed any woman capable of the depravity to which she has sunk. I allow no traitors to live in my midst. When the bards came to extend your invitation, I had no idea of the events transpiring here. No way of knowing…" His voice catches. "I hoped to find my son here. Instead, I find not only a traitor, but a *female*." He straightens his shoulders. "It's an abomination."

"But it can't..." Miriam echoes quietly, still apparently at a loss, and unhappy for it. "It's not possible."

"When?" Rihad turns on me and pins me with his snakelike eyes. "You say you came to seek retribution for your house's warrior knight. But you have a Divh. When did you get it? How?"

I refuse to look at my father, but there's no strategic value in lying to Rihad. If nothing else, Miriam will know, *should* know, that a woman's position can be gained by doing something other than serve a murderer. Even if I'd held my position as warrior knight for only a few short days, I'd done it. And if I can do it...

I firm my resolve, then speak.

"Lord Merritt died. In my arms. I was the first one to reach him. His Divh collapsed some distance away, then disappeared. I..." I shake my head. "I assumed he was dead when he left this plane."

"It," my father snaps, but I pay him no mind.

"As I held my—Merritt's arm, his warrior band changed. It turned as if to liquid, or as a snake, and before I could draw back, it had peeled away from Merritt's arm to slide up mine." I grimace, recalling the moment as if it'd been dredged up from the depths of time, though it happened a bare two weeks earlier. "It...hurt."

My father explodes. "You should have died in the attempt! It is against every edict of the Exalted Imperium." Something else seems to finally occur to him. "Where is *Nazar*? The other guards? Surely they would not have let you—"

"Hold, Lord Lemille." Rihad crosses over to his throne and settles into it, looking down on me as if he's been charged with solving a particularly perplexing riddle. "We are in your debt for your service and fervor. But you're not being entirely honest with us, I think."

He slides his glance to Miriam, who nods once. Rihad curls his lip. "I thought so. Would that your intuition could cut with a sharper blade, Councilor Miriam. For us to not realize that there was a woman in our midst..."

She appears unfazed by his rebuke, and once again I wonder how much she truly knows. "But there is a misdirection that I *have* perceived," she says, her eyes flashing. "Lemille, share the whole truth with us. This girl is your daughter."

"No, she's not!" My father's denial is less alarming the second time. As he squares off against Miriam, my thoughts slip ahead to my own death.

Will they kill me by the time-honored form of execution, beheading, or will they simply call the guards in to slit my throat? I could run straight out of the First House—escape the way I did before, summoning Gent to carry me far away. But I had the advantage of surprise then...and a head start. This time I'd never reach the open air, where I could safely summon Gent. I'd be running directly into the arms of the guards.

I grit my teeth. The way of the warrior is death, Nazar has told me, too many times to count. I knew it when the band bit its way into my arm. I knew it when I first cut my hair and donned the attire of a man. Silently, I pray that Nazar and Caleb fled once they saw me disappear with my father. Nazar might have, I think. Caleb, I don't know. He's already displayed a perilous tendency to make unwise choices. And he isn't exactly anonymous with his missing arm.

"Talia of the Tenth House." Rihad's voice seems to have acquired added resonance, and it quiets my own thoughts as well as my father's and Miriam's squabbling. "Either way, you cannot die this night."

That sets Father off again. "She *must*," he blusters. "It's the rule of the Imperium."

"And we must ever follow the orders of the Exalted Imperium," Rihad says, derision dripping from his words. He leans forward, studying me like I'm a particularly poisonous beetle. "Oh, she will die, must die, as you say. But not tonight, I think. You weren't watching the battle at the Tournament of Gold today, Lemille. You didn't see what your *daughter* did."

"The petals." Miriam's words are so low as to be a whisper, but

I hear her. She stares at me with renewed interest. "The connection with your Divh. But a woman...even a direct descendant of the first line." She frowns. "It simply cannot be."

Rihad continues as if Miriam hasn't spoken, trampling over her words. "She beat multiple warriors, Lemille, or her Divh did. One she should have killed outright to save me the trouble. The others, however, were men of strength and worth."

My father's scoff is absolute. "She could do no such thing."

"She could and she did, in so doing capturing the attention of the masses, I'm afraid. For Merritt of the Tenth House not to show his face tomorrow would cause...significant unrest. I can't allow it."

Beside Rihad, the great fireplace seems to sputter and pop, and I find my gaze drawn to it as the Lord Protector speaks. A shadow cast in the flames surges up with each crackling sizzle, and I imagine more than see the creature who was there before, staring at Rihad from the center of the blaze. A figure with his face in shadow, cloaked in fire...

"Talia!" Rihad barks the word so loud, I jump, and I force my attention back to him.

He still leans forward, his right arm bent, resting his elbow on his knee. "You will fight tomorrow, and you will fight honorably—or dishonorably, it makes no difference to me. But you will die, know that for certain. As will your attendants at the moment of your demise. Whether you fall by the hand of one man or many, it will be done by this hour tomorrow night." He waves out toward the coliseum, far across the open plain.

"The Tournament of Gold is intended first and foremost as a skill competition between the very best warrior knights. It can be much more than that, however. It is also an opportunity for men to kill, if they are lucky..." He twists his lips. "Or be killed, if they aren't."

I lift my chin. If my life is ash, what I say here won't matter. "There's no honor in killing for sport. Surely some of the warriors left in this tournament believe that."

"A true warrior knows no honor other than to his lord." This time, it's my father who speaks, not Rihad. Apparently, he's regained his backbone, at least enough to spit words at me. "Which you would know if you were a man and had any shred of worth to you."

I stiffen, but the matter is already settled in Rihad's mind. "The men of the First and Second are mine to command," he says, a smile playing at the corners of his mouth. "You'll face both in equal combat. And your partner in the team competition shall be Kheris of the Third." He laughs as he sees the expression on my face. "At least you know his serpent well. Your Divh will have to be careful that it doesn't face three opponents on the tournament field, not two."

"She shouldn't even be allowed to compete," whines my father. For once, I almost agree with him. The mercy of a quick death seems far preferable to what awaits me in the coliseum.

"*She* won't," Rihad holds up a hand, in a voice now stony with command. "Merritt of the Tenth House will. And there he'll also die—a second time—for the greater glory of the Protectorate. Guards!"

He eyes me as the men march into the room. "This night, you'll be the esteemed guest of the First House," he says, his lips flattening into a thin smile. "I trust you will be comfortable."

CHAPTER 40

The dungeon of the First House is deep and complex, but that shouldn't surprise me. What does surprise me, however, is how unusual it is. Rihad has hewn pathways through the rock that all, eventually, must end up opening onto the enormous cavern fed by the waterfall. I know what's down there now, but from the chittering cries beneath me, it seems that Szonja isn't the cavern's lone occupant. Depending on what other wild animals Rihad has let roam free in the vast underground space, it would make for easy disposal of any unfortunate captive when Rihad tires of housing him.

Still, it also makes for a pleasant vista, I expect, when the sun is high in the sky. As long as whatever is below stays below. For long minutes, I remain far enough back on my ledge, beyond the bars, to avoid whatever animals lurk down there. The cell is quite livable, I decide. It contains nothing but a stone floor and one of the ubiquitous jugs of water, but it's still...habitable. I'm wearing enough clothing to turn some of it into a makeshift pillow and blanket, but I have no thoughts of sleep. Instead, at length, I venture out onto the ledge and sit, my feet dangling over the edge.

Szonja doesn't stir in the stillness below, but I have a sense of her anyway. I wonder if there's any other human prisoner in the other dungeon cells. The place has an abandoned feeling to it, and I suspect Rihad cleaned house prior to the tournament. At the Tenth House, we don't even have a dungeon. We've never had a need for one.

I sigh, thinking of what the Tenth House manor must look like now, in high summer. I left the animals in the capable hands of the chamberlain, and the lambs would now be steady on their feet, the foals gaining size and strength. Even the chickens would be deeply pleased with the weather. The spring has been long and wet, but now there would be sunshine every day. Sunshine and grain and safety. I received as much as well, as long as I'd lived in that house. Safety, perhaps not always. But sunshine and enough food to grow strong. And even my mother...

I swallow, pushing thoughts of her away. My mother was always kind to me, even as she was a follower of the Light, and moreover of my father. But she'd still done me an immense service at the moment of my birth, and probably many times thereafter until she died. She'd kept me *alive*...I can't imagine the price she must have paid for that, especially since she'd borne my father no more children after Merritt.

Yet another reason why he's hated me so well, for so long. Had he killed me as the law had dictated he could, even should, he firmly believes the Light would have granted my mother several more children. I suspect not, but there's no denying that Merritt's birth assured my continued survival.

And my mother did her part as well, returning to the Light two years ago, after yet another illness. Her death allowed Father to remarry—which he did, though his second wife's first child was also a female, the two of them now banished to one of our lesser holdings. Maybe now they'll be allowed back to the manor house.

If they're smart, they'll stay away.

"Merritt."

I scramble back from the edge of the precipice, startled at the sound of my brother's name echoing over the surface. The abyss distorts the word and sends it back to me in odd waves. I can see nothing in the gloom for a long moment, and I don't trust myself to respond. Then a lamp flares in the distance, and I nearly cry out. How quickly I've begun to yearn for light again! It seems almost like a benediction.

"Merritt." The voice comes again, strangely harder now, but I recognize it. Fortiss. I step forward.

"I'm here. Here." I say the words as a normal conversation and instantly regret them when the lamp flickers out. How many guards does Rihad have stationed in the cavern? Have I just broken some protocol that would result in me being taken to another cell, one not so friendly? And below me in the murk, I hear a long, fluttering shudder. The sound of a winged creature shifting against the cavern wall. I've even disturbed Szonja.

I sigh but creep closer to the edge of the precipice, glad to have some company in the darkness. The drift of sound below me and to my right lets me know that Szonja has moved, the deep ruffling noise conjuring up images of her broken wing, stretching in the mists. The air smells sweet here, and I wonder how far we are from the oiled stones.

"Why do you stay here, Szonja?" I murmur, too low for the creature to hear me. The sound of my own voice is comforting in the darkness.

"Who are you talking to?"

Fortiss's voice sounds directly above me, and he laughs as I startle back, stumbling. "Stand aside, I'm coming down."

A moment later, he drops down on light feet, and I feel rather than see the mists shift beside me. He straightens and scowls at me, while I stand as far away from him as the ledge allows. "What did you do to anger Rihad? He hasn't stowed a man down here in years."

My eyes widen, the need to tell my tale warring with my need to keep the fragile bond between us. He doesn't know?

Of course he doesn't know. He wouldn't be here if he did. In fact, once he knows for sure...

I tighten my jaw. The way of the warrior may be death, but I've damned well died enough times today already.

"I suspect you'll hear about it in the morning," I say, pitching my voice deliberately low. He's seen me in this space as Talia. In the darkness, his ears might tell him something more than his eyes could.

"But I want you to tell me now. I could help."

I snort. "Not likely, but I thank you. You should go, though. There may be guards."

He shakes his head. "Just because I honor my uncle's rules—usually—doesn't mean I don't know how to elude the gaze of the guards. Besides, I wanted to come." He peers at me curiously through the gloom, and I can barely make out the confusion on his face. "You sound…a little odd."

I rub my hand over my mouth, trying to mask my voice. "It's been a long day." To forestall his questions, though, I know I must tell him…something. "I'm not Merritt," I sigh. "I'm just one of his, um, company. Lord Lemille didn't send me to the Tournament of Gold. When he showed up yesterday and realized my lie, he said as much to Rihad. And here I am."

Fortiss's shock is plain. "You're not—but who are you? You have a Divh, and clearly a first line one. Whose house do you represent?"

It's a good question, and I don't have the answer to it, but I stumble on anyway. "The Tenth, still. I…I was with Merritt when he died. I took on the sacred charge of his Divh to avenge his death."

"To avenge…" He pauses. "But if you're not Merritt, who are you? What's your name?

I shake my head. "I'm no one," I say hollowly. *A lie. A cheat.* "You know, just call me Merritt. He's the only reason I am here."

Before Fortiss can say anything more, I rush on. "Tomorrow, I fight, though I dishonor the Tenth by being here under false pretenses. There's nothing more I can do about that."

Szonja shivers in the darkness beneath me, and I turn, warmed to see her giant, thoughtful eye now level with our ledge, her gleaming snout angled up, her lips pulled back. A stream of smoke wafts out between her teeth.

Fortiss follows my gaze.

"What?" he asks. "What do you see out there?"

I swerve back toward him, startled. It's one thing that he couldn't see her when we were both above the oiled rocks, but here? So close? "You cannot see the, ah, beast that roams this cavern?" I ask. "It's right...well, here."

Szonja twitches away but only slightly as I tug Fortiss closer. He frowns, peering into the mist. "I've heard it whispered that Rihad has enchanted the space. But the Lord Protector is no spell caster, for all that he believes in premonitions and dreams. I don't know what the guards have told you, but don't you believe it, either." He turns to peer at me. "And you're wrong about him, still. He didn't kill your lord."

"Shut up, Fortiss." I pull his hand up and press it against the smooth plane of Szonja's muzzle. The dragon, for her part, remains perfectly still.

Fortiss stands riveted to the spot. "What is this magic?" he murmurs, his voice heavy with confusion. I can feel the cool, slick scales too, solid beneath my fingers. Szonja twitches again, and the mist curls and scatters away, causing Fortiss to pull his hand back with a hard jerk. He turns on me.

"What's going *on* here?"

"What do mean?" I protest, edging backward. There's something different about his tone, now. He keeps shaking his hand, but he's not looking to where Szonja is regarding us solemnly through the darkness. He's staring at *me*.

"Who are you?" he demands.

The unexpected question catches me completely by surprise, and my hands go to my face, my hair, anything that might have betrayed me in the near darkness. "I don't..."

"Your hand," he says harshly. "I've touched you before, and not as a warrior. Here, in the First House. I've *touched* you. I *know* you."

I can't hide from his accusation, but the panic in his voice would have made me smile in another situation, another time. Not here, though, not now. I can already feel Fortiss pulling away from me, doubt and suspicion replacing the comradeship in arms between us that had always been a lie anyway. He's not my people; this isn't my place. Could never be my place. The moments I've shared with him have been stolen and will stay that way, for all that I'll treasure them for however long I have left to live.

"You have." I draw myself up, saying the words that've been chanting in my head since I saw my father at the feast, echoing in my mind like a dirge. "I'm Talia of the Tenth House, Fortiss," I say, stepping back almost unconsciously, as if he might take a swing at me. "Merritt is...was my brother. He died on the road to the Twelfth House. It's been me all along. I'm sorry that I lied to you. I had no—"

"Talia?" Fortiss stiffens in confusion at the feminine name, though he's the one who called me out. "What are you *talking* about?"

"I'm Talia, Fortiss." I frown when he doesn't say anything. "I'm female. A woman. I'm not sure how else to describe it."

"No." He does take a sharp step back from me now. "No, that can't be possible. You have a Divh."

I smile. This would get old, having to explain it to people. Fortunately, I won't have to do it for very long. "I don't know why or how it happened. I was with Merritt when a warrior, I don't know of whose house, loosed the arrow that killed him. My brother died in my arms. When he did, his band slipped off his arm and traveled to mine." I lift my right hand self-consciously to my left upper arm again, reliving the moment. "It moved of its own will. I didn't know it could do that."

"It can," he says hoarsely. "If the son is with the father when the father dies. Otherwise, it can be transferred safely by the house lord's will alone." He shakes his head like a bear coming out of hibernation. "But you can't—females are *forbidden* to control a Divh. By order of the Exalted Imperium. To do so is death."

I gesture to the darkened abyss. "Which is why I'm in this dungeon."

"But..." He struggles against the idea with too much fervor, the same way Miriam did. I eye him curiously. Have I simply grown used to my new reality because I've personally been living it these past few weeks? It no longer seems wrong or forbidden or even particularly special that I bonded with Gent. It seems right and true. The way it should be.

"You went to the plane of the Divhs," Fortiss finally finishes.

"Yes. A field in a blue mist, with high walls all around. I couldn't see the sky. I could barely see in front of me. Then the mist thinned, and there was a sound, a roaring. And all at once, Gent came out of a large opening, and—"

"Stop...stop!" Fortiss slaps his hands to his ears and turns away, as if my words cause him physical pain. "What you say isn't possible! Not for *you*."

Bitterness rings in his words, and I close my mouth to stifle my retort. Fortiss is a bloodline descendant of a great and proven warrior, and he doesn't have a Divh. I am a woman born into a world where I am fit for nothing but service or motherhood. And I *do* have a Divh. My band practically throbs on my arm, as if Gent is turning toward me across the vast distance from his island home.

But Fortiss has no band. He's not yet a true warrior knight. He's never been given the chance.

As if he can sense the change in me and recognize it for the pity it is, he pulls back farther.

"Have a care," I murmur. "You're close to the edge."

"Don't dare to tell me what to do, *Talia*," he growls, his voice now harsh with anger. "You've lied about everything since you've *come* here."

Now it's my turn to stiffen. "I didn't ask for this."

"You *lie*," he snaps again, his rage coming at me like a wave. "You can't tell me that you didn't hold your brother in your arms and crave that which made him special. You can't tell me that you didn't secretly mourn the loss of the greatest gift your family has ever had, the one thing that singled you out among all the others in your house. You wanted that band more than life itself, didn't you? You wanted what Merritt had by the right of his birth, that you could never have, not truly. You—"

"You're wrong!" I nearly scream the words, but I don't care who hears us. The pain that wells up inside me is like a waterskin full to bursting, and when it does, it will send my body flying in a million different pieces.

"I didn't want Merritt's band, I wanted my *brother*. My brother! Laughing, alive, free. I wanted his joy and his smile and his truth and his life, not his dead body slipping away from me. I didn't want his band. I didn't know I could have his band. Because you," I jab a finger at him, "and people like you have spent your entire lives *telling* me I couldn't. That I couldn't stand and walk among warriors. That I couldn't be strong enough to be chosen by a Divh. Well, you're wrong, Fortiss. You're all wrong. There are things that I see that you have closed your eyes to, refusing to acknowledge the truth. There are things I can do that you can only dream of, until you open those eyes."

"You are a *disgrace*," he snarls back. "The punishment for a female stealing a band, attempting to control a Divh, is *death*."

"Then bring it! That's Rihad's solution, if you're wondering. He'll let me fight tomorrow because it suits him, but death is the assured result. Understand this, though: I'm not attempting to *control* a Divh, Fortiss, I'm *connected* to one. And it's been noticed at your precious tournament—you know it has. I've won fairly in the trials, for all that they are supposedly barred to me. Rihad knows it too, which is the only reason why he can't kill me outright. Instead, he'll let the men who fight me do his killing for him."

"You lie." He's still seething, but at least he's quieter now.

"About this? No." I shake my head. "Tomorrow, I die a warrior, which I suppose is more than I deserve. But at least I'll face that death *as* a warrior. Everyone else who follows Rihad's command on that field can live as cowards for all I care."

"You're *wrong*. Rihad won't order the men to kill you, Talia of the Tenth,"—He says my name like it's a vile curse—"no matter the filthy way you got your band. He might want it, but he won't command it. He *won't*."

Fortiss remains furious, and beyond him, I can see Szonja again, her beautiful head turned to regard us, her intelligent eyes filled with an emotion I cannot describe. Pride. Sorrow. Pain. She's not watching me so much as Fortiss.

There *is* a connection there, I realize suddenly. A connection that perhaps they both can find their way to, if they only try.

I swing my attention back to Fortiss and blink into the darkness.

He's gone.

CHAPTER 41

In what seems an impossible feat of workmanship, two new wooden towers have been built overnight to accommodate the Tournament of Gold's final four-man battles.

All along the path there are cheering crowds, from the First House gates at the base of the mountain to the coliseum. Now, as we stand on our platforms, the coliseum heaves and swells like a living thing. There's never been a four-man battle in the past three hundred years. There's never been a melee of Divhs, and the wide marshy plain between the stands and the First House's mountain fortress is teeming with men as the warrior knights from yesterday's battles gather here, waiting for another turn at glory.

This is a day that will forever change the world, Rihad boasts in his announcements to the crowd, dutifully carried from crier to crier around the stadium. This is a day no one will ever forget.

I can tell at a quick glance my father does not stand among Rihad's cabal of spectators. No doubt he is drinking himself drunk back at the First House, lost in his schemes of how to capitalize on my imminent death. The idea of the warrior band transferring back to him sets my teeth rigid.

No. That cannot happen.

I scan the wide field and the stands beyond, noting Caleb and

Nazar's presence with the other warrior knight retainers. I'm glad but not surprised that Caleb is there, but my heart nearly breaks to see Nazar by his side. I've not been allowed to speak to either of them, and guards have ridden close the entire path to ensure that I don't.

I've no idea if Nazar has been called yet to answer to my father, but ultimately, the man is a priest and answers to no one but the Light.

Still, my priest and my squire clearly remain alive, and for that, I'm grateful. Both men's horses are festooned with green and silver sashes as well, the sight of which brought a sudden rush of tears to my eyes when I first stepped out into the sunshine.

Now those sashes are flying in the stands, along with banners of gold and black, sky blue, purple, sand and red. Banners of victory and hope in this mockery of a tournament. No one will know that it's a foregone conclusion who will win this battle and who will lose.

Kheris stands on the platform to my right, ready to fight. My partner, who I know would as soon kill me with his own hands as consign himself to the limits of the tournament. He's been scowling at me since the moment I took my place with the other combatants for this round. I don't think he knows I'm female, simply marked for death. That's enough for him.

The horns blast, and as one, all four warriors upon the stands curl our right hands to our hearts. We raise our left hands high into the air, and the coliseum erupts to a fever pitch of screaming as we hold our positions one moment...two...then summon our Divhs.

The roars of giants replace those of the crowd.

Gent's awareness billows in my mind like an unfurling sail, and I can immediately see through his eyes as he swings his head left and right, taking in the unfamiliar positions of the other Divhs —and the fact that there are three, not one to fight. Instantly, he seems to grasp the nuance of primary and secondary target. The ones to the far end of the field are the first wave of attack, but the serpent to his right is also a threat. My own skin prickles as he stares at Kheris's Divh, the memory of the acidic poison on the creature's skin raking through both my mind and Gent's once more.

Then the monsters at the far end of the field race toward us.

I look to the man standing opposite me on the far platform, tied to the multihorned bull. Cheric of the First House isn't looking at me but at a space beyond me, staring at the monsters pounding across the dirt. That's wrong, though. The way of the warrior is strategy, and the strategy of one warrior against many is a careful dance of both the long sword and the short.

Nazar's words flow back into me. *"To beat one man means you could beat many, if your gaze is true and your heart ready."*

All at once, confusion leaves me. I hear Gent's answering call, an undulating cry of both happiness and excitement. He welcomes the battle, I know. He welcomes the race, anyway.

For myself, I know what I must do. I lift my arms slightly, in the merest hint of the movement of this dance, and flow through the steps.

The Divhs clash in a sudden blaze of bodies and spirits.

The other two warriors have clearly been better prepared for this than we have. As one they attack Kheris's snake, leaving Gent to swerve around in a wide arc, his opponent completely ignoring him. The serpent twists and writhes, and though I have no love for Kheris or his creature, I can't let his Divh fail the way he would surely let Gent drop. To do so will mean quick death to us both.

Instead, I lift my hand and edge it backward. On the field, Gent changes course. He runs at both of the other monsters from behind. They can't see him and aren't expecting him in the face of the giant serpent's full-on defense. Gent grabs the head of the bull and cracks it hard into the mouth of the much larger tusked cat, the second snapping instinctively down, maiming his own partner.

After that, Kheris's snake rights itself and tears into the cat, the bull apparently impervious to her acidic skin. The cat's screams shake the stadium, and Gent swings around to the bull, who's still reeling from the blow to his head. Neither my Divh nor I hesitate as we did in our first battle. My mind and his immense form race forward in the spirit of the one cut, attacking and attacking again, and the bull suddenly sees Gent everywhere it looks, so large is Gent in its field of vision. Gent battles the bull down to the dust of the tournament field, and suddenly, after a long, deafening blast of horns, I come back to myself.

Kheris and I have won the first battle.

I brace myself for the serpent to turn on Gent, yet Kheris doesn't move. The battle is done, it seems, and he's not attacking me...but why? Almost belatedly, I punch the sky with my hand, sending Gent back to his own plane. The horns sound again, and Kheris's snake disappears as well. I slump backward, grateful that Kheris isn't standing right next to me. We've survived, and the crowd is on its feet, stamping and cheering. But there are no petals at my feet, nor swirling in the air. We don't have time for pageantry in this match.

We're escorted back to the warriors' dais, and I watch the other four warriors ride out to battle. Before they even gain the top of their platforms, Kheris is at my side. I brace myself for the much larger man to simply kill me on the spot, but he says nothing to me as he stands beside me as the tournament protocol demands of him. Beside him, I feel like a dwarf mushroom next to an oak.

The second battle takes longer than the first, the warriors already making adjustments to their fighting style based on what they saw in our match. Still, these pairings don't work in perfect sync with each other. Their Divhs aren't connected with them the way Gent and I are, the way I'd even felt with the dragon Szonja.

Unable to wonder any longer, I turn to Kheris. "You didn't try to kill me, and you could have just now. Or at least made the attempt. You want to wait until the final round?"

I've managed to startle him, but he sneers down at me. "I'd kill you where you stand if it were the will of Rihad," he rumbles. "He decided to wait until deeper in the tournament. And so, I wait."

I glare right back. "I don't want to kill you, but I'd still rather not die in the next round if I can avoid it. Instead, I'll give you that chance to win you crave so much."

He barks a short laugh.

Unfazed, I continue, "You see these Divhs? They don't fight together. They don't assist each other. Not the way Gent attacked your enemies from behind when your serpent was cornered."

He bristles. "My Divh is stronger than that cow you control."

"I don't care. They're both stronger working together than either working apart." As he considers that, I press my point. "If you have a need in this next battle, allow your Divh to hear me. Only if you have a need."

He looks as if he wants to argue, but he's seen what the others have seen. The reaching of Gent's long arm across the field, the swirl of petals in the air.

"What sort of sorcery is this?" he growls.

I roll my eyes. Whatever it takes to live through another round, I'm willing to do. Whatever it takes to keep Gent alive.

"The sorcery that would allow you to have your glory in the end. I won't kill you, Kheris. I wouldn't even if I could. But I'll let you take your chance at killing me. If you want that chance...let your Divh hear me."

"Warlock," he curses under his breath, but he turns away from me as the battle ends on the field. There are now only four warriors left, and we climb again to our positions in the tower.

"There's been a change in the tournament, to keep the crowd happy," the guard says gruffly as I mount the stair. "If you win this round, and the expectation is you will handily, you won't fight Kheris here. You'll face him as opposing captains in the melee, out on the open field."

I roll my eyes. *Rihad and his meddling.* "I've never fought in a melee. My horse hasn't either. That won't make for good sport for anyone."

The guard shifts uneasily. "By order of the Lord Protector." Then he glances at me down his long nose. "He can't let you die till the end, Merritt of the Tenth. You have too much support." With a quick grin, he pulls back his sleeve. Wrapped around his forearm bracer is a familiar green-and-silver sash. "The melee is another story. It's never been done. Accidents can and will happen. You'll still be honored, though, even in death." He curls his hand to his chest.

"Comforting."

Then the man is gone, and four warriors stand once more upon the platforms.

I stare across at the warrior from the Second House, the exact opposite of Hantor—where Hantor was foolish and scrawny, this man is a monster. He stares back, grinning.

My mind clears. It suddenly occurs to me that all the warriors might have been given different messages by the guards who attended them. It *then* occurs to me that I alone could be preparing for my death during the melee, while my opponents are still hoping to kill me in this battle.

The moment the attack begins, I realize how right I am.

The monsters both rush Gent, this time leaving Kheris's fighting serpent twisting in confusion. I feel the outrage of the snake even as Gent deflects the first attack, making his arms as deadly as a long sword and fighting with both arms to cut and to slash. Kheris has never had to barge in on a fight, apparently, and so his serpent turns and turns again, not able to do anything but score the backs of the other Divhs as they pound on Gent.

Gent, for his part, roars in pain at one particularly vicious swipe of the shaggy red wolf-like beast he's opposing, the creature's teeth sinking into his shoulder. I can feel the spurt of blood at my own collarbone, as the wolf holds fast. After a long, sickening moment, Gent sends the creature reeling with a punch to its face. Then Gent staggers back, in full retreat.

Suddenly, the serpent screams.

At *me*.

A flood of awareness washes through me as the serpent races across the tournament field toward Gent, splitting apart the other Divhs briefly and shooting past my Divh. Kheris must have realized that with me dead too soon, he and his Divh would surely fall next. His only choice is for me to survive this round.

Either way, his Divh is right before me, and my mind flashes immediately to Fortiss's demonstration with Lord Rihad's Divh. If Fortiss can guide a Divh not his own...by the Light, so can I. With a flick of my hand, I reach out, and Gent swings his mighty paw. He grabs hold of the serpent's tail and swings her—she's a *her*, I realize—around, her hood full and her mouth stretched wide, poison dropping from her jaws and glistening on her skin.

She catches the other Divhs in full arc, slashing and puncturing with her teeth, clearing a swath for Gent to regain his feet. At the last moment, he releases the serpent, and she piles into both monsters with Gent roaring in behind. As she ducks and spins away, he follows up with punishing blows to the faces, heads, and necks of the other Divhs. The ground shakes as they all topple to the ground. Kheris's snake wraps herself around the wolf, and Gent pounds away in blind outrage at the bull until the trumpets finally sound above.

The battle is over.

Gent stands and turns quickly this time, not to be denied. But he doesn't turn first to me. Instead, he turns to Kheris on the far platform and raises both arms to the warrior, in silent testimony of the act that has quite possibly saved the tournament for us, if not our lives. As I stare, a swirl of dark blue and white petals surge around the giant man, a maelstrom of color. Then Gent turns to me, and the crowd roars.

Petals are everywhere. They burst into the space around me, but also in hundreds of places around the tournament stands, and the wind whips them into a soaring storm.

It takes four tries for the horns to quiet the crowd enough for Rihad to announce the next stage of the tournament: the melee. My guard was right in one thing at least—there will be no one-on-one fight between Kheris's serpent and Gent. The crowds are already streaming out of the coliseum to spread out along the great plain. I instantly see the value of this. From the ground, they'll be able to see nothing but enormous clashing Divhs. I could die a hundred times over and no one would know how.

For a moment, fear attacks me in the cut of one timing, but I am ready with a lifetime of fury to push it back. Fury at being denied everything, at being forced to scrape and cower, my life hanging by a string. I will fight in this twisted battle of Rihad's, because I *can* fight.

Before, it was denied to me. But I will be denied no more.

By the time my escorts come to usher me off the platform, I'm ready.

"Your horse has been prepared," the first man says as we clomp down the steps, the same guard who'd spoken to me before. "Your squire rides with you."

"My—" I widen my eyes, thinking of Caleb astride his sturdy gelding. Caleb, fierce and brash, ready to run headlong into any fight, so convinced that he could win by the strength of his will alone. How can I let him risk his life for me? How will I live with myself if he's hurt?

As if in answer to my thoughts, a smile creases the guard's gruff, weary face. "He would not be denied," he says. "He's determined to ride into battle with his warrior, he says, and to face death as only a warrior can. He's a good man."

I nod, my heart thudding with so many emotions for my bright and irrepressible friend—pride, fear, worry, and above all *gratitude* —I'm surprised it doesn't burst. "He's the best man I know."

There's no more time for words as the guard resumes his clomp down the stairs, but my thoughts are not so easily stifled. The image of Fortiss leaps to my mind—unbidden, unwanted. His glorious golden eyes, his heart-swelling touch, his warm and vibrant laugh...his ultimate, damning disdain.

Did he watch me fight this day, one of the very few who knows my true nature? Did he worry about me at all—or even, like the guard, silently cheer for me? Or is that battle already lost forever?

I shouldn't care. I don't. I won't.

I do.

CHAPTER 42

The other warriors are already lined up to fight the melee in long lines of men and guards, and each of the winners of the fighting pit tournaments has been provided with a horse and spear. Caleb's own long sword is already drawn. Instead of his gelding, however, he sits upon Nazar's mare. Seeing that makes me feel better, if only slightly. Caleb can't balance a spear with only one arm, but a sword is an extension of his arm, and his center is strong. He will hold.

Darkwing stamps and whinnies, and I meet the gazes of the men who line up to be captained by me. These aren't my allies, nor are they my friends. How many of them have been ordered to kill me in the first rush of the attack? Many, I suspect. All, more likely.

Nothing I can do about that now.

As we ride, I watch the men's eyes slide off me like water off a fish, eddying to the right and left. They won't follow me. They can't. Even though I've won the tournament beside Kheris, there are too many among them who are under the Lord Protector's sway. Too many among them who bristle at my youth and lack of knowledge—and who'd lose their minds entirely if they knew I was female. There will be no time to convert them, not this day.

I need to try something else.

I turn to Caleb. "Go into the men. They respect you," I say as he looks up at me with surprise. "Tell them this as if you have studied the strategy of the melee your entire life."

"Um...I've never fought in a melee."

"Neither have they. Neither have the men opposite us. Therefore, to win we must take the strategy of the long sword and apply it to the concept of one against many. Each of our men are one, but they shouldn't fight one against one. That's the conventional thought, and it's what'll be expected, but it will fail. Instead, they should each choose four opponents as their enemies, and chase those four specifically from side to side, left and right. The outliers of one man's foursome will also be the outliers of another man's. In this way, each of our opponents will have two enemies, not one."

I stop, pointing to the far side of the melee gathering, where the youngest winners of the pit battles, boys of twelve and thirteen, are massing on foot. Why are they even here? If they get caught in between the foot soldiers, or Light forbid, the mounted combatants, they'll be crushed. "The boys should stay out of the battle entirely, fighting only on the fringes."

Caleb nods, his breath coming more quickly now. "What of the Divhs?"

"The Divhs will appear behind the warriors. It's what they're accustomed to doing. So we'll create a wide path for them, driving the enemies away to the left and right, so the Divhs don't trample us in their coming run. The warriors will fight first with lance to cut a path open, and then with their minds once the Divhs arrive. When the Divhs are clear, they'll fight once more with the lance and sword...I think. No matter what, the soldiers and boys will be the most at risk. You must ensure their safety."

I look up and see I've nearly reached my mark. "Go."

Caleb peels away from me as I line up across the wide swath of open space from Kheris, who sits staring at me like a man possessed. He'll get his chance at last, first of all the others. He and I are positioned several steps forward of the nearly five-score men in the melee. Fifty or so remaining banded soldiers, fifty more men of worth who have not yet received their Divhs, but whose mettle has been proven in the fighting pits. The excitement in the air is palpable, as is the dread. There'll be severe injuries from this tournament game, beyond what might happen to me, I think. It's too many men. Too many men and too many Divhs for safety.

Rihad now stands at the head of the line, Fortiss at his side. He rides in procession down the long line of men, shouting to them.

"Men of the Tournament of Gold, we salute you," he cries. "May you fight honorably and well. The melee will continue until the blasts of trumpets and fireworks signal the end. If you cannot hear the one, you will see the other. Look and listen for my command! We want no foolish injuries here." He reaches the center of the line, where Kheris and I are positioned. I gaze stonily at Rihad, whose sly grin fills up his whole face. Beside Rihad, Fortiss refuses to look at me at all. "Though there will be injuries and there may be deaths. Such is the nature of war."

He raises his left hand to the sky, his right fist curled to his heart. All the men who are warriors except Kheris and myself do the same, then Rihad drops both hands back to his bridle.

"Kheris of the Third House, Merritt of the Tenth. I command you to battle!" Rihad shouts. Behind us, a huge swelling roar of excited men erupts, made ever greater as the crowd joins in.

Rihad and Fortiss turn and gallop back to the stage. As they ride, a growing clamor of shouting men and rattling weapons sounds from all sides of the wide field, while spectators strain forward to see above each other and search the skies for the first appearance of the Divhs.

Now Kheris and I lift our hands to our hearts and the sky as well. The big man glares at me with far too much hate for any one face. I return his stare, my mind strangely clear once more, the anger within me bright and true. The sun is behind me in the western sky, which puts it in the face of Kheris's line. I will fall back, I decide, feigning weakness as Kheris comes on, then as his own focus sharpens with the eagerness of an easy kill, I will plunge

Darkwing forward full force. This is the strategy to win in the first rush. After that, it will be the Divhs' battle to fight.

A horn blasts through the air.

As one, we drop our arms.

The sky booms with the force of a thousand cannons, and men scream all around me, flush with the fire of war. I can hear Gent's roar of excitement before I feel his connection sharpen to crystal clarity in this plane, and though I don't turn back to see where he's landed behind the converging warriors, I know the truth. *He's here!* He's with me. For a brief, blessed moment, I immerse myself in his waves of joy and pride that he has come to fight by his warrior's side—

Then the madness of the battle consumes me.

Kheris launches himself at me with the fury I expect, and I fall back, forcing my men to cleave around me and spin to the right and left. I can almost feel Kheris's glee, and I wait one, two, a third moment longer before I surge forward. I see him, yes, but I also see through Gent's eyes, his head swinging from right to left as he races forward at the head of the line of monsters to all his foes beyond. I thought I would be able to see both above and below, but I can't focus on Kheris. I see only the creature right in front of Gent, not Kheris's huge serpent but the giant spider-legged beetle of a Seventh House warrior, every inch of her body dripping poison.

Gent swings his hands close together like a battering ram and collides with the creature head-on. I feel my Divh's surprise at the ferocity of the hit, and the satisfaction of it as well, and I realize— he doesn't truly understand this fight, doesn't seek it, but he will do anything I ask. Whatever it takes to protect me. And that bond has brought him here, huge fists flying, horns bristling, his howl shattering the sky. I don't know whether to laugh in exultation or weep in shame.

The battle on the ground rages forth as well. Kheris races his horse directly by me—*by* me, not into me, and I pull Darkwing to the left in time for it to be a clean pass. Kheris doesn't swipe his arm to knock me off my horse, however, and he doesn't turn to plow me over with his much larger steed. Instead, his eyes hold the near-and-far gaze I suspect I also project, his body twitching at the neck and shoulder and arm. He pulls his sword, and—attacks a man at my right.

My right! Kheris is *defending* me.

Belatedly, I jerk my own sword out of its scabbard as well and instantly realize the truth of our situation. We can't fight effectively like this, not simultaneously on the ground and in the sky, in the minds of our Divhs. A hot burst of pain blossoms on my shoulder, and I blink back into focus.

Hantor is before me, attacking and slashing, and I allow both mind and spirit to snap together and take him in the quick attack after a sudden slash. I am neither bigger nor stronger than Hantor, but he's not expecting me to pull my short sword with my left hand even as I heft my long sword with my right. I cut in, sharply, and clip his shoulder just at the neck. He wheels away, his horse staggering against his sudden cut of the reins.

Around me is chaos. The fighting men have split, as Caleb directed them to do, drawing their enemies into two clusters of battles with the long sword, the boys at the periphery and the seasoned guardsmen cutting down their foes with bloodthirsty glee.

The warrior knights, though, are slowing, steadying, their minds torn in two with the need to both protect themselves and guide their Divhs as well, in perfect point and counterpoint. One of the great lions falters and falls, and an attacking bull leaps for its throat, the two of them tumbling end over end as their warriors on horseback wheel and jerk in their saddles, their weapons going wide as their minds are consumed with the heat of another battle.

My own gaze fractures. Gent crashes his fist hard into a spitting lizard's jaw, sending it spinning, and pain bites through my gloved hands as the poison eats into an open wound on Gent's paw. The flash of agony clears my head and centers me, but the moment of distraction exacts its price.

A warrior of the First House breaks through the field and

pounds up to me on a horse as white as snow, even in the churning dust. He does to me what I would have done to him if I'd been quicker, attacking down the long sword, the angle of his blade pressing forth, and I realize he's stopped controlling his Divh; his mind is no longer split.

He's fully in the moment, his Divh left to its own battles even as I struggle to balance my sight between Gent's multifaceted gaze and the world directly before me. The blade of the man's sword slices along my arm, skidding away from a direct cut at the last minute but laying open a deep cleft of flesh and muscle that jolts me to my core. I've never been injured like this—I've never felt such pain.

Somewhere high above me, Gent screams.

Another of the First House is approaching in direct assault from my side, and my first thought is Darkwing. Beautiful, valiant Darkwing, who rears and darts away, his hind legs bunched for flight. The stallion springs in rapid movement as the short sword —a dagger, really—comes out of nowhere and plunges into my right thigh. I feel the sudden surge of lifeblood spew forth and know that this, I cannot stanch. This cut is thick and deep and true.

The way of the warrior is death.

My vision swims, and I see what Gent sees—Gent, as he swings two small Divhs together and tosses them both aside like garbage, then turns and lumbers toward me, furious and panicked, but nearly blind when it comes to seeing fine detail. Blind! I've forgotten his sight in this plane.

His pain isn't at all physical, but it swamps him, swamps us both as if it is. *He can't find me.* No matter his might and strength, his overwhelming need is to keep me safe. Only, he can't reach me. No one can reach me.

I've learned the way of the warrior. But in the end, I am no warrior.

I don't have the strength. I haven't had the time.

A flash of gold and black bursts before me, and the nick of a blade against my collarbone adds a spray of blood to coat my face and black my eyes. Darkwing spins beneath me, confused and terrified; I don't know how I stay astride him. My sight careens wildly between what I'm seeing and what Gent sees, and I barely note the sand-colored flash that comes upon me next. It's not Kheris, but—

Another stripe of pain lances my fingers. My sword falls away.

Gent's rage consumes me.

My gaze switches to the high view, where my glorious Divh glares around fiercely, trying to make sense of the heaving riot of riders and soldiers at his feet. And suddenly, it's not my thoughts that fill my mind, but those of a mind I've never felt so clearly before. One that I've touched, but never fully known. *Too many riders, too many horses! I will trample them. But there in the center is my beating heart, my very life. I must reach her! Must make her whole.*

"No," I gasp, but Gent can't, won't hear me. He surges away from the battling Divhs just as a cry screeches from on high and something rushes at him from the sky.

I gape, looking up as well. Rihad's winged scorpion is attacking! It has entered the battle.

And there, in the distance, I see something else. A wedge of horses thundering across the plain, heading straight for the far edge of the battlefield, where I know the youngest soldiers are fighting for their lives.

But these aren't the mighty battle horses of the warrior knights and soldiers. These are fresh horses unburdened by ceremonial saddles, with riders tall and straight, hair streaming in the wind as they hold their swords high, one of them lifting a horn and sounding a clarion call that lifts above the chaos. The Savasci have also entered the battle—and they have come to *fight*.

I can't see Fortiss from where I'm clinging to Darkwing. I don't know if he's guiding Rihad's creature. But I wheel Darkwing around, trying to focus. The field opens up around me, and...something is wrong here, definitely wrong.

There are too many men collapsed, broken and bloody, on the ground. Silent, unmoving.

Dead.

Not just soldiers either, but warrior knights I recognize, from the Fourth and Sixth Houses, their eyes staring wide in surprise at the sky. I knew Rihad was looking to ensure his control, but this... this is carnage. What can be gained by it?

Screams of the monsters flood my mind, and I jerk my gaze up, past my own pain to focus on the far battle. Divhs litter the ground there as well. Dead, dying, their bodies becoming ephemeral in the rising heat of the marshy field as they return to their own plane. I stare in horror, struggling to understand. The Tournament of Gold isn't about death and dying, it's—

My mind shifts back to Gent's perspective, and I see something different. Not all the Divhs are dying, at least. Those of the Eighth House and the First are rolling strong, the Second too. And the Third. Those are the ones attacking to kill, not to maim or merely overcome. Those are the ones attacking to destroy, both on the ground and in the sky. The wolf of the Second House and the bull of the Seventh are once more a team, dragging down a set of smaller Divhs I've not seen before in the tournament, the Divhs of lesser warrior knights, I'm certain, collapsing under the attack of the much greater first-blooded monsters. They thrash and whirl, but surprisingly, there's no real telling who is the aggressor and who the defense, not if you don't know what to look for...

Not if you don't know.

All at once, I see the beauty of Rihad's plan. There will be no survivors of this battle except those that Rihad has carefully chosen. Those warrior knights loyal to him to the end will as one decry the savage treachery of their fellows, claiming that *they* were the ones turned upon, *they* were the ones assaulted. Rihad will then pledge to restore the glory of the Protectorate by creating new bands, new Divhs—all of which he'll ultimately control. In one horrific melee, he'll have both destroyed his greatest opponents and swung the gratitude of the masses to him.

Another cry cuts across my thoughts, and Gent turns to take the full brunt of Rihad's monster's attack. The scorpion's cruel pincer-like appendages slash through the air, its wings erupting in a wild fury as it slams fully into Gent's body.

Exactly at that moment, a new pain erupts in my side, strong enough to lift me off my saddle. It does lift me off, in fact, the broad cleaving sword of an Eighth House soldier skewering me and wrenching me from Darkwing, who screams and surges away to avoid being trampled by the rush of three warriors who've borne down on me from behind.

I land hard on the dusty ground, the world around me bathed in blood. I haul myself up, finally regaining my feet, knowing that the Eighth House soldier has dismounted as well to finish me off. I stare at him, backing away, but there's nowhere to run. A flash of metal cuts through the air, catching the bright sunlight—

Pain rips through me. A chasm of fire stretching wide to swallow me whole.

"Talia!" The agonized, unmistakably feminine cry is distant—but I hear it. I hear it. Pride surges through my blood.

I stagger one step, then another. The ground is suddenly too close, and I fall down to meet it. Images flash before my eyes: Merritt's joyful leap as he surged into the sky that final time. My mother's quiet smile as she brushed my long, unruly hair. Nazar, wise and calm, his grace and wisdom so obvious now when before, I had never seen it, never imagined its harrowing truth. Fortiss's face, half-masked in the darkness, before he knew me for what I really was. Caleb, brave and fierce.

My heart swells, and I struggle to rise, then cower as a horse veers too close to me. The full-throated cries of the Savasci grow louder, renewed as they surge nearer and another wave of attacks bursts from the roiling crowd.

But there are so many who wish to see me dead. A gauntleted fist cracks into the side of my head, another knife slash tears through what remains of my sleeve, ripping it to shreds. My thoughts spin off in new directions and I feel the surge of panic again welling up.

Gent—Gent is trying to find me, to reach my broken body. Gent who, though scraped and bloody from Rihad's massive Divh, is even now battling his way through the mob to protect me.

I pray to the Light he won't make it.

I roll forward on my face, my hand stretching out to where I know my beautiful Divh will eventually come. My worry that my father might reclaim my warrior band melts away as a new, far more horrible possibility looms. Gent *can't* die with me. And he will. The bodies of warriors surround me, their eyes dead and their Divhs dead with them. It can't be this way for Gent, I think, as I taste copper and salt, my lips wet now, my face streaming with tears. He cannot die.

My right hand lifts to my heart, then higher still, to where the warrior's band is clamped around my left arm. I curl my fingers around it as my Divh thunders up from the far distance, tossing men and horses aside like toys with his immense, sweeping arms.

"Gent," I manage, though my mouth is filled with blood. The sound of the battle dims with the pounding of my heart in my ears. My hand slips on the warrior band, but I force my fingers beneath it, tugging with all my strength, the pain merely another wave of fire blackening my bones. "Gent, you cannot die."

The scream of my Divh fills the whole world, anguish, pain, and loss crashing around me as he drops to his knees a hundred strides distant from me, his shadow blocking out the sun. At last the warrior band comes away in my hand, pulsing with a life I can no longer share with it. Relief fills me, staving off the pain for a moment more, and I put my last crystalline burst of energy into a force as strong as any command I will ever utter.

"Gent," I whisper through chattering teeth. "I release you."

CHAPTER 43

I crumple as the air snaps around me, and the sun blazes down on my body once more.

"Tal—Talia." Caleb's voice is frantic in my ear, and I flail back to consciousness, worry surging up in my throat along with my own blood. Someone stands beyond him, tall and straight. Someone...almost familiar.

"Go," I gasp, as my mind grapples with what he'd called me. What had he said—it seems wrong now—wrong. "Caleb, leave, they'll come to finish me. You must get away."

"No." He flops down at my side and wraps his right arm around me, firmly pulling me into his embrace. "No, Talia, you *can't die*."

His words strike an impossible echo with what I'd just told Gent, what I told Merritt weeks ago, then I piece together what he's said. My skin seems to crack with the effort it takes to smile. "Talia," I mutter. "Did you call me Talia on the open field?"

"You're an idiot," Caleb groans as he rocks me, protecting me with his body. "You should have run, you could have run..." I struggle to meet his gaze, and see those eyes are filled with anguish now. "But Gent *left* you. How can he have left? He could have protected you—"

"I let him go." The pain is somehow lessening now, everything blurring into one sensation as blood drains out of me and onto the open field. I open my hand, and the sentient band pulses there, shimmering with life.

Caleb gasps. "You didn't."

"I'm going to die." The words fill me with a peace I hadn't expected. "He shouldn't."

"You *can't*." Caleb looks to the west and the bright sun, and I let a little more of the world back into my awareness. With it comes a wash of pain, but I struggle up, trying to make sense of what I'm seeing.

"What's happening?" I whisper.

Shuddering Divhs and dying warriors, still scrabbling to hold onto life, and horses and soldiers lie everywhere on the field. But the battle still rages on in pockets. The marauder women are in the thick of it, and a few of them have come to surround me on horseback, their blades and axes pulled. No one else is close.

"I don't know," moans Caleb. "It was a melee, a fight, then Rihad's winged monster showed up and everything...shifted. The men of the First and Eighth Houses turned in earnest on the others, whether they were on their official side or no. They fought not to best or pin, but to kill." He grimaces. "They succeeded."

"They can't—" I wince as I try to sit up further, and taste more of the bright coppery tang of blood. Gent is gone, and my heart surges with relief. But everywhere else, there's carnage. Nearest to me is Hantor's bone creature, its eyes wide and glassy, a line of blue blood trailing from his mouth. Even as I stare, it disappears, and my breath stops. *Hantor...* "This cannot be."

Suddenly, Rihad's winged scorpion screeches in earsplitting fury, and Caleb jerks around, jostling every wound open on my body. I nearly swoon, and darkness rushes in, narrowing my vision to pinpricks.

"What in the..."

Pulling his arm from me, Caleb grabs the glass around his neck and fixes it to his eye. I can't see anything in the roiling dust.

"Rihad is down," Caleb cries. "The guards are fighting with Fortiss!"

I sag back, my heart twisting anew. That's why Rihad's Divh screamed. Fortiss must've finally realized that what was happening on the tournament field was not the result of crazed monsters and men, but the careful plan of the Lord Protector.

He'd seen the truth of Rihad, and he'd driven his blade into the man. It's too late—far too late, but...

The air around Caleb and me shudders again, and my squire collapses back to the ground, dragging me with him. With a resounding boom, the sky turns black, the sun completely blotted out. I roll into a ball with Caleb, certain this is the end.

"Go," I scream, but my words barely come out as a whimper. "You must go."

"Watch *out*—" Caleb throws his body over me as the ground shakes violently enough to bounce us up a few inches, and then we crash suddenly down.

It happens again, and again.

I blink, trying to see through the dust, but there's nothing but Divhs in a wide circle around us—upright Divhs this time, ones I've never seen before. Enormous clawed and taloned, leathered and furred, feathered and scaled Divhs, each of their thunderous feet pounding hard into the ground, loud enough to bring the very heavens down.

Life. The earth seems to cry out with every stomp. *Life.*

"Ahh!" I jerk rigid. An immense bolt of fire rips through me, and I scream as salt and dust assault us in a whipping gale. The warrior band I'm still gripping splits in my hand, tearing straight down the middle. I blink at it blearily, trying desperately to understand. But...how? Only the Lord Protector has the power to split his band! It is Law!

Law or not, one half of the sentient band falls away from my fingers, while the other half races back up my injured arm, leaving a searing trail of pain in its wake, to wrap tightly around my bicep once more. And before my eyes I see it return to its full, untorn size

—exactly as the Lord Protector's has done since the dawn of the Protectorate.

"*No.*" I cough blood and seem to burn from the inside out, even as Caleb shrieks in agony beside me.

"Get it off me!" he bellows, dropping me to the ground to claw at what remains of his left arm. There's a burning trail across the front of his clothes and my hand is now empty. I know what's happened before he does, but I can't speak, dizzy with pain, blood loss, and confusion as the stomping continues and the mighty beasts around us roar. How is it I'm still alive? How is it I'm—

Then a familiar enormous foot plants itself not twenty paces from my head. I know that ebony claw, that swath of thick green hide. I look up—and up still further, unable to stop the tears now coursing down my face.

Oh no... Oh no, no, no.

"Gent, *no*," I scream, half-sobbing. "You can't be here!"

A rush of wind rips across my face, my body, driving dirt into my mouth and eyes. Then Caleb is howling again, and an enormous claw scrapes the ground out from beneath me, toppling me into Gent's palm.

A palm he curls to his heart as he roars.

Not death, his mind pounds against me, his enormous heart beating as one with mine. *Not death, not death. Life.*

I can't see anything then for a few minutes, but we are running forward, running and stomping and howling, only it's not just Gent but an *army* of Divhs, more than I've ever thought possible could be in one place. They burst into the group of battling men and monsters and separate them, scattering and even trampling the banded soldiers and warrior knights, and knocking the exhausted Divhs end over end. The soldiers still left fighting immediately break ranks in the face of this newest threat. The battle seems on the edge of finally, blessedly ending—no more dead and dying warriors, no more thrashing bodies of Divhs littering the open plain.

Then Rihad's winged scorpion surges up into the air, freezing all the Divhs with its piercing scream.

I crawl up in Gent's paw, realizing distantly that the worst of my wounds are no longer bleeding, that my breath is coming more easily. And I know: somehow, Gent did this. My Divh. His protection is not only shielding me...but *healing* me as well. How is it we know so little of the wonder of these creatures, after all their centuries of service? I dash the blood from my eyes to see more clearly as my Divh swings around.

Rihad kneels over Fortiss, one hand on his shoulder holding him to the ground as his other is raised high. As I watch, however, Fortiss surges up and claps his hand over Rihad's left bicep, then wrenches something away. High above them both, the scorpion bellows again, but there's another screeching roar that follows hard upon that scream.

A howl of rage that comes from deep within the mountain.

Gent swings around. The side of the cliff well behind the First House suddenly shatters, and the percussive *boom!* of exploding rock knocks us backward. The knot of Divhs lurches to the side, and the Divhs of the Eighth and First Houses scream in fury, adding their cry to that of Rihad's creature.

Before I can see anything more, Gent's paw contracts again, cradling me to his chest. He pounds over to the high walls of the coliseum and drops me on to its tallest wooden tier of seating. I land on the sun-blasted surface with a bone-rattling crunch.

Then Gent turns, roaring, and dives back into the fight.

I struggle to my feet, dizzy with pain, and stare at the new creature rising above the mountain.

A dragon nearly two-thirds Gent's size arrows through the sky, one glorious wing outstretched, and one horribly bent. Her speed is astonishing, however, and she plows into the side of the winged scorpion, sending it cartwheeling. I turn, watching the aerial attack continue over the far end of the coliseum. Szonja can't win this battle—she can't. Her talons can rip and tear, she may even summon fire, but the moment the winged scorpion realizes she can't truly fly...

Suddenly, another Divh bounds toward me on my coliseum perch, an ungainly giant with the hard-beaked head of a falcon, the muscled torso and arms of a man, and legs as thick and hairy as an ape's. It seems like it'll charge straight through the wall of rock, but it stops at the last moment, hurling something down. I try to duck but am unable to escape the heap of body that crashes into me.

Caleb. Apparently dead.

"*Caleb.*" I have no voice left, my throat is filled with rocks, but I wrap my arms around his shattered form. I pull the squire into my body, as he's so recently done to me, and realize he still breathes. He shakes, in fact, convulsing. I hold him, not knowing what else to do as I search the skies for the dragon and the winged scorpion that have soared beyond the clouds.

"Szonja," I whisper.

In the far distant reaches of my mind, I feel her return touch. Hers and someone else's...Fortiss, bold and valiant Fortiss, her new warrior knight. Fortiss, whose wildly beating heart now gallops in frantic rhythm with my own.

Keeping Caleb with me, I pull myself over to the walls of this highest rampart of the coliseum and gaze down.

I fumble for the glass around Caleb's neck, yanking it free to place it against my eye.

In the midst of the battlefield carnage, Fortiss and Rihad are frozen in fierce combat, for all that they aren't touching each other. Ringed round them are two layers of guards, clearly at a loss for how to proceed. They cannot break the connection between the two men, but it's as if they're as locked as much in place as the warrior knights are. Blood runs down Rihad's face and Fortiss's arm. Fortiss's tunic has burned clean away at the shoulder too, revealing a bicep which now bears the unmistakable cuff of a warrior band.

He has finally chosen to fight. To rip off the band Rihad had stolen from his father and claim it as his own. Szonja has answered his call. And the battle of their respective beasts is so strong, the two men are caught in their thrall.

The screeching rage of the flying beasts above catches me again. As I look up, they cartwheel through the sky, slashing and ripping. Szonja's poorly healed wing makes her flight awkward and seems to require her constant correction. However, the uneven angle of her attack is precisely what's causing the winged scorpion the most trouble.

They snarl and fight in the sky. I sense the touch of Fortiss in the distant part of my mind, the part that holds the fragile connection with Szonja.

And I realize with horror...he's *losing* that connection. Fortiss isn't yet strong enough. He hasn't fought with his Divh at all, and he's not truly connected with her—or maybe he's just reeling from the act of being banded. Either way, he's not yet strong enough to fight this fight—he's not enough!

But I am, I know with absolute, unshakable certainty.

I am enough.

Suddenly, the words tumble forth as if directly from Nazar's teaching, and I push them out to Szonja like an offering. Szonja, beautiful Szonja, whose scream in the sun-bright sky now takes on a new and bloodcurdling ferocity. A scream that is echoed on the bloody battlefield not only by Gent, but by howls of all descriptions.

"Body and soul," I breathe, slowing my heart, standing tall as I look into the heavens with both my form and spirit, hitting from a place of emptiness as I direct Szonja to fly at Rihad's Divh again and again, accelerating strongly despite her shattered wing. Fortiss's mind reaches for me too, adding his strength to my fiery intensity.

I press harder, my mind as Szonja's mind, my eyes her eyes. The cut of no conception and no design is the one strategy that cannot be defended against, not completely, because it combines the best of improvisation and the best of strategy in a hit without hitting, a cut without cutting, a thought without thinking.

I pour my thoughts forth, barely moving, my whole body wrung out, as the battle crashes across the heavens, each cut more vicious than the last. But then, finally, with one last, driving thrust, Szonja closes her vicious maw around the winged scorpion's neck, and the two of them plummet to the ground, far to the west of the coliseum. Another muffled *boom!* rocks across the plain.

For one long, sickening moment, there's nothing but silence.

Fortiss is there, I am there, our link unbroken as I see what he sees—Rihad on his knees, torn and bloody, his mouth working though I cannot hear his words. Is he sending his injured Divh back to his own plane? Is he conceding?

I cannot see at first through Szonja's eyes—there is only blackness. Blackness...and then sky.

Sky!

My heart seems to swell to several times its normal size, and I'm swamped with an elation so great, so terrible, I nearly pass out from its ferocious joy.

A moment later, her jaws opened wide and stained with the blood of her enemy, Szonja's screech of rage and glory fills the air.

The air snaps tight around me once more. A sudden, whipping gale blows me back from the coliseum's walls, and I crouch down against the stone, huddling Caleb close against the ferocious wind.

When the storm passes, I peer out again. My hand shakes Nazar's eyeglass, throwing everything in motion.

But I can still witness the truth of the battle below; I can still see the truth.

It is finished.

Fortiss stands at the edge of the battlefield, looming over Rihad. The Lord Protector is out cold at his feet, blood at his mouth and staining the front of his robes. Fortiss turns to stare across the wide field. The guards drop to one knee.

Then, around Fortiss, billowing forth like a sea kept too long from high tide, the crowd of Trilion suddenly flows. They stop at the very edge of the carnage, where the dead warriors lie, their own Divhs long gone, and kneel to Fortiss as well. He is the symbol they know, the heir to the ruling House. He is the man they will follow, now that Rihad has fallen. He is their leader—and he can remain their leader, as far as I'm concerned. I don't want the burden of all these people. I only want…

I blink, realizing the truth of it.

I want to be what I am.

A warrior knight. First-blooded and firstborn.

Below me, a huge, resounding cheer goes up.

Then, beyond the tide of humanity and across the wide plain, one Divh steps free from the collection of giants gathered there. He turns and points. Not to Fortiss…but to me. My heart surges again in my chest as I recognize my beautiful silver and green goliath, feel the touch of his mind on mine, the view of ocean and flowers and an endless, sun-drenched field.

Gent extends his long arm toward me, and I, in turn, high atop the coliseum, reach out to him.

Then thirty other Divhs extend their arms and wings and claws toward me as well—and roar.

Somewhere far across the sky, Szonja adds her scream to their song.

I stand, arm outstretched, totally still as the people of Trilion, spectators and villagers alike, rise up and cheer anew. Then I drop my arm…and the monsters disappear.

I sag.

"Talia."

The gasp behind me seems to come from far away—so far away—and I turn with a startled cry as Nazar tops the stair, the old priest seeming barely winded as he rushes toward me, staff in hand, his long robes flowing out behind him.

Nazar only speeds up as he sees the boy crumpled at my feet.

"*Caleb*," he moans, and in these two words, I've heard more emotion from the priest than in all the time I've known him.

Nazar casts his staff down, and together we crouch toward

Caleb, shoulder to shoulder as we peel the boy away from the wall. Caleb is curled tight, protecting his stumped arm, his body still awash in violent tremors. I exchange a glance with Nazar and lay a hand first on Caleb's foot, then his leg, talking the whole while.

"Caleb," I soothe, and Nazar adds a low murmur to my words, speaking in a language I don't know as I babble, "Caleb. It's all right, you're all right. I'm here, Caleb. It's okay."

I make it all the way up to the boy's shoulder, and with Nazar's help turn him over to face me. He goes willingly, burying his face against my shoulder as he convulses again.

Then I realize that these aren't the pain-scorched throes of a broken boy.

Caleb…is *crying*.

I jerk my gaze to Nazar, and the priest settles back on his heels. There's no longer a look of worry on his face, though. In its place is an expression of fierce pride.

"It is good," Nazar declares, his face creasing into a tired smile. "It is of the Light."

In my arms, Caleb merely sobs harder.

"Mistake," he manages, his entire body shaking. "There's been a—a terrible mistake."

I gape at him but cannot yet break in past the wracking agony of his cries. Finally, Caleb hiccups a shuddering breath and seems to collapse in on himself. I set him back from me, searching his face, as he shivers with silent sobs. "What mistake, Caleb? What happened? Are you injured? Are you—"

"This!" With his mouth contorted in a wash of pain, he reaches with his right hand and lifts the torn and tattered cloth of his left tunic sleeve, pulling the material up and over his shoulder to reveal the most slender of warrior bands, clamped tightly into his skin.

"It slid onto me from your—from your band," he manages, his breath coming too quick, too harsh. "And then…and then that Divh…that hodgepodge, mashed-up, incredible Divh…" He shakes his head and turns to Nazar, then back to me, his eyes wide and shining with disbelief.

I know that disbelief. It wasn't so long ago that I suspect I wore that same stunned, confused, and deliriously bleary look. I smile, a smile so wide it makes all my bruises ache. "What's his name, Caleb? What's the name of your Divh?"

"Marsh. His name is Marsh," he says, the words barely a whisper. "He chose *me*, Talia, to be his warrior. *Me*."

"And he chose well." Nazar places a hand on Caleb's shoulder, and in the priest's worn and dust-streaked face, I see the resolve of decades of truth and training, hear it in his voice. "There is no one who fights so long and so well as you, warrior Caleb, and no one who—"

But Nazar's words are cut off by the sound of the crunching earth, a steady, rhythmic thudding and heavy woosh of wings that could only be a Divh—or two of them. Gent and his fellows have already left, and Nazar's and my gazes lock, knowing this as the sudden threat it must be. The ear-shattering pounding reaches a crescendo as I pull Caleb to the side. Nazar grabs up his staff, whirling around with a shout—

And freezes.

I can only stare as the old man's face slackens in shock, his eyes fixed up, up on the enormous beast who even now leans down toward him, our great height at the top of the coliseum rendering us nearly even with the Divh's bulky form. Its sharp, golden beak glints in the light, its snowy white plumage bursting around it to cover its head. Its piercing black eyes, cunning and intelligent, stare at Nazar with an unyielding gaze, while its powerful lion's body, coated in midnight blue fur in stunning contrast to its mighty spread of snow-white feathers, practically vibrates with excitement. The quietest, questioning trill escapes from its beak as it tilts its head to lean down more closely to us.

A clatter makes me blink, and I realize that Nazar has dropped his staff. The priest steps forward once, twice, then lifts his ruined left arm free of his cloak, reaching high. The scrap of what is left of his warrior band, buried in his wrist, flashes in the bright sun, while the mighty creature dips its beak toward him, exhaling another soft, chittering trill.

Nazar's eyes are mirror bright, but his face is calm, and his voice, when it comes, is resolute. The single word he speaks carries on the breeze, rich with power, purpose, and a warrior coming home.

"*Wrath.*"

CHAPTER 44

There is no victory celebration this night.
Too many warriors have died; too much has changed. Too much and not enough.

Under Fortiss's order, Caleb and I are carried back to the First House on litters, taken to dignitaries' rooms.

My father remains at the First House, closeted with most of Rihad's advisors. He has done nothing wrong, after all. He is no prisoner here. Somehow, I know, he will turn this to his advantage. Tonight, I'm too exhausted to care.

Rihad hasn't awoken, but he also hasn't died; he remains under heavy guard. He's still a first line warrior knight, still part of the sacred trust of the Protectorate. And, until the Imperium hands down official rule, still safe.

For now, however, Fortiss is the Lord Protector of the First House, by full agreement of the council and the remaining House warriors, few though there are. The lords of all the houses will be summoned, but, again for now—it is enough. Fortiss will pass temporary judgment on Rihad, and that judgment will be harsh. It's plain to all that the master of the First House has broken the first law of this land, which is never to turn warrior on warrior in true battle.

That isn't the way to ensure the Protectorate stays strong. It's the way to ensure it would be broken. And broken it is now.

Broken is apparently what Rihad wanted.

Nazar's quiet words state the carnage succinctly as he speaks to me in the half-darkness of my room.

Of the original fifty-odd elite warriors who fought in the Tournament of Gold, thirteen remain, including Fortiss. Four of those are from the First House, two from the Eighth.

Of the surviving warriors, all but three were under the orders of Rihad to turn on the other combatants during the melee and destroy them. Their fates are for cooler minds than mine to decide, but in the end, they were soldiers following orders. They did as they were trained, nothing more.

The one defector had been Kheris. He'd contracted with Rihad not only to fight, but also to slay me. According to Nazar, he changed his mind during our shared fight, and was responsible for the three warriors who did survive to still be standing, along with their Divhs.

The priest pauses in his accounting, watching me with palpable interest. He draws on his long pipe, a thin tendril of smoke wafting through the room. "There are three additional discoveries of import that have been shared with Lord Protector Fortiss," he says, nodding as I glance toward him. "The first is that Caleb is now a banded soldier."

That makes me smile. "As he should be," I begin, but Nazar continues.

"The second is that the bodies of two women were found among the dead—women who bore weapons and battle armor. Women who'd fought like men."

I close my eyes, my heart aching that not all of the fearless Savasci escaped Rihad's killing field. *I'm sorry, Syril.*

"You knew these women," Nazar says. It's not a question.

When I don't reply, he sighs. "The blasphemy of their act has only been outdone by your own, it would seem. Trilion has become a city of whispers and gasps."

I frown at him. "Mine?"

"Yours. You, Talia of the Tenth, a first-blooded and firstborn warrior who has, by all accounts, commanded the Divhs who won the melee...are a woman."

That declaration makes me sit up in my bed, despite the spinning pain the movement causes behind my eyes. My tunic has been cut off my body and what's left of my wounds is sewn and bandaged. There's now a thick blanket over my chest and legs, my arms free. The right is heavily wrapped below the elbow, and the left is bandaged tight all the way up to my warrior band, which gleams anew against my arm, a pulsing, living thing.

"How is it that people know—beyond whoever stitched me up?" I ask, frowning. "I could be killed, Nazar."

"You would be killed, executed, were this the Imperium or if Rihad still ruled. But it isn't the Imperium, Rihad is imprisoned, and your Divh saved the warriors who were left on both sides of the battle. That battle would have otherwise raged on, I suspect, until everyone was dead. And you somehow managed to call forth a new army of Divhs—"

"No," I interrupt him. "I didn't do that. Gent did. The Light did—I have no idea. But not me. I had nothing to do with that."

Nazar just studies me implacably, falling silent as I lean back against the pillows, utterly spent. "I didn't do it," I insist again.

Several moments pass where neither of us speaks, and I'm too weak to ask what Nazar is thinking. But I know the truth. Those Divhs came because of something other than me—they couldn't have done otherwise. I'm merely...

A warrior knight, Nazar's words echo in my mind. *First-blooded and firstborn.*

As if he can hear my thoughts, the priest speaks again. "How it came to pass is perhaps of less importance than that it did come to pass. And the way of the warrior requires humility of spirit and strength of heart, Talia. You have both." He takes another long draw from his pipe. "Fortiss has formally offered you command of the Court of Talons, should you wish to accept it. He feels somewhat outnumbered, though from all appearances, the council wasn't aware of Rihad's decision to use the tournament melee as a field of death for the Protectorate's greatest warriors."

"Command of the..." It's too much. I can no longer hold my mind around the words. I close my eyes as Nazar continues to speak and sink back into slumber.

I wake hours later to utter silence. Gloom hangs heavily in the room, and a fire burns in the grate, though the windows are open to the just-dawning sun. It's not a cold morning, but I gaze at the fire a long while, savoring its warmth.

At length, however, I simply have to move. The First House is quiet, and I slip out of bed, reaching for the heavy robe that Nazar has left me. I pull it over my shoulders, wincing at the pain. I don't know how I've managed to survive to see this new day. I don't want to know. But still, it feels right. It feels good.

It is enough, for this moment...and so am I.

I emerge from my room, startled to find two guards at the door —more startled still to see them wearing the tournament sashes with my colors—half those colors, anyway. The green has been cut away. Only silver remains.

The men drop to one knee, confusing me further, until I urge them back up again. I am no lord here; I have no house. But I'm grateful for them just the same.

"Thank you for..." I trail off, not knowing what to say. "Thank you."

"The great hall is a flight down and to the left, Warrior Talia," the man on the right says. "Lord Protector Fortiss directed us to take you there when you woke. If you're able."

I purse my lips, mystified at the new titles. Lord Protector Fortiss. Warrior Talia. Is that who I am, in truth? No longer a lie. A cheat. No longer a daughter or a wife or a servant to a greater lord.

A warrior. With a banner sewn of silver.

I could get used to that.

"And, ah..." I clear my throat. "The banded warrior, Caleb? Is he somewhere close?"

"The Lord Protector knew you would ask." The same guard nods. "But he's still in the throes of the delirium caused by his banding. He's being watched over."

I wince, remembering my own reaction to the band, the days of queasy pain that followed. Silently, I gesture to the guard to take me to Fortiss. Later, when he's rested, I'll visit Caleb. We turn down the staircase, the unexpected height of the step sending a jolt of pain through my body. There's still so much healing to be done...in every corner of the Protectorate.

We find Fortiss in Rihad's inner chambers, with the fire roaring behind him. He sits, alone, at a table he's pulled into position in front of Rihad's grand throne. Before him on the table rests Merritt's shattered gray arrow. I look around the room, unable to keep from shuddering. It's been mere days since I last stood in this room, betrayed by my father, sentenced to death by Rihad, rejected by both blood and all that I believed to be honorable in this world.

Fortiss looks up as I approach, and the guards bow to him and leave the room to take up their positions with the other men stationed outside the doors. Fortiss smiles wearily as he watches them go, then turns his gaze to me.

"My apologies, Warrior Talia," he says stiffly. "The first of so many apologies I owe you. It's you who should be sitting here, not me."

I can't help it, I laugh, then immediately regret the act as my ribs protest. I wince, pressing a hand to my waist. "I have no desire for that seat," I say honestly. "And you...oh, Fortiss. You didn't know."

"I should have known." Fortiss's words are bleak, his face suddenly haggard as our eyes meet. The guilt of so much death weighs heavily upon him, and nothing I can say will change that. It's his path and whatever there was—is—or might ever be between us, it's too early to know.

But I want to know, I realize. My heart leaps to be so close to him, my fingers tremble with the desire to drift through his hair, along his skin. And deep beneath the sorrow shimmering in his eyes, I think I see an answering fire. I hope I do.

I hold his gaze, sharing his path, his pain with him. It's all I can do, now. But I can do that much. He doesn't break our contact for a long moment, and I pour all the strength I still have into him, knowing that there will always be more.

"You're feeling all right?" I murmur. "After your banding?"

A quick smile brightens his face, erasing yet more of the pain. "I am. It was so long in coming and felt so natural, I recovered quickly. Being thrust into battle before my band had even cooled helped as well, strangely enough. But here." He drops his gaze once more to the book in front of him. "Come closer, if you would. I...you should see this."

I stride across the grand room, struck by how different it seems without Rihad in it. Brighter, lighter. A place of hope, not despair. I stop in front of Fortiss, and he points to the open book. "I can't read it."

I frown and lean close. The book is opened to a page inked with an elaborate, scroll-like lettering, a language I have never seen. I reach out and touch the page and lift it to see the next—more lettering, more words, all equally indecipherable.

"Is the whole book like this?"

"Yes. And three more besides. I began to sound out the words, but the fire leapt in the grate." He gestures to the roaring fire behind Rihad's throne. "I thought I should wait until I understood it more completely."

"The fire." My eyes widen as I take in the flames now crackling cheerfully. I've seen what's emerged from that fire. "Ah..." I hedge. "Have you spoken to the council about it?"

"They claim no knowledge, but I suspect some of them are lying. It'll take time to figure out who and how."

I nod, then finally move myself to speak. "I don't know these words, Fortiss. But I know what they summon. And if you knew that, perhaps you can work backward to what the words say?"

"But how..." He listens, clearly horrified, as I explain what I saw in this room the first night he'd found me in a servant's clothes.

"That was *you* who jumped?" His scowl deepens. "Off the lookout perch?"

"It's not like I had much choice." I tap the book. "But the thing that Rihad was talking to—it was darkness cloaked in fire, a lizard coiling around itself, snakes writhing at its feet. It seemed—quite large. Rihad had to stand back and crane his head far back to see it all."

Fortiss stares at me, his face now quite pale. "Wait here."

He pushes away from the table, then strides over to the door to summon the guard. The man leaves at a run, returning with another book. Fortiss opens it to a full-color illuminated page, and I flinch back with a grimace.

"Is that what you saw?" he prompts.

I nod again, staring at the gruesome image, fire and shadows and twisting snakes. "What is it?"

"I don't know," Fortiss says, turning the book back toward himself. He pages forward. "My father kept these books, handed down over the generations, a full and complete record of the battles of the Western Realms. The Imperial soldiers called these things the Kot'lok—but no one knew their true names."

"Evil," I translate the ancient word, staring at the images.

"Evil from the Western Realms. And there's more." Fortiss nudges the great book. "Councilor Miriam has come to me, with enough evidence to convict Rihad of treason a dozen times over—evidence which, she says, she was holding against a visit from the Imperium that never came. She had decided she couldn't do anything to risk that evidence." He grimaces. "Not even try to save you."

I lift my brows at that. Miriam did know more than she was letting on, all this time. Of course she did. Is that knowledge enough for me to trust her? Not even a little. But it's a place to start.

"According to Miriam, Rihad has kept private counsel with

outside ambassadors since the time he took sole control of the First House upon my father's death. She first assumed these ambassadors were from the Exalted Imperium. She later realized her mistake, but could never identify them. I think they were these...things."

I wave at the first book with the strange writing. "We need to get that translated."

"I've checked. There's no one in the First House who knows the language of the Western Realms. And the warriors from the Eighth are gravely wounded; most have not yet awakened, if they ever will. We'll have to go to their holding on the western border, with a brace of new warriors, to see if there is any who can share this information with us. And we have to act quickly."

I wince, once more seeing the chaos of the melee in my mind's eye. I wonder if I will ever stop seeing it. "Rihad wasn't wrong, in staging the melee. Such a staggeringly bold attack would have been all too easily explained as him saving the Protectorate from traitors. But with Rihad the traitor..."

I pause, staring at the book. Could someone within the Savasci know the language of the Western Realms? Possibly—at least some of it. I smile to think of the warrior women and wonder if they are safe in their cavern below the falls, or if they've already returned west. I hope...I hope they have left this place of death and betrayal. Still, I also can't help hoping that we'll meet again.

Right now, however, our path lies not only to the west, but to the east as well.

"We've got to warn the Imperium," I begin, even as Fortiss holds up a hand.

"We will...but first, we must protect ourselves." He turns to me. "Whatever Rihad was planning, he wanted it to catch us unawares, and we can't let that happen. We'll need your battalion of Divhs, Talia."

I squint at him. "My battalion...no. That's not what they are. Those Divhs aren't mine to direct, Fortiss. They're not banded to me. And they're gone, in any event."

He stands, looking suddenly far older than I remember him. Then again, I probably don't look all that hale and hearty either. "Follow me."

Fortiss leads us out the door and down the long hallway to the overlook. When we arrive, I find it's not empty. A brace of ten soldiers awaits us, wrapped in silver. My soldiers, I realize with a start. The men I hired before the tournament commenced.

"Lady Talia," the nearest one says, lifting his fist to his heart. The men behind him do the same. I find my own hand lifting as well, returning the time-honored salute. *My soldiers.*

Beside me, Fortiss's attention quickly goes to the sky. As the wind rustles around us, he lifts his left arm, curling his right hand over his heart.

There, in the full dawn of a new morning, the great dragon Szonja appears.

"If you would," he says to me, his eyes shining as he watches his glorious Divh stretch her wings—one straight and true, the other bent but no less beautiful. She's already healing.

I frown but raise my left arm as well, pointing toward the wide plain. I curl my right hand to my heart. *Gent,* I call in my mind.

The sky shudders, and a moment later, Gent appears, tall on the open plain between the First House and Trilion. He lifts one long arm to me, reaching across the space, his wild, ululating call rife with happiness.

Then the air seems to bow outward, and I gape.

Fully thirty Divhs now stand arrayed around Gent, all with arms, wings and claws lifted...reaching out to me. Suddenly, a thousand pinwheels of blue and white flowers burst around us, soaring high in the rising breeze.

Unable to stop my startled laugh, I turn to Fortiss, who's beckoning a guard forward. The man offers him something I can't quite see at first—and then I blink.

It's a sash of silver.

Fortiss takes it, then turns and holds the beautiful cloth out to me.

"Your company of Divhs, Warrior Talia, seems more than enough to form the newest house of the Protectorate," he says, and his voice seems to cascade over the edge of the First House overlook, spilling to the wide plain below. "The Thirteenth House. Will you stand with the Protectorate, against whatever may come? Will you wear the winged crown?"

I can't speak for a moment, but when I do, the sound of my voice surprises me. It's easily as strong as Fortiss's, and it is certain —more certain than it's ever been.

"Yes," I say, and I take the cloth of silver. "Yes. I, my soldiers, and all the Divhs of the Thirteenth House will stand for the Protectorate, against whatever may come. Together, we will fight."

Fortiss gazes back at me, and in his eyes, I see something more than what had been there before. Something full and deep and filled with possibility. He bows his head slightly, his gaze never leaving mine. Once again, something powerful and sure shifts in his eyes, a promise newly formed.

"Together," he says, "we cannot fail."

My soldiers pound their fists against their chests, and I reach out for my company of Divhs, the same way I have reached for Gent across the battlefield, feeling our connection deepening as the sky is blanketed anew in blue and white. As one, my Divhs howl with joy, and I recall Gent's cries as he cradled me to his chest a scant day before, surrounded by this mighty army that our bond has somehow raised.

Lifting both my hands high, I meet the Divhs' outstretched arms and claws and wings across the far distance. And as I gaze at these protectors of this house, my house, I realize that Gent was right about something else as well.

In the end, after all the battles and the pain, the plans and the strategies, the way of the warrior is not death after all.

It's life.

Beautiful. Powerful...

Fierce.

Thank you for reading COURT OF TALONS! To learn more about Book 2, CROWN OF WINGS, and get a FREE bonus scene from Book 1 featuring Fortiss, sign up for my email list at www.jenniferchance.com (look for the signup at the bottom of the page!) or drop me an email at jennifer@jenniferchance.com. You can also find me online at Facebook.

If you enjoyed this work, please leave a review at Amazon, Goodreads, or BookBub! Reviews are the best way to share books with new readers.

Author's Note

For those of you curious about the sacred book of war Talia quotes within these pages, I owe a profound debt of thanks to The Book of Five Rings (also known as A Book of Five Rings), a text on kenjutsu and martial arts. It was originally written by the Japanese swordsman Miyamoto Musashi around 1645, and has been translated many, many times. Any misunderstandings of its text in my work are, of course, my own.

Acknowledgments

Thanks to my editor Sally OKeef, whose copyediting expertise was incredibly valuable, and proofreader Holly Thompson, as well as the extraordinary Toni Anderson, Lizzie Bemis, and Sabra Harp, who valiantly took on this book at various stages and wrestled its inconsistencies to the ground. Any remaining errors are definitely my own. Thank you to Geoffrey Girard for his exquisite storytelling and world building insights and assistance...this book would not exist without you. And thank you to Dar Albert for my gorgeous cover that perfectly celebrates the beauty and fierceness of this world. Writing COURT OF TALONS has been an absolute joy.

Also by Jennifer Chance

Fang & Fire Series

Court of Talons

Crown of Wings

Gatekeepers of the Gods

Courted

Captured

Claimed

Crowned

Boston Magic Academies

Touch of the Mage

Blood of the Mage

Heart of the Mage

Soul of the Mage

The Hunter's Call

The Hunter's Curse

The Hunter's Snare

The Hunter's Vow

Witchling Academy

Teaching the King

Tempting the King

Taming the King

About Jennifer Chance

Jennifer Chance is the pen name of Jenn Stark, an award-winning author of paranormal romance, urban fantasy, and contemporary romance. Whether she's writing as Jenn or Jennifer, she loves writing, magic and unconditional love.

Thank you for taking this adventure with her. If you're feeling social, you can find her online at https://www.jenniferchance.com or visit her on Facebook at https://www.facebook.com/authorJenniferChance/!